Also by Ann Tatlock
in Large Print:

A Place Called Morning

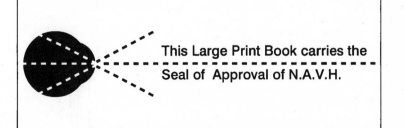

This Large Print Book carries the
Seal of Approval of N.A.V.H.

A Room of
My Own

A Room of My Own

Ann Tatlock

Thorndike Press • Waterville, Maine

Copyright © 1998
Ann Tatlock

Published in 2002 by arrangement with
Bethany House Publishers.

Thorndike Press Large Print Christian Fiction Series.

The tree indicium is a trademark of Thorndike Press.

The text of this Large Print edition is unabridged.
Other aspects of the book may vary from the original edition.

Set in 16 pt. Plantin by Myrna S. Raven.

Printed in the United States on permanent paper.

Library of Congress Cataloging-in-Publication Data

Tatlock, Ann.
     A room of my own / by Ann Tatlock.
        p. cm.
     ISBN 0-7862-4720-7 (lg. print : hc : alk. paper)
     PS3570.A85 R66 2002
     813'.54—dc21   2002029084

To my own Papa
Edward L. Shurts
and to the memory of my mother
Jane T. Shurts

I love you both.

Acknowledgments

A number of people deserve my thanks for their unique contributions to this book:

Viola Blake, a dear friend, who shared with me her childhood memories of the Depression and gave me a flavor of the times.

Les Stobbe, my agent, who believed my work to be worthy of publication and didn't give up until he found a publisher who agreed.

The editorial and marketing staff of Bethany House, especially Sharon Madison, who was kind enough to call me the minute she finished reading the manuscript just to tell me she couldn't stop crying, and Sharon Asmus, my editor, who skillfully lopped off all the rough edges and polished the manuscript into its present form.

Martha Shurts and Carol Hodies, my sisters, who as children "spun the globe" and dreamed with me, and as adults encouraged me through all the years that the fulfillment of my dreams appeared doubtful.

And special thanks to Bob, my husband, who helped with the research for this book by reaching into the seemingly inexhaustible depth of his knowledge of trivia to answer my endless questions about history, civics, and politics. More importantly, through your companionship and your support of me as a writer, you made all my dreams of love and work come true.

Chapter One

Aunt Sally once told me that the rays of the sun are really ladders of light, traveled both by the souls of the dead who climb them to heaven and by the angels who descend them on missions of mercy to earth. Mother said Aunt Sally was talking nonsense, but then Mother was always exceedingly proper and not very imaginative. I myself was fascinated to think that heaven and earth might be connected in this way, and while I was in no hurry to see a dead soul on its way to eternity, I always rather hoped I might spy an angel headed earthward. Whenever the rays of the sun streamed in through the windows of our house, I paused to look for angels.

And that's exactly what I was doing on the May afternoon that, unknown to me, would prove to be the beginning of a pivotal time in my life. School had let out early for the summer that year due to lack of funds, which was why I was at home on a Monday. I was lying on the floor in Papa's study near the spot where the afternoon sun slanted in through the west windows. It wasn't very ladylike to be sprawled all over the floor in my cotton dress, my head resting on one angular elbow, my bare legs — pale and gangly — stretched out across the Persian rug. I was aware of the impropriety of it — "Young ladies don't loll about the floor as though they were rag dolls," Mother would have said had she seen me — but I couldn't resist. Not only did I want to see an angel, but I loved this room because it was Papa's. It was warm with my father's presence. He was there among the myriad books that crammed two bookcases and overflowed onto the floor. His collection consisted primarily of medical books, but he also had books on art and poetry, music and history. Papa was there in the dusty piles of medical journals that he claimed to read cover to cover, although no one ever saw him do it. He was there in the sagging couch where on a rare occasion he napped and in the wing chair where he sat at night to listen to recordings on the old Victrola. A mismatched footstool bore the marks of heel prints from the shoes of his resting feet. His presence hovered about the desk where he sat very early in the morning for what he called "the first order of the day." Later that summer when I started spending the nights on the couch in this room, I would sometimes awaken to see Papa hunched over his Bible, the small desk lamp burning back what was left of the night. The worn condition of the book, the

10

ragged cover, the heavily marked pages gave testimony to his daily ritual.

Papa's study was in a perpetual state of disarray, a condition Mother wouldn't have allowed in any other part of the house. But since this room was Papa's, she allowed it. The general disorderliness was part of what I liked about the room; it gave it a lived-in feel, and it was my father who did the living in it. I felt secure there, knowing that as long as Papa was with us, there was nothing in the world to be afraid of. Papa took care of everything. He had even brought people back from the brink of the grave when other doctors had given up hope.

When I asked Papa what he thought about Aunt Sally's sunray theory, he replied simply, "Well, we know that people go to heaven and we know that angels come to earth, so they might as well travel by sunray as anything else, I suppose." He took off his wire-framed glasses and began to polish them thoughtfully before adding, "You might have some difficulty convincing the theologians of that one, however."

I never thought very much about theologians, though I thought quite often about God. On that May afternoon while I was lying on the floor hoping for some sort of heavenly visitation, I recall I was rather

11

angry with Him. Mildly irritated was how I thought of it at the time, as it seemed a sin to be outright angry with God. But I was still reeling from the news shouted from the headlines five days earlier that the Lindbergh baby had been found dead in the woods near their home. Ever since his kidnapping on the first of March, I had prayed earnestly for his safe return, only to learn that all the while I was praying, he must have been dead already. I couldn't understand how such a thing could happen, how God could have watched the whole thing taking place without doing anything about it. That a child had been murdered was bad enough, but that it was the only son of Charles Lindbergh was unthinkable. Lindy was one of my heroes. His picture, cut out of a magazine, was one of two pictures stuck in the frame of my dresser mirror. I took what happened to him personally, and when little Charlie was found dead, I felt I had lost a member of my own family.

I sighed deeply several times as I lay there on the floor, a sign of my disapproval for God's failing to intervene. But my last sigh was punctured by Mother's voice calling to me from the other room.

"Gin-*ny!*"

The emphasis on the second syllable signified Mother's disapproval of me, and I scrambled up from the floor of Papa's study and stumbled into the parlor where my mother stood, hands on hips, waiting for me. Her cotton dress was covered by the apron that she wore almost constantly no matter what kind of housework she was doing. That afternoon she'd been washing the laundry down in the basement, directly beneath the parlor — and the piano.

"Ginny, what *are* you doing in there? You know you're supposed to be practicing, and I haven't heard a single note out of the piano in the last fifteen minutes."

I looked up at the imposing figure of my mother. She was a tall plain woman, with a shape that was decidedly middle-aged. Her midriff bore the remains of four pregnancies; her arms and legs were thick and matronly, and the chin that cupped her round face was just beginning to sag. Her hair — still a rich chestnut color with only a hint of gray — was worn invariably parted in the middle and pulled straight back into a bun. Her narrow lips were pale, her cheeks colorless; she refused to highlight any of her features with cosmetics. She wasn't homely. Her features were well proportioned, and there was nothing unpleasant about her. She might even have been feminine and rather pretty had her morals allowed it. But she did her utmost to appear austere and without gender, and to her credit, she succeeded quite well.

As she hovered over me now, her face was a combined portrait of annoyance and hurt, as though I had insulted her personally by leaving my post. I could hardly tell her I'd been watching the sunbeams for angels, so I mumbled some excuse about giving my fingers a rest.

"Giving your fingers a rest?" she echoed. "After ten minutes of playing? Honestly, Ginny, how do you expect to master the piano if you refuse to practice?"

I slid sheepishly back onto the piano bench, bent my fingers over the keys, and struck a harsh-sounding chord. "All right, Mama," I sighed. "I promise to practice another half hour if you promise to call me Virginia."

We had struck the bargain before. Neither of us was very good at holding up our end.

"Well, Ginny, Virginia — whatever your name is — you'll never get anywhere in life if you don't discipline yourself. I don't want to have to come up here again. I'm already behind on the laundry as it is. Now, I expect to hear another thirty minutes of music coming out of that piano."

Good luck, I thought as she turned and left the parlor. She might hear a certain amount of noise coming from the instrument, but it was questionable as to whether it could rightly be called music. Mother believed that all proper young ladies should play the piano. Both she and her sister, Aunt Sally, had begun lessons before their feet could even reach the pedals, and though neither was of concert material, they played well enough to be asked often to accompany various soloists and choral groups at church. Mother didn't want to face the fact that I would never be so honored, that, in fact, when it came to music I had no talent whatsoever. I must have taken after my father, who, though he loved music, couldn't "carry a tune in a bucket," as the saying goes.

I was well aware of my deficiency, and so was my piano teacher, Miss Cole. Generally, after I had played my lesson for her, Miss Cole gave me a blank stare, followed by the comment, "My dear, did you have the opportunity to practice this week?" She had long ago given up offering me any false encouragement. My brother, Simon, at nine years of age was a far better musician than I.

Miss Cole had been coming to our home for an hour a week for more than two years, ever since the start of the Depression. Her elderly father was under Papa's care, and the only way Miss Cole could pay the bill was by giving free piano lessons to Simon and me. If her father didn't die soon, she would no doubt be obliged to give lessons to my two younger sisters as well.

Not a few of Papa's patients paid in services or produce in those days. Everyone had a garden, as did we. Mother and I and our hired girl, Emma May, spent a good portion of the summer and early fall canning the produce from our own garden and half that from our neighbors'. And because we lived in a Midwest city in the heartland of Minnesota, we were surrounded by farms. Some of the farm families came to Papa for their medical needs — though they were tough old birds, men and women alike. Mostly they waited to come in from the farm or call Papa to come out there until they were almost too close to the edge of death to be called back or until a woman was so close to giving birth that Papa arrived just in time to give the newcomer his initiatory slap. From these people we got chickens — sometimes dead, sometimes alive — plenty of eggs, prime cuts of beef, and thick slabs of bacon. They also paid in apples, potatoes, plums, pears, and string beans, most of which we canned so the produce wouldn't spoil before we could eat it.

"Well, we won't starve," Mother often said, "but how I'm supposed to add up apples and potatoes in the ledger is beyond me." Mother kept Papa's books because Papa didn't care enough about money to do it himself. If Mother weren't on top of things, sending out the bills and following up when they went unpaid, she said we'd all be in the poorhouse for sure.

Anyway, about Miss Cole. She was a spinster. There's no use trying to pass off my piano teacher as single or unattached. Miss Cole was definitely a spinster, and all the negative connotations of the word clung to her like lint. I envisioned her life as one of lonely monotony, a daily waiting upon an invalid father while the dream of the handsome prince became more and more implausible. She must have been all of thirty, but to a thirteen-year-old such as I, she seemed terribly old and far past the age of marriageability. She wasn't homely, only rather plain, with regular features and colorless hair. But even her appearance I considered a detriment. At least when a woman is ugly she leaves a definite impression upon others. When she is only plain, no one much notices her at all.

In my adolescent opinion, Miss Cole's case was hopeless. I felt very sorry for her and thought it would be just as well if she curled up and died right along with her ailing father, because without a husband and children, she couldn't possibly have anything to live for.

Miss Cole was in my thoughts that afternoon while I fumbled my way through the maze of notes on the music sheet before me. As I played I felt a bit weepy and almost talked myself into shedding a tear or two. Had I succeeded, the tears would not have been for my lonely piano teacher but for myself. I was imagining my own adult life without the companionship of a husband, and it seemed a tragedy too great to bear. Of course, I revelled in the sweet sorrow of my own solitude, specifically because I didn't really believe it could happen to me. I was destined to marry and that was that.

Before I could actually produce any tears, though, my journey into sentimentalism was cut short when my sister Claudia hollered, "Mama, someone wants Papa!"

An interruption! I hadn't heard the knock, but I stopped playing and perked up my ears. Rather than going directly to the office door at the side of the house, people sometimes came to the kitchen door when they needed Papa. I thought it must be one of the few blacks in our city, because they invariably came around to the back. Papa tried to convince them to come straight to his office like everybody else, but he wasn't successful. Not only would they not present themselves at the office door, but they wouldn't set foot in the office at all. When one of their own was ill or hurt, they sent a messenger to fetch Papa and bring him back to the patient. They were afraid of what the response might be if white folks saw them in the waiting room of Dr. Eide's office.

Not that they hadn't affected Papa's practice already. Papa was the only white doctor in town who would tend to blacks, or "Negro folks" as we called them then. When word got out that Papa was taking care of Negroes, some of his white clientele refused to come to him anymore. Papa just shrugged his shoulders and said if that was the way those white folks felt about it, he'd just as soon not bother patching them up and putting them back together again. Mother, too, stood by the blacks, saying they made a greater effort to pay Papa for his services than did their fair-skinned counterparts. Papa always said our door — front or back — was open to anyone who needed help.

But the man who appeared at our back door that afternoon was not what I had at first expected. He wasn't a black man, nor did he appear to be one of the hobos that came around more and more frequently looking for work, a handout, or a plate of food. Whoever he was, I'd never seen him before.

I arrived in the kitchen just as Mother came from the basement, her washing once again interrupted. Emma May was also in the kitchen, up to her elbows in bread dough. My youngest sister, three-year-old Molly, sat in a high chair at the table drinking a glass of milk. My other sister, Claudia, took Mother's wet hand as she stared up wide-eyed at the figure beyond the screen door.

"Yes?" Mother asked cautiously. "What can we do for you?"

"Please, ma'am," the stranger pleaded, "there's a man who's been badly hurt. If the doctor could come —"

"I'll get him!" I volunteered, and before Mother could say anything, I had run the length of the wide front hall and burst through the door into the waiting room of Papa's office. Fortunately, the room was empty save for old Mrs. Greenaway, who came nearly every afternoon just to have Papa assure her she was still alive.

"Papa!" I hollered. "There's someone at the back door. Says a man's been hurt bad."

In a moment Papa appeared from behind the door that led to the examining rooms. I had probably caught him in the middle of an exam or a consultation, but Papa didn't look annoyed, only concerned.

"Do you know who it is?" he asked mildly.

I shook my head. "Never seen him before. But he looks scared, Papa. Maybe you'd better hurry."

Papa glanced at Mrs. Greenaway as we left the waiting room together and hurried to the kitchen. Since Mother had not invited him in, the poor man still stood beyond the screen, clutching his fedora. Papa opened the door, and before he could utter a word, the man spoke again.

"Please, Dr. Eide, there's a man who's been in an accident. I don't think there's much hope but — can you come?"

"Where is he?" Papa asked.

The man looked embarrassed as his nervous fingers kneaded the rim of the hat. "Down at the camp, sir."

"Just a moment," Papa said. "I'll get my bag."

Mother, with Claudia in tow, followed Papa out of the kitchen while I brought up the rear.

"William!" Mother whispered harshly once we reached the hall. "He's one of those hobos from down by the river."

Papa shook his head and opened the door to the waiting room. "No, I don't think he is, Lillian. He appears to me to be a man of some education."

Papa was right, I thought. The man's suit was wrinkled and in need of cleaning, but still, it was a suit. The hat he clutched in his hands wasn't the trademark cap of the hobos. He had made the effort to shave that morning, and the fact that he had a full set of teeth was a dead giveaway. I'd never known a hobo whose mouth didn't have gaps where there should have been teeth. On top of that, his speech was far more refined than the mangled grammar characteristic of the tramps. This man had mentioned the camp, but he wasn't one of the regular residents of the hobo jungle.

"But you've got patients to take care of here," Mother protested.

Old Mrs. Greenaway looked up from her magazine and lifted her linen handkerchief to her mouth. She gazed at us with a pained expression that appeared to ask, "If Dr. Eide doesn't tell me I'm alive, how will I know?"

Papa looked from Mrs. Greenaway to Mother. "Nothing that Harold can't handle by himself." To his elderly patient he said, "I'll be leaving you in good hands, Mrs. Greenaway. Dr. Bellamy is a first-rate doctor."

Before either Mrs. Greenaway or Mother could utter a word of protest, Papa disappeared into his back office and returned with his medical bag. He rushed out to the kitchen with the three of us still tagging him like unwanted shadows.

"Come on," he said to the stranger at

the door. "We'll take the car." As the two men made long strides across the yard, Papa hollered back to Mother that he'd be home as soon as he could.

Mother stood at the screen door and watched the two men hurry to the garage in the alley. She shook her head and sighed. Claudia still clutched Mother's hand, and Molly, a milk mustache cresting her upper lip, let the half-empty glass sit idly on the kitchen table. Emma May's hands were silent in the dough. For a long moment none of us said anything, nor even moved. We seemed to know instinctively that Papa's going with this man would somehow change our lives.

And it did. Especially mine.

Chapter Two

Papa was a whistling man. He whistled in the morning while he shaved. He whistled as he moved about his office checking supplies in the medicine cabinet and looking through his appointment book. He whistled at night while waiting for Mother to heat his habitual glass of warm milk before going to bed. Invariably, he whistled whenever he came home from visiting a patient. After parking the Buick in the garage, he'd move swiftly, lightly, across the backyard, whistling all the way.

"Papa's home!" we'd yell when we heard the shrill notes signaling his return.

The strange thing about Papa was that he almost always whistled Christmas carols. Because he was virtually tone-deaf, you sometimes had to listen carefully to recognize the tune, but generally he was able to hit enough notes for the listener to eventually identify the song. Papa also appreciated the great hymns of the church and, after a lifetime of singing them, knew the words to dozens by heart. I loved to sit next to him during worship services so that his great booming off-key voice came showering down upon my head, making me feel warm inside.

And yet, in spite of the vast number of tunes that must have been lodged in Papa's mind, when his lips pursed in a whistle, it was a Christmas carol that came out. Sometimes this particular habit of his was annoying, especially in the spring and summer when Christmas was as far from most people's minds as the face on the dark side of the moon. Even when we had all the windows thrown open against the heat and sweat had glued our clothing to our backs, Papa went about whistling "Deck the Halls" and "O Holy Night."

"Oh, really, William," Mother sometimes chided, "how can you possibly be thinking about snow at a time like this?"

Papa would smile indulgently and reply, "Well, now, Lillian, I don't guess it was snow I was thinking about."

And off he'd go, filling the air with a joyful noise that caused family, friends, and patients alike to stare at him with raised brows and suppressed smiles.

But on the day he was called down to the hobo jungle, Papa didn't come home whistling. Though still fairly light outside, it was already late in the evening when he returned. I saw him from the kitchen window where I stood at the double sink washing dishes with Simon. He came trudging across the yard as though he were almost too tired to move one leg in front of the other. His gaze was lowered to the ground. He glanced neither at the garden nor at the day's laundry that I had hung on the line hours earlier.

In keeping with Papa's appearance, my announcement was subdued. "Papa's home," I noted quietly.

Simon, short for his nine years, stood on tiptoe to peer over the windowsill. Mother, sitting at the table, set her coffee cup back in the saucer and said, "Goodness knows, it's about time. What on earth could have kept him so long?"

Dr. Hal, who was just finishing his supper, wiped at his mouth with a cloth napkin. "Must have been a pretty bad case, Lillian," he said. Dr. Hal was the son of one of Papa's cousins. He had just completed medical school a year before, and Papa invited him to join his practice for a time before venturing out on his own. Papa figured he could use the help, and Dr. Hal could use the experience. Dr. Hal accepted the invitation with little persuading. During the Depression it seemed safer to join an already established practice than to try to set out on one's own. He slept on a rollaway bed in the back room of the office and took his meals with us. His real name was Dr. Harold Bellamy, but I always called him Dr. Hal. A thin, narrow-faced but handsome young man, he was quiet and well mannered and serious about his work. I might have taken a crush on him if he hadn't been family. My best friend, Charlotte, did have a crush on him, but that wasn't saying much. There were few members of the opposite sex who didn't strike her fancy at one time or another.

Mother rose to greet Papa at the door. "William," she said kindly, "you've been gone for hours. You must be starved. Sit down and I'll have your supper on the table right away."

Mother allowed Papa to kiss her cheek briefly before he slumped down into his usual chair at the head of the table. He generally returned his medical bag promptly to his office, but that night he simply set it down on the floor beside him and sat staring solemnly at his own two hands folded in front of him on the table. His hair, the color of sand and thinning on top, leaped out from his head in all directions. His wire-framed glasses straddled his nose halfway down the bridge, waiting to be pushed up. His cheeks were ruddy with the color of youth, and yet that night his round face appeared heavy with age. I had never seen him look so weary.

"Hi, Papa," I greeted him from the sink, sending him a smile.

He raised his eyes with a start, then

smiled wanly in return when he realized who had spoken. "Hi, Ginny," he said. He nodded toward Simon. "Hello, son."

Simon was rubbing a plate with the dish towel. "You look tired, Pa," he remarked.

Papa nodded in agreement. "I'm a little tired."

"Tough case?" Dr. Hal asked. He pushed his plate away and pulled his coffee cup in front of him.

Papa sighed loudly and undid the top button of his shirt. "There was nothing I could do," he confessed mournfully. "The man was dead when I got there." Taking off his glasses, he began polishing the lenses in a circular motion with his handkerchief. Then he set the glasses down on the table and rubbed his eyes with his large palms. I had the feeling he was trying to wipe away whatever it was he had seen at the camp.

Mother set a plate of food in front of him. Papa acknowledged it with a nod, replaced his glasses on his nose, and picked up his fork.

"What happened, William?" Mother asked quietly. She slid into the chair catercorner to him.

Papa, the food untouched, laid the fork back down. "The man was trying to hop a train when he slipped and ended up under the wheels. Sliced one of his legs off completely. He just didn't have a chance, not with an injury like that. Some of the fellows down at the camp tried to staunch the flow of blood. They did an admirable job too, considering. But the poor man had bled to death long before I arrived."

I heard Mother gasp and felt her eyes on my back, but I didn't turn from the sink. I wanted to appear preoccupied with the dishes so Simon and I wouldn't be sent from the room.

"How dreadful," Mother said quietly.

"I'm sorry, William," Dr. Hal offered. "That's a tough thing to have happen."

Mother continued. "But you've been gone for hours. If there was nothing you could do . . ." Her voice trailed off, her question unasked.

"I — well, how do I explain?" Papa replied. "I left and called the coroner from the nearest service station, but then I went back to the camp. I've spent the past few hours just talking with people."

"The men at the camp?" Dr. Hal asked.

"Yes, but I had no idea . . ."

When Papa didn't continue, Mother suggested, "Why don't you eat your supper, William? You can talk about it later."

But as though he hadn't heard her, Papa exclaimed in tones that were almost agonizing, "How could I not have known what was going on down there?"

From the corner of my eye, I saw Dr. Hal lean forward over the table. Soothingly, he asked, "What did you see, William, and what can I do to help?"

I heard Papa sigh again. How I longed for the sound of his whistle. "There aren't just a few hobos living down there anymore. You know that patch of land between the river and the railroad tracks?"

Dr. Hal grunted his acknowledgment.

"There must be — I don't know — a hundred people, probably more."

"There's a hundred men living down there?" Mother asked.

"Not just men, Lillian," Papa explained. "Mostly men, yes, but women and children, too. There's even going to be a baby born there in the next couple of months."

The kitchen was quiet. Simon and I cast sideways glances at each other and held our breath, still hoping not to be noticed and sent away.

One of the chairs creaked softly as Mother leaned back in it. "That's no place for women and children."

"It's no place for anyone, Lillian," Papa corrected quietly.

"Are you telling us there's a Hooverville down there?" Dr. Hal asked.

"Looks that way, Harold," Papa said, nodding. "It's a regular little community with street names and everything. President

Hoover, though, might be gratified to know that this particular camp doesn't bear his name. The residents are calling it Soo City."

"Soo City," Dr. Hal echoed, trying out the name. "And have they really gone so far as to build houses and streets?"

"Well, only in a manner of speaking. Not houses, really. Shacks is more like it. Made out of odd bits of wood, cardboard, even flattened tin cans. A few people have set up tents. One or two seem to be living out of abandoned cars."

"Oh, William," Mother whispered.

"Of course there's no sanitation," Papa continued. "No toilets or baths; no running water. The perfect environment for the breeding of disease. I didn't notice anything contagious going around yet, but I did notice in some of the children — in some of the adults, too — the first signs of pellagra."

"The Red Death?" Dr. Hal asked incredulously. "Are you sure?"

"I've never seen it before, but I'm pretty sure. The listlessness, the red splotches on the skin —"

"But that's just found in the South, isn't it?" Mother interrupted.

"Not anymore, Lillian. It's found anywhere people are starving."

"Good heavens, William! Do you mean

to tell me those people are starving?"

"Not quite, but very nearly. Some of them, anyway."

"Where exactly do they get their food? Just how are these people surviving?" Dr. Hal asked.

I turned in time to see Papa shake his head. He still hadn't touched the food on his plate. "Some of the men earn a little money going around door to door and offering to do odd jobs. A few of the men even have regular jobs, I guess, except their hours and wages have been cut back so much they were finally no longer able to pay the rent or the mortgage on their homes. They ended up being evicted and their furniture carted off or left out on the sidewalks. Many of them have sent their wives and children to live with relatives, but as I said, there are some women and children there — I guess those folks had no relatives to take them in. So anyway, as far as food goes, there's the breadlines where they can get soup and a sandwich once a day. They tell me they also get wilted vegetables and other unsalable food at the IGA, and when they have to, they scrounge for food in the garbage cans behind the restaurants downtown."

"And they get their water from the river?" Dr. Hal guessed.

"Sometimes, yes. But fortunately the

owner of the service station where I stopped to use the phone — it's about a mile from the camp — is allowing the men to haul back a certain number of gallons of water every day. At least they get a little clean water that way."

"And the city inspectors, the department of public health — they're allowing it?" Mother's voice was agitated when she spoke.

"Apparently so," Papa replied. "Dick Mason — that's the man who came to the door this afternoon — he says one of the sheriff's deputies patrols the area regularly. He doesn't say much, just shows up and looks around. Apparently making sure no one's disturbing the peace. But they haven't been asked to leave and I'm not sure why. They could be run off the property as a menace to public health, certainly. They could be arrested for vagrancy. But so far, they've pretty much been left alone."

"Just who in the world are they, William?"

"That's what I was trying to find out, among other things. Far as I can tell, they're just people who have nowhere else to go. They've all lost their homes or farms. Some are from around here. Some are from as far away as either coast. The man who died this afternoon — he was

Dick's brother-in-law. The two men used to be in business together in upstate New York, but of course they lost everything in twenty-nine. They scrounged around looking for work up there for a couple of years, but without much luck. Finally they decided to take to the road in search of work elsewhere. They had a car, but it gave out about two hundred miles from here. Since then they've been walking and riding the rails. Somehow they ended up down there in the camp. They were planning to move on today, but — well, it was the end of the line for one of them."

Simon stopped drying a handful of silverware and said, "Roger Stimson's father says all the unemployed are just a bunch of good-for-nothings. He says they could get jobs if they really wanted to work."

"Simon!" I hissed his name between my teeth, sure that our hour of departure had arrived.

But instead of sending us out of the room, Papa responded to Simon's statement patiently. "Well, son, I'm afraid a lot of people take that stance on the unemployed, but it just isn't so. I would bet that all the men I met down there today would jump at the chance to work if there were any jobs available. Right now there just aren't any jobs. But that doesn't make these people lazy, and they're not good-for-nothings either. Many of them had decent jobs and lived in homes not too different from ours but lost them because of circumstances they couldn't control. No, Simon, I suggest you not listen to the opinions of Roger's father."

"Yes, sir," Simon responded sheepishly. He dropped the silverware into a drawer and reached for the pot I was handing him.

"Well," Mother said, getting up and pouring herself another cup of coffee, "I'm sorry for what's happened to those poor men and women, but I hope you're not planning to spend a lot of time down there."

Papa took the first bite of his dinner and chewed thoughtfully. Finally he said, "Well, Lil, I was thinking maybe I could make a run out there once or twice a week. Those people need medical care same as anyone else."

"Then they can take advantage of the free clinic — that's what it's there for."

"I'm afraid not, Lil. To be treated at the free clinic you have to prove residency, and that's one thing these people can't do."

Mother stirred milk into her coffee and sat down again. "Then what about the Red Cross? Remember that drought last year that hit the belt land so hard? The Red Cross fed thousands and no doubt offered medical help too. Can't they do the same here?"

Papa had his mouth full, but Dr. Hal jumped in to answer Mother's question. "That drought was a natural disaster, Lillian. The funds of the Red Cross are for war and natural disasters. What we've got here is an economic disaster. I'm afraid that's not the same thing at all. Besides, the problem is so pervasive. People are losing their jobs and their homes all over the country. There probably isn't much the Red Cross can do."

Papa swallowed and nodded in agreement. "Harold's right, Lillian. These people are pretty much on their own, I'm afraid."

"Thanks to Hoover," Dr. Hal added, "no federal aid. Every man's responsible for pulling himself up by his own bootstraps. Hoover doesn't realize that's a little hard to do when your boots are so worn there's not enough leather left to hold on to."

"I'm sure Hoover is doing what he thinks is right," Papa said quietly. "But help's got to come from somewhere. Those of us who can help in some way need to be doing it."

"But, William," Mother protested, "think of the diseases that must be festering down there in that filth. Think of what you could bring home to the children. You said yourself —"

Papa smiled and said in his most re-

36

assuring tone of voice, "Lil, I'm a doctor. I work around disease all the time. Now, don't worry."

"But, William —" Mother began again.

"What is it, Lillian?" Papa asked tolerantly.

"We have four children."

I heard Papa chuckle, a decidedly weary chuckle. "Yes, dear, I'm well aware of that."

"And, as you know, these times are difficult for everyone. We're no exception. If you spend much time down there — well, those people can't pay. We're hardly in the position to be peddling your services for free."

"Now, Lil, if I stop by the camp once or twice a week, I hardly think that will send us to the poorhouse. I have a good stable practice, and what's more, Harold is here to help. I understand your concern for the children, but really, there isn't anything at all for you to worry about." Papa patted Mother's hand and smiled, as though the matter had been amicably settled.

But Mother pursed her lips. There was something else on her mind that she didn't dare speak aloud. Papa would have his way whether Mother liked it or not, and Mother was resigned. But I knew my mother well. I knew what she was thinking. While she was truly sorry for those poor people in the shantytown, her first concern was for the welfare of her own family — both how we fared financially and how we appeared to our neighbors. Mother didn't like Papa's lackadaisical attitude toward money. She didn't like his willingness to give medical care for free. But worse yet, to have him, a respectable doctor, mingling with the likes of those people down by the river — why, it just wasn't proper!

Chapter Three

Charlotte's house was just a few streets over from ours. It was a small brick structure, about half the size of my family's rambling Victorian affair, but large enough for the Besac family, as Charlotte was an only child. Mr. Besac, a traveling salesman, was seldom at home, so Charlotte and her mother were usually the sole residents of the place anyway.

The sidewalks between Charlotte's house and mine were a well-traveled path for me, because she and I had declared ourselves best friends ever since our first-grade teacher assigned us to eraser duty together. I felt almost as much at home in Charlotte's house as in my own.

Although school was out for the summer, it was generally after noon before I was able to escape to Charlotte's to play. Mother didn't believe in allowing children to become lazy during the summer vacation — an idea I wholeheartedly disagreed with at the time — and so she devised regimented programs for her offspring to follow. Instead of the three R's, summers revolved around what I thought of as the two L's: learning and labor. My mornings and sometimes a good portion of my afternoons were spent at the piano learning to play, at the sewing machine learning to sew, in the kitchen learning to cook. And I wasn't to get away from book learning. The primary textbook for those hot summer days was the Bible. I was expected to read a certain number of chapters daily, and every Sunday Mother chose a verse or two that she expected me to memorize and recite aloud by the end of the week.

Mother also compiled a list of what she called "fine literature" that I had to work my way through before school started again. Everything from Louisa May Alcott to Charles Dickens to Nathaniel Hawthorne. Generally I checked a book out of the library three or four times before I finally finished it, and Mother could never understand why it took me so long to read a single novel. What she didn't know was that during much of the time I was supposed to be devoting to fine literature, I was actually devouring issues of "True Story," which Charlotte passed on to me when she finished reading them. I figured everyone had to have a vice or two, and surely one could do worse than reading romance magazines.

That was the learning side. The labor side consisted of an endless cycle of household chores that still makes my head spin to think about. We had just finished our annual spring cleaning, a ritual that left every muscle and bone in my body aching from overwork. Mother, Emma May, Simon, and I stripped the walls bare in each room and scrubbed them with strong soap and household ammonia in water. We carried all the rugs, large and small, out to the clothesline, where Simon and I sighed and sneezed and scowled as we beat the dust and dirt out of them with carpet beaters that looked like oversized whisks. Then, on hands and knees, the four of us scrubbed the floors with huge wooden brushes and Fels-Naptha soap. Mother and Emma May then washed all the curtains in the house by hand while Simon and I cleaned the windows with a potent mixture of warm water, ammonia, and vinegar. After the curtains were washed, they were stretched out to dry on the curtain stretcher. Simon and I gave an exaggerated yelp every time we pricked one of our fingers on the pins, hoping Mother would have pity and excuse us from this chore. She never did. Thankfully, spring cleaning lasted only about a week.

But even afterward, the usual chores remained. On Mondays when Mother did the laundry, I hung up the damp clothes and linens on the lines in the backyard. Sometimes on Tuesdays I helped with the ironing. On Wednesdays I dusted and polished the furniture, and on Thursdays I swept the porch and the sidewalk. Fridays were bed-changing days, when I was responsible for putting fresh linens on all the beds. Every day I was expected to wash dishes, clean my own room, and help tend the garden, where I did everything from planting the seeds to pulling the weeds to canning the vegetables after they'd been picked.

Needless to say, I was not an idle child.

The day after Papa's first visit to Soo City, I had dutifully completed my daily projects before heading out to see Charlotte. I was anxious to tell her about the community living down by the river that Papa discovered. Charlotte was constantly telling me about her own father's travels through his Midwest territory, but I was ready to bet he'd never come across anything quite like Soo City.

I skipped along the sidewalk, wondering how I could embellish the story a bit to make it all the more sensational. Perhaps I could say Papa saw rats and snakes and spiders crawling all over the people's shacks, all over the people *themselves,* and the men and women of the camp were so used to it they didn't even care. Charlotte would turn absolutely white, maybe even faint, if I was convincing enough.

Charlotte's mother was sitting on the porch swing when I arrived at their front steps. Mrs. Besac was just about as different from my own mother as she could be. In the twenties, when Mother was attending temperance rallies and campaigning against the evils of drink, Charlotte's mother was visiting speakeasies and going to parties where she rolled down her stockings and danced the Charleston far into the night. Charlotte said her mother didn't go to these parties with her father, but with a series of men Charlotte knew as Uncle Joe, Uncle Fred, Uncle Al. There was a whole string of uncles, she said, that showed up when her father was away on business. They'd hang around for a while, then disappear again.

I was both puzzled by and in awe of Mrs. Besac. Imagine rolling down your stockings and dancing until all hours of the night! Actually, I *couldn't* imagine such a thing. No woman in my family would dream of such mad behavior. I thought Mrs. Besac must be terribly courageous and fun loving, but at the same time I wondered why she rarely smiled.

For a onetime flapper, she now appeared oddly subdued, sitting there on the porch swing in her plain white cotton dress with her bare feet tucked up beside her. Her full lips were painted the color of cherries. Her fingernails — and even her toenails, from what I could see — were polished in a matching color. Her narrow face was powdered and rouged, and her marcelled hair hung in brisk waves over her ears. Pinched between the index and middle fingers of her right hand was the slender Lucky Strike she was rarely without. She lifted the cigarette to her mouth and inhaled deeply. She held the smoke in her lungs for a moment and gazed skyward, then let it out slowly, wistfully. In her left hand was a sweating glass of lemonade, which she used as a chaser for the nicotine.

When she saw me, her face registered no emotion at all. She simply looked at me as one might stare at a harmless curiosity. Then, as though she finally recognized who I was, she pushed at her marcelled hair with the hand that held the cigarette and said, "Hello, Ginny. Hot enough for you?"

I climbed the porch steps and saw that in spite of the powder her forehead glistened slightly with small beads of perspiration. Now that she mentioned it, I realized my own dress was beginning to cling to my back.

"It's pretty hot for May, isn't it, Mrs. Besac?" I agreed.

Mrs. Besac nodded slightly and took another sip of the lemonade, her lower lip meeting the smudge of lipstick on the rim

44

of the glass. I waited for her to invite me in to see Charlotte, but she said nothing. Instead, she continued staring off beyond the porch railing as though she were waiting for someone. Finally, not wanting to invite myself into the house, I asked, "Is Charlotte home?"

Mrs. Besac, taking a drag of the Lucky Strike, frowned at me. She blinked her eyes against the smoke. "Who?" she asked.

"Charlotte," I repeated.

She formed her shiny lips into an O and exhaled swiftly, but all the smoke had already escaped. "Oh, Lottie. Yeah, she's upstairs. Go on up."

Ever since Charlotte and I had announced our intention to go by our full given names rather than by Ginny and Lottie, neither of our mothers could seem to remember who we were. We constantly had to remind them to call us Virginia and Charlotte — they, who had given us the names in the first place.

"Thanks, Mrs. Besac," I said.

The woman managed a bland and unconvincing smile. "Sure, Ginny," she said.

I resisted the temptation to correct her, but just to be annoying, I let the screen door bang behind me as I stepped into the house. Maybe that would show my displeasure at her insistence on calling me by a childish nickname.

I ran past the parlor where Charlotte and I often danced ourselves into exhaustion doing the Lindy Hop and the Charleston, the Black Bottom and the Susy-Q. We were usually heavily made-up and decked out in her mother's cast-off clothes and long strings of pearls. Our imaginary audience was composed of all the males we were sweet on at the moment, and we believed ourselves to be both stunning and mischievous as we jumped around like a couple of baboons gone mad. Of course, we would generally end up on the floor in hysterics, and now I'm glad there were no actual onlookers to witness our illusions of grandeur.

Charlotte was in her room, a spacious pink-and-white place with frilly curtains, a four-poster bed, and an otherwise assorted collection of furniture that she claimed to have inherited from various aunts and grandparents. On top of the chest of drawers an ancient electric fan worked noisily to create a current of air through the room. Every time it turned one way it ruffled the curtains, and when it swung the other way, it sent a shiver through the pages of the magazines scattered across the desk.

Charlotte, looking cool in spite of the heat, sat at the vanity table picking through a shoe box filled with bottles, tubes, and compacts of cosmetics her mother no longer used or wanted. Since my own mother wore no makeup, I had no castoffs at home to experiment with. It didn't matter; Charlotte had plenty.

"Finally!" she exclaimed when she saw me in the doorway. "I thought you'd *never* get here."

My friend loved to speak in italics. You could just see certain words come out all slanted under the weight of emphasis she placed on them.

"Sorry," I apologized. "I'm having trouble with the dress I'm working on, and Mama made me rip part of it out and start over."

Charlotte wrinkled her slender nose. "I hate to sew," she announced.

"So do I."

"Then why do you do it?"

"Have to."

"How come?"

"Mama says I have to learn."

"I'm glad *my* mother can't sew."

I shrugged. Charlotte was lucky, but I didn't want to say so. I didn't want to let her know I was envious of her freedom. She didn't have to cook or sew, and she could read "True Story" right in front of her mother, and Mrs. Besac didn't say a word.

"Know what?" I asked, my voice loud with exaggerated excitement.

"What?" Charlotte asked. She was looking for a particular shade of lipstick among the myriad of tubes in the box.

"You know that hobo jungle down by the river?"

"Yeah?" She twisted the end of a tube to make the lipstick pop out like a wagging tongue.

"Papa says it's turned into a whole city. There's hundreds and hundreds of people living down there — women and kids, too. All of them living like bums in cardboard boxes and eating food they've dug out of garbage cans. . . ." I went on to tell her all I could remember from Papa's description, embellishing the facts whenever possible. When Charlotte ran the lipstick over her upper lip and capped the tube without coloring the lower one, I knew I had her attention. I rambled on for at least ten minutes, arms flailing dramatically.

When I finished, Charlotte narrowed her eyes and, hissing through one red and one pale lip, said, "Oh boy, if only my pop weren't off in St. Louis, he'd march right down there and shoot every last one of them. You think he wouldn't, but I'm telling you he would. They don't come around here looking for food anymore when they know *Pop's* home." She laughed shrilly, then continued. "You shoulda seen it when they came around and *Pop* was here. He chased them off the back porch with his rifle, calling them lazy bums and pampered poverty rats. Pampered *poverty* rats!" She laughed again, her dual-colored mouth wide with glee. "You should see how fast those bums can run! They may be lazy, but start to swing a rifle at them and they're slicker than greased lightning!"

I thought Charlotte might want to go down and spy on the camp, but she didn't suggest it. Probably the idea of the rats and snakes put her off. Truthfully, I wasn't much eager to wander over there myself. The hobos that came to our back door looking for food had always frightened me, and I couldn't imagine coming across so many of them at once.

At the same time, although I couldn't understand it, I felt myself wanting to defend these folks who had snuffed out Papa's whistle and sent him home all wrapped up in weariness and concern. I dragged a straight-backed chair across the room and sat down at the vanity table next to Charlotte. I looked at her reflection in the mirror. She had come to realize her omission and was pursing her lips together to even out the color.

"Papa said some of those people used to be just like us," I said, "but they lost their jobs and their homes, and they don't have anywhere else to go."

Charlotte rolled her eyes. "They're bums," she stated flatly. "Take my word for it. They could find work if they wanted to. My pop's still working, isn't he? And we still have a house and a car and clothes and stuff. Pop says it'll take more than a little depression to keep him from supporting his family. Listen, let's do the globe, huh?"

Soo City forgotten, Charlotte pushed aside the box of makeup and set in its stead her spinning globe, our forecaster of future romantic adventures. The standard ritual was to take turns placing an index finger lightly on the globe and then, with eyes shut, give the globe a furious spin. The spinner's finger was obliged to travel up and down the surface of the globe as it was turning, passing over the equator numerous times before the globe finally came to rest. When the spinner opened her eyes, the magic orb revealed where she would spend her honeymoon. More often than not, Charlotte or I would find ourselves stranded in the middle of the Pacific Ocean thousands of miles from anywhere. But we were not disheartened. We simply spun again until the globe set our feet on dry land.

Charlotte wanted to honeymoon in Africa. Her plans for her future husband and herself included sailing the Nile, wandering off into the wilds of Kenya on safari, and visiting the pyramids of Egypt. Of course, she intended to be rather old when she married, maybe as old as twenty-six or twenty-seven. She wanted to remain single for a long time so she could have adventures before settling down.

"But going to Africa with your husband sounds like an adventure to me," I'd argue.

"Sure," she'd say, "but I want to spend a good long time shopping around, so when I go to Africa I don't end up with a dud."

My own dreams centered around Europe. I pictured my husband and me snuggling together in a gondola in Venice and taking midnight walks along the River Seine in Paris.

Charlotte may have had an inkling, but I myself was clueless as to what actually took place on a honeymoon. I invariably envisioned a couple all decked out in their finest, sitting on a hotel balcony and gazing up at the moon. The husband would interrupt the blissful silence at calculated intervals to call his wife "Honey" and other terms of endearment — hence, the term honeymoon. That such an event might be hampered by bad weather or an invisible new moon never occurred to me. In my imagination, the night was always clear and star studded, the moon as round and luminous and exotic as the blue moon

I'd once seen rising up over the city of Minneapolis.

And so we spun, hoping the globe would take us to the place of our dreams. But even if it didn't, even if the globe predicted that we'd be gazing at the moon in some desolate place like Mongolia or Siberia, we decided that even there we'd find romance, as long as our husbands were handsome and rich.

On that particular afternoon, Charlotte landed somewhere in the East Indies — Borneo, I think — while I found myself headed for Honduras. "I'll never go there," I murmured, lifting my finger defiantly from the globe.

"Yes, you will," Charlotte said firmly, "if that's where your husband wants to go. It's either that or stay an old maid."

"I suppose," I sighed, though I really did have my heart set on Europe.

"Come on, let's see who we're going to go with." Charlotte pulled out of the vanity drawer a little jewelry box that played "Let Me Call You Sweetheart" when you opened the lid. My friend instructed me to go first.

Again I shut my eyes. I fumbled with the lid, and while the notes sang ". . . call you sweetheart, I'm in love with you . . ." I pulled out one of the folded pieces of paper from inside.

"What's it say?" Charlotte asked.

"Two," I replied.

"Charlie Chaplin."

"Yup."

"Some honeymoon."

But I was glad. If I had to spend my first days of marriage in a place like Central America, Charlie Chaplin was the man I wanted to be with.

"Okay, my turn," Charlotte said. She screwed up her face into a tight knot while she slid her hand into the box. She unfolded the paper and smiled satisfactorily. "One!" she cried. "That means Al Capone."

Charlotte was in her gangster phase. Later in the summer when the Olympic games were being held in Los Angeles, she'd turn her allegiance from gangsters to athletes. But for the past couple of weeks, ever since we saw *Scarface: The Shame of a Nation*, she found something enormously appealing about the men of the underworld. Had she selected paper number two from the jewelry box, she would have been traveling to Borneo with the whole Klondike O'Donnell gang.

"Goodness, Charlotte," I said, "I can't understand why you like these guys." Just a month before, number one had been Clark Gable and number two, Gary Cooper. Paper number three had been, and still was, Mitchell Quakenbush. He was the most recent object of Charlotte's affections at school.

Charlotte sighed moonily. "For one thing," she said, "some of them are richer than the Rockefellers."

"Ill-gotten gains," I reminded her, borrowing my mother's phrase.

"But think of the adventures!" she continued, undaunted. "Just imagine how exciting life must be for Bonnie, gallivanting all over the place with Clyde. Why, he must be the bravest man in all the world. He and Al Capone."

"And Bugs Moran and John Dillinger," I added.

"Yeah, them too."

"But, Charlotte, if you marry someone like that, you'll have to go around robbing banks and killing people. Not only that, but you just might get killed yourself!"

My friend fingered the globe absently while considering this. "I don't know if it has to be that way, Virginia," she said.

" 'Course it does. That's how they make their living."

Charlotte spun the globe and stuck out her lower lip. "Well," she declared, "there must be some way to be an outlaw without robbing and killing."

Sometimes Charlotte didn't make much sense to me. But then, even though we were best friends, there were few things we saw eye to eye on, not the least of which was men. Just as I couldn't share her enthusiasm for gangsters, she couldn't understand my infatuation with Charlie Chaplin. To her, he was just a silly little man with a too-small derby, an overactive cane, and oversized shoes that were always pointed out in the ballerina's second position. Worst of all, he was a tramp, disgustingly similar to the hobos that lived in the jungle down by the river. She didn't think much of any of the comedians of the day, saying there must be something wrong with the whole lot of them — Chaplin, Buster Keaton, Harold Lloyd — because not one of them could walk more than a short distance without falling down.

But I liked them, especially Charlie. Granted, he wasn't dashing in his tramp getup, but I'd seen pictures of what he looked like out of costume, and I thought him exceedingly handsome. Even as the tramp, he was appealing in his own sweet way. I think it was the way he regarded his leading ladies with tender devotion that struck a chord with me. I had seen *City Lights* five times the previous year, and I found myself envious of the blind girl, the object of Charlie's affections, as she enjoyed Chaplin's lingering kiss upon her hand. How I longed for such a kiss of wholehearted devotion and admiration to be planted on my own hand someday.

Had I picked either of the other two papers in the jewelry box, I would have been honeymooning with Charles Lindbergh or Danny Dysinger, my own current interest at school. He had left to spend the summer on his grandparents' farm, but that didn't keep me from dreaming about him. Not that I had much reason to think he might be sweet on me in return. The one event that gave me any hope at all was that he had bid on and won my box lunch at the end of the school year. Our class had held the box luncheon as a fund-raiser for the Lower Street Mission. Most of the lunches went for a dime or less, but whatever the boy bid, the girl was expected to match. The proceeds — I think it was all of six dollars — went to the mission to help with the ever increasing crowds gathering in the breadline. On the last day of school, we received a letter from the mission thanking us for our contribution.

Anyway, Charlotte and I were not to be deterred by the fact that Mitchell and Danny paid us little attention, that Charles Lindbergh and Charlie Chaplin were married, or that Al Capone was in prison. For us, romance knew no barriers.

"All right, then," Charlotte said, lifting the globe to the floor and pulling the box of makeup forward again, "let's get down to business."

Now that we knew where we were going and who we were going with, we had to get ourselves all fixed up to go. What a pair, Charlotte and I. We were a couple of adolescents straddling the line of maturity with one foot in childhood and the other in adulthood. We were much younger than we imagined, trying to act much older than we should have. Just weeks before we had taken an oath together that we would no longer play childish games like jacks and marbles, jump rope and hopscotch. We put away our dolls, and we buried our Little Orphan Annie secret decoder pins in the backyard in a ceremony as solemn as high mass. We wanted to put the fairy tales and fantasies of childhood behind us. We were ready for adult responsibilities and adult joys — like being in love. We were ready to face life as it really was.

Or so we thought.

"What do you think I should wear on my wedding night?" Charlotte asked.

"I have no idea," I replied.

Charlotte shrugged. "Well, by then I'm sure the styles will have changed. I'll worry about that later."

We scrutinized our faces in the mirror while considering the cosmetics we would experiment with that afternoon. There was no doubt Charlotte was prettier than I, though she was good enough never to say so. I knew it and she knew it and we both knew that the other knew it, but it was an unspoken fact that we silently accepted. She could have passed for older than thirteen, as her face no longer carried the fullness of childhood. Her features were well formed, almost sharp. She had high cheekbones divided by a narrow nose, and she could already bat her large brown eyes coquettishly. Her teeth were perfect, her jawline firm, and her creamy white neck long and slender. Her dark hair hung in waves to just below her ears, much like her mother's, except that Mrs. Besac's waves were the result of a permanent and Charlotte's were natural.

My face, on the other hand, seemed more reluctant to lose its childish appearance. It was as round as a dinner plate, and while I knew I had cheekbones somewhere, they hadn't bothered to begin showing themselves yet. Freckles dotted my slightly pug nose, and my braided hair was what I called fickle — it couldn't decide whether it was blond or brown and so lay in a rather shadeless area in between. I wanted to bob my hair as Charlotte had done to hers, but Mother insisted that proper young ladies wore their hair long and pulled back. My eyes, though a nice

shade of blue, were set a bit too close together, and my lips were flat and narrow so
that my mouth appeared little more than a
colorless line. Being the eternal optimist,
however, I had great hope that I might
someday, somehow, grow into beauty.

"What do you think of these earrings?"
Charlotte asked. She had clipped a pair of
rather gaudy dangling things to her earlobes and was turning her head from side
to side for inspection.

"Where did your mother get those?" I
asked.

"Oh, I don't know. Some uncle or other.
They're always giving her jewelry and
stuff."

"Well, those might work for Africa."

"I think Al would like them, and that's
all that matters."

"Anyway, you're supposed to be doing
the makeup first. We'll pick out the earrings later."

We were a couple of perfectionists when
it came to primping. We applied compact
powder and rouge with the care of an
artist. We painted our lips slowly so as to
stay within the lines. We darkened our eyebrows with the blunt end of an eyebrow
pencil and sometimes used the same
utensil to plant a Hollywood glamour-star
mole on our cheeks.

We further ornamented ourselves with

the contents of a second box on Charlotte's vanity table — jewelry. Again from Mrs. Besac we had inherited a variety of rings, necklaces, and bracelets, as well as several pairs of matched and mismatched earrings. We examined each piece of jewelry discriminately — as though we hadn't seen it a hundred times before — and discarded some as too plain or gaudy while slipping others over our wrists, onto our fingers, around our necks, and onto our earlobes. The result resembled a parody of the magazine advertisements for a national jewelry store.

Once painted and bejeweled, we then sniffed Charlotte's collection of half-empty perfume bottles like a couple of connoisseurs sniffing wine. Just the right one had to be chosen to please the acute senses of husband number one, two, or three. Once decided upon, the perfume was sprayed or dabbed generously behind each ear and upon the wrists.

Finally, to complete the preening process, we settled upon our heads one of the half-dozen or so hats that had also come down to us from Charlotte's mother. They were all outdated and rather worn, but Charlotte and I pretended not to notice. That afternoon she chose one of those close-fitting cloches that were so popular in the twenties. They made a woman look like she had a rather large bell pulled down over her ears. On Charlotte it looked very stylish. The brim bordered her face like the frame around a piece of artwork, and the curly ends of her bobbed hair lay pressed against her cheeks like an extra bit of frilly adornment. For myself I chose a large floppy affair that boasted a tuft of peacock feathers sprouting from the hatband.

An expectant hush followed as we stared long and hard at ourselves in the mirror. Did our faces reflect the essence of beauty we so greatly desired? Had nature kindly endowed us with the features that assured a woman of a life of romance? These were important questions that required no small amount of consideration.

Suddenly, surprising even myself, I wailed, "Oh, it's just no use, Lottie!"

"It's *Charlotte*," my friend retorted. "And *what's* no use?" *She* was obviously pleased with what stared back at her from the mirror.

I grabbed the braid that hung down my back and held it up to Charlotte. "I'll never look good as long as I have to wear my hair like this!"

Charlotte pulled one side of her mouth back and peered through narrowed eyes at the plait that lay across my palm. She nodded her understanding.

In probably the first comment I ever

made that revealed my envy of her, I said, "I want my hair bobbed like yours."

Turning to look at herself in the mirror, she said simply, "Then cut it."

"You know Mama will never give me permission."

"Then we'll have to do it without her permission."

We each looked at the other in the mirror for a long moment. Finally I said, "You mean . . . cut it ourselves?"

She rose resolutely from her seat. "I'll go get Mama's scissors."

Her absence gave me a minute to reflect on what I was doing. Months ago, when Charlotte had had her own braid shorn, I had begged Mother to let me cut my hair, too. But Mother was adamant. Bobbed hair was not proper for young ladies. I hated the braid that hung girlishly down my back, but if I cut it off I'd surely be in trouble for at least a year.

Charlotte walked back into the room with a large pair of shears. Snapping the blades twice in the air, she commanded, "Take the hat off. Let's get to work."

"I don't know, Charlotte," I faltered. "Mama will kill me."

She sat down in the chair beside me and looked me straight in the eye. "Virginia Eide," she said somberly, "you don't want to be an old maid *all* your life, do you?"

I sighed. Faced with such a prospect, the worst of all possible fates, I felt I had no choice. I couldn't let my mother's disproportionate sense of propriety interfere with my future happiness. If I didn't stand up to her, if I didn't become the navigator of my own destiny, I'd end up like old Miss Cole — alone and lonely, going about from house to house trying to make a living by teaching tone-deaf children how to play the piano.

I removed the hat.

"Go ahead," I whispered. "You'd better do it."

Without a word, Charlotte unraveled the braid and brushed out my hair until it hung limply down my back. Then she walked from one side of me to the other and studied me with a frown. I half expected her to hold up one thumb like a painter, but she didn't. Satisfied, she picked up the scissors and laid them against my neck. In spite of the summer heat, the metal felt cold against my skin. I almost pulled away but managed to fortify myself with images of all the tight-lipped spinsters I knew who sat like a blight upon my picture of the perfect world. Far be it from me to join their ranks, even if it meant taking drastic action.

In a moment it was all over. Long strands of my hair lay in tangled piles on the floor. That which remained on my head came to an abrupt halt just below my ears. The sudden change was jarring, and I wasn't sure I liked it. Stifling the terror that was rising up in my chest, I raised pleading eyes to Charlotte and asked, "What do you think?"

Charlotte nodded confidently. "It's going to be good," she assured me. "It looks a little blunt right now, but so did mine when it first got chopped off. All you need are a few curls. Now, let's see." She pursed her lips in thought. "I know! Mama used to roll her hair in rag curlers before she got the wave. Bet she still has those somewhere in her dresser. Meet me in the bathroom. We'll fix you up right!"

For the next half hour, Charlotte wet strands of my hair with warm water and carefully rolled it in long strips of cloth. Neither of us said much. For my part, I was too busy alternately praying my hair would look good when we took the curlers out and wondering whether the nuns at the orphanage would take me in if it didn't.

Finally, just as Charlotte got the last of my chopped tresses all tied up into knots, we heard the grandfather clock in the downstairs hallway strike five. My stifled terror quickly erupted into panic. "Oh, gosh!" I cried. "I've got to be home in half an hour!"

"Don't worry," Charlotte said. "I'll have you ready by then." She ran out of the bathroom.

"Where are you going?" I hollered after her.

"I'll be right back!"

I was a sorry sight with those rags sticking out all over my head, and I was afraid my friend recognized her mistake and was running off to heaven-knew-where with no intention of ever coming back. If I had to walk home through the streets of our neighborhood looking like this, my life would be ruined for good.

I was just about to burst into tears when my faithful companion returned with a magazine in each hand. "Fan!" she cried, handing me one. And fan we did, Charlotte waving a "True Story" magazine to dry one side of my head, I using a "Saturday Evening Post" to dry the other.

Finally, when our arms were too tired to flap any longer, Charlotte felt my hair and announced, "I think it's done." She untied all the rags and, with the skill of a trained beautician, brushed the tight curls into flattering waves.

When she finished, I couldn't believe what I saw. "Oh, Charlotte!" I said. "I look . . . I look *good!*"

" 'Course you do," she replied, as though there had never been any question.

I couldn't turn away from the mirror. For the first time in my life, I really did feel pretty. "I had no idea —" I started, but before I could finish my thought, the clock struck the half hour.

"You'd better run home, Virginia!" Charlotte warned.

"Oh! Oh, gosh!"

"Want me to save your hair for you?" she asked, nodding toward her bedroom.

I shook my head. "No, no. Throw it away. I don't want it."

Then Charlotte said what I longed to hear. "Gee, Danny Dysinger's just gonna go wild ape when he sees you!"

"Yeah!" I agreed happily. But then I added, "And Mama's gonna be mad as a wet hen, I'm afraid!"

When I left Charlotte's house that afternoon, Mrs. Besac was still on the porch swing, still gazing out after that shapeless someone who seemed not to want to appear. A newly lit Lucky Strike burned between her long fingers; a thread of smoke lifted into the warm air and disappeared. The lemonade glass, long empty, lay on its side beneath the swing amid a scattering of lipstick-stained cigarette butts.

Though I was already late, I purposely stopped on the porch and offered myself up to Charlotte's mother for her inspection. If she liked my hair, there was a small chance that Mother might, too — once she got over the initial shock. After a moment passed without Mrs. Besac realizing I was there, I knew I'd have to say something to draw attention to myself.

"Good night, Mrs. Besac," I said shyly, wondering what she would say, what comment she might offer in praise of my new appearance.

But she had no compliments to give. She barely glanced at me as she offered a dour, "Oh, good-bye, Ginny. See you tomorrow, I suppose."

Disappointed, I trotted off the porch, wondering why she thought she'd see me tomorrow when she had not seen me today.

Quickening my pace, I hurried along the sidewalks of our neighborhood. Most people were inside for the dinner hour, but a few sat on their porches, radios propped up in a front window, waiting for "Amos 'n Andy" to come on (a show we weren't allowed to listen to in our house because Papa said it was demeaning to Negroes). No one greeted me by name. I suppose they simply didn't recognize me, but I preferred to think they'd been stunned into silence. I could almost hear their thoughts: *My, my, that can't be little Virginia Eide. Why, she's all grown up and lovely as a fresh blossom!* I smiled to myself, but when I reached the walk in front of my own house, my fanciful thoughts were swallowed up by the more practical emotion of terror. I lifted my eyes to the house that had always been my home, the beautiful white clapboard house with the mansard roof and the gingerbread trim on the porch. I loved that house. It had always been a sort of refuge, calling to me with open arms, inviting me into its warmth with the words, *This is where you belong.* But now it only appeared chilling and foreboding, and if it was saying anything at all, it was crying out, *Run! Run as fast as you can!*

I moved toward it with a sense of dread, a murky cistern of nausea settling into the pit of my stomach. Literally weak-kneed at the thought of facing Mother, I had to stop a moment on the porch to catch my breath. All the makeup and jewelry had been taken off at Charlotte's to lessen the impact of my appearance. Nevertheless, I knew the bobbed hair alone would be shock enough. I tried to tell myself that this great stride toward beauty was worth any amount of Mother's wrath, but by the time I pulled open the squeaking screen door, I realized I wasn't convinced.

Mother's voice reached me from the kitchen. "Ginny, is that you? You're late! I'm waiting on you to set the —" Her sentence was abruptly cut short when she came out into the hallway and laid eyes on me. For a moment I was certain she would faint. Her face blanched to the same pale whiteness that Grandpa Eide's had been when he was laid out in his coffin, and she seemed almost to totter on her feet as though she might end up in a crumpled heap upon the floor. But just as quickly she gathered her wits about her, drew herself up into one huge giant of maternal indignation, and bellowed, "Virginia Jane Eide!"

Well, I reflected, at least she remembered to call me Virginia. But before I could find much comfort in the thought, she continued. "Have you taken full leave of your senses! What have you gone and done to your hair?"

Rather foolishly, I replied, "Charlotte cut and curled it, Mama. Don't you think it's pretty?"

"Charlotte cut it," Mother echoed angrily. "*Charlotte* cut it! Somehow I knew she'd be behind this. I've half a mind to keep you from that Charlotte Besac. Honestly, I don't know why I've let you associate with her this long. I thought maybe you'd be a good influence on her, but I suppose it's true that bad company corrupts good morals. She's bound to turn out no good, that one — just like her mother."

"Mama," I cried, "you can't mean that! Charlotte's my best friend, and she's a good person, too, no matter what you say. And what's the matter with Mrs. Besac? You just don't like her 'cause she wouldn't join the Women's Temperance Union when you asked her to!"

"Don't argue with me, Virginia Jane!" Mother cried.

Then and there I decided I really did prefer that she call me Ginny after all.

"And anyway, never mind about the Besacs. It's you that's got me nettled now. If you weren't so big, I'd take you right over my knee and spank you! Honestly, what would compel you to do something like this? I can't spank you but I can send you to bed without your supper. Go on upstairs. Go on," she said, waving both arms like an agitated policeman directing traffic. "I don't want to see you again till morning."

I started up the stairs but had only climbed a few when I heard the scrambling of my siblings' feet on the hardwood floor of the hall. The commotion had drawn them from the parlor where they were playing. The three of them stood there in the wide front hallway, lined up like stairsteps and gazing at me with mystified looks on their faces.

Simon, with all earnest concern, asked,

"Gee, Ginny, was you in an accident?"

At the prospect of my having been hurt, Molly's lower lip quivered and she began to cry.

Before I could explain, Papa rushed out of his office, carefully but firmly shutting behind him the door to the waiting room. "Lillian," he said, "a half-dozen people have their ears pressed up against the waiting room wall. Now, what on earth is going on here?"

Mother pointed one accusing finger up at me and said, "Just look what your daughter has done to her hair!"

Papa looked up and studied me a moment. Finally he asked, "Got yourself a new 'do, Ginny?"

"Charlotte cut it for me, Papa," I said demurely. "I wanted to have my hair bobbed like all the other girls." Then I added hopefully, "Do you like it?"

"Never mind that," Mother interjected. "What's right for other girls and what's right for you are two different things."

"Well, now," Papa said, coming to my defense, "if it's what the other girls are doing, I don't see anything wrong —"

"You let me handle this, William," Mother said, cutting him off. "No daughter of ours is going to go prancing around in public looking like some cheap flapper."

To Mother's obvious irritation, Papa

71

gave a brief chuckle. "Well, you can hardly keep her indoors until it all grows out again."

"Maybe not," Mother said, "though I've half a mind to do just that."

"Now, Lillian —"

"Go on upstairs, young lady," Mother ordered. "No supper for you tonight, and that's just the beginning. You won't get off easily this time."

"Now, Lillian —" Papa tried again, but it was no use. Mother had spoken, and that was that. When it came to the patients, Papa had the final say, but when it came to the children, Mother was not to be overruled.

When I started up the stairs, Mother turned the last remnants of her wrath on the younger ones. "Didn't I tell you ten minutes ago to wash your hands for supper? Come on, now, Molly, stop your blubbering. There's no use in tears. Simon, you and Claudia set the table, will you? And leave off one place setting. Your older sister won't be joining us tonight." Molly belched out a final howl as Claudia and Simon led her off to the kitchen.

When I was halfway up the stairs, I realized that Papa still stood at the bottom looking up at me. I turned and paused a moment, long enough for him to give me a wink and a nod. He liked my hair. I knew he did. I smiled at him in return. Then whistling "Joy to the World!" he returned to his patients. He and Dr. Hal would be eating a late supper, as usual.

I ambled to my room and made a beeline for the dresser mirror. I had to re-assure myself I'd done the right thing. The mirror told me that I had, in spite of Mother's explosion.

Turning my gaze from my own face, I rested my eyes on the two magazine photos I had stuck in the mirror's frame — one of Charles Lindbergh, the other of Charlie Chaplin. I thought of them as My Two Charlies. "Well, what do you guys think?" I inquired. After all, as Charlotte said, it was what the men thought that mattered. I had a feeling that like Papa, My Two Charlies rather approved of the bob.

I blew them both a kiss, then lay down to dream of gazing at a Honduran moon while Charlie Chaplin kissed my hand and called me Honey.

Chapter Four

A few days later I was pacing the floor of my room, trying vainly to recite a poem by Thomas Campion. Memorizing three poems by this sixteenth-century wordsmith was part of my punishment for cutting my hair. My sentence also included sewing one skirt and two aprons more than what I was originally supposed to stitch that summer, reading two more library books, mastering three more piano pieces, attempting six more recipes, and committing to memory — in addition to the usual weekly scripture — the third chapter of Second Timothy, which talks about the sins of silly women (such as myself, I presumed). In other words, Mother was trying to keep me too busy to get into trouble again.

Campion alone almost made me regret cutting my hair, but not quite. I was determined to take my punishment without so much as a whimper so that Mother wouldn't think I was bothered by it. Strutting back and forth in front of the mirror as I performed for my two Charlies, I recited dramatically, "To music bent is my retiréd mind, / And fain would I some song of pleasure sing. . . ."

I didn't understand the meaning of the words that tumbled pell-mell from my lips. Campion might as well have been writing in Latin, for all I understood his poems. I was used to memorizing the vintage English of King James, but Campion was one step beyond James in poetic oddities. Nevertheless, I stumbled through the baffling lyrics again and again, hoping that when it came time to recite them to Mother, she'd be just preoccupied enough with other things that I could substitute my own fillers should I find myself drawing a blank.

Surprisingly, in spite of Mother's threats, I was not forbidden to see Charlotte. I think that was Papa's doing. Mother may have disapproved of our companionship, but Papa liked Charlotte, and he knew it would have broken my heart to be separated from my best friend. When Mother laid out my punishment the morning after the hair-cutting incident, not a word was said about Charlotte. But later in the day when I took a message to Papa in his office, he said, "Oh, by the way, Ginny, I heard there's a new Buster Keaton picture showing down at the bijou starting this weekend. You and Lottie won't want to miss it, I'm sure." That was Papa's way of letting me know I was allowed to continue associating with my accomplice in crime.

When my sorry delivery of Campion was

interrupted by the doorbell, I knew it was Charlotte, for I was expecting her. I had talked her into going to the Saturday matinee of the Keaton movie Papa had spoken of, *The Passionate Plumber.* She had balked at first, retorting, "Just how in the world can there be anything passionate about a *plumber?* It's just going to be an hour of Buster Keaton going around fixing toilets and falling down." But with a little persuasion on my part — I reminded her it was possible Mitchell Quakenbush would put his money down for the same show — she agreed to go.

Hearing Charlotte's voice in the hallway, I blew my usual farewell kiss to the two Charlies and hurried down the stairs. Charlotte was there talking with Simon, who hid his hands in his pants pockets but couldn't hide the flush on his cheeks. Simon was a shy fellow, bespectacled and bookish, the spitting image of Papa when he was a boy. Not your usual rough-and-tumble type, he was rather frail, thin, and sallow skinned. His penchant for reading and his enjoyment of piano playing didn't bode well when it came to being popular among the neighborhood boys. He had a few friends, but he largely preferred his own company to that of the other kids. It seemed he was never happier than when he was curled up with one of Papa's medical books. His future seemed already certain, though he was only nine years old.

The attention of a young lady invariably left Simon tongue-tied. When I met up with my friend and my brother in the hall, Simon was trying to say something to Charlotte, but it sounded as though his teeth were all tied up with rubber bands. He looked up at me helplessly, then made his escape back to the piano, where he hammered out his embarrassment on the keys. Above the music I hollered, "Mama, Charlotte's here! We're going down to the picture show now."

From the kitchen I heard, "All right. But I want to hear at least one stanza of Campion when you get back."

"All right, Mama." I rolled my eyes at Charlotte, who smirked and shook her head. The last time she was punished by her mother was on her seventh birthday when she threw her still-lighted cake across the dining room because it had white icing instead of chocolate. I was there at the time and awfully sorry to see that pretty cake flattened against the wall, shards of the shattered plate slicing through it like so much shrapnel. I happened to like white icing and could hardly stand the thought of the cake being ruined. Even so, Charlotte's only punishment was to clean up the mess. If I had done such a thing, I'd still be paying the penalty.

Before we could escape the house, Papa showed up in the doorway of the waiting room patting the breast pocket of his white jacket as though he were looking for a pen. He appeared to be on the verge of hollering for Mother's help when he spotted Charlotte and me.

"Ah, hello, Lottie!" he chirped amiably. "I understand you've gone into the beauty parlor business."

"Oh!" Charlotte exclaimed and started to laugh so hard she couldn't speak. With a hand clamped over her mouth, she backed out the front door and down the porch steps with me trailing her. We giggled our way down two blocks before we could stop laughing.

Finally Charlotte said, "Your pop's so silly, but he's nice."

I nodded my agreement.

"He hasn't been back to that hobo jungle, has he?"

I nodded again. "Yup, he's been back. And he says he's going to go down there once or twice a week for as long as he's needed. He tried to find a couple of other doctors down at the hospital to give him a hand, but he hasn't had any luck so far. None of them are too excited about going down to that place."

"I can't blame them," she replied.

"Who'd want to — you know — *touch* people like that. It'd be worse than touching lepers."

I laughed. "I don't know why you think that. Papa says none of them have any contagious diseases. And not a single one of them has leprosy."

"Dr. Hal's not helping out down there, is he?"

"Nope. Papa needs him at the office and for making house calls."

Charlotte sighed with relief. "Good thing. I wouldn't want anything to happen to Dr. Hal."

Her words sent an unexpected shiver of concern through me. Frowning, I demanded, "What do you mean by that? What could happen?"

"Well, you know. All sorts of bad things could happen — *do* happen — in a place like that. I mean, hobos *love* to kill people for their money. Don't you read the papers?"

Actually, I didn't read the newspaper, and I knew Charlotte didn't either.

Nevertheless, she continued as if she did. "There's stories all the *time* about the sheriff pulling bodies out of the river — men that've been robbed and beaten to death by the tramps. You'd better tell your Papa not to take any money with him when he goes down there."

"I never heard of any hobos killing people for their money. You're just making that up."

"Am not."

"Are so. Besides, these people aren't really hobos. They're just a bunch of people out of work."

"What's the difference?"

"There's a big difference."

"No, there isn't. Hobos are people out of work."

"Yeah, but hobos are regular bums. Hobos were bums even when the whole country was rich. The people down in Soo City aren't like that."

"Virginia Eide, you don't know what you're talking about."

"I do so. Papa says they're just the same as us except they lost their jobs in the Depression."

"I don't believe in the Depression. That's just another lie grown-ups tell so they don't have to work."

"You don't believe the country's in a depression?"

"Naw. People got tired of working, so they quit."

I considered Charlotte's theory for a moment.

Before I could respond, she said, "I bet your mama doesn't like it."

"Doesn't like what?"

"Your pop going down to that shanty-town."

"No, not really. She says he's going to bring back some terrible disease and make us all sick."

"Probably will, if the hobos don't kill him first."

Charlotte's words gave me a whole new reason for not wanting Papa to go to Soo City. Like Mother, I hadn't been keen on the idea since he'd announced his intentions earlier in the week. But unlike Mother, I wasn't worried about Papa bringing back any diseases. Papa was around sick people all the time; a few more wouldn't matter. Also, being somewhat less conscious of appearances than Mother, it didn't bother me that my father would stoop to mingle with those some might consider the lowest of the low. Papa's regular patients had never been exactly wealthy. But what really bothered me, though I'm ashamed to admit it, was Mother's point about these people not being able to pay. They wouldn't even be able to supply us with chickens and vegetables. And that meant less for me. The raise in my allowance I'd been hoping for seemed ever more unlikely.

But now I suddenly had a far graver reason for objecting to Papa's charity work. What if by going to Soo City he really was in danger? What if some hobo really did try to kill him for his money?

Charlotte and I walked along in silence, the unseasonably hot sun beating down on our backs and causing the bits of shale in the sidewalk to sparkle. The glare of the light was almost blinding. I squinted and scratched my head and ran my hand down the length of my bobbed hair. I told myself that terrible things happened to *other* people, not to people like Papa, so I needn't worry about his safety. Besides, Papa always said that God was taking care of us. Surely He'd be good enough to send a few extra angels down the sunray ladder to protect my father if it looked like anything bad was going to happen.

I had myself mostly convinced of Papa's safety by the time we reached the theater, and when the houselights went down and the movie flickered on the screen, I had forgotten completely about my father and the shantytown. I loved to sit in the middle of a movie house filled with laughter. It made me feel like a part of something wonderful. I enjoyed comedies even more than the romantic pictures that made women cry, and fortunately for me, in those days the comedians were hard at work trying to keep people laughing. Unlike Charlotte, I believed there really was a depression going on, but I wasn't any more aware than my friend of the real consequences of our country's economic troubles. I didn't know that many of those who laughed with me in that movie house were there simply to escape from the fears that had plagued them since the day in 1929 — remembered as Black Thursday — when the bottom began to fall out of the stock market. Ten years old at the time of the crash, I was old enough to know that something had happened but not old enough to fully understand what it was. I heard that men were jumping out of windows and women were crying and fainting in the streets, but the reasons behind the calamity were a mystery understood only by the adult mind. I had no idea that the ripples of Black Thursday would ever reach me. And in fact, three years later, the Depression seemed still not to have touched me at all. Something might be happening to other people, but life went on in our house just the same as always. I did recall that the bank where Papa deposited our money closed sometime in 1930, and Mother, who rarely cried, wept over that. Yet I couldn't see any visible changes in our daily routine. The same amount of food appeared on our table, the same number of dresses hung in my closet, and Papa always seemed to have a sufficient amount of cash in his wallet. He even started giving me an allowance of a quarter a week when I turned twelve. Whatever this Depression was, my family seemed immune to it. It wasn't anything I needed to be concerned about.

And so I laughed at Buster Keaton as the straight-faced little fellow made a fool of himself for the sake of other people's happiness. I laughed easily and innocently, not afraid of the lights coming on again, not afraid of having to go back out to face the real world. To me, the real world was grand. I wanted to grasp it and hold it to me and take from it everything it had to offer. From where I stood on the threshold of adolescence, life appeared full of promise and possibility, and I was anxious to meet it head on.

"That was pretty good, wasn't it?" I asked Charlotte as we flowed with the crowd back out onto the simmering sidewalk.

"It was all right," she said blandly. She'd never admit that she liked a Buster Keaton movie, though my left ear was still ringing from her shrill screams of glee.

I turned toward the direction of home, but Charlotte stopped me by saying, "I don't feel like going back yet, do you?"

I shrugged. "What do you want to do?"

She answered with a question of her own. "How much money do you have?" I reached into the pocket of my dress and pulled out a nickel. "Good," she said. "Just enough for a cherry Coke over at Pete and Jerry's. We can get two straws and split it."

"Well, all right," I agreed, but hesitantly. Pete and Jerry's was a small ice cream parlor in a rather run-down section of town. Charlotte and I had been there once or twice on the sly, but not since the previous summer. I knew Mother wouldn't want me to go there, and I envisioned myself, if found out, being slapped with three more Campion poems and the entire book of Second Timothy. But I followed Charlotte anyway as she headed toward the heart of downtown.

We had crossed one street and were only halfway down the next block when Charlotte stopped suddenly. She pressed her forehead up against the window of an empty shop and peered inside. "Look, Virginia," she said, "this is where Mama used to love to come and shop for clothes. It's gone out of business, and they didn't leave so much as a garter belt behind. Take a look."

I pressed my own forehead against the surprisingly cool glass and cupped my hands like horse blinders beside my eyes. Charlotte was right. The place was completely empty. Mother and I had never shopped there, but I did remember passing by the display window now and again and catching a glimpse of the sleek clothes on the mannequins. "I wonder what happened," I whispered.

"I don't know," Charlotte said. "Wilma — that was the owner — she always had a pretty good business going. Least it seemed so."

"Maybe she moved the store somewhere else," I suggested.

"Maybe," Charlotte agreed.

We looked at the sign in the corner of the window. It said "For Lease" and gave a phone number. Usually when businesses moved, they taped their new address to the front door of the old place. But Wilma had packed up and vanished without a forwarding address.

"Oh well," Charlotte said resignedly. "Won't Mama have a fit when I tell her!"

We continued walking. Up ahead we saw a shabbily dressed man accept a coin from a better dressed one. The scruffy man lifted his cap in appreciation and stuck the coin in his shirt pocket.

"He's a beggar," Charlotte whispered from the corner of her mouth. "Just walk right by as if you don't see him."

"But all I have is a nickel anyway," I said.

"That's a gold mine to him. Stare straight ahead," Charlotte ordered.

I couldn't imagine that the pathetic-looking figure now walking toward us would ask for a handout from two young girls. But suddenly I remembered what Charlotte said about hobos killing for money, and I wondered whether this beggar would accost us and slit our throats for the sake of a nickel. I wished I had gone home rather than agreeing to go to Pete and Jerry's.

But the man passed by without giving us so much as a glance, and while I breathed a sigh of relief, Charlotte waved her hand under her nose.

"Whew! Beggars stink, don't they?"

I hadn't noticed. I was too happy to be alive with my nickel safe in my pocket.

"There's another one over there," she continued, nodding toward a man on the other side of the street. "They're all over the place."

There had always been panhandlers in this part of town, but once again Charlotte was right. Two on the same block was a rare sight. As we continued to walk, we not only passed two more panhandlers, but three shoe shiners, a couple of kids hawking pencils, and a man on a street corner selling apples.

"Bothersome, aren't they — all these sidewalk salesmen," Charlotte remarked with a slight tilt of her chin. "That's what Mama says. She says back in the old days people ran respectable businesses in their shops. They didn't go out into the streets and try to shove their goods into people's faces."

"Did she say what changed it?" I asked.

"The Depression, of course."

"I thought you didn't believe in the Depression."

"I don't, but Mama does."

"I don't know, Charlotte. I mean, they're always talking on the radio about the Depression."

Charlotte shrugged.

"And what about all those people down at the shantytown —"

"But look at us, will you?" she interrupted. "Are we starving? Are we poor?"

No. As I'd already realized myself, we weren't starving, and if we were poor we didn't know it.

We moved along past empty shops with "For Rent" signs in the windows, past stores that were holding closing-out sales, past employment offices with "No Help Wanted" signs nailed to the doors. Charlotte began to speculate aloud as to the whereabouts of Mitchell Quakenbush (he hadn't in fact shown up at the theater), but I scarcely heard a word she said. I was still a little nervous about going to Pete and Jerry's, but more than that, the farther we walked the more convinced I became that something terrible was happening right here in the streets of our hometown. The city was quieter, more subdued, than I had ever known it to be. There were fewer cars in the streets, fewer pedestrians on the sidewalks (not counting the panhandlers and two-bit salesmen), and fewer businesses that were actually open for business. I suddenly felt as though I were walking through the belly of a dying man.

"How much farther to Pete and Jerry's?" I asked.

"You know where it is," Charlotte replied with a hint of annoyance. "Around this corner and down another couple of blocks. Say, look at that line of men over there. Goes all the way around the corner and down the next block. I didn't know there was a movie theater down there."

When we turned the corner, we discovered that the men were not in line for a late afternoon show. On the other side of the street from where we stood was a morbid red brick building. A crude sign over the door identified it as the Lower Street Mission. Charlotte and I stared dumbfounded at the line that snaked backward from the mission door. It was an ill-clad, unshaven, forlorn group of men that stood there one behind another like obedient schoolchildren waiting for milk. They were eerily quiet, the only evidence of life their constant agitated fidgeting beneath the hot sun. With eyes downcast and shoulders slumped, they wiped at their foreheads with soiled handkerchiefs, the rims of their caps, or sometimes with just the back of their hands. The line seemed barely to move at all. Every few moments the men shuffled forward half a step or so. One man, better dressed and more confident than the others, went down the line handing out what looked to me like Bible tracts. I figured he was a volunteer with the Mission. Food was never dished out at a mission without a side order of the Gospel. The men in line received the pamphlets dully. Some glanced at them and stuffed them into shirt pockets. Others tossed them aside.

"What on earth are they doing?" Charlotte whispered.

"It's a breadline," I replied just as quietly. The aura of anger, humiliation, and despair hung so heavily about these men that it dissolved any trace of joy that had clung to me from my film trip into make-believe with Buster Keaton.

"Oh yeah, a breadline. I've heard about them."

"Don't you remember? This is the mission where we sent our money."

She nodded. "Well, I hope they appreciated it. Come on, let's go. I'm as hot as your mama's temper and dying for that cherry Coke."

The occasional wind had carried one of the pamphlets to our side of the street, dropping it gently almost at our feet. I picked it up and caught Charlotte by the arm. "Just a minute. Listen to this. It says, 'Workers of the world unite. You have nothing to lose but your chains.' I don't remember that being in the Bible."

Charlotte nodded knowingly. "I think it's in the Old Testament somewhere, probably in Exodus. Isn't that where all the slaves got together and left Egypt?"

"Oh yeah." I narrowed my eyes, trying to remember if this was something Moses had announced to the Hebrews to get them riled up enough to walk out on Pharaoh. Though I'd read the story numerous times, I didn't recall this particular verse. But, I reasoned, it was hard to remember the details of all the Bible stories. There were so many.

"At any rate," Charlotte continued, "the man handing out these tracts is knocking on the wrong door. These men aren't workers, they're beggars — the whole lot of them."

"Well, maybe not, Charlotte," I said, rising to their defense.

"What do you mean, maybe not? They're standing around waiting for a handout, aren't they?"

"Yeah, I guess so, but — hey, who's that man there?"

"What man where?"

"The one with the tie."

Charlotte pushed out her jaw and squinted. "If you mean the one with the wing-tip shoes, I've never seen him before in my life."

He *did* have on wing-tip shoes. What was a man wearing a tie and wing-tip shoes doing in a breadline?

"I know that man," I stated with certainty.

"Yeah, well, it's no secret that you favor tramps. He looks a little bit like Charlie Chaplin."

"I don't mean —"

"Come *on*, before I die of thirst."

It was her turn to grab my arm and pull me along, but we'd gone only a couple of steps when from the corner of my eye I saw one of the men stagger and fall forward onto the hot asphalt of the street.

"Charlotte, look!" I cried. I pulled my arm from her grasp and instinctively started across the street toward the man who had fainted. I have no idea how I might have revived him had I reached him, but I couldn't get that far, for the crowd of men that gathered around him. I stood in the middle of the street with my fingertips pressed to my lips.

"Go on, little miss, get out of the road 'fore a car comes along and runs you over."

I looked up into the face of a rough-looking fellow, a man who seemed hardened by the years, but when he spoke his voice was gentle.

"It's just the hunger and the heat that got him. Happens all the time. Go on now, you run along 'fore you get hurt."

I turned to go, but as I turned I saw again the familiar-faced man, and this time he noticed me, too. A look of recognition, then of fear, or perhaps embarrassment, flashed across his face. He quickly turned his head away and coughed, but the cough sounded contrived. It almost seemed he wanted to hide from me.

"Come *on*, Virginia!" Charlotte called. "The sun's starting to burn the skin right *off* me."

Without a word I joined her, and in spite of the heat, we ran the remaining two blocks to Pete and Jerry's. When we arrived, panting and holding our sides, we found the door locked.

"Drat!" Charlotte cried. She actually stamped her foot on the sidewalk as she repeated her exclamation. "Drat and double drat! Just what in the world is going on around here? Pete and Jerry's has shut down, too."

I didn't answer. My mind had just called up a memory of the familiar face waiting for a bowl of soup. I saw myself holding Papa's hand as we took our weekly pre-Depression walk to the bank to deposit money. I always felt a chill run through me as we entered the lobby of that plush establishment. The place reeked of wealth, and I knew that beyond the marble counter where the tellers stood, there was a huge vault that held all the money in the world. Sometimes Papa would take me into the office of the president, who was an acquaintance of his. The man sat there looking very splendid in his double-breasted suit and his wing-tip shoes.

His wing-tip shoes. That down-and-out fellow outside the Mission had once been the president of Papa's bank!

As Charlotte had so aptly put it, just what in the world *was* going on around here? How could it be that bank presidents ended up in breadlines, that our streets were crowded with beggars, and that Wilma, Pete, and Jerry had all disappeared overnight?

Chapter Five

The Depression began to seem real to me after I saw the breadline at the Lower Street Mission. Just a few days later it really hit home when Mother told me that Uncle Jim had lost his job down at the grain mill and that now he and Aunt Sally and two of my cousins, Rufus and Luke, would be moving in with us. About a year earlier the oldest boy, eighteen-year-old Jimmy Jr. had hopped the Soo Line with some friends and was traveling the country in search of work, along with about 200,000 other boys and young men. Uncle Jim and Aunt Sally received an occasional postcard, but they knew that by the time a card arrived from, say, Omaha or St. Louis, Jimmy Jr. had long since moved on to someplace else.

At first the prospect of relatives living with us seemed rather exciting, but that thought lasted only until Mother told me to clear my things out of my room because it would soon belong to Aunt Sally and Uncle Jim.

I was too stunned to speak for a moment. My room had always been my room, from the very beginning. I had grown up in that room, journeying all the way from infancy to adolescence. That room was where I dreamed my dreams and hoped all my hopes. It was where I opened my eyes on each new day and closed my eyes in sleep at night. It was the place to which I retreated when I wanted solitude. It was my refuge, the only little space in all the world that was wholly mine.

When I found my voice, I discovered it to be several decibels higher in volume than usual. "They can't have my room, Mama! It's *my* room!"

Mother looked at me without so much as the slightest expression passing over her face. "Your aunt and uncle need the room, and so they will have it. The decision's been made and it's final."

"And just where do you expect me to sleep?" I cried. "In the bathtub? On the kitchen table? Outside on the porch swing?"

"Certainly not," Mother said calmly. We were in Mama and Papa's bedroom at the sewing machine. Mother was inspecting the apron I had just finished — one of the punishment garments. She snipped a piece of thread that was dangling from the hem and said, "You'll move in with the girls. They're still small enough that the three of you will fit nicely in their double bed."

"Mama! You can't expect me to share a bed with Claudia and Molly! I'll be kicked and drooled on all night. I'll never get any sleep. I'll grow sick from exhaustion. I'll —"

"Nonsense," Mother interrupted. "You'll do just fine, all three of you."

"Oh, Mama," I groaned, picturing myself squeezed into that dark little closet of a room with my two sisters. Because my own room was on the east side of the house, it caught the morning light, and sometimes when I sat on the bed reading or memorizing poems, the sun shone in across me, and I could almost feel the airy footsteps of angels as they climbed down the sunbeams to earth. The room my little sisters shared was on the north side of the house, and because of an enormous red maple just beyond its single window, it got little light at all. "Oh, Mama!" I exclaimed again. Tears came to my eyes, and I couldn't keep them from slithering down my cheeks, though I was ashamed for Mother to see me cry. I was trying so hard to convince her I was grown up, and shedding tears would only work against me. But I couldn't help it. My room — the one little alcove of the house that was all mine, that had always been mine — was now lost to me, and I felt I was being exiled to a strange land.

Mother surprised me by patting my hand and saying kindly, "I'm sorry, Virginia. Truly I am. I know I'm asking a lot of you, and if there were any other way —" she paused and shook her head — "but there isn't."

I sniffed and dabbed at my wet cheeks with the back of my hand. "What about Simon's room? Can't they have *his* room?"

"Your cousins will be moving in with Simon. Even then, one of them will have to sleep on a pallet on the floor. Probably Simon, since he's the youngest. So you see, you're not the only one making a sacrifice."

I wondered what sacrifice Mother and Papa would be making. Sure, the relatives moving in might be an imposition for them, but at least they would still have their own room, their own bed. Quietly, I slid a spool over the spool pin and began threading the machine. I had intended to start work on a skirt that morning — the pattern was all cut out and ready to be stitched — but I suddenly felt completely drained of energy. Had Mother not been there beside me, I would have run to my room, flung myself across the bed, and howled like a newborn.

After a moment I asked dully, "Why can't they stay in their own house, Mama?"

"I told you. Your uncle Jim lost his job a few days back, and since he and Sally are already in debt, they won't be able to keep up with the rent. They can't stay there."

"But can't Uncle Jim get another job?"

Mother sighed heavily. "Not likely. Not in these times."

"Well," I asked hesitantly, "how long will they be here?"

"I can't answer that, Virginia. I just don't know. But it could be quite some time, so don't get your hopes up that you'll be getting your room back anytime soon."

I pressed the bobbin into the bobbin case and sniffed again. My mind stumbled over itself in an attempt to come up with a solution to this problem, a solution that the grown-ups had somehow overlooked. "Surely, Mama," I said feebly, "surely there must be some way Uncle Jim and Aunt Sally don't have to lose their home —"

Mother shook her head. Wisps of hair stuck out from her bun and floated about her head like gossamer. I noticed there were a few more gray strands than before. In fact, she looked older and more tired than I had ever seen her. "There's no other way, Virginia. You don't expect me to send my own sister to live down in that shantytown, do you? Down there with the others who have lost their jobs and their homes? No. As long as your father and I have our health and our senses, no family of ours will go hungry or without a roof over their heads."

I rose from my chair and went to gather the pieces of my skirt from the floor where I had cut them out, thinking I would begin to stitch them together. But Mother changed my plans.

"Leave that until later, Virginia," she said quietly, not lifting her eyes to look at me. "You'd best start cleaning out your room this morning. They'll be coming the end of the week."

Today was Wednesday. That meant I had only two more days to call my room my own.

Mother continued. "You might as well start by cleaning out your closet and carrying some of your clothes up to the attic to store them there. That closet in the girls' room won't hold all three of you girls' clothes."

"But how am I supposed to wear my clothes if they're up in the attic?" I asked. I stood there with two pieces of my skirt in my hands. The cloth became wrinkled as my hands closed into fists of frustration.

"Just keep aside what you need and store the rest. Heaven knows you have more clothes than any child ought to have anyway."

Then why am I slaving over this sewing machine making more skirts and dresses for school? I wondered. I wanted to throw the question at Mother, but I knew better. My tears dried on my cheeks, and my sadness was swallowed up by anger.

I loved my uncle Jim, but in that moment I sided with my maternal grandparents in their opinion of him. Though it had all taken place long before I was born, I knew from Aunt Sally's stories that Grandfather and Grandmother Foster were strongly opposed to their daughter marrying Jim Dubbin. "He's working class," they had protested. "He'll never make a decent living, never give you a decent home."

But Aunt Sally had married Jim Dubbin anyway. They had eloped one night when Aunt Sally was only seventeen years old. Not even Mother, who was older by three years, was married yet. According to Aunt Sally, Grandmother Foster had cried straight through for a week and had even worn mourning clothes for a year, but the way Aunt Sally liked to embellish a story, I was never sure whether that last part was true or not.

She told me all this with a look of victorious joy on her face, as though she had outwitted her parents at their own game.

"They said I'd never be happy, but they were wrong," she boasted. "Jim and I have been together all these years, and I can't imagine any two people being happier than we are. Oh, I know I don't have all the fancy things my own mama and papa had — a big house, fancy dishes, pretty clothes. But" — she waved a hand gleefully — "who needs all that finery? Jim's always worked hard and we've never lacked for anything. We have three fine sons, and I wouldn't choose to live any other way."

My grandfather Foster had been a rather wealthy businessman and what Aunt Sally called "a big man about town." She described both her father and mother as educated and sophisticated and "always strutting about town like a couple of peacocks with their feathers all puffed out." Maybe my grandparents impressed a lot of people, but I had a feeling that one person who wasn't terribly impressed was their own daughter Sally. "The quality of a person's character isn't measured by his bank account," Aunt Sally was known to say.

And yet one of the first things I learned in life was that a wing down at Mercy Hospital had been named after my grandfather because he had donated the largest amount of money toward the hospital's expansion fund. More than once Mother had taken us children down to that wing of the hospital to show us a bronze plaque on the wall bearing Grandfather's name and the year the wing was completed, 1924. Evidently Mother, unlike Aunt Sally, was rather proud of her father's accomplishments.

My grandparents were both still living, but sometime before the Depression they had moved back to Grandmother's native Georgia to escape the long harsh winters of the upper Midwest. It was never talked about, but I suspect they lost some or all of their fortune in the crash, as it was about that time that the flow of extravagant gifts from Georgia to Minnesota stopped.

When Aunt Sally first related to me the story of her nuptials, I couldn't understand my grandparents' stubborn objection to Uncle Jim. So what if he was a working man? Papa worked. He worked long hours every day. All my friends' fathers worked. For that matter, Grandfather Foster himself worked! It appeared to me that all men worked unless they were bums. Wasn't everyone who worked a part of the working class? And if a man worked and wasn't a bum, wasn't he respectable? Just what was it that made Uncle Jim different?

I still didn't understand fully the reason my grandparents rejected Uncle Jim, but when I learned that the Dubbins would be moving in with us, I thought perhaps Grandfather and Grandmother Foster had been proven right at last. There must be something wrong with Jim Dubbin. He couldn't provide for his family. And because of him, the Dubbins and the Eides were all going to be miserable, especially me.

I went to my room, and feeling intensely sorry for myself and quite sure that I of all the people in the world had been the most ill treated by the Depression, I started to pull my clothes out of the closet and threw them across the bed. "I'll run away," I muttered as the tears came again and I sniffed angrily. "I'll run away and live with Charlotte — they have plenty of room there. Probably no one around here will even notice, since there's going to be such a crowd in this house." But even as I declared my resolve to run away, I knew, of course, it was a futile plan. Mother would only find me and drag me home by the ear, and three more poems by the unfathomable Campion would be drilled into my reluctant brain.

For the next couple of days I divided up my garments, taking some up to the attic to be stored in boxes, moving the rest into the closet in Molly and Claudia's room. I gathered up my toiletry items, my knick-knacks, my books, my secret stash of "True Story" magazines and carried everything into the room on the north side of the house. Claudia and Molly sat on the double bed, each of them clutching a doll with a porcelain face and porcelain hands and real human hair. The dolls had been given the rather dubious names of Gardenia and Petunia. (Aunt Sally, who loved flowers, had named them.) They had been a gift to me and to Claudia from the Grandparents Foster a few years back, just before Molly was born. I gave mine to Molly when she became old enough to appreciate it and I too old to play with it any longer. Now four pairs of eyes — those of my sisters and the glassy eyes of the dolls — stared up at me in puzzlement.

"Whatcha doing, Ginny?" Molly asked.

"Moving in. You know that — Mama told you."

"You mean," Claudia asked, "you're going to live in here with us?"

"I'm afraid so."

"And sleep in here with us, too?" Molly asked.

"Yes, that too."

A gleeful cheer arose from my sisters, and the porcelain hands of the dolls began to clap at the bidding of their owners.

"Well," I said, "I'm glad somebody's happy about it."

"It'll be fun, Ginny," Claudia said. "We can tell stories every night."

"And you can sleep on this side of the bed," Molly added, "so I don't have to be afraid of the ghost anymore."

"What ghost?"

"The ghost Simon said stands by our bed and watches us when we're asleep," Claudia explained.

Molly added, "Mama says there's no such thing as ghosts, but Simon said —"

"Simon's just telling you a story," I said. "But if it'll make you feel any better, I'll sleep on that side of the bed. I just hope the two of you won't push me out of it. I don't care to wake up in the morning and find myself on the floor."

"Ginny," Molly asked, "why are you moving in here? Don't you like your own room anymore?"

I sighed. "Yes, I like my old room, and I wish it was still my room. But I have to move in here because Uncle Jim's a —" I wanted to say that Uncle Jim was a bum, but I couldn't quite get the word out. As angry as I was with him, the word just didn't fit the man I knew.

"Uncle Jim's what?" Claudia asked.

"Is he dead?" Molly asked, horrified.

I laughed at my younger sister's quivering lower lip, set in motion by the slightest fear or provocation. I pinched her lip playfully, kissed her forehead, and assured her that Uncle Jim wasn't dead. "You know what happened. Mama already explained everything to you. Uncle Jim lost his job, so he and Aunt Sally and Rufus and Luke all have to move in with us."

"Where did he lose it?" Molly inquired.

"What do you mean, where did he lose it?"

"Whenever I lose Toonya" — she held Petunia up for me to see — "Mama tries to make me remember where I might have lost her. Maybe we can help Uncle Jim find his job."

"Well, it's not that he lost it, not that way, it's just that — oh, never mind. You two are just too young to understand. You have to be grown up, like me. Now, listen, instead of just sitting there like a couple of bumps on a log, how about giving me a hand?"

The last items I brought over from my old room were My Two Charlies. I stuck them into the frame of the dresser mirror in my new room, high enough so that neither Claudia nor Molly could reach them. "Sorry, fellows," I apologized as I fitted them between the wood and the glass. "I know you don't like these new surroundings any more than I do, but there's nothing I can do about it. Like Mama says, I suppose we're just going to have to grin and bear it."

I still carry in my mind a picture of the Dubbins walking up the street toward our house on the day they moved in. They had never owned a car. Papa intended to pick them up, but he was called out to see an ailing patient just at the agreed-upon hour. Mother didn't drive, though she somehow got word to her sister that Papa would meet them with the Buick as soon as he could. But the Dubbins didn't wait. Rather than spending another few hours in the rented house they could no longer afford, the Dubbin family walked across town with their few possessions crammed into a half-dozen beat-up old suitcases. Whatever happened to all their furniture and household goods, I never knew. Perhaps they had tried to sell some of it, or perhaps they had given some away. Yet again, maybe they had simply left it all in the house and walked away from it. I don't know.

I spied them coming up the sidewalk when they were more than a block away — a forlorn group of refugees, victims of an economic debacle as shattering to human life as any war. Even from a distance I could see that the four of them tried to walk with dignity. In spite of the heat, they were dressed in their finest clothes — Uncle Jim and the boys in slacks and white shirts, suspenders and bow ties; Aunt Sally in a yellow dress with an artificial lace collar, a pair of buffed pumps strapped across her tiny feet. Both the boys wore caps, but Uncle Jim wore a fedora, and Aunt Sally had on the white straw hat with the cloth flowers on the brim that she'd worn to church every Easter for the past several years. Had it not been for the suitcases and the fact that it was a Friday afternoon, they might well have passed for a respectable family on their way to Sunday morning services. And yet, as it was, their attempt at dignity actually made their small parade appear all the more pathetic. It was obvious they were a family on the move — on the move because they had lost what they had, on the move from the place they had once called home to a place they would never really call home. Because they, like so many others, were a defeated army. They had tried to stand up against calamity, but the enemy had been too big, just too overwhelming for them.

I called to Mother and she joined me on the porch.

"Oh!" she exclaimed at the spectacle of her own flesh and blood tramping like displaced Okies up the sidewalk. "Now, why didn't they wait for William to pick them up, I wonder?"

I had no answer and knew she didn't expect one.

She waved a hand and called out, "Gracious, Sally, why did you hike all the way over here in those high-heeled shoes of yours?" She hurried down the porch steps, took one of the suitcases from Sally, and put an arm around her shoulder. "That's a good way to wear out the soles before their time, and heaven knows we have to make things last as long as we can. Well, come in, come in, everyone. You must be roasting, walking all that way in this heat. I've got some cold lemonade in the icebox. Virginia, get out some glasses, will you, and pour some lemonade. Well, wait a minute, before you do that — here, take this suitcase and show your aunt Sally and uncle Jim to their room. Rufus and Luke, you follow me."

None of the Dubbins had uttered a word so far. The weary and solemn-faced troupe climbed the porch steps and filed silently into the house while I held open the screen door for them. Aunt Sally did attempt to smile at me as she passed by, but the slight upturning of her lips was overshadowed by the dull sheen of sadness in her eyes. Uncle Jim, his own eyes averted, took off his fedora and offered me a taut nod. The cousins looked cross and out of sorts, and I was rather surprised when Luke stuck out his tongue at me. A year younger than I, Luke had always been more or less cordial toward me, though obviously disinterested in my feminine world. Now he poked his pale tongue at me as though his family's misfortune were all my fault. I frowned and fought the temptation to return the gesture.

I was the last to enter the house, dragging one of Aunt Sally's suitcases with me, and by the time I got into the hallway, Mother was already ascending the stairs, throwing words over her shoulder as she went.

"Now, boys, we're going to put you in with Simon. I trust you'll be comfortable there. We want you all to make yourselves right at home here, of course. Anything you need, you just let us know. Ginny, are you coming? Let's get these folks settled in so we can start enjoying that lemonade."

"Yes, Mama," I replied. I looked up shyly at my aunt and uncle, who were waiting for me to lead the way. "You'll be in my room," I said. Then, though of course they had seen the room before, I added, "I hope you'll like it."

I started up the stairs when I heard Aunt Sally behind me begin to say something.

"Ginny, I'm —"

I clutched the banister with my free hand and looked back over my shoulder. "Yes, Aunt Sally?"

My aunt's face was red from the heat and moist with perspiration. The hair that poked out from under her hat was matted to her skin. For a moment I thought she was going to say she was simply too tired to climb the stairs. I reached out to take her other suitcase, but she smiled bravely and waved a hand.

"I'm fine, Ginny," she said. "I was just

going to say that I'm sure your room will be lovely."

"Oh," I muttered. I turned and we walked the remainder of the distance to my room — their room — in silence.

When we had put the suitcases down beside the bed, Aunt Sally asked, "But where will you be?"

"In with Claudia and Molly. I've already moved all my stuff over there."

"Ah, I see. Well, it's very kind of you, Ginny, to give us your room."

"Oh," I muttered feebly. "I don't mind. I mean, I'm glad to let you have it." I wondered whether they could tell I was lying.

Aunt Sally went to the dresser and removed her hat. Unlike Mother, who insisted on wearing her hair in the unvarying severe bun, Aunt Sally wore hers in a fashionable short cut. Now it lay matted to her head, but she gave it a cursory brush-through with her fingers and patted it back into place. I often wondered at the difference between my mother and my aunt. Where Mother was dark complected, Aunt Sally was fair. Where Mother was tall and large boned, Aunt Sally was short and diminutive. She might have appeared frail had it not been for her natural exuberance and unbounded energy. And unlike Mother, Aunt Sally didn't consider it a sin to add a little color to her cheeks and lips, or to wear fashionable dresses of bright material. Personality-wise, where Mother was quick to reprove and correct, Aunt Sally was quick to laugh. She was the carefree one, the one always ready with a song or a story or a shriek of unbridled glee.

Except for now. As she turned from the mirror toward Uncle Jim, the look of sorrow on her face was completely foreign, so completely out of character that even her features seemed twisted and changed.

Uncle Jim dropped his eyes from Aunt Sally, tossed his fedora onto the bed, and sat down on the edge of the mattress. His red face became redder still, and I could see his pulse thumping in his temple as he clenched his hands together. When he spoke for the first time since arriving, it was through clenched teeth.

"It's a crying shame, Ginny," he said, "just a crying shame to kick a little girl out of her room like this." It was defeat more than sorrow that settled over Uncle Jim's face, the same defeated look of the men standing in the breadline, the look of men who had lost everything and had been reduced to seeking a handout.

"Oh no, Uncle Jim!" I cried. I lifted my hand to my chest. My heart ached so with pity I thought it might burst. "I don't mind at all! Really, I don't. It'll be awfully fun to have you and Aunt Sally and the cousins

113

here, really it will. And you'll get another job soon, I'm sure of it, Uncle Jim, I'm —"

I stopped when Uncle Jim went into a fit of coughing that drowned out my words. Aunt Sally stepped over to her husband and, sitting down beside him, patted his back. Uncle Jim had been coughing half his life. Papa said it was because of the grain dust down at the mill. He said it was destroying Uncle Jim's lungs. "One good thing about Jim's losing his job," Papa had said, "maybe he can find a job that won't kill him in the end."

I wanted to run to Uncle Jim and throw my arms around his neck and tell him everything would work out for the best somehow. I wanted to tell him that he could stay here in my room for as long as he wanted, years and years if need be, and I wouldn't mind at all — no, not one bit. I wanted to comfort him and Aunt Sally and peel away all the sadness so that the jolly people they were inside — the happy people I'd always known — could come out again.

But the picture of the two of them sitting on the edge of the bed that stifling afternoon was enough to drain away my own hope, and I quietly slipped out of the room, leaving them alone while I went to the kitchen to set the table with large glasses of cold and bittersweet lemonade.

Chapter Six

That same week Mother let Emma May go. Now that Aunt Sally would be around to help, Mother figured she could do without a hired girl. I suppose, too, she thought the money she spent on Emma May should more rightly go toward the upkeep of the family that had increased overnight by four.

Emma May had been with us for three years, and we all hated to lose her — especially Molly, whose lower lip worked overtime on Emma May's last day. Emma May herself took the news calmly, though not without a few tears. She was a shy and retiring girl who never said much, but when she did speak she always tried to be positive, and the comments she made when Mother apologetically dismissed her were in keeping with her optimism. She had been secretly hoping, she said, to marry her sweetheart and set up a home of her own by year's end. Now that she had lost her position, perhaps her young man would view this as a suitable time to pop the question — Depression or no. After all, he was earning a small but steady income as a clerk for the railroad, and Emma May had always heard that two could live as cheaply as one. So with a brave smile and a promise to stay in touch, she left us.

Her absence was the reason Mother and I both stood kneading separate mounds of bread dough on the kitchen counter the morning after the Dubbins moved in. It was a task that Emma May had perfected — nothing tasted better than a slice of her bread straight from the oven with a big slab of butter melting on it — but now the chore had been handed down to me. Mother was showing me how to knead the dough properly by pressing it down and away from me with the heels of my hands, then turning it a quarter circle and repeating the process until the texture of the dough was smooth and elastic. She encouraged me by saying it would strengthen my fingers and make me better able to play the piano. Mother was a woman of indefatigable hope.

Aunt Sally was working in the garden that morning, watering and pulling weeds. The patch of land on which the Dubbins' rented house sat had been too small for a garden, so Aunt Sally was eager, she said, to get down on her hands and knees and work with the earth. I was happy to see her out there communing with nature. If she weren't doing it, then I'd have to do it, and weeding the garden was one of my least favorite chores.

Papa and Dr. Hal were with patients in the office. Simon was at the piano practicing. Rufus and Luke had run out after breakfast to explore the neighborhood and to elude chores. The girls were in the parlor having a tea party with Gardenia and Petunia. And even though it was mid-morning, Uncle Jim hadn't yet appeared for breakfast.

As we worked, Mother asked, "Well, how was your first night with your sisters? Not so bad, was it?"

Certainly it hadn't been the best night I'd ever had. The girls were asleep by the time I got upstairs and had left me only a foot of room on the ghost side of the bed. Before getting in, I had to rearrange the two of them, but even then I gained only a few more inches for myself. Then there was the heat, made worse by the fact that there were three sweaty bodies in the same bed. The one electric fan in the room did little to keep us cool. Every time I fell into a restless sleep, Molly woke me up again by throwing an arm around me. It was almost enough to make me want to curse Uncle Jim again, but when I remembered how he looked as he sat there on my bed, I just couldn't be angry with him.

I told Mother that I had slept fine.

"I'm glad, dear," she replied absently as she sprinkled a little more flour across the counter. "I know it's going to take some time for all of us to adjust, but — well, there you are, Jim! Good morning. Have a seat and I'll fix you some scrambled eggs and toast."

"No thanks, Lillian," Uncle Jim said, though he pulled out a chair and sat down at the table. "Just a cup of coffee will do."

"Nonsense," Mother said. "You have to have something more substantial than that." She poured him a cup of coffee from the pot on the stove and set it before him. "Now, it won't take me a minute to cook something. You do like your eggs scrambled, don't you?"

Without waiting for a reply, Mother went about the task of gathering what she needed to make yet one more breakfast that morning. Uncle Jim sipped his coffee without looking up at us, but I couldn't help looking at him. In the few weeks since our families had last been together, he seemed to have taken a great leap in the aging process. His thin face appeared thinner still and more elongated. Heavy lines creased his forehead and curved around his brow, almost meeting the crow's-feet at the corners of his eyes. He hadn't bothered to shave, and his purplish beard looked like a bruise across his cheeks. His dark hair, combed straight back from his face, had some gray I'd

118

never noticed before. And his dark eyes, once so lively they almost twinkled, now appeared sunken and somber.

He pulled a cigarette out of the pack in his shirt pocket, tapped the filter end against the tabletop, and stuck it between his pale lips. He then reached into the same pocket with one index finger and fished out a pack of matches. Striking the match head dully against the friction strip, he ignited a small flame, which he lifted to the tip of his cigarette. He squinted while he inhaled to get the tobacco burning. I watched the taut sad line of his mouth as he exhaled, sending a small funnel of smoke twirling up toward the ceiling. Then he pinched the tobacco seed off the tip of his tongue and rolled it off his fingers onto the floor.

His brand of cigarettes was Spud Menthol. I had seen them advertised in *Life* magazine with slogans like "Be Mouth-Happy" and "Join the Mouth-Happy Club." But on that first morning of the Dubbins' long stay with us, Uncle Jim looked anything but a candidate for the Mouth-Happy Club. All the sadness of the previous afternoon settled over me again as I watched him silently smoking and sipping his coffee.

After a few more puffs of tobacco, he started to cough — a barking hack that reminded me of the time Simon had whooping cough. Mother shook her head as she pushed down the handle of the toaster.

"You'll have to let William listen to that cough again," she suggested. "Maybe there's something he can give you."

"I doubt it," Uncle Jim said listlessly. "He's already told me the old lungs have taken in too much grain dust."

"Maybe so, but it might help, too, if you didn't smoke quite so much."

My uncle shrugged. "Everyone smokes, Lillian. Never hurt no one."

"Papa says all that smoke turns your insides black," I offered. "Says you might as well poke your lungs onto a stick and toast them over a fire like a couple of marshmallows."

Uncle Jim snickered and peered at me in amusement. His response to Papa's theory was to take another long pull on his cigarette and to let the smoke out slowly. Then he tapped his ashes onto the saucer.

"Where's Sally?" he asked, changing the subject.

"She's out working in the garden." Mother stepped to the window and looked out. "Looks like she's watering the tomatoes."

"Hmm. Sally always wanted a garden."

"Well, now she has one," Mother responded pleasantly.

"And she can work in it as much as she wants," I added.

Nothing more was said until Mother set the plate of eggs and toast in front of Uncle Jim. "Would you like some jam with that?" Mother asked. "We've got enough preserves to last from now till 1940, I bet." She gave a brief laugh and wiped her hands on her apron. She'd been trying hard to keep everyone's spirits up since the Dubbins arrived, and I had to admire her for that. To support her, I tossed out a little chuckle myself so she wouldn't have to laugh alone.

But Uncle Jim just sat there staring at the plate of food as though he couldn't comprehend what it was, as though he'd never seen scrambled eggs and toast before. Slowly he lifted his head. His eyes traveled from the plate to the face of his sister-in-law.

"Lillian," he said quietly, "I owe you an apology."

Mother frowned and cocked her head. "Why, whatever for, Jim? I can't imagine what you mean."

Uncle Jim crushed the cigarette out in the saucer. Simon's piano playing was all that was heard for a moment while Uncle Jim shook his head slowly, his eyes averted. Then suddenly he looked up at Mother

121

again and exclaimed, "Your parents always were against me marrying Sally, and they were right. She deserved better."

"Nonsense!" Mother snapped. "You're a good husband to Sally and a good father to the boys. Better than a lot of men might be. I, for one, have always been glad you're part of our family."

I raised an eyebrow. According to Aunt Sally's version of the story, even her own sister had tried to talk her out of marrying an uneducated laborer. I believed Aunt Sally, as Mother always placed great emphasis on education and breeding. Of course, Mother herself had dropped down a notch or two economically when she married Papa. William Eide would never see the wealth that Clarence Foster had accumulated. But at least Papa was educated and held a respectable position.

As time passed, though, Mother must have forgotten her initial objections to Jim Dubbin because she was obviously genuinely fond of him. She continued. "Besides, I think my parents long ago repented of anything they might have said at the time you and Sally married. They like you, Jim. I'm sure they do."

Uncle Jim, his food untouched, went on shaking his head. "Even so, even if they did come to accept me, what will they think now? I've lost my job and I've lost the house. I can't even support my family —"

"If I'm not mistaken," Mother interrupted, "you're not the only man with troubles lately. It's the times, Jim. It's just the times."

"But I'd still be working if I hadn't been so loud-mouthed about organizing a union down there."

"Well, I don't know about that, Jim —"

"It's the ones who wanted a union that were laid off. Those who kept their mouths shut are still on the job."

Mother went back to kneading the ball of dough. She asked, "Is that what they said when they let you go?"

Uncle Jim rapped once with his knuckles on the table, a brief tap of annoyance. "Naw, of course not." He spat the words out as though they tasted bitter in his mouth. "They couldn't say it had anything to do with union work, but we all know that was the call. Well, they may have fired me, but they haven't seen the last of me yet. I'm gonna go on working with the organizers till the mill decides to recognize the union. Maybe eventually those of us who lost our jobs for union activity can get hired on again. Then I can get Sally and the boys back into a house and get out of your way, Lil."

"You're not in my way, Jim," Mother responded. She turned to face Jim, her eyes wide with concern. "You know I want you here. Sally is my only sister. We're family, Jim. All of us. You'd do the same for William and me if the tables were turned. You know you would."

"But the tables aren't turned, Lillian. Will won't never be without work, being a doctor like he is."

Mother sighed. "Eat your breakfast, Jim," she said quietly. She went back to her kneading. "Then go on out to the garden and help Sally. You'll feel better as soon as you make yourself useful around here."

Uncle Jim ate reluctantly while Mother and I put the smooth full-moon balls of bread dough into glass bowls, which we set in lukewarm water in the sink so that the dough would rise. Then we started cutting up vegetables for soup.

Later, when Jim went out to join Sally in the garden, I asked Mother, "Aunt Sally always told me she was happy being married to Uncle Jim. Do you think she still is?"

"Certainly she is," Mother replied. "Just because they've run into hard times doesn't mean they don't love each other anymore."

"Mama?" I asked. "Are you and Papa happy together?"

"Of course!" she answered briskly, as though the question were ridiculous, the answer obvious.

I went on chopping carrots. Mother, kindly, had claimed the onions for herself. Simon went on playing adeptly. I envied him and at the same time felt anger toward him for the talent he'd been born with. I knew Mother must — however unconsciously — compare my playing with his, and that made me appear all the more inept. I chopped and listened and looked at my aunt and uncle working quietly together in the garden.

"Mama," I asked, "how old do I have to be before I can go out with a boy?"

Mother brushed away an onion tear with the back of her hand and replied, "You know very well you have to be sixteen."

Three more years to go. It seemed like an eternity. I wondered whether Danny Dysinger would wait that long for me, or whether he would go after other girls in the meantime.

To my surprise, Mother sensed my concern and disappointment. She cast me a sideways glance and smiled a smile that was rather coy for Mother. "I know how you feel," she assured me. "I was already sweet on your father when I was your age."

"You were?" My squeal of surprise was sincere.

"Oh yes. I used to write 'Will and Lil' all over my school books." She laughed out loud at the memory, a joyful sound at odds with the tears running down her cheeks. "I was terribly silly in my youth. Of course, your father barely knew I existed back then. He didn't start coming around to court me — that's what we called it in those days — until we were seniors in high school, and even then he didn't propose to me until eight years after that. He wanted to be established in a practice before he took on a wife and family. So you can take my word for it, I know how hard it is to wait. But sometimes that's what we're called to do."

"How did you finally get Papa to propose to you, Mama?"

Mother laughed again and brushed away a couple more tears. "Well, what could I do but pray? Every night I asked God to convince your father to propose to me. Finally he did."

It must have been just as she said. Mother probably didn't reveal her feelings to anyone but God. Papa himself was no doubt clueless as to how Mama felt about him. Even though they were courting, Mother, who wouldn't be caught dead flirting, probably acted as though she couldn't care less whether Papa proposed to her or not. She had allowed herself, admittedly, to scribble "Will and Lil" on her school books, but I suppose that was as close to being romantic as my mother ever dared venture.

And yet, there must have been a time when she had fallen in love. She must have known at least some inkling of the thrill of romance, since she had, after all, gotten married. People didn't get married, I reasoned, unless they were in love. Mother must know *something* about that greatest of all mysteries, the experience for which Charlotte and I had already done a great deal of pining.

"Mama," I asked, "what's it like to be married?"

"My, my." She clicked her tongue and shook her head. "You're just full of all sorts of questions today, aren't you?"

"Charlotte says it's the greatest thing in the world to be married."

"And just how might she know, I wonder?"

"Oh, I don't know, but I'm sure she's right. I'd never want to end up an old maid like Miss Cole."

"I imagine Miss Cole's very happy as she is."

"Oh, I don't think so, Mama! I mean, how could she be?"

"We can be content in whatever situation we're in, as long as we trust the Lord for what's good for us."

This oft-repeated phrase from Mother always struck fear in my heart — fear that

God was going to decide that spinsterhood was good for me. I wanted Him to work with me, not against me, when it came to marriage. After all, if Mother could pray for Papa to propose, surely I could pray to marry and receive a favorable answer.

"Well, but anyway, Mama," I continued, "isn't it nice to be married?"

"Of course," she said simply. She scraped the onions off the cutting board and into the pot of water boiling on the stove, then pulled apart a stalk of celery.

"But, well — what's it *like,* Mama?"

Mother frowned a moment as she laid two sticks of celery side by side on the cutting board. She raised her long serrated knife over the doomed vegetables and went to work with the swiftness of an executioner. Finally she said, "Well, Ginny — I mean, Virginia — *this* is what being married is all about" — she paused and gestured with her hands — "what we're doing right here. It's cooking and cleaning and raising children. It's about taking care of your home and family."

Narrowing my eyes, I peered at Mother. I didn't know whether she was purposely being evasive or whether she simply wasn't aware of how dull she was making marriage sound. I had no intention of growing up only to do more of what I was doing now. "But, Mama," I protested, "there must be more to marriage than that. There must be something nice about being in love and being together and — oh, I don't know, just being with the man you love."

Mother lifted her eyebrows and sighed. "I suppose," she said. Then she pulled a linen handkerchief from her apron pocket and dabbed at the perspiration on her neck. "Not even noon yet and already it's hot enough to melt a mountain of steel. I can remember some hot summers, but this one has outdone them all."

I was beginning to get frustrated, and I wasn't about to let Mother change the subject — not until I got a suitable reply. "But, *Mama*," I cried, "surely there must be something *romantic* about marriage."

Mother laughed and sighed simultaneously. "Oh, Virginia," she said, "you're such a dreamer."

But of course. Of course I was. What was the use of living if one wasn't going to dream? I couldn't help feeling rather sorry for Mother — she seemed to have no idea what made life both wonderful and worthwhile.

Chapter Seven

On the tenth of June, Violet Sharpe committed suicide. As a maid in the household of Anne Lindbergh's mother, she was to be questioned a second time by police in their investigation of the kidnapping of baby Charles. Apparently unable to handle the thought that she was a suspect, she evaded the police by swallowing cyanide chloride. She was discovered near death in the pantry by Mrs. Lindbergh's mother, and a moment later died in the woman's arms.

For a few weeks I had forgotten I was angry with God, but this incident reminded me. I commiserated with Charlotte and found myself tempted to agree with her when she said such tragedies proved God to be only a myth, anyway.

"Mama says if there really was a God, the world wouldn't be in such a mess," Charlotte said.

I considered Mrs. Besac's philosophy. It appeared sound enough on the surface. The world certainly was a mess, what with the murder of innocent children and the Depression and people like my uncle Jim losing his job and his home. Every morning we were given an update on the worsening situation by Dr. Hal, who, along with his toast and coffee, religiously ingested Walter Lippmann's syndicated comments in the local paper. Shaking his head and frowning, Dr. Hal could be counted on to make such discouraging announcements as, "Well, according to the American Federation of Labor, more than thirteen million people are out of work now."

One of the defining events of the Depression had begun only a couple weeks earlier out in Washington, D.C. According to reports we heard on the radio, a horde of veterans from the Great War had gathered to demand payment of the bonus bill Congress had passed back in 1924. The news had it that somewhere between fifteen and twenty-five thousand veterans were living in encampments along the Anacostia River and in a number of abandoned buildings on Pennsylvania Avenue. They were determined to stay put until they received the bonus they believed was rightfully theirs. The money was supposed to be in an endowment fund until 1945, but a Texas congressman in 1929 had introduced legislation for immediate payment of the bonus. His idea gained support from several other congressmen, from the Hearst newspapers, and from that popular radio priest from Detroit, Father Charles Coughlin.

The one person who wasn't keen on the bill was Herbert Hoover. I didn't know much about Hoover beyond the fact that he was president, but from bits and pieces of conversation among the grown-ups, I did gather that he wasn't doing his job — at least not to most folks' satisfaction. The majority of people blamed him for both the Depression and for our inability to pull out of it. They only laughed at his assurances that the country had "passed the worst" and we would "rapidly recover." I remember Uncle Jim saying, "Prosperity may be just around the corner, but that man Hoover has no idea just how far it is from here to the corner!"

Actually I felt a little sorry for Hoover. I couldn't imagine that our country's troubles were entirely his fault, and I didn't think it fair that he should have to shoulder all the blame. I recalled him saying sometime in the winter of 1931, "No one is going hungry, and no one need go hungry or cold." Since I myself was neither hungry nor cold, I had no argument with him.

Meanwhile, the situation across the country was growing worse, and our own city was experiencing the first rumblings of discontent. I guess I was still protected by the naivete of youth, because it took me a while to see what was happening right under my own nose. Uncle Jim was at the center of the coming upheaval at the grain mill, but as usual I had no idea what was going on until a man Uncle Jim introduced as a union organizer came around to our house one evening to talk with the grown-ups. The meeting must have been prearranged, because before the man showed up, Mother had six glasses set out on a silver tray and informed me that when the company came it would be my job to pass around the iced tea and offer sugar and lemon.

The man appeared at our front door at about eight o'clock that warm June night. Mother had already put Claudia and Molly to bed. Simon and the cousins were out back kicking a ball around the yard. They'd been instructed not to bother the grown-ups. Only I, who was expected to play hostess along with Mother, would have any interaction with the adults — and that, if Mother had her way, would be limited.

As Aunt Sally seated our guest, Uncle Jim hollered into the doctors' office for Papa and Dr. Hal to join them. While the others gathered in the parlor, Mother put ice into the glasses and poured the tea, then removed her apron and hung it on the pantry door. She smoothed her skirt and patted at the stray hairs that had escaped her bun, then indicated with a nod that I was to follow her into the parlor with the tray.

When we entered the room the stranger popped up from the couch like a jack-in-the-box springing to life.

"And this," Uncle Jim said, looking from the man to Mother, "is Lillian Eide, my sister-in-law. Lillian, this is Rex Atwater of the Grain Millers Union. He and I've been working together for the past several months."

"How do you do, Mr. Atwater," Mother said.

"Pleased to meet you, ma'am," the man responded.

"Oh, and my niece Ginny," Uncle Jim added, looking at me.

"Pleased to meet you," the man said again, this time in my direction.

"How do you do," I replied, echoing Mother.

"Well, I guess you've met everyone, then, Rex," Uncle Jim said. Mr. Atwater looked about the room, nodded his assent, and sat down again. Uncle Jim settled himself on the piano bench and crowned one knee with the opposite ankle. He took a cigarette out of his shirt pocket but didn't light it. Dr. Hal was seated, legs crossed, on the end of the couch opposite Mr. Atwater. Papa was in one of the wing chairs that had been dragged from the front wall to a position closer to the couch. He patted the arm of the matching chair to invite Mother to sit by him. She accepted the offered seat and folded her hands primly in her lap, then glanced across the room to where Aunt Sally sat in the rocking chair. Aunt Sally was pushing unconsciously at the floor with the balls of her feet so that the chair moved in brief nervous spurts. A two-toned squeak accompanied the rocking, a high squeak when the chair moved backward, a lower squeak as it sighed forward. When Aunt Sally noticed Mother's disapproving frown, she let the chair come to an abrupt rest. The final squeak was followed by a jarring silence.

Mother turned her attention to our guest. "It's another warm night, Mr. Atwater, so I've made iced tea instead of coffee," she said. "May I offer you some?"

"Much obliged, Mrs. Eide," the man said, hitching himself forward to the edge of the couch to accept the drink. "Iced tea would be just the thing to hit the spot."

I stepped toward the man and held out the tray of perspiring glasses. As Mr. Atwater reached out a small but solid hand to select one, I asked, "Sugar and lemon, sir?"

He smiled. "No, thank you, little miss. I prefer it without."

I smiled politely and moved on to offer a glass to Dr. Hal. While Dr. Hal was spooning sugar into his tea, Uncle Jim said, "If you don't mind, Rex, I'm just going to turn it over to you and let you explain to the folks just what your plans are and why you wanted to come here tonight."

Mr. Atwater cleared his throat as though readying himself for a long speech. I stepped to Papa with the tray. He took a glass and winked at me. I smiled at him in return.

"Well, I reckon Jim's told you some of what's been going on down at the mill," Mr. Atwater began.

"Enough for us to realize that it's the union that cost him his job," Aunt Sally interjected abruptly.

I glanced over at my aunt to find her glaring at the union organizer with steely eyes. For an odd moment, I noticed an uncanny family resemblance between Aunt Sally and Mother.

Mr. Atwater cleared his throat again and rolled the glass of iced tea between his two small palms. "Yes, ma'am, and I'm sorry about that. That's very often part of the price that's paid when you're forming a union. But our hope is that the men who have been laid off for union activities — there's been plenty of them — will be put

136

back to work once the union is formally recognized. I've seen it happen before, and I hope it'll happen again."

"You know there's been at least fifty of us laid off for actively supporting the union, Sally," Uncle Jim explained, waving the hand that clutched the unlit cigarette. "Of course, the mill owners won't admit they're kicking men out because of the union." Here Rex Atwater agreed with Uncle Jim by shaking his head. "Why, that old Emerson Thiel and his boys will give any excuse for getting rid of the workers willing to help the union. But the fact is, they're afraid of us being organized. Thanks, Ginny." Uncle Jim took a glass of tea and I moved on with the tray to Aunt Sally, who took the last glass without taking her eyes off her husband.

My mission completed, I stepped to the edge of the room, not quite sure what to do now. I wanted to stay and hear the conversation. I wanted to have my curiosity satisfied as to what was happening down at the mill, but I could hardly spend the evening standing in the parlor doorway with a serving tray in my hands. Almost involuntarily, my eyes moved toward Mother. She signaled me to take the tray back to the kitchen.

Obediently, I carried the tray down the hall and laid it on the kitchen table. The voice of Uncle Jim droned on in the parlor. I strained to hear his words as I placed the remaining lemon slices in the icebox, but I couldn't make out much. Latching the icebox door, I figured there was only one way to get an invitation to join the grown-ups, and that was to invite myself.

When Mr. Atwater began talking again, I bet on Mother's unwillingness to interrupt him to send me out of the room. I stole back into the parlor and slid as quietly as a shadow onto the piano bench next to Uncle Jim, who, listening to our guest, shifted his weight unconsciously to make room for me. I sat ramrod straight with my ankles crossed and my hands folded in my lap, staring intently at Mr. Atwater as though my presence had been expected there all along. Mother's stern gaze fixed on me, and from the very corner of my eye I could see her jerking her head slightly and trying to catch my attention, but I merely sat placidly, ignoring her.

". . . and at these other mills," Mr. Atwater was saying, "we've been able to institute the eight-hour day, a minimum wage, workers compensation, and health and welfare insurance. We want to bring about these same standards at the mill here in this city. So we've been working for the past several months just to get the mill workers to agree to supporting the union.

It hasn't been difficult to convince most of them of their need for collective bargaining. They realize that each man on his own has little or no power against the mill owners, and that if they don't become organized, nothing's going to change in their favor. They'll go right on working long hours for too little wages and no benefits."

"So are you saying," Papa asked, "that most of the men want the union?"

Mr. Atwater nodded. "I'd say we've got maybe eighty-five, maybe ninety percent of the men on our side."

"Then why haven't eighty-five or ninety percent of the mill workers been laid off?" Aunt Sally asked tersely.

"Well, Mrs. Dubbin, not all the men have been so outspoken as your husband. You see, it's the ones who pushed the hardest for the union who have been pushed right out of the mill."

Papa, as was his habit, took off his glasses and rubbed them with his handkerchief. "Of course the mill owners don't want the union," he stated flatly.

" 'Course not," Mr. Atwater confirmed. "In my twenty years of organizing, I've yet to meet an employer who's not opposed to unions from the git-go. To them a union means they've lost the upper hand. It means they have to pay more money for fewer hours of work. But we've got to convince them that the union will be profitable for them, as it will. We've got to convince them that employers and employees are all in this together, and that more is accomplished when the employees are satisfied and well taken care of."

"Have you started negotiations yet?" asked Dr. Hal. He finished off his tea and set the empty glass down on the coffee table in front of the couch.

"Not yet," Mr. Atwater replied. "You see, Dr. Bellamy, I've got two men working with me from the Grain Millers Union and one from the A.F. of L. Like I said, all we've been doing so far is recruiting workers to support the union. We feel we're ready now to begin negotiations with the mill owners."

Mr. Atwater paused to take several swallows of his iced tea. With each swallow his Adam's apple traveled the distance of his throat and disappeared beneath his chin the way the weight on a carnival strongman game slides upward to hit the bell. When he had satisfied his thirst for the moment, he plucked a handkerchief from his shirt pocket and rubbed it once along each side of his neck just below his ears. Mr. Atwater was a small, pockmarked man with nervous hands and reticent blue eyes that flitted from face to face like a butterfly in a garden of flowers. He had dressed informally to meet us — just a short-sleeved summer shirt, gray slacks, and a pair of worn leather shoes that looked like they'd hiked plenty of picket lines. His thinning hair was combed straight back from his forehead, and his ears stuck out from the sides of his head like a pair of ornamental wings. Nothing about his appearance suggested conviction or strength of character, and he certainly didn't seem the type to lead men in acts of defiance for the sake of justice. Yet his voice held a steadiness, a sureness, that said he had — somewhere in the hidden regions of his soul — what it took to do what was right for the working man.

"Yes," he repeated, "we intend to start negotiations beginning of next week, and we're hoping for the best."

"But expecting the worst?" Dr. Hal asked.

Mr. Atwater sighed and set his glass on the table not far from Dr. Hal's. "Yes, Doctor, you could say we're expecting the worst. The signs are there already — what with the recent layoffs and all. Thiel and his boys have got one great advantage — for every man they lay off there's twenty out there waiting to take his place. It's no skin off the noses of the mill owners to lose some of their workers, even if they've been around a long time like Jim. The Depression has offered a ready supply of men who'll work gladly for any amount of pay, fair or no."

"Then isn't this a bad time to be trying to organize a union, Mr. Atwater?" Papa asked.

The union organizer shrugged. "It's not the best of times, granted," he agreed. "But we can't bring our work to a halt just waiting for the Depression to end. No telling how long it'll last. No," the man shook his head, "we've got to go right on trying to gain justice for the workers."

Mother spoke up then. "You say you're expecting the worst, Mr. Atwater. Exactly what does that mean?"

"Well, ma'am," he said while lacing and unlacing his fingers, "it means we expect we'll have to strike."

Mother raised her brows in dubious surprise. "Do you think it'll come to that?"

"I'm afraid it probably will. Like I said, I've been doing this kind of work for twenty years, and most times nothing gets done without a strike."

"That seems to be the standard means for getting the union recognized?" Papa asked.

"Yes, sir," said Mr. Atwater politely, almost apologetically. "It's generally the alternative we end up having to take."

The room fell quiet while the grown-ups

142

contemplated this. The clock on the piano behind me ticked off the seconds, and with each passing minute the tension in the air seemed to grow and expand. From the backyard we could hear the shouts and laughter of the boys as they played. The muffled voices of passersby on the sidewalk reached us, as did the distant tinny music of our neighbors' radio playing on the porch across the street. So still was the small group gathered in our parlor that the room actually pulsated with the chirping of the cicadas amid the gathering dusk. The silence was broken only when Uncle Jim tried unsuccessfully to stifle a cough. Aunt Sally offered him the remainder of her iced tea, which he accepted with a nod.

When Uncle Jim had stilled the spasms in his chest, Mother spoke up. "Well, Mr. Atwater, could I ask you what precisely this has to do with us? I realize that Jim, of course —"

"We're looking for help, Lil," Uncle Jim interrupted, his cheeks burning red from the exertion of coughing. "If it comes down to a strike — and like Rex said, it probably will — we're going to need all the help we can get."

Mr. Atwater's hands stopped fidgeting a moment and rested in the air, fingertip to fingertip. "There's a great deal that goes on behind the scenes of a strike," he explained. "It's not just a crowd of men showing up and picketing outside the mill gates every day. It takes a lot of planning and a great deal of help from people who aren't employed by the mill but who sympathize with the union. Have any of you folks been involved in a strike before?" When he was met with a round of head-shaking, he continued. "Well, then, let me explain a little bit about what happens. Right now we've got our union headquarters in an abandoned garage, but we'll need a lot more room than that once the strike gets underway. That's no problem because there's plenty of empty warehouses not far from the mill. In fact, we already have one picked out. Soon as negotiations fall through, we'll rent the place and set up our strike machine. We'll open a commissary where the men will be fed three meals a day. We've already got promises of food coming from sympathizers — we've got a relief committee working on that — and we're working on putting together a women's auxiliary to take care of the cooking and cleaning up." Here Mr. Atwater glanced at Mother and Aunt Sally. "There'll be cots set up for the men who have nowhere else to go. We'll have a lecture hall for daily pep talks, and we'll provide a room for recreation. Our picket line strategy will be to send at least a couple hundred men out at a time, day and night, on two-hour shifts. We'll form teams of about twenty men. Jim here has volunteered to be a team captain." Mr. Atwater nodded at Uncle Jim, who nodded in return.

"One problem we've got is the grain delivery. We've been talking with some of the members of the railroad union, trying to persuade them not to haul grain into Thiel's mill should we call a strike. They'd have to go on strike themselves, but seeing as how they're union men too, we hoped they'd be sympathetic to our cause. Well," Mr. Atwater shook his head, "right now it doesn't look good. They claim they're sympathetic, but that it's not in their best interest to support our strike. That means Thiel's going to be getting his grain as usual, and to Thiel, grain is the same as money. He won't want his grain to just sit around and rot, so he'll bring in scabs to work the mill. And when scabs are brought in, things get ugly. We'd like to hold a peaceful demonstration — in fact, we'd like to bypass a strike altogether and sit down like gentlemen and discuss our grievances. But things in this old world don't much work out that way. If we strike, we can hardly just step aside and wave the scabs on through the picket line. We're going to have to fight for our rights, plain and simple.

"Now, I'm not going to lie to you folks. Two things are bound to happen when we strike. The first is that men will get arrested. But we've already got a lawyer working with us, and the grain union will put up money for bail when the time comes. The second thing that will happen is that men will get hurt. Plenty of men, most likely. I myself have been beaten up by more billy clubs than I can count, and I've even been shot once or twice by sheriff's deputies."

Mother and Aunt Sally gasped audibly. Papa frowned as he always did when he heard of someone being hurt. As for me, my admiration for the man soared. I couldn't believe I was in the company of someone who'd taken a bullet in the flesh. I couldn't wait to tell Charlotte.

Mr. Atwater continued. "We're going to need to organize our own hospital inside the strike headquarters."

"Why not just take the wounded to Mercy?" Papa asked.

"We might as well take the men straight to the city jail as take them to any of the city hospitals," Mr. Atwater explained. "You see, once they're in the hospital, they're held for police questioning, and then as soon as they're well enough — sometimes before — they're hauled to jail till the strike is broken. We've lost too

146

many good men that way in the past. But you see, if we can patch them up right in our own headquarters, we can send them back out to the picket line when they're ready, and they can avoid jail. Of course, there may be times when we can't give a man the care he needs — say he's shot in the chest or something. In that case, we'll see to it the man is taken to the regular hospital for care."

"Shot in the chest!" Aunt Sally cried. She tipped the rocking chair forward with one angry squeak so that her face, registering obvious horror, was only a few feet from the union organizer's.

Rex Atwater squeezed his hands together and looked sheepish. "Sorry to upset you, ma'am," he said. "It doesn't happen very often. Last time I was shot it was just a flesh wound to the forearm. Nothing serious."

"But —"

Aunt Sally was unceremoniously interrupted by Dr. Hal. "So I take it you're looking for a doctor or two to man this strike hospital."

"What we're hoping for, Dr. Bellamy, is at least one more doctor to serve as a kind of backup to what we already have. The doctor who used to be the company physician down at the mill, Dr. Wilson — you might know him?" Papa and Dr. Hal nodded to indicate their acquaintance with the man. "He's agreed to be our principal man at the strike hospital. We also have four nurses lined up to be on duty around the clock. It won't be easy. It'll mean a lot of work and a lot of sacrifice on the part of these medical people. My concern about Dr. Wilson is that he's getting old and doesn't have the energy that a younger man might have."

Dr. Hal pulled back one side of his mouth in a half smile. "You mean, perhaps, a man of about my age?" When Mr. Atwater said nothing, Dr. Hal looked over at Papa. For a moment the two doctors seemed to be speaking to each other without words.

Finally Papa leaned forward in his chair and said, "I'm in full sympathy with what you're trying to do, Mr. Atwater. Naturally, I'd like to see men like my brother-in-law get a better deal for themselves. But I'm afraid my schedule won't allow me to take on a duty such as what you've just proposed." From the corner of my eye I saw Mother sink back into her chair in relief. Papa continued. "However, I'd be willing to let Dr. Bellamy volunteer his services from time to time, if he'd be inclined to do so."

Mr. Atwater looked eagerly at the younger man. Dr. Hal held his palms up

148

and said, "I'll be glad to help, if I can. I can't be there around the clock, of course, but maybe I could fill in if you need an extra pair of hands."

"That's all we're asking, Dr. Bellamy. Much obliged," Mr. Atwater said.

"When do you think this . . . this strike will start?" Aunt Sally asked breathlessly.

"I'm afraid I can't answer that, ma'am," replied the ever polite Mr. Atwater. "I've seen negotiations go on for weeks, and I've seen talks break down before they even got started."

"Oh, Jim," my aunt cried, turning to her husband, "why didn't you tell me it might come to this?"

Instead of answering the question, Uncle Jim said quietly, "We could use your help on the women's auxiliary, Sally. The men would appreciate your fine cooking."

"But, Jim —"

"I'm going to be out on the picket line, Sally, if it comes down to having to strike. I made up my mind a good long while ago. I could use your support."

Aunt Sally gazed silently at her husband for a moment. Then she nodded so slightly the movement of her head was almost imperceptible. "All right," she said finally. She turned to face the union organizer. "I'll help in the commissary, Mr. Atwater." Her words came out on a sigh of strained resignation.

Rex Atwater nodded respectfully. "Thank you, ma'am. We'd be grateful for your help."

Aunt Sally looked over at Mother. But refusing to acknowledge her sister's expectant gaze, Mother addressed the little man on the couch. "I'm sorry, Mr. Atwater, but I don't see how it would be possible for me to take part in this — undertaking. I have four children to take care of, two of which are barely more than infants. I'm —"

Mr. Atwater interrupted with a wave of his hand. "I understand, Mrs. Eide. We have no intention of taking mothers away from their children. But I'm pleased Dr. Bellamy here and Mrs. Dubbin have both expressed their willingness to help. With Jim to boot, that's more than I have a right to ask of any family." He cleared his throat again and raised his glass to sip the water from the melting ice cubes.

Uncle Jim put the cigarette between his lips and I thought he was finally going to light it, but he didn't. He took it out again.

Mr. Atwater went on. "Now, I want to tell you straight out before you get involved that you're going to hear rumors saying those of us trying to organize the mill are Communists. Those rumors follow us wherever we go. I am not and never have been a member of the Communist Party, nor are any of the other organizers

150

I'm working with. We are backed by the A.F. of L., and you all know they won't have anything to do with the Communists."

Dr. Hal thrust out his chin knowingly. "I suppose the mill owners want to accuse you of being Red so they don't have to recognize the union."

"That's about the way of it," Mr. Atwater replied. He chuckled and shook his head. "I've been called a Commie by every grain mill owner from here to South Dakota and back, but I wouldn't side with the Reds if my life depended on it. No, I'm just trying to see the working man get a fair shake within the ranks of capitalism, that's all."

Uncle Jim said, "I happen to know that some of the men down at the mill are in fact what you would call 'fellow travelers.' That is, they have Communist leanings, though they may not actually belong to the Party."

"Sure," Mr. Atwater agreed. "They're down there, all right. I can spot them like so many flies on a wall. There's not a mill or a factory in this country that doesn't have its fellow travelers as well as its card-carrying members. It's a real popular thing right now. All the time Hoover is tooting his horn about prosperity being right around the corner, the Communists are swearing there's a revolution right around the corner. They think the United States of America is going to end up touting allegiance to Moscow. They're pretty sure of themselves right now, since it looks like capitalism has failed. Well, capitalism might have taken a pretty bad tumble, but it isn't like Humpty-Dumpty who can't be put back together again. In my opinion, the economy's eventually going to come back stronger than ever — the way a bone that's been broken ends up being stronger after it's healed." He smiled at Papa and Dr. Hal, obviously proud of his medical analogy.

Papa smiled briefly in return. "So you're asking us to turn a deaf ear to anyone who might want to label you a Communist?"

"Yes, sir. For your own sakes and for the sake of the mill workers, I'm asking you to pay no mind to those rumors. They only hurt what we're trying to do."

"Well, I for one have no doubt you're not a Communist, Mr. Atwater," Papa assured him. "But I can see how you might have a hard time convincing a lot of people of that. Even if Mr. Thiel himself doesn't think you're a Communist, if he says you are, there are plenty of people in this town who'll believe him — just because he's Emerson Thiel." Papa paused and shook his head. "If I hear any such rumors, I'll do my best to squelch them."

"Thank you, Dr. Eide," Rex Atwater said with a nod. "I'd appreciate that."

As the grown-ups went on to talk about Communist infiltration of legitimate unions, I tried to remember what I'd learned in school about Communism. I recalled our teacher speaking about life in Russia with disdain, saying we ought to thank our lucky stars we were born in America where we could live in freedom. She said the Russian people weren't even allowed to believe in God anymore, and that the churches had been shut down at the time of the revolution in 1917. She made it clear to us that Communism was a way of life to be avoided at all costs.

In spite of my earlier impressions of Rex Atwater and my admiration of his having been shot, I suddenly felt a bit mistrustful. His insistence that he wasn't a Communist led me to think that he certainly must be one — at least that was how it always worked in the movies. The person you're sure is the good guy turns out to be the bad guy in the end.

Maybe it was all the talk about violence, or maybe it was just the heat, but I suddenly felt sick at the thought of Uncle Jim being mixed up with this man and his mission. My personal opinion — unspoken, of course — was that Uncle Jim ought to start looking for another job and forget all about this union stuff.

Aunt Sally must have been feeling the same way because I heard her sniff and saw that she was wiping at her eyes with Uncle Jim's handkerchief. When she noticed me, she smiled bravely and pretended to be only dabbing at beads of perspiration, but I knew it was tears that moistened her cheeks.

Finally Mr. Atwater rose and said, "Well, I'm afraid I've taken up too much of your time —"

"Not at all," Papa said, getting up himself from the wing chair and stretching his legs. "I only wish there was more we could do. . . ."

Mr. Atwater reached out his hand to shake Papa's. "You've done plenty already, sir," he said.

"Can I offer you a fresh glass of iced tea?" Mother asked stiffly. I knew she wanted only for the man to go.

"Thank you, no, ma'am. I really best be on my way." He shook hands with Dr. Hal and Mother and was about to turn to Aunt Sally when Uncle Jim intercepted him.

"Thank you for coming, Rex," Uncle Jim said, leading the union organizer out to the hallway before the latter could notice Aunt Sally's tears. "Listen, nine o'clock tomorrow morning, right? Down at headquarters."

"I'd appreciate your being there, Jim."

"I'll be there."

A few more words were exchanged at the screen door before we heard it squeak open and slam shut again. Then Uncle Jim appeared in the entrance between the hall and the parlor. He chewed at his lower lip and his eyes were wide and expectant.

"Well," Papa said to Uncle Jim, "looks like you've got your work cut out for you."

"Looks like it," Uncle Jim echoed.

Papa turned to Dr. Hal. "Shall we do that inventory on the medicine cabinet and then call it a night?"

"I'm right behind you," agreed Dr. Hal.

The two doctors started toward the hall. Papa stopped when he came up beside Uncle Jim and put a hand on his shoulder. "Just be careful, Jim," he said quietly.

"I'll be careful, Will."

My father patted my uncle's shoulder and, with Dr. Hal following, walked away whistling "O Holy Night." In the parlor, Uncle Jim, Aunt Sally, and Mother stood silent and unmoving, like a trio of statues. I sat equally motionless on the piano bench, holding my breath and waiting for someone to say something. The clock behind me went on ticking away the time.

Finally Mother said, "I don't care for the thought of violence, Jim."

"I don't much like it myself, Lillian, but

155

I hate injustice even more."

"But, Jim," Aunt Sally cried, the hand-kerchief to her lips, "men could end up . . . dead." The last word came out in a whisper.

"Could be," Uncle Jim agreed. "It's been known to happen in a strike." With those words Aunt Sally's tears began to flow freely.

Mother said, "Now, Jim, men are always quicker than women to settle their differences with violence. I'm going to ask you to think this through for a minute. You've a wife and three sons. You've already lost your job. Are you sure it's worth the risk to go on fighting for a union?"

Without hesitating, Uncle Jim replied, "I've thought about it for a long time, Lil, and I don't have to think anymore. It's worth the risk."

Aunt Sally gave a sharp cry and ran from the room. Neither Uncle Jim nor Mother tried to stop her, and neither went after her. Instead, they remained to consider each other without speaking.

Finally, in what seemed an attempt to justify himself, Uncle Jim asked, "What kind of man would I be, Lillian, if I weren't willing to fight for my own rights and for a better life for my family? As long as there's a chance I can get my job back — with better wages and benefits, too — I've got to try."

Mother sighed deeply and dropped her eyes to the floor. Then she looked at my uncle kindly and said, "You're in a hard position, Jim, and I don't envy you. You need the support of your family, so I'll tell you that in theory I support you. I hope everything turns out for the best for all the men down at the mill. I would only ask, along with William, that you not do anything foolish."

"I'll be careful," Uncle Jim promised. "You have my word."

"In the meantime, let's pray that a strike can be avoided."

"And that if we have to strike, we'll win."

"Yes, well — come on, Virginia, help me clean up the kitchen, and then it'll be time for you to be off to bed."

As we washed and dried the dishes, Mother said nothing about my staying in the parlor to listen. In fact, she said nothing at all. When we had finished and I was ready to go upstairs to join my little sisters in bed, I saw Uncle Jim leaning against the frame of the front door, staring out at the quiet street and the starry night beyond. He had one hand in his jeans pocket. With the other he was holding the Mouth-Happy cigarette he had finally lighted. He took deep breaths and blew the smoke out through the screen. He was so lost in thought that he didn't hear me when I said good-night. I supposed he must have been thinking about the future, and I wondered myself what was in store for him. Would he catch a billy club across the skull or take a bullet in the chest? Would he lead the strikers on to victory? Were the Communists right after all, and rather than prosperity looming right around the corner, it was a political take-over?

I shivered at the thought. Then and there I immediately dropped for good the Besac philosophy that God was only a myth. It sounded a little too much like Communism to me. It was tempting to toy with atheism when I was angry, if only to make God aware of my displeasure at some of His decisions. But I could never, when it came right down to it, dismiss His existence altogether. I knew He was there, and I believed He was willing to offer help to those who called on Him. And I planned as soon as I slipped into bed to call on Him and to keep calling until sleep came. Because at that moment I felt at last as though the ripples of Black Thursday had not only reached us, but that all of us were in danger of drowning beneath its waves.

Chapter Eight

Charlotte showed up at our house when, according to the clock on the piano, I still had fifteen minutes left of my half hour of practice. We had plans to go to the Saturday matinee, as usual. *Strangers in Love* with Fredric March and Kay Francis had just opened at one of the theaters downtown, and we were both anxious to see it. But I'd had a busy morning, and the fact that I'd had to start over half-a-dozen times while trying to recite to Mother Thomas Campion's "When Thou Must Home" set me behind in my schedule. Claudia and Molly were in the parlor with me, forcing poor Gardenia and Petunia to dance to the tunes I was banging out on the piano. Claudia saw Charlotte first out the front window and cried, "Lottie's here, Ginny! She's sitting on the porch steps with Rufus."

At once my fingers picked up speed as I tried to rush through the song I was practicing — until I realized that rushing the song wouldn't speed up the clock. "Tell her I still have fifteen more minutes to go," I called to Claudia. "Tell her we'll still have plenty of time to get to the theater."

Claudia obediently pressed her nose up

159

against the screen and yelled louder than necessary, "Lottie! Ginny says she still has fifteen more minutes to go! She says you'll still have plenty of time to get to the theater!"

In a moment, Charlotte's own voice came from the other side of the screen. "That's all right, Virginia," she said mildly, almost too sweetly. Her words were meant for me, but her tone of voice, I knew, was for my cousin. I went on playing but looked over my shoulder to find her smiling at me from where she stood between the porch swing and the window. She licked the tips of her fingers and patted at her wavy hair. "Take your time," she continued. "I'm just out here having a little *tête-à-tête* with Rufus."

I rolled my eyes and turned back to the piano. Where Charlotte got some of her expressions was beyond me. She was always trying to sound like a sophisticated debutante, and what was most frustrating was that she very often succeeded. I sat there agitated and sighing and fumbling over the keys for the remaining fifteen minutes, then rushed out to the front hall, hollered to Mother that I was off to the movies, and made my escape past the squeaking screen door to where my best friend and my cousin sat tête-à-têting together on the front steps. Charlotte had that coquettish look on her face that surfaced whenever she spoke with Mitchell Quakenbush or any of the other boys she happened to be sweet on.

The broom that Rufus had been sweeping the porch with leaned against the railing, neglected. "Aunt Sally asked me to tell you to finish sweeping the sidewalk," I lied, grabbing the broom and handing it to Rufus. "Charlotte and I are going downtown and won't be back till dinnertime."

Rufus took the broom but made no effort to get up from the steps. "In a minute," he mumbled.

"What's the rush, Virginia?" Charlotte complained. "Rufus was right in the middle of telling me a story, and it was *so* exciting." To my cousin, she purred, "Go on, Rufus, what were you saying?"

Before Rufus could continue, I said, "If we don't leave now, we'll miss the beginning of the movie."

"Just the cartoon and the newsreel," Charlotte said, her voice reverting from kitten to angry alley cat. Then she laughed coyly. "Honestly, I don't much care about cartoons or the news, do *you*, Rufus? I'd *much* rather hear the end of your story."

I wasn't certain just why I didn't like Charlotte flirting with my cousin, but I didn't. Maybe it was because she was so much better at getting a positive response from boys than I. It seemed a bit traitorous on Rufus's part to succumb to her charms. He could have at least pretended for my sake that he didn't find her so attractive. Had we not been related and had I tried myself to gain the attention of this young man, he probably would have gone right on sweeping the porch and the sidewalk and been halfway down the block by now.

"Well, I'm going now," I announced stubbornly, pushing my way between Charlotte and Rufus and pounding down the steps. "I'll save you a seat, *Lottie,* should you decide to come."

"Vir*gin*ia! What in the world's the *matter* with you?" she cried. "I just wanted to hear the end of the — oh, good-*bye,* Rufus!"

"Be seeing you, Lottie," Rufus replied.

I had reached the street and could hear Charlotte's hurried footsteps coming up behind me and the whisk of the broom as Rufus went back to sweeping.

"Ginny!" Charlotte huffed loudly as she reached me. Her own use of my nickname didn't escape my notice. "What's come over you?"

"I just don't want to be late for the movie, that's all," I said evenly.

"Well, good heavens, the rate you're going you'd think Fred March himself was going to be there in person. We've got plenty of time, I tell you. Slow *down* or I'm going to wear through the soles of my shoes before we reach downtown."

I slowed my pace and we walked in silence for a moment. Then Charlotte sighed moonily and said, "I didn't know your cousin was such a good-looker."

Through clenched teeth, I muttered, "He's all right, I guess."

My opinion was understated. Rufus plainly was a handsome boy. He was blond and fair like his mother, and tall and lean like his father. He had eyes as blue as a clear-day sky, a narrow, well-formed nose, and teeth that were perfectly straight. And strong hands. I liked strong hands on a man. I was sorry that he and I were kin, and I was sorrier still that he had never paused in the middle of a chore long enough to tell me a story. In the weeks since he'd moved in with us, he'd never even commented on my bobbed hair. I was just his kid cousin, not a girl to be admired like Charlotte. And as I said, even if we weren't related, it was doubtful he would have admired me.

Charlotte continued, "Must have been a year ago I saw him last, but now that he's moved in with you, I can see him a whole lot more. Do you know how old he is?"

"Fifteen, I think."

"Oh!" Charlotte thought a moment, then

said, "Does he have a regular girl?"

"Naw." I shook my head. "Not that I know about, anyway."

"Uh huh." Charlotte remained outwardly calm, but I knew her so well I could practically hear her heart beating wildly in her chest.

Not wanting to talk about Rufus just then, I changed the subject by asking, "What does your mother say about Communists?" Not that I agreed with Mrs. Besac's opinions about God, but because Mother had more than once called Charlotte's mother a woman of the world, I thought Mrs. Besac might have better insight into political affairs than she did spiritual matters.

"Communists?" Charlotte echoed dully. For a moment she seemed startled by the abrupt change in the course of our conversation, and she shook her head as though trying to find the path I'd suddenly veered down. Finally she said, "I can't remember her saying anything about them. Why?"

"Do you think they're going to take over America?"

My friend peered at me quizzically, two small lines forming between her brows. "Well," she answered with a hint of sarcasm, "to tell you the truth, I can't say I've spent a whole lot of time contemplating *that* question."

I frowned back at her and threw up my hands as though reprimanding a child. "Don't you know there are Communists right here in our country, right here in this city, who are saying there's a revolution right around the corner?"

"I thought pro*sper*ity was supposed to be around the corner."

"Not according to the Reds," I replied, trying out the word Dr. Hal had used.

"Well, whatever it is, I just hope there's *something* around the corner. Things are getting pretty boring as they are."

"But don't you know what it means if the Communists take over?"

"They can't take over."

"Why not?"

"Because we're too strong for them."

"How do you know?"

"Well, we beat them in the Great War, didn't we?"

"Did we fight them in the Great War?"

Charlotte shrugged again. "Must have. They're the enemy, aren't they? If we beat them once, we can do it again. You sure worry about stupid things, Virginia. Why are you even thinking about the Communists?"

I told her then about the visit from Rex Atwater the night before and the possibility of the strike down at the mill.

When I finished, Charlotte asked, "Your

165

uncle Jim's going to march in a picket line?"

"Looks like it," I replied.

"Well, that *is* exciting."

"It's dangerous, is what it is. Don't you know that men in picket lines get beaten up and shot and sometimes killed?"

My friend's dark eyes widened in wonder. "Will you tell me when the strike starts?"

I sighed. "Yeah, I'll tell you." I had forgotten momentarily that she was in her gangster phase and any tussle with the law appealed to her.

"But what's this got to do with Communism?" she asked.

"Nothing, I guess. Except that that union organizer, Mr. Atwater, said so many times he wasn't a Communist that it made me start to think he *was* one."

"Oh." Charlotte paused to pull a leaf out of the buckle of her shoe. Instead of tossing the leaf aside, she twirled it between her thumb and index finger while she thought. Finally, she asked, "Is this Rex Atwater a handsome man?"

I shook my head vigorously. "No. He's kind of small and funny looking."

"Is he rich?"

"I don't think so. He didn't dress like he was rich, anyway."

"Well, if he's not handsome and he's not

166

rich, why would the Communists want him?"

I couldn't argue with her, and yet it seemed to me there was something faulty in her reasoning. Since I couldn't quite put my finger on what it was, I simply replied, "Well, I just hope you're right."

"Of course I am. People go on strike all the time. It doesn't have anything to do with Communism."

We had almost reached the box office of the theater when Charlotte, steering our conversation back to the original subject, asked somewhat shyly, "What did you say your cousin's last name was?"

"I didn't say."

"Well, what is it?"

"Dubbin."

"His name is Rufus Dubbin?"

"Yup."

We handed our money to the young woman behind the glass and received our tickets. The price of our admission had jumped from a dime to a quarter when we turned thirteen, but we were proud to pay the difference. Inside the lobby other kids were clustered around the concession stand, stocking up on soft drinks, candy bars, and popcorn in the last few minutes before the show. Charlotte and I breathed deeply of the aroma of popcorn.

"Want some?" Charlotte asked.

"Yeah."

"Got any money left?"

"No. Do you?"

"No. I tell ya, when I start dating, any boy wants to take me to the movies better have enough money for *two* bags of popcorn *and* a soda, *and* he better have money left over for a cherry Coke afterward."

"You're asking a lot."

"Not if he's rich."

"There's a depression on."

"That's no excuse."

We made our way down the aisle and chose a couple of seats in the middle of the theater. The movie house was filling up all around us with popcorn-chewing, gum-snapping, soda-guzzling kids.

Charlotte laced her fingers across her stomach and looked pensive. "What do you think of the name Charlotte Dubbin?" she asked. It was another pastime of ours, sounding out what our names might be when we married.

"I like Charlotte Capone better."

"Hmm, yeah." She sank down in the chair so that her head was resting on its rim. "Rufus Dubbin is kind of a silly name, isn't it?"

"Not as bad as Mitchell Quakenbush."

The lights in the theater started to go down. The kids around us let out a howl. A piece of popcorn flung from several rows behind landed in my hair. I picked it out and ate it.

"Let me have the next piece," Charlotte said.

"Sit up higher so you can catch your own."

The curtains across the front wall parted, and in another moment the screen came alive with the flashing images of the latest newsreel. The black-and-white shots were of men's shoes — all kinds of shoes in various stages of dilapidation. Scruffy oxfords, dirty loafers, worn boots with flapping soles. And the shoes were walking, walking, endlessly walking. A commentator's deep voice boomed, "All across the United States men are beating the pavement, desperately looking for work. . . ."

Charlotte leaned over and whispered, "I've been thinking about that."

"About men looking for work?"

"No, about going through life with the name Charlotte Quakenbush."

"What about it?"

"I've decided it's just no good. I can't go around introducing myself as Mrs. *Quak*enbush and expect people to respect me. I'm just going to have a crush on someone else soon as school starts up again."

"What about Rufus?"

"I'm not that keen on being Mrs. *Dubb*in, either, but I'll keep Rufus in mind. Just in case."

Chapter Nine

With Charlotte's illogical assurances taken to heart, I forgot all about the threat of a Communist revolution — at least until the sheriff came around to talk with Papa about the Reds who were trying to take over the grain mill.

It was another warm evening with just a whisper of a breeze that didn't so much as ruffle the lace curtains in the open windows or disturb the leaves of the red maple in the front yard. Papa and I sat together on the porch swing while Simon straddled the railing just in front of us. My brother and I relished these moments with Papa, as they were all too rare. That his office was in our home meant he was generally close by in proximity, but what we children wanted — his attention — was more often than not focused somewhere far away. Not that that was how Papa wanted it. That's simply the way it was when a person was a doctor. The office hours posted on his shingle meant nothing. Papa was never off duty. He could be called upon to meet the needs of an ailing patient at any time, day or night. Illness and accidents didn't pay attention to the clock. They didn't care whether they called a man away from his family on a Sunday afternoon, at two in the morning, on the evening of his son's or daughter's birthday. In fact, it seemed that most of humanity's ailments actually preferred to rise up at the hour of greatest inconvenience. How thankful Simon and I were when calamity decided to rest long enough to allow us a little time with Papa.

The time we had with him was spent, for the most part, simply talking. For days we saved up all sorts of things to tell him — news of our latest accomplishments, our dubious adventures, our disappointments. Papa always listened with both ears, nodding intently, injecting grunts and other sound effects at all the pertinent spots, and finally plying us with questions to show the depth of his interest in our lives. When we had exhausted our storehouse of information about our own lives, I always begged Papa to tell us stories about his childhood, which he proceeded to do with all the alacrity of a seasoned storyteller. Simon, the budding physician, preferred to talk about Papa's work, pleading for all the gruesome details. Papa laughed and said there wasn't much that was gruesome about sore throats and fallen arches.

That particular night our household was unusually quiet. Earlier, Mr. Turbin from the next block came by and said his wife had slipped on the cellar stairs and hurt her ankle, but Dr. Hal volunteered to take the call so Papa could stay home with us. Mother was upstairs giving Claudia and Molly a cool bath before putting them to bed. Uncle Jim was off at one of his endless union meetings, but my suspicions of Mr. Atwater had subsided, and I wasn't much worried at the moment about Uncle Jim's activities. I don't remember where Aunt Sally and the cousins were — with so many people in the house I tended to lose track of everyone — but it seems to me they must have been out for the evening.

So there was no one to disturb the three of us except the occasional passerby. Those were the days when neighbor knew neighbor, and to walk past a group of porch-sitters without offering a greeting was unthinkable. Our three-way conversation was interrupted at odd intervals when someone might call out, "Evening, Doc Eide. Evening, Ginny, Simon."

And Papa would lift a hand and say something like, "Evening, Mr. Harper. Nice night for a walk, isn't it?"

And the passerby would respond, "A bit hot yet, but not too bad a night at that."

And Papa, always the medical man, then asked, "How's young Albert's stomach? Did the bicarbonate of soda help?"

And the man would say, "Much obliged,

Doc, it did the trick straight off."

In this friendly fashion, Papa kept updated on the health of many a patient during the course of an evening.

Through the warm still air there came to us the music of a neighbor's radio, the rumbling of traffic through distant streets, the singing of the cicadas as twilight fell. I rested my head on Papa's shoulder while listening to him talk. The swing we occupied together moved lazily as he pushed us with his one foot anchored to the floor. I thought I could stay there for the rest of my life — surrounded by the last light before nightfall, cradled in the motion of the swing, listening to Papa's strong yet gentle voice — and be completely satisfied.

That was why, when the sheriff's car pulled up in front of our house and the badge-wearing man himself came up our walk, it was an interruption that didn't so much pique my curiosity as make me angry. What had calamity been up to now to separate us yet again from Papa?

"Evening, William," the sheriff said as his heavy boots pounded up the porch steps.

"Evening, Clem," Papa said. He didn't bother to stand but extended his hand, and the sheriff shook it briefly. "Everything all right?"

The sheriff removed his cap and pulled

the back of his hand along the edge of his dark sweat-matted hair. "If you mean has someone been hurt, no. I'm not here because someone needs doctoring. But I would like to talk with you, Will, if you have a minute."

"Sure, Clem. What can I do for you?"

The lawman glanced at Simon and me and said, "Might be best if we was alone."

Papa nodded. The arm he'd been resting on the back of the swing came around me in a half hug. "You two run along inside for a few minutes. This won't take long."

"Aw, Papa!" Simon protested.

"Go on now, son. I'll finish the rest of the story later."

Simon hopped off the porch railing with an audible huff and turned his eyes away from the sheriff as he passed by him into the house. Before getting up from the swing I took a moment to look up into the face of Sheriff Dysinger, Danny's father. I wondered whether Danny would grow up to be so big and ugly. The sheriff was probably more than six feet tall and evidently heavier than he cared to admit, for he wore his uniform at least a size too small. The buttons of his shirt strained to stay together, and one of the front shirttails hung out over the belt that was lost beneath the man's ample belly. When he put his cap back on, fitting it over his round head with one hand on the brim and the other on the back, I noticed two full moons of sweat beneath his arms. His face hung heavy as a hound dog's, his nose was bulbous and ill defined as putty, and his chin was a series of ripples captured finally in the knot of his tie. If he stood as a portent to Danny's future appearance, I thought perhaps I ought to think twice about pursuing a romance with the boy.

I rose and asked politely, "How's Danny enjoying his summer out on the farm, Sheriff Dysinger?"

The man seemed pleased that I would ask. "Well, now, he's having himself a really fine time. His grandpa says he's one strong worker, that one. I'm afraid he won't be wanting to come home again once school starts."

"That's nice," I replied dully, revealing no hint at all of my feelings for this man's offspring. "Well, good night, sir."

" 'Night, Ginny." He leaned his hefty body against the porch railing that Simon had just vacated and crossed his arms across his wide chest.

Simon had gone into the kitchen to get something to eat, but I for one wanted to hear what the sheriff had to say to Papa. I figured that the night had become just dark enough that I wouldn't be noticed if I crept into the unlighted parlor and sat in one of the wing chairs beside the open window. There was no danger of Papa seeing me. Though he was right outside the window on the swing, he was facing the street. I kicked off my shoes and tip-toed into the parlor, hoping that Sheriff Dysinger wouldn't notice any shadow of movement in the room beyond Papa's head. I crept stealthily to the wing chair, avoiding every squeaky part of the floor, and reached my destination with success. Curling up in the chair with my head only inches from the window, I didn't have to strain at all to hear the two men as they spoke. In spite of the falling darkness, I had a pretty good view of the sheriff and a side view of Papa.

Sheriff Dysinger had paused to light a cigarette, but when he had the tobacco burning he said, "So he's out at one of them union meetings right now, is he?"

"He should be back within the hour, I'd say, if you'd like to talk with him," Papa said.

The crunching sound of an apple being bitten into came from the hall, followed by Simon's footsteps on the stairs. I hoped he would go directly to his own room and not wonder where I was.

Outside, the sheriff was shaking his head while he inhaled deeply on the cigarette. The smoke came out while he spoke. "Tell you the truth, I'd rather he not even know I came around tonight. This is strictly off the record. I'm here to talk to you friend to friend."

If Papa and Sheriff Dysinger had a friendship going, it couldn't have been a very strong one. The sheriff wasn't exactly a regular visitor around our house, and I even remembered some harsh words on his side when it became common knowledge that Papa was supporting Sid Jeffers for sheriff in the last election.

Papa, in spite of the dubiousness of their relationship, said kindly, "If that's how you want it, Clem."

"I suppose, Will, you're fully aware of what's going on down at the grain mill, seeing as how Jim's so involved."

"Well, I know the men are trying to organize a union, and I know they're in the middle of negotiations with Mr. Thiel and his sons and the board of directors. But I'm afraid I don't know any of the particulars beyond that. I'm pretty busy —"

"I'll get straight to the point here — we've got trouble on our hands. A bunch of men have come into this town under the pretext of being union organizers, but those of us in law enforcement know what they really are."

"And what might that be, Clem?" It was a rare day that sarcasm crept into Papa's voice, but I thought I detected it just then.

"Now, William, you know as well as I do that whenever there's talk about workers' rights, them doing the talking are Communists."

"Well, not necessarily —"

"They might not admit it themselves, might not come right out and say they're members of the Communist Party, but that's what they are all right."

Papa chuckled softly and shook his head. "That Mr. Atwater sure was right about one thing," he remarked.

"Rex Atwater?"

"Yes, Rex Atwater. Of the Grain Millers Union."

"You know him?"

"Wouldn't say I know him. I only met him once."

"How'd you happen to meet him?"

"He came around to the house not long ago. Jim invited him."

"What'd he want?"

"He was just looking for help and support for the union."

"He didn't persuade you to help him in any way, did he?"

"Clem, with a schedule like mine, there's not much more I can take on. I'm afraid there's really nothing I can do for the man."

"Good thing for you, Will. I'd advise you

not to get involved."

"Well, now, like I say, it's my schedule, not my convictions, that's keeping me from getting involved. I fully support what the men are trying to do down at the mill. A union can only be good for both employees and employers alike."

"We're not talking about a union here, William."

"Then just what is it we're talking about, Clem?"

The sheriff flicked the butt of his cigarette onto the grass, then leaned forward from the porch railing toward Papa. "Aren't you aware of what's happening in this country?"

Papa, undaunted, looked directly at the big man. "Fill me in, Clem," he said flatly.

"The Reds, William. The Reds." The sheriff managed to send shivers down my spine, the way he pronounced the word. Maybe Charlotte didn't think we had anything to fear from the Communists, but evidently the sheriff thought we did. He let out an expletive before continuing. "They've even got a candidate on the ballot for the November election. A Mr. William Z. Foster. Till yesterday you could see his name painted on the side of the Landlaw Building downtown, along with the message 'Vote Communist.' I had to send one of my deputies out there to paint it over. What's more —" Sheriff Dysinger paused and pulled a small folded newspaper from his back pocket. He tossed it onto the porch swing beside Papa, who picked it up and opened it. "That's one of their newspapers. The *Daily Worker*, they call it. They're selling these and all their other Red propaganda on every street corner in town. They're here, William. I'm telling you, they're right here in this city, every which way you turn."

Papa calmly laid the paper aside after giving it only a cursory glance. The swing moved briefly back and forth while Papa gathered his thoughts. "Well, Sheriff," he said quietly, "the Communists have been standing on street corners peddling their literature since 1919, and I'm sure they've been right here in our own city since that time, but that doesn't mean they're organizing the union at the grain mill. Mr. Atwater says he's with the Grain Millers Union and that what he's doing is backed by the A.F. of L. Frankly, Clem, I see no reason not to believe him."

Sheriff Dysinger shook his head and lighted another cigarette. "We don't intend to have a repeat of Gastonia around here," he said. He paused to pluck a tobacco seed off the tip of his thick cowlike tongue. Rubbing his fingers together to rid them of the seed, he continued. "You know very well it was the Commies that ran that strike down in those Gastonia mills in twenty-nine. That's a recorded fact. And it's also a fact the Reds have been leading strikes in Kentucky, Rhode Island, Pennsylvania. I'm not making this up, William. I'm talking particulars, here. And I'm telling you, it's not going to happen in this town. Now, by law I can't stop the negotiations, and I can't stop the strike if those mill workers want to go on strike, but I can do my best to see they don't win that strike. No, sir," the sheriff said, pointing to his badge with the fingers that pinched his cigarette, "it's my job to uphold the law around here, and the law of the land is capitalism."

Papa, growing obviously weary of the conversation, shifted his position in the swing. "I can't argue with you there, Clem. I know the Communist Party has something of a following here in the U.S., but I'm of the opinion that capitalism isn't in any real danger. I just don't believe it is. This country was built on free enterprise, and it's going to take a lot more than a few radicals selling newspapers to change things. Oh, I know the idea of a revolution is attractive to some people right now — the country being in the mess it's in. But once the situation gets better — and it will — I'm of the opinion that this whole frenzy about Communism is simply going to be forgotten."

Sheriff Dysinger was quiet while he took another long drag of his cigarette. It was only half smoked, but the sheriff decided he'd had enough, or else that he would use it to make a symbolic point. This time, instead of tossing the butt into the yard, he let it fall to the porch, where he crushed it beneath the toe of his boot. His huge foot swiveled back and forth at the ankle for an unnecessarily long time. "I hope you're right, William," he said finally. He blew the last of the smoke out the side of his mouth. "But in the meantime, I can't just sit around and hope that Communism will fade away."

The two men were quiet again. My eyes fell to the gun in the holster resting on the sheriff's hip, the handle dimly reflecting the porch light. As though he knew I was gazing at the weapon, Sheriff Dysinger's hand moved to the gun and gave it a slight pat. It made me nervous to see his hand resting there, but then he withdrew it and removed his cap again to wipe away the sweat that was sliding down either side of his face.

"I can appreciate your concern," Papa said, "and since we're in two different areas of public service, I can appreciate, too, that your duties are different from mine. But I'm wondering, Clem, exactly what it was that brought you here tonight. Are you hoping I'll try to convince my brother-in-law not to be involved in the union?"

"Actually, Will," Sheriff Dysinger replied, securing his cap back on his head, "my concern is for you."

"For me?" Papa's surprise was genuine. "Like I said, I'm not involved in what's going on down at the mill."

"No, but you've gotten yourself involved in something else. I hear you been visiting out in that shantytown by the river."

Papa propped an elbow up on the back of the swing and cocked his head as though he hadn't quite understood the sheriff's words. "The shantytown?" he echoed. "Yes, I've been tending to some of the people out there, but forgive me for being dull, Clem, I'm not quite making the connection between the mill and the shantytown."

Sheriff Dysinger cracked his huge knuckles, then flexed his fingers by his sides. "The connection is this," he explained. "The same people that are trying to stir up the mill workers are out there trying to stir up the unemployed. Now, just a minute — hear me out, Will. One of the favorite tactics of the Reds for winning people over and for stirring up trouble is organizing what they call Unemployed Councils. They claim the councils are designed to help the men find food and jobs, but their main concern is to organize protests and food riots and whatnot. All they really do is rile up the men to make demands on the government that the government can't meet. A bunch of jobless men in these Unemployed Councils have been marching in cities all over the country — well, I don't have to remind you of that hunger march in D.C. last November and that one in Detroit just this past March. Four men killed in that one and more than sixty injured. Yes, killed and wounded by law enforcement officials, but that's what's got to be done to keep these Communist demonstrations from getting out of hand. Like I said, we don't want to see that kind of thing happening around here. The Reds get out there and get people all worked up, and it only leads to no good.

"Now, so far we've been turning a blind eye to that shantytown because the mayor asked us to. He knows those people don't have anywhere else to go. We could pick them up on vagrancy, we could drive them out for health reasons, but we haven't done it. All we're asking is that they live there peaceably and orderly. First sign of trouble, we're going to have to run them out."

Papa swung silently a few minutes before asking, "And you say you think the Communists are trying to organize an Unemployed Council down there?"

"We know they are."

"I haven't heard anything about it."

"They've got no reason to tell you."

"I don't know, Clem. The men down there speak pretty freely with me about their situation."

"A man known to sell these Red newspapers has also been seen in the shantytown. Our deputies that patrol down that way have seen him. He can only have one reason for being down there, Will."

"I see," Papa said. "But if indeed he's trying to preach Communism or get those men to form some sort of Unemployed Council, I'm not sure he'll have much luck. The people I've tended to in the shantytown don't seem to me the type to have any interest in such things."

"I wouldn't be so sure of that. A poor man's a desperate man. They don't always see things the way you and I see them."

"Maybe so, but I still don't think there's anything I can do about it. I deal with people's physical welfare, not their political persuasions."

The sheriff scratched the back of his thick neck, then crossed his arms once again across his chest. It was a habit that relieved the pressure on his shirt buttons, and I wondered if he did it for that reason. He said, "I just want to give you fair warning to stay away from that place. I'd hate to see you getting mixed up in any kind of trouble."

"I appreciate your concern, Sheriff," Papa replied, "but I can't imagine how I might get mixed up in any trouble. I'm just there to tend to people's medical needs as much as I'm able."

"There's them that might mistake your motives, Will," the sheriff warned.

But Papa laughed outright at the comment. "Just who do you have in mind, Clem?"

The sheriff hitched up his pants and frowned. He looked as though he'd taken offense at Papa's laughter. "No use playing the fool, William," he said. "No one quite knows who to trust anymore, not in this day and age."

Papa's head moved slightly from side to side. I couldn't see his face but I knew he was amused. "Like I said, Clem, I appreciate your concern, but as long as there are people in the shantytown who need me, I'm not going to stay away."

Just then I heard Mother's footsteps on the stairs. I held my breath, hoping she wouldn't find me eavesdropping in the parlor.

Outside the window the sheriff leaned forward again and looked at Papa through narrow eyes. "I don't get it, Will," he said. "I mean, what's in it for you? I know those people aren't paying you a dime for your trouble."

But before Papa could answer, Mother appeared at the front door. She greeted the sheriff with a hint of surprise in her voice. I saw the sheriff take off his cap before he greeted her in return.

"What brings you out tonight, Sheriff Dysinger?" Mother asked. I hadn't heard the screen door squeak open, so I knew she stood talking to him from inside.

"I was just gabbing with William about his doings down at the shantytown."

"Oh?"

The sheriff stood and stretched. "But it's getting late and I'd best be moving along."

"What about the shantytown?" Mother asked.

Before the sheriff could respond, Papa rose from the porch swing and extended his hand. "Well, thanks for stopping by, Clem," he said.

The sheriff took his hand. "Think about what I've said, won't you, Will?"

"I'll do that."

"William?" Mother asked.

"Good night, Clem," Papa said.

"Good night, Will, Mrs. Eide."

His boots landed heavily on each porch step as he walked away, and I wondered how I would make my own escape from the parlor without getting caught.

Fortunately for me, Papa said, "Come on out and sit with me awhile, Lil."

I got up quietly from the wing chair as Mother and Papa sat down together on the swing. The last words I heard were Mother asking, "What did the sheriff say, William?" and Papa answering, "Nothing of any great importance, just a lot of hot air, like one of his campaign speeches." Mother said something else, but by then I was on my way up the stairs in my bare feet, relieved that I'd been able to get away unseen, but headed for a restless night on the ghost side of the bed, fighting off the very real phantoms of fear that plagued me in the form of the sheriff's warning.

Chapter Ten

Of all the chores that defined the summer days of my youth, the one I minded least was hanging the freshly washed laundry on the clotheslines in the yard. We had a rather primitive Maytag washing machine, but Mother still insisted on scrubbing the worst of the clothes on a washboard before throwing them into the machine. She didn't think anything mechanical could work as hard as she did, so for hours every Monday morning she and Aunt Sally scrubbed piles of laundry by hand until their skin was red and chapped and their fingers wrinkled like prunes. After the clothes and linens had been washed, Mother pushed them through a wringer while Aunt Sally turned the handle, squeezing the water out. When they finished a load, I was called upon to carry the results up to the clotheslines to dry in the sun.

We didn't worry much that summer about rain interfering with our laundry's drying process. Except for Mondays, in fact, we worried that we weren't getting enough rain. We longed for rain to bring us cooler temperatures, and the farmers longed for it to moisten the earth and to keep their topsoil from blowing away. But very little rain fell, and we sweltered in the heat while Kansas blew into Nebraska, and Oklahoma and Texas traded places.

But, as I say, on Mondays I enjoyed standing out in the morning light, pinning up the laundry to dry. Sometimes I'd pause and lift a pillowcase or one of Mother's dresses to my face and press the cool dampness of it against my cheek and forehead. I can still remember the fragrance of the soap that clung to the fabric, and I thought it sweeter than any flower or perfume I'd ever smelled. Its scent was not just fragrant but clean, and it had miraculously transformed a whole household of dirty, sweaty laundry into something wonderful.

Too, while I worked I dreamed of Charles Lindbergh landing his plane right there in the alley behind our house and whisking me away to soar through the skies with him. Or I pretended I was the Gypsy drudge — the beautiful young girl kidnapped by the Gypsies and forced to work as a slave — who was rescued by a valiant Charlie Chaplin in *The Vagabond*. No one watching me from another yard could know the strange dichotomy of my thoughts, could know that I stood there amid the damp clothes simultaneously enjoying what was and longing for what was not.

They never came, of course — neither of the Charlies. But toward noon on one particular Monday, the Fourth of July, 1932, while I pinned the last clean pillowcase to the line, a man did rush into the backyard, causing my heart to skip a beat while an involuntary gasp escaped me.

"Sorry, miss," the man said hurriedly. "I didn't mean to give you a fright, but is this the house of Doc Eide?"

I nodded dumbly. I knew at once by his appearance that the man was a resident of Soo City. His unkempt clothes smelled dreadful and looked worse, a stark contrast to the fresh clothing I had just hung on the line. The wrinkled shirt and pants appeared slept in, and the cap the man twisted in his hands was dirty and frayed. The man himself wasn't in any better condition. His unwashed hair fell below his collar, his skin was dry and leathery, and he hadn't shaved in at least a couple of days. Remembering what the sheriff said to Papa a few days before, I wondered whether this man might have joined the Communist group for unemployed people. If so, if he were in sympathy with the Reds, no telling what kind of crazy and dangerous stunts he might pull.

"Would you mind calling him, miss?" the man asked, impatiently trying to break through my stupefied gaze. "He's needed down to the camp."

Without saying a word, I started walking backward toward the house, never taking my eyes off the man. I carried the clothes basket in my arms to act as a barrier between him and me, though its actual benefit as a means of protection was questionable. When I reached the back door, I set the basket down and hurriedly stepped inside. Mother was in the kitchen fixing lunch while Aunt Sally rolled dough for green tomato pies. "Mama," I said, "there's a man here says he needs Papa."

Mother, in spite of the heat, was stirring a large pot of soup at the stove. She stepped to the kitchen window to see who was waiting in the yard. At the sight of the man, she sighed and shut her eyes a moment, as though wishing the man away. "I suppose he's from the camp," she said, opening her eyes. "Do you know what he wants?"

"He didn't say. He just said someone needed Papa."

Aunt Sally, still clutching the rolling pin, moved to the window and glanced out. "He looks anxious, Lillian. Better see what he wants," she suggested.

Mother wiped her hands on her apron and went to the screen door. Without opening it, she called out tentatively, "Can

I let the doctor know what you've come about?"

The man stepped closer but cautiously. "I beg your pardon, ma'am," he said, "but there's a baby coming down to the camp."

"A baby!" Mother exclaimed.

I tugged at her sleeve. "Don't you remember, Mama? Papa said there was a woman expecting a baby down there."

"Mercy," she whispered irritably. To the man she said, "Are you the father?"

The man shook his head. "Oh no, ma'am, not me. The old man's down by the riverbank, pacing and ringing his hands. We — those of us down to the camp, that is — decided someone would have to fetch the doctor for him."

Mother turned to me and instructed resignedly, "Run and get your father, Virginia."

I ran to alert Papa, bursting into the waiting room with such force that everyone sitting there jumped in alarm. I didn't stop to apologize, even though old Mrs. Greenaway clutched at her heart as if I had caused it to arrest. When I told Papa about the man in the yard, he once again left Dr. Hal in charge of the office while he grabbed his medical bag and hurried through the front hall.

As soon as he entered the kitchen, Mother stepped forward to meet him. "I had Virginia call you because there's a woman and a baby involved."

"Of course," Papa replied hastily.

"You know how I feel about —"

"I've got to be going, Lillian. Don't worry about anything."

"But if it weren't for the fact that it's a baby —"

"I might be gone awhile," Papa said as he strode across the kitchen. "I've left Harold in charge of everything."

"Please be careful, William."

Papa recognized our visitor as soon as he opened the screen door. "Well, hello, Sherman," he called cheerfully. "They have you pulling stork duty today, do they?"

The man responded gratefully to Papa's friendliness, thankful, I'm sure, that someone had arrived who didn't regard him with suspicion. "Yessir," he replied. "Old Everhart's got himself all tied up into knots with worry, so I was sent to fetch you."

Papa joined the man and, putting his free hand on Sherman's shoulder, hurried him along. "Come on, then. We'll take the car."

Aunt Sally went back to rolling out the pie crust, but Mother stepped to the door and rested one hand upon the screen. She watched the two men move across the yard, past the shirts and dresses and linens that hung on the line like reminders of better days. I saw her lips move, and I think what she spoke silently was my father's name. Evident there in her profile was a look of unmistakable concern that I had never quite seen before, and she struggled visibly to keep herself from calling out to him, from calling him back.

Aunt Sally saw it, too. "Don't worry so, Lillian," she said. She blew a strand of hair out of her eyes as she worked. "You look as though he's going off to war."

Without turning to look at Aunt Sally, Mother said so softly that I could scarcely hear, "It's just that I have a bad feeling. . . ." But she didn't finish her sentence, and her voice trailed off.

As she stood there with her hand upon the screen, I recalled Mother telling me that years ago she wrote "Will and Lil" all over her school books, and I think for the first time I understood that my mother and father were together not because that was how it had to be, but because they had chosen it. She was as far from romantic as a person could be, but Mother did love Papa. And Papa loved her. It was not the stuff of Hollywood, the land of happy endings, but the stuff of real life, in which a part of loving meant you had something to lose.

I went to Mother and put my arms about

her waist. Her hand dropped from the screen and rested against my back. We watched together as the Buick rumbled through the alley and disappeared.

I remember it was the Fourth of July because Rufus and Luke brought firecrackers and sparklers home from somewhere, which we lighted that night after dark. In those days the city didn't plan a fireworks display, but anyone who felt so inclined shot off Roman candles and whatnot from their yards, which meant an odd assortment of lights littering the sky at any one time, as well as an inevitable number of accidents taking place on the ground. Very often Papa was called upon to take care of minor burns. The greater mishaps, such as hands left without fingers in unexpected explosions, went directly to the hospital.

American flags waved from front porches all up and down our street. I saw the patriotic gesture as ironic — people had been complaining about our country all year long, but now that it was Independence Day, they went right ahead and celebrated as usual. Maybe it wasn't hypocrisy that led to the flags and the fireworks. Maybe it was hope. Hope that prosperity would indeed return in spite of all the indications that the economy was continuing to worsen.

Papa had come home whistling late that afternoon after being down at the camp for only a few hours. He announced that he had helped deliver a healthy baby girl, which I thought was a fine thing. Ever since Claudia and Molly were born, I believed all babies should be girls. I'd been eight when Claudia arrived, ten when Molly came — old enough to remember what it was like to hold them when they were only minutes old. To me they were the most miraculous things I'd ever seen, all pink and warm and perfect. I wondered what the newborn down at Soo City looked like. I pictured her tucked into a cradle just like the one my little sisters had been laid in, dressed in a tiny hand-stitched gown and covered with a homemade quilt. But then I realized there was probably no cradle, no hand-stitched gown, no quilt. That child's house, according to Papa, was made from an odd assortment of wooden boards and sheets of corrugated tin. Fancy baby items had no place in a home like that.

"Is she a pretty baby, Papa?" I asked. We sat together on the porch swing after the fireworks and sparklers had fizzled out and all the others had gone inside to bed or to get something cold to drink. I hoped none of our neighbors had burned a hand or otherwise injured themselves, because I didn't want Papa to be suddenly called away.

"Cute as the dickens," Papa answered. Then he looked sideways at me and smiled. "Of course, not half as pretty as you were when you were born."

I wrinkled my nose to say I didn't believe him, but secretly I hoped he thought I'd been the most beautiful baby he'd ever seen.

"Were her mama and papa happy?"

"Oh yes, certainly," Papa replied. Then he added, "But it was a happiness mixed with a little sadness too. When you have a child, you want to feel you can give her the best of everything, but — well, these parents won't be able to do that. Not for a while, anyway. These aren't the best of times to be raising a family."

Papa's comment weighed on me and pulled my brow into a frown. "But, Papa," I remarked, "*you're* raising a family in these times." I looked up at him with something akin to fear in my eyes. The thought occurred to me, probably for the first time, that my brother, sisters, and I might be a burden to Papa.

My father understood my unspoken words. "Yes," he said, smiling kindly as he patted my short hair. "But, you see, we're a little better off than some. I've never given much thought to money, certainly never had any desire to be rich, but I can't deny that life is better when you have enough money for the things you need. It frees you up from the terrible burden of worrying about the basics — like where your next meal is going to come from and whether or not you're going to have a bed to sleep in."

I thought about how it was Mother who kept the books and tried to collect delinquent payments, and how she always said we'd all be in the poorhouse if it weren't for her.

Papa paused and pushed the swing slightly with the ball of one foot. My own legs were long enough that with both feet planted on the porch my bony knees stuck up like twin snow-capped mountains every time we swung forward. I thought about how Papa and I had been swinging together on this porch swing ever since my legs were so short that my feet barely hung over the edge of the seat.

Papa continued. "We're very blessed, Ginny, and that's something I never take for granted. I know how fortunate I am to have all that I have — and the best that I have is you and your brother and sisters."

Papa's words relieved me of my momentary guilt. Papa saw me as a blessing, not a burden, and that was a wonderful thing. Had I been more mature I might have wondered why our family was so blessed when others suffered, but at the time I simply took our good fortune for granted.

"And you're glad you have Mama, too, aren't you, Papa?" I asked.

"Oh yes." Papa smiled. "Very, very glad."

"We're just about the best family in the world, aren't we?"

"If not the best, then we're pretty close," he agreed.

That settled, my mind wandered back to the family so recently expanded down in Soo City. "The little baby that was born today — does she have any brothers or sisters?" I asked.

"Two brothers."

"Then it's especially nice that she's a girl."

"Uh-huh," Papa agreed absently.

"Do you know what they named her, Papa?"

"I believe they named her Caroline Sue. Yup, that's it. Caroline Sue Everhart."

I mistook the spelling of her middle name. "Did they name her after the Soo line, Papa?"

Papa chuckled mildly. "I don't believe so, though that might have been appropriate after all. She came into the world just as the three-thirty-five to Chicago passed by the camp. Her first cries were all but drowned out by the train's whistle." He chewed his cheek a moment and cast a distant glance somewhere far beyond the porch rails, reflecting. "She must have thought the world an awfully noisy place, poor thing."

We swung in silence for a moment, looking out over the dark street and listening to all the night songs of nature mingled with distant radios and the rumbling of our neighbors' voices as they gathered on their own porches to talk.

"Think her family will have to live down by those tracks for long?"

"I don't know," Papa said. "I hope not."

"Mama says no child should have to be in a place like that."

"No child and no woman — no man, for that matter. Someday I hope such places won't exist."

"Do you think so, Papa?"

"Yes, I think so."

"I hope by the time little Caroline knows she's alive, she'll be in a nice house with pretty curtains and a big front porch and a yard with a flower garden and everything."

"I hope so too, Ginny."

For a moment I sat quietly, pondering the makeshift city in which Caroline had begun her life. "Is it very awful there?" I asked. "Down in the camp, I mean."

Papa considered my question. Then he

said, "Pretty awful, yes."

"Mama doesn't like you going down there."

"No, I'm afraid she doesn't."

"Why not, Papa?"

"Oh, I guess she worries about things."

"What kinds of things?"

Papa pushed his glasses farther up his nose and scratched his thinning hair. "Things she doesn't need to be worried about," he answered.

He didn't know I'd heard his conversation with Sheriff Dysinger, and I didn't dare ask him anything directly about Communists in the camp. I chewed my lip a moment while I thought of how to phrase my next question. "Are there — do you think there's any bad people down there by the river?"

Papa shook his head slowly. "No, no bad people. Just people down on their luck."

"Then Mama shouldn't worry so much?"

"No, she shouldn't worry so much."

"And there's nothing to be afraid of?"

"Of course not," Papa said, patting my shoulder. "There isn't anything to be afraid of."

I wanted to believe Papa, but I couldn't reconcile his assurances with what I'd heard the sheriff say. If there really was no danger, why would Sheriff Dysinger warn Papa not to go down there? And too, there was the sheriff's final unanswered question nudging at me as though it hung still in the air around the porch swing: "What's in it for you, Will?"

"Papa?" I asked.

"Hmm?"

"Why do you do it?"

"Why do I do what?"

"Why do you want to go to an awful place like Soo City?"

Papa took off his glasses and polished them while he thought. He put them back on his nose and tucked the handkerchief in his shirt pocket. Then he said, "Did I ever tell you the old story about the Jewish rabbi who was given a special tour of heaven and hell, with God himself as the tour guide?"

Papa had told me many things about the Jews. He said they were God's chosen people. He said the first Christians were Jews, and that if we traced the roots of our faith to the very beginning, they would go all the way back to Abraham, Isaac, and Jacob. He said the Jews were to be respected for their special place in history and in the unfolding of God's plan for the world. But I couldn't remember Papa ever telling me about a rabbi getting a tour of heaven and hell.

"No," I said. "I don't think you told me about that."

The cicadas sang. A lone car passed in the street. Papa followed its taillights with his eyes until the car turned a corner and disappeared. Then he said, "Well, it seems God took this rabbi down to the netherworld first to show him what it was like. It wasn't a place of fire, as you might expect, but just a regular room where a lot of people were sitting around a big round table. It was obvious to the rabbi that the people were famished, even though in the middle of the table there was a huge pot of stew with more than enough for everyone. Seems the problem was that the only eating utensils the people had were spoons with very long handles — so long that once a person scooped out a bit of the stew he couldn't reach his mouth with the end of the spoon. The rabbi could see that these people were in a terrible predicament and were really suffering.

"Then the Lord told the rabbi that he wanted to show him heaven. Turns out God took him into another room that was exactly like the first one. There was the large round table and the pot of stew and the long-handled spoons. But the people sitting around this table were plump and happy. They were talking and laughing and just having a good old time. The rabbi couldn't understand it. He scratched his head and tugged at his beard and just about turned blue in the face trying to figure out why this place was different from the first. 'It's simple,' God finally told him. 'These people have learned to feed each other.' "

Papa and I swayed together in the swing. I waited for him to continue, but he remained silent. Finally I figured he was finished, that this story was the answer to my question, though I couldn't quite make the connection. I didn't much like it when grown-ups answered my questions with parables. Not only did the use of parables leave room for errors in interpretation, but it also meant that I had to think harder than otherwise.

Finally I said rather hesitantly, "So I guess you're feeding the stew to the people in Soo City."

Papa nodded. "Something like that."

I wasn't satisfied. Maybe he had uncovered the riddle of the long-handled spoon, maybe he knew what he was supposed to do with that strange utensil, but what was he getting in return? Who around that shantytown table was feeding Papa? It was supposed to be a mutually beneficial deal, after all, and I could only imagine that Papa was getting slighted.

My father, it seems, could sense my uncertainty. "Don't you understand, Ginny?" he asked kindly. "There's nothing noble about what I'm doing. I go down to Soo City simply because it makes me happy."

Made him happy? To work in that filthy place and not get a dime for his efforts?

Sometimes I thought Papa a little odd. This was definitely one of those times.

Chapter Eleven

Charlotte was laid low with a cold, so I was entertaining myself by dancing and singing along with our floor-model Philco radio on the afternoon Papa announced he was taking me with him to Soo City. "Happy Days Are Here Again" was coming in over the airwaves, and I was flapping my arms and singing so loudly I didn't even know Papa was in the parlor with me until the radio went dead. I stopped in midtwirl and discovered my father with his hand on the radio knob. Before I could apologize for the noise — I was sure he was there to tell me that all the patients in the waiting room were complaining — he said, "Put your shoes on, Ginny. I'm going down to Soo City to make my rounds, and I want you to come along."

My surprise left me as immobile as Lot's wife when she turned into a pillar of salt. With arms still suspended in midair, I could only manage to mutter, "You do?"

"You've been wanting to see the baby, haven't you? Well, she's three days old now, and it's time I got back there to check up on her and her mother."

At once an odd combination of fear and

curiosity seized me. I didn't particularly want to go traipsing through a place that Papa himself described as awful, and I was still decidedly leery of the people who populated the camp. If Sherman Browne, the man who had rushed into our yard while I was pinning up clothes, typified the citizens of Soo City, they weren't a group I wanted to mingle with. Besides, what about Mother's dread of disease and her whispered premonition of disaster? What about the sheriff's warning of Communist organizers getting the men all riled up to no good? Papa's assurances that there wasn't anything to fear somewhat assuaged my anxiety for *his* safety, but I wasn't so sure I wanted to test the waters myself.

And yet a morbid inquisitiveness drew me to observe firsthand these people living in squalor down by the river. I found myself facing an opportunity not open to the other neighborhood kids. Think of what I would have to tell Charlotte.

Before I could make a move to run upstairs and get my shoes, Mother rushed into the room, wiping her hands on her ever present apron. "William!" she exclaimed. "Did I hear you say you were taking Virginia down to the camp with you?"

Evidently my parents hadn't discussed this matter between themselves. I don't know whether Papa had been thinking about it for a while or had decided to take me on the spur of the moment. He was generally a predictable type, but sometimes he had his whims.

"I see your ears are as sharp as ever, dear. Yes, I'm taking Ginny down to the camp with me today." In a lower voice, he continued. "I think it'll do her good."

Mother cast a worried glance in my direction, then indicated with a nod of her head that Papa was to step with her out into the hall. Their slight change of location, however, didn't keep me from overhearing their conversation.

"What do you mean, it'll do her good?" Mother asked anxiously. Ironically, I was pondering the same question myself.

"Just that," Papa replied simply. "Ginny's growing up."

I acknowledged my father's words with gratitude that someone had noticed I was growing up — even if that person generally couldn't remember to call me Virginia. "It's about time she was introduced to those less fortunate than herself."

"But, William," Mother protested, "that camp is no place for a young lady."

"I can't think of a better place for our daughter to learn a few facts about the harsher side of life. I won't have her pampered, Lillian. Besides, I could use her help."

"Doing what?"

"Oh, this and that," Papa remarked evasively. "Whatever the situation warrants at the time."

"I'm sorry, but I just don't think this is a good idea. It's bad enough that you insist on going down there yourself, but to take Virginia —"

"Trust me, Lillian. Everything will be fine. She'll be with me every minute. I promise not to let her out of my sight. Not that any harm could come to her anyway, even if she were to wander the camp by herself. It's no more dangerous than the streets of our own neighborhood."

"But —"

I stepped to the doorway between the parlor and the hall in time to see Papa lay one finger gently across Mother's lips. He smiled. "I appreciate your motherly concern, Lillian. I love you for it. But I'm Ginny's father, and I have some idea, too, about what's good for her. Now, have I ever steered you wrong?"

Mother took Papa's hand from her lips and said quietly, "No, William."

They both turned to look at me. "Don't worry, Mama," I said. "I want to go. I want to help Papa if I can."

Mother sighed resignedly. "Run and get your shoes, then."

A few minutes later, with the tinny radio

tune still echoing in my brain, I was sitting with Papa in the Buick as we headed for the camp. Since we lived in a neighborhood on the edge of town, our house wasn't far from the spot on the river that the hobos had long inhabited. I'd estimate the distance was between two and three miles. We didn't say much on the way. Papa's only comment, delivered with a chuckle, was, "Sometimes your mother worries overly much."

I didn't know what was ahead, but I decided to try to enjoy the brief ride until we got there. Our car was a 1929 four-door sedan, olive green with wooden spokes on the wheels. The seats were real leather instead of cloth, which was pretty grand for those days, perhaps even a bit highfalutin. The fact was, though, that Papa bought the Buick secondhand and had gotten a good deal. The previous owner had had possession of the car for only nine days when the stock market crashed and wiped out the man's modest fortune. The hapless victim returned the car to the dealership, left the keys on the front seat, and simply walked away from it. The equally hapless salesman was glad to sell the car to Papa at a greatly reduced price just to get it off his hands. Even though most of the other doctors in town drove sleek black Packards, we were all proud of that Buick — except for Papa, who saw it only as the quickest means for making urgent house calls. When it came to possessions, Papa was strictly utilitarian. As for me, I always felt like the Queen of Sheba whenever I rode around in our car because, though it may not have rivaled the transportation of other doctors, it was undoubtedly the nicest automobile on our block.

Nevertheless, I was hard put to enjoy my brief ride in it that afternoon. The leather seats were so hot I felt like a strip of bacon in a skillet. My dress scarcely acted as a buffer between my skin and the seat, and I wondered that I didn't start to sizzle and spit out grease. We drove with the windows down, our only hope for some small bit of relief, but the inrush of air was not only hard to breathe but made annoying whips out of my hair that stung my cheeks and forced me to travel with my eyes shut. Papa generally whistled while he drove, but that day even he lacked the gumption. His gentle stream of notes wouldn't stand a chance in the face of the hot wind blowing over us. Lacking Papa's usual entertainment, I listened subconsciously to the music of my own mind.

By the time we turned off the main street out of town and bumped along a rutted dirt road that crossed the railroad tracks and led on down to the river, Papa's shirt and my dress were glued with sweat to the simmering leather interior. The wheels of our car kicked up a great cloud of dust that tumbled along like an angry storm in our wake, and soon we felt gritty all over from the powdery dirt. The suggestion of earth was on our tongues like the aftertaste of unwashed vegetables. I longed for water but said nothing. We passed through a wooded area, then came to a clearing where I saw the first of the shacks on the edge of Soo City. Papa pulled the Buick into the shade of a tall maple and turned off the engine. I breathed a sigh of relief and pushed my tousled hair back from my sweaty forehead. "All ashore," Papa said. "You can help me first of all by carrying one of the bags."

He had brought along two medical bags. One, he explained, for his medical supplies, the other — a larger bag — for cans of food and a few other items. He gave me the bag with the medical supplies, saying it was lighter.

As I followed him toward the encampment, I noticed a hand-painted sign on a square of wood nailed to a tree. "Welcome to Soo City," it read. Then beneath that in smaller letters: "The Soo Line brings us, And the Soo Line takes us away. Blessed be the name of the Soo."

I gasped at what appeared to be obvious

blasphemy and looked up to Papa for an explanation, but he strode face forward toward the shacks without glancing up at the sign. I figured he had seen it so many times before he didn't even notice it now.

"First, we'll check on that pretty little baby," Papa said as we reached the first pitiful dwellings. "Her house is down this way a bit."

I thought Papa awfully generous in equating any of these shacks with what we thought of as a house. The fact is, we were walking amid the contents of the city dump, all rearranged to resemble a town. As Papa had said after his first visit to Soo City, the place was a sea of flimsy structures made of cardboard, two-by-fours and other scraps of wood, flattened tin cans and sheets of corrugated tin, even old rusty signs that had once been tossed onto the junk heap. One outer wall of a shack advertised the joys of drinking Coca Cola by featuring the smiling faces of a family sitting in a shiny new convertible. The wall of another shack showed a clean-shaven, obviously well-to-do businessman smoking a certain brand of cigarette. The pictures seemed terribly strange in the middle of these surroundings and served to magnify the wretchedness of the little makeshift town.

All the dwellings had windows cut into

them, and though none of the windows had glass, most of them were rigged with some sort of shutters so they could be closed up in bad weather. I was surprised to see that a few odd windows were adorned with curtains — nothing fancy, just old sheets and scraps of material — but curtains nevertheless. I saw it as a desperate bid toward normalcy. A number of the houses also had round tin chimneys poking out of the roofs, indicating that there was some means of cooking inside.

Scattered amid these ramshackle structures were several old tents held up with mismatched pieces of rope and even string. One tent was simply a couple of old blankets sewn together and tossed over a line. Here and there a few Tin Lizzies and dilapidated pickup trucks were parked with flattened tires and rusted exteriors. They were more for shelter, I supposed, than transportation.

Also, as Papa had described it, the camp was laid out in streets, dry dirt streets that like the road leading into the camp spit up little clouds of dust when you walked on them. There was one main street that ran parallel to the river, with smaller streets crossing it. The smaller streets started at the river and stopped about three hundred yards away, near the railroad tracks. Whoever painted the Soo City sign had painted street signs as well, giving them names like Hoover Avenue (the main street), Prosperity Place, and Recovery Way. The streets, I noticed, were clean and free of clutter, and outside the front doors of some of the shacks whisk marks in the dirt gave evidence that the ground had been swept. Here was the city dump, all right, but the inhabitants at least made an effort to keep it orderly.

As we made our way down Hoover Avenue, the place was eerily quiet, the ambiance that of an inhabited ghost town. A few lean chickens strutted dispassionately between the shacks. Here and there a stray dog sauntered along the dusty roads, sniffing at open doorways, looking for a handout from the one group of people least able to oblige. Squirrels scrambled over tin roofs that threw the sun blindingly back at itself, and birds of various kinds pecked vainly at the ground, looking for seeds. Soo City seemed unable to offer up sustenance to any living thing. Not to animals and not to people.

Men sat cross-legged on the ground in groups of twos and threes around small fires. They stared glassy-eyed at the tin cans they had set to heat in the flames. The gray smoke drifted straight upward into the windless air. Occasionally a rumble of conversation reached us, punctuated by laughter, but it was the laughter of the lost: crisp, sarcastic, and trailing off into sighs.

Soo City lacked the bustle of a thriving community, though it was dotted with people going about their daily business. One young fellow, wearing overalls and grease-stained to his elbows, worked under the hood of one of the pickup trucks. Another older man fumbled with a propane stove, trying to get it to work. Still another was using a rock as a hammer to nail a piece of cardboard over a hole in a wall. Other men, less motivated or perhaps enervated by the heat, simply sat on the threshold of their shacks smoking cigarettes, their movements deliberate and weary. Some read newspapers. One man slept directly on the ground with a folded paper over his face. No one smiled, except briefly when they called out their greetings to Papa and me.

"Afternoon, Doc! Got yourself a helper today?"

"Afternoon, men. I'd like you to meet my daughter, Ginny."

"Virginia," I whispered to Papa, and though I knew he had heard, he didn't correct himself. I smiled shyly at the strangers while caps were removed and the men muttered variations of "Glad to know you, miss" and "Howdy do?"

217

"Anyone got any complaints?" Papa asked.

"Not today, Doc. 'Preciate you asking."

"Let me know if you do."

We walked on. In the next moment the eerie quiet was abruptly punctuated by the rumbling of an approaching train. It had probably left the station only moments before and was just now picking up speed. I heard it — and felt it — before I saw it. The train seemed to be coming out of nowhere, pressing down on us like an unexpected storm, sending its weighty vibrations through the dry ground. As the rumbling grew louder and the train drew nearer, the earth trembled beneath our feet. Shacks shivered; curtains swayed. The train whistle split the air with its cry, leaving me startled and half deaf, and suddenly there it was, this iron monster rolling its tons of dead weight toward the camp. I was certain that it was bearing down on us and that before we could make a move to save ourselves, Papa and I and the entire camp would be flattened as though by a steamroller. But at the last moment the train followed the curve of the tracks and only skirted the town rather than running through it. As its many freight cars rolled by, the entire camp was absorbed by its passing. There was no more eating, no more doing, no more conversation, even no more thoughts. The train absorbed every-thing, overwhelmed everything so that it alone existed. The thunderous weight, the groaning and screeching of wheels against track, the sudden furious wind coughed up by the motion of the rushing cars, the throbbing that seeped right through the bottom of your feet so that your insides rattled. The black leviathan blew its whistle again, though it scarcely needed to warn us of its presence, and belched billows of black smoke into the air. Finally the ca-boose appeared, rolled by, and passed on with one final ear-shattering squeal of pro-test, as though casting censure toward the people who had illegally hopped its back and stolen its name. At last the rear end of the caboose disappeared, and while the rumbling became a distant storm again be-fore dying out altogether, the soot from the train's smokestack settled over the town like one last lingering insult.

"How often does the train go by?" I asked Papa.

"About every hour or so."

"Day and night?"

"Not so often at night, maybe every few hours."

"What if it jumps the tracks, Papa?" It seemed to me the small inward curve of the wheels wasn't nearly enough to keep that huge train running on those two smooth rails. Soo City had escaped disaster this time, but one false move and someday that overgrown serpent would be dragging its belly right through the middle of the camp.

"It's always possible, I guess," Papa said, "but we just have to hope it doesn't happen around here."

Even so, even if that train stayed where it belonged, I didn't like it. "Doesn't the noise bother these people?" I asked.

"I guess they get used to it."

"I never would."

"You would if you lived here."

I was glad I didn't live there.

The first woman I saw was washing her family's clothes in an old tin basin. She was a plump woman, with matted hair held firmly in a grip of bobby pins and a web of varicose veins on the back of her thick legs. Her gray dress was soaked through with perspiration. She was turned away from us, so I couldn't see her face, though I could well imagine the weariness etched upon it. We passed close enough for me to notice that the water in the tub was gray and without suds. Apparently she had no soap to use. When she finished washing a piece of clothing, she didn't need to rinse it. She just wrung it out with her hands and threw it over a line of rope strung up between the roof of her own shack and that of her neighbor's. She had no clothespins to hold the clothes on the line. The shirts and pants and dresses that dripped there in the sun were faded and worn, and I supposed they weren't much cleaner now than when the woman had started. And surely they didn't smell like Mother's clean laundry when I hung it up on the line on Monday mornings.

Only slowly — I think it was after I saw those pitiful clothes hanging there like so many weathered scarecrows — did I become conscious of the song that insisted on replaying itself like a broken record in my brain.

So long, sad times.
Go 'long, bad times.
We are rid of you at last. . . .

The woman threw another pile of clothes into the dirty water, stuck her arms in up to the elbows, and went on scrubbing.

Howdy, gay times.
Cloudy, gray times.
You are now a thing of the past. . . .

Walking toward us down Hoover Avenue was a young man about the age of my cousin Jimmy Jr. He must have been young because his skin was smooth and firm and the whiskers on his face were soft like down rather than stiff, but his eyes were middle-aged, and the slump of his shoulders was decidedly old.

'Cause happy days are here again!

He passed us without seeing us, and I pulled my eyes away from his face only to have my gaze shift to another face — an older man smoking in a doorway — that really wasn't a human face at all but a portrait of despair.

The skies above are clear again.
Let us sing a song of cheer again. . . .

He lifted a cigarette to his lips, inhaled deeply, then let his hand fall again to his knee. It hung there, sagging at the wrist, fingers dangling downward like the udder of a cow ready to produce but with no one to milk it. A full and idle hand.

Happy days are here again!

Oh, Papa! But before I could cry out, we had reached the house where the baby had been born, and Papa was giving me last-minute instructions. "Now, be polite and friendly, just as though we were visiting the Mobleys," he said, referring to our next-door neighbors. He knocked gently on the piece of knotty wood that served as a door. After a moment it opened a crack and a face peered out timidly from the darkness inside. The apprehensive eyes brightened when the woman recognized Papa.

"Dr. Eide! How kind," she said, throwing the door open wide. "Come to see Caroline, have you? Come in. Come in."

Papa had to duck his head to get into the dim little shelter. I followed, and once inside thought immediately of a playhouse I used to have in the backyard, long since toppled in a violent windstorm. Charlotte and I had fixed that place up with a throw rug and a table and chairs. We'd hung curtains in the windows and tacked pictures from magazines on the walls. We often had tea parties there, with Charlotte pretending to be the guest, and I the hostess. We'd sit at the table sipping imaginary tea and flashing imaginary diamonds and nasally uttering such inanities as, "Darling, you look simply divine" and "Charmed, I'm sure."

But this woman wasn't pretending, and she didn't even appear to have any chipped cups and saucers like the ones Grandmother Foster had given me to play with. Curtains of a sort did frame the shack's two windows, but the dirt floor had no rug, and the only things hanging on the walls were a few items of clothing suspended from nails. A table and two cane-bottom chairs were pushed up against one wall. A mattress covered with sheets — apparently the only bed in the house — lay on the ground by the opposite wall. Here and there a few packing crates held household items like dishes and cooking utensils. The woman must have done her cooking outside over an open fire because there wasn't a kerosene or propane stove inside.

The most pitiful thing in the shack was the woman herself. I wanted to be polite but couldn't help staring at her. She was thin and pale, and though rather tall, she couldn't have weighed more than ninety or, at most, a hundred pounds. Her sleeveless cotton dress, ringed with sweat along the collar, revealed arms not much thicker than my own. Her oval face was so gaunt as to be almost skeletal, and her large eyes sat deep in their sockets. Her thin fine hair was parted in the middle and pulled back into a careless knot. Because of her complete lack of color, she reminded me of an artist's preliminary sketch that hadn't yet been painted. She might have been pretty once, but now she just looked hungry and tired.

"Mrs. Everhart," Papa was saying, "this is my daughter Gin— um, Virginia. She's helping me out on my rounds today."

"Well, now, isn't that fine?" Mrs. Everhart exclaimed, sending a smile in my direction. I noticed that she still had strong white teeth. She held out one slender hand to me. "Pleased to know you, Virginia."

"How do you do?" I responded automatically. Her hand felt light as air in my own, almost as though she weren't really there at all.

"Tom has taken the boys into town with him," the woman said to Papa, "so Caroline and I are spending a quiet afternoon together." Papa nodded and followed the woman's gesture toward a packing crate in one corner of the room. From the crate we heard a soft cry and then the cooing of a baby. The woman continued. "I do believe she knows you're here, Doctor. She's happy to see you again."

With a smile Papa set the large medical bag down on the floor, rolled up his sleeves, and gently lifted the tiny newborn out of the packing crate. The child was naked save for a diaper fashioned from what once might have been a pillowcase. "Well now, Miss Caroline," Papa crooned, "let's just see how we're doing today. Ginny, hand me my other bag, will you?"

While Papa briefly examined the child — listening to her heart with his stethoscope and so forth — Mrs. Everhart invited me

225

to sit at the table. As I settled myself in one of the cane-bottom chairs, I wondered where it had come from. Was it something the Everharts had taken away with them when they left their home — wherever that was — dragging it all the way to Soo City so they'd have something to sit on when they arrived? Or had they found this chair, these few bits of furniture, somewhere around the city? In the junkyard, or maybe just on some sidewalk in the residential district, which seemed to be where the furniture of so many displaced people ended up these days. I was curious, but I didn't want to ask. Primly folding my hands in my lap, I wished I could be doing something to help Papa rather than just sitting.

Mrs. Everhart sat in the chair opposite me and asked kindly, "Would you like some water, Virginia? I'm sure you must be thirsty, the heat being what it is." I almost accepted the offer until I remembered where the water came from — the river. Or, if she was lucky, her husband had hauled a bucket from the comfort station a mile away. Neither prospect seemed particularly inviting.

"No, thank you, ma'am. I'm not thirsty, really," I declined politely, though in fact I could still feel the grit of the road on my teeth, and I was longing for a tall glass of Mother's lemonade.

"Fit as a fiddle," Papa cried happily as he finished his examination.

"Thank the Lord for that," Mrs. Everhart responded.

"Yes," Papa agreed. "Now, Virginia, would you like to hold her for a moment while I dig a few items out of my bag here?"

I looked at the child's mother. She smiled gently. "Go ahead," she invited.

I took the baby from Papa and held her on my lap with her small, wispy-haired head resting in the crook of my arm. Papa was right. She was a beautiful child. Unlike the woman who bore her, Caroline looked healthy, with full and rosy cheeks and chubby little fists. It was almost as though Mrs. Everhart had given all the best of her health to the baby, while leaving only enough life in her own body to go on living. Just the opposite of Mother, who with each baby simply kept getting bigger and seemingly more robust.

Caroline reminded me of Molly when she was born, and I wished that I could take her home and care for her and spoil her and dress her up in all sorts of frilly baby clothes just as I had done with my sisters. But she would have to stay here, sleeping in her packing crate and wearing whatever clothes her mother could piece together from hand-me-downs and rags. It was a less than fortunate beginning, and as I gazed at the baby's wondrous and innocent little face, I understood the happiness tinged with sadness that Papa had told me about.

In another moment my attention was turned to Papa who, after rummaging through the larger medical bag and lifting something from it, exclaimed, "Ah-hah! Here it is. A little something for Miss Caroline."

I recognized the item as a wooden rattle that had occupied a place in my siblings' cradles, as well as my own. Each of us had in turn grasped its wooden handle with our infant hands and gnawed at the bulb with our toothless gums. It had disappeared sometime after Molly became a toddler. Papa must have searched the attic high and low to find it again.

The mother accepted it with evident joy. "Oh my! Oh, how kind of you, Dr. Eide." She took the rattle and placed it in her daughter's tiny hand. The baby's fingers curled around the handle while the mother looked on with obvious pleasure. "It's Caroline's first gift. Thank you, Doctor."

"You're most welcome," Papa said. "And this," he continued, holding up a jar of a yellowish powder, "is for the boys."

The woman frowned in spite of the smile that refused to fade. "Why, what on earth is it?"

"Brewer's yeast," Papa stated matter-of-factly, as though it were an item found in every mother's cupboard. "Stir two tablespoons into a little water three times a day and have the boys drink it. They won't like it, but they need it. It'll give them strength. See that they drink it all."

"I'll do my best."

"After this is gone, I'll bring some more."

I played with the baby for a few minutes, amusing her with the hissing song of the rattle, while Papa asked the woman about her own health. Then satisfied that all was well — or as well as could be expected — Papa rolled his sleeves down and snapped shut the two medical bags.

"I trust Tom got over his case of nerves the other day," Papa said, referring to the man's hand-wringing and pacing of the riverbank the day Caroline was born.

Mrs. Everhart laughed. "Yes, he's fine, thank you. He's much obliged for your help. If he'd known you were coming by today, he'd have stayed home to thank you himself."

Papa waved a hand. "You tell Tom he's more than welcome, and he can call on me anytime anyone needs a doctor. Well, Ginny, if you'll put Caroline down for her nap, we'll be moving on."

I reluctantly carried the baby back to the

crate and gently laid her down. Carrying both bags, Papa stepped toward the door and I moved to follow him, but the woman stopped us. "Just a moment, please. I have something —" She lifted a small wooden box from a crate that served as a bedside table next to the mattress. From the box she pulled a shiny item that she held in her extended palm for Papa to take. From where I stood I could see it was a silver brooch, shaped like a flower, with an opal at the center of it. Like the Coca-Cola sign featuring the convertible, it seemed jarringly out of place, an odd little nugget of luxury in the midst of squalor. "For your wife," the woman explained quietly.

Papa looked at the brooch, then lifted his eyes to the woman's face. He put the bags down, cupped the woman's hand in both of his own, and curled her fingers around the piece of jewelry. "The day's going to come," he said gently, "when you or Caroline will have a pretty new dress, and you'll need something to ornament it with. This nice pin will be just the thing. You keep it for that day, Mrs. Everhart."

For a moment the woman's face appeared fuller, her eyes brighter. I think when we stepped out of the shack that afternoon, Papa left behind not just a rattle and a bottle of brewer's yeast, but also what he knew to be the best medicine —

a little bit of hope.

On the way to our next patient, we ran into Dick Mason, the man who had come to our door and called Papa down to Soo City the first time. He was still living in the camp, evidently thwarted in his plans to move on by the sudden death of his brother-in-law and traveling companion. He looked more like a hobo now than he had two months before. Though he was still clean shaven and still had all his teeth, his clothes were a little more worn, his shoes a little more scuffed, and his face had taken on the characteristic weariness of the men who live hand to mouth.

Nevertheless, like the others whose fate had brought them to Soo City, he greeted Papa cheerfully. Papa handed me the smaller of the bags, and the two men shook hands.

"How are you, Dick?" Papa asked.

"Can't complain," came the reply.

Papa introduced me and the man shook my hand as well.

"Pleasure to meet you, Virginia," he said. "I think I might have seen you at the house, but we weren't properly introduced."

"Yes, sir," I responded.

"Helping out your father today, young lady?"

"Yes, sir," I repeated.

"What do you think of our little community here?" he asked, his eyes scanning the shacks that stretched out in every direction. "More than a hundred homes at last count, and we're expanding all the time. We can be proud — not every community can say they're growing these days."

I nearly failed to detect the sarcasm in his words, he slipped it in so subtly, and I was left wondering how to respond. But Papa saved me from having to answer by steering the man on to another topic.

"I've been meaning to ask you something, Dick," he said.

"Go ahead and shoot," Mr. Mason replied easily.

Papa put a hand on Dick's shoulder and guided him down Hoover Avenue. As I trailed along behind, I heard Papa say, "I've heard rumors to the effect that there've been men coming around here trying to organize an Unemployed Council. Any truth to the rumors?"

Dick Mason gave a brief laugh, which I thought a good sign until he said, "Not only have they been coming around, but one of them lives here now. Built himself a shanty and moved in the other day. He tries to pass himself off as just another man out of work. He never comes right out and says he's Red, but everyone knows why he's here."

"Is he having any luck? I mean, are the men listening to him?"

"Some are. People are hungry. Men are tired of being out of work. After a while, they'll start to listen to anything that promises a change."

Papa nodded. "But do you think he's actually going to be able to get the men to form a Council?"

Mr. Mason ran his fingers through his hair, which badly needed a wash and a trim. "Hard to say," he replied. "I'd guess the majority of us, myself included, don't want anything to do with a Red, even if it means sure starvation. But every time a man goes out looking for work and comes back here no closer to a job than when he left, he gets just a little bit more worn down. You know what I mean, Doc?"

Papa nodded his understanding.

Dick Mason continued. "It's pretty easy to swear by capitalism when your stomach's full, but when a man gets desperate, no telling what he might do."

The two men continued strolling in silence while I followed along on their heels. Walking behind Mr. Mason, I couldn't help but notice the stale odor of sweat and dirt that trailed him like a foul cologne. *So this is what we would all be like if we didn't take baths,* I thought. Mother was right after all. It was necessary to bathe if one wanted to remain respectable.

"You told me once that the sheriff's deputies patrol around here," Papa said.

"Yes, there's two or three that come around on a regular basis. They don't say much, just kind of walk by to make sure we're staying in line — no one's turned bootlegger or anything like that. Not that we never see moonshine around here." Mr. Mason laughed briefly. "Amazing, though, how some men are always able to get their hands on the liquor, even when they haven't got a penny in their pocket for food."

Papa nodded his agreement but didn't pursue the topic. He asked, "Are the deputies aware of the latest newcomer to the community?"

"The Red?" Mr. Mason lifted his shoulders in a shrug. "I doubt it. Why?"

Instead of answering directly, Papa seemed to change the subject. "Dick, are you planning to move on anytime soon?"

Again the man lifted his shoulders, this time in resignation. "One place is about the same as the next, Doc. I might as well stay here for the time being."

"Would you mind keeping an eye on this man for me — by the way, do you know his name?"

"He says it's John Jones, but there's no telling. He's got good reason to go by an

234

alias. And if you ask me, a name like John Jones has a bit of a fishy smell to it."

"Well, keep an eye on Mr. Jones for me, will you, Dick, and keep me posted on his activities around here?"

"Sure, Doc."

"Appreciate it, Dick. Listen, my wife's been canning again, and she's just about got us buried under a mountain of Mason jars. I'm trying to clear her some shelf space by getting rid of some of last year's goods." Papa placed the medical bag he was carrying on the ground and opened the latch. He reached inside and, sure enough, pulled out a couple of Mason jars. "Could you use some tomatoes, Dick? And how about some peaches? They're last year's crop but they're still good."

Mr. Mason knew — and I knew he knew — that Papa wasn't trying to help Mother with her shelf space. It was a lame story, but Mr. Mason appeared grateful anyway.

"Well, now, Doc, I think I can help you out by taking a couple of those jars off your hands," he said, accepting the goods from Papa.

Papa closed up the bag. "Let me know if you need anything, Dick."

"I'll do that. And in the meantime I'll keep a close watch on our friend Mr. Jones."

We left Dick Mason with a jar in each

hand and moved on to the shack of a man called Mr. Lucky. Papa said that wasn't his real name, but everyone called him Mr. Lucky because he was always telling people that their luck would soon be changing for the better. The man was one of the original hobos of the camp and hadn't worked since long before the Depression, so no one knew what kept him so upbeat. But his belief in better days ahead was unassailable.

Before Papa knocked on the door, he cupped his hands and instructed me to find the rubbing alcohol in his bag and pour some over his palms. I did as I was told. Little drops of alcohol seeped through Papa's fingers and formed muddy pearls on the otherwise dry ground. Papa rubbed his hands together vigorously, then laced his fingers and kept on rubbing as though he were rinsing his hands under water. Just as suddenly as he started, he stopped. "Towel, please," he requested. I looked again in the bag and pulled out a small white towel. Papa took it and patted his hands dry. "Thank you, nurse." He smiled as he returned the towel to me, while I just about burst with a sense of importance.

Then we were ready to turn our attention to the next patient. Mr. Lucky, who to me seemed not so lucky at all, had burned his hands trying to put out a fire. He had kindled a small flame inside his shack so he could heat up a can of beans, but somehow the flames had gone wild and threatened to burn down his home. He put it out before all was lost, but evidence of the recent fire remained in the form of scorch marks on the walls and the odor of burnt wood in the air.

He invited us into his slightly charred shack with great enthusiasm, saying he would gladly shake both our hands if his own weren't quite so sore. Papa said he had come to check on the burns and to change the bandages.

"Do as you like, Doc," the man said cheerfully. "If you say it's time to change the bandages, then it's time to change the bandages."

It was past time to change the bandages, and Papa and I both knew it. Normally, Papa would change a patient's bandages daily to keep the wounds from becoming septic, but since he couldn't get to Soo City every day, things like this just had to wait. Mr. Lucky may not have been shaking people's hands, but he certainly had been doing everything else, because his bandages were soiled and in a sorry condition.

In fact, everything about Mr. Lucky seemed to be in a rather sorry condition. His white hair was a mat of knots, his beard a burial ground for the remnants of his last meal. His clothes were nearly rags, and he smelled alarmingly worse even than Mr. Mason. Yet the smile never left his face, revealing browns stumps that had once been, I assumed, two neat rows of choppers. While Papa removed the bandages and washed Mr. Lucky's palms with an antiseptic, the man talked merrily about President Hoover's predictions of prosperity around the corner. Papa and I let him chatter away. I resisted the temptation to repeat Uncle Jim's remarks about just how long a hike it was from here to the corner.

Just as Papa was twining clean gauze around the man's right hand, a dog pushed open the door of the shack with his nose and sauntered in. I didn't know whether to be afraid or amused, though the mutt — a big long-haired creature that must have been part collie — seemed harmless enough.

"Ah, T-Bone!" Mr. Lucky cried happily. "Back from scavenging, I see. Any luck, my friend?" The dog gave one miserable bark and, after pawing at the dirt and circling a couple of times, curled himself up in a corner of the shack. Mr. Lucky sighed. "Well, these are bitter times for man and beast alike, I'm afraid. You know things are bad when there's not enough out there even for a dog. But we keep our hopes up, don't we, T-Bone?"

The dog lifted his head and again responded with a crisp bark, then laid his long muzzle on his front paws. The poor thing panted and drooled in the heat, creating slimy puddles on the shanty's dirt floor.

"Why do you call him T-Bone?" I asked.

"Ah, you see," the man's bright eyes widened as he looked at me, "that's because he's always dreaming about steak, though he's blessed to get so much as a bone. But one day" — he turned to the dog — "one day you'll be eating steak. Isn't that right, T-Bone?"

The dog didn't bother to lift his head again. He merely wagged his tail once, then shut his eyes. He seemed to lack the optimism of his master.

Papa, who had just finished wrapping the man's hands, said cryptically, "Speaking of bones —" Again he reached for the medical bag out of which had already come a rattle, a container of brewer's yeast, and two Mason jars of canned food. I wondered what on earth he was going to pull out this time. This making the rounds with Papa was turning into a regular magic show.

Whatever it was he pulled out, it was wrapped in a piece of newspaper. As he folded back the wrapping, Papa explained to Mr. Lucky, "The butcher's daughter has ringworm. This soup bone was part of my payment."

He tossed the bone toward the dog, who jumped up and yelped in delight. He took the gift in his mouth, carried it back to his corner, curled himself up again, and began to gnaw hungrily at the bits of fat and grizzle still clinging to the bone. His tail thumped wildly on the hard-packed dirt as he chewed.

"Well, now, Doc, that's right good of you to think of T-Bone like that," Mr. Lucky exclaimed. "I'm obliged to you, I'm sure."

I was busy wondering what Mother would have thought had she known Papa had just thrown part of his pay to a shanty-town dog. She could have made a nice pot of soup with that bone. But Papa gave me a look to tell me that this was to be our secret. He then went into his brief spiel about how Mother was busy canning and could Mr. Lucky help us out by taking a couple of Mason jars off our hands? He placed two jars on a lopsided table that was the only other piece of furniture in the room besides the chair Mr. Lucky was sitting in. "Now, this one's peaches," Papa said, tapping one of the lids, "and the other is pears. You don't need to heat them up, so you won't have any reason to start a fire."

Mr. Lucky laughed heartily. "I swear, Doc!" he cried. "You do think of everything!"

Papa snapped shut the latches on both the bags and rolled down his sleeves, saying he'd return again in a couple of days.

"I expect I'll still be here, Doc, a couple of days from now, but I can't promise anything after that. Soon as prosperity comes, I'm gonna grab my share of it."

"Of course you are, Mr. Lucky," Papa agreed amiably. "A castle for you and a doghouse for T-Bone."

Mr. Lucky laughed again, a deep rich laugh filled with eternal optimism. Then he lifted one bandaged hand in a farewell gesture and said, "God bless you, Doc. And God bless you, little girl."

We moved on then, going from shack to shack while Papa tended to heat rash and coughs, toothache and poison ivy. Nothing serious or contagious, just as Papa had said. We did visit a few people, including a couple of children, who showed early signs of pellagra — the Red Death. But that wasn't catching, I knew, since it resulted from malnutrition. Mother didn't have to worry about that in our family. Papa left jars of brewer's yeast for those who had the red splotches on their skin. Elsewhere he dispensed jars of canned goods, small bags of rice, a piece of candy or two for the children, and always a little bit of hope.

Sometime during our trek through this haphazard city, we came across Sherman Browne. He sat barefoot and cross-legged on the ground, his shoes on top of a piece of cardboard. He was tracing the soles with a lump of coal — no doubt picked up along the railroad tracks that bordered the north edge of Soo City. When he finished he took a pocketknife out of his back pocket and began to cut along the lines, his tongue sticking out one side of his mouth in concentration. That he had so frightened me when he came running into our yard a few days before was unthinkable now. He was just a harmless little man who'd been reduced to stuffing cardboard in his shoes.

When Papa greeted him, he looked up at us with a genuine expression of delight. "Afternoon, Doc!" he said. He lifted a hand for Papa to shake but didn't bother to stand up. "Nice to see you around here again. Anyone sick?"

Papa shook his head. "Nothing serious. Just the usual complaints. I think you've met my daughter Virginia?"

"I believe I had the pleasure up to your house last Monday," the man replied, tipping his cap. "Howdy do, Virginia. Name's Sherman Browne."

"How do you do, Mr. Browne?" I responded.

"Anything I can do for you today, Sherman?" Papa asked.

Sherman chuckled and lifted up his shoes so we could see the soles. Both had holes in them larger than silver dollars. "Not unless you're a cobbler after hours," he quipped.

Papa laughed and rolled back on his heels. "I'm afraid my skills are limited to medicine, though I'd like to help you if I could."

Sherman put the shoes down and said, "That's all right, Doc. The cardboard works pretty good. Only problem is, it doesn't last near as long as leather." The man let go a good-natured chuckle and scratched his head with fingers that were blackened by the coal. As he scratched, his cheerful expression slipped into one of consternation, or perhaps it was puzzlement. His eyes took on a faraway look as he said, "You'd never guess to look at me that I used to be able to spiff myself up real nice — shiny shoes and all — every Saturday night to take my girl out to the picture show, and every Sunday morning to go to church services. Seems like a long time ago now."

Sherman Browne was right about one thing: I never would have imagined such a thing. I never would have seen him as anything other than just another transient resident of Soo City. To suddenly be made aware of his former life — a better life — was something of a jolt. To picture him all spiffed up to meet his girl, shiny shoes and all, was too great a task for my imagination.

"Where's your home, Sherman?" Papa asked.

"Little place called Mayfield, up to the north of here. Had my own lumber business. I was just really getting started when the crash came, and I lost it all. Darn shame, too. I think I could've done real good if things had kept on going as they were. I'd just begun to put some money aside so my girl and I could get married. 'Course, the crash changed all that, too."

"What's your girl's name, Mr. Browne?" I asked.

He looked at me and smiled. "Her name's Mary Lou. Prettiest little thing I ever set eyes on."

"Where is she now?"

"Up in Mayfield with her folks. She promised to wait for me. I hope she does."

Papa said, "She'd be a fool not to, Sherman. That's my best opinion."

Sherman looked up at Papa with gratitude. "Thanks, Doc," he said. "A man can use a word of encouragement now and again."

Papa gave Sherman the last jar of peaches, looked at his watch, and announced it was time to go home. I didn't say as much, but I was glad. The heat had drained me of all strength, the tearing past of two more trains had left my insides all the more rattled, and I had grown more and more thirsty over the last couple of hours. Never had I wanted more desperately to go home. But as we walked back through the camp on our way to the car, we found ourselves momentarily sidetracked by music. Not radio music, but live music. Between a couple of the shacks three men sat huddled together on upturned cinder blocks, one with an accordion, another with a guitar, and the last with a harmonica. Not only were they playing, but the two whose mouths were free were singing, and though they would never make Carnegie Hall, they weren't too bad for a group of ragamuffin minstrels. When they saw Papa, they stopped playing as though on cue, right in the middle of "Brother, Can You Spare a Dime?"

"Afternoon to ya, Doc," the harmonica player called. He was a short, stocky man with curly red hair and a blue bandanna tied around his neck.

The two other musicians called out similar greetings as Papa and I approached them.

"Good afternoon, men," Papa said. "Getting yourselves in tune?"

The accordion player, a dark Italian-looking fellow, said, "We thought we'd croon a little to keep our vocals geared up. You never know when you might be called upon to play at a dance or a wedding. Say, who's that with you?"

Again I was introduced, and again caps were removed and I was greeted politely.

As though the existence of their group required an explanation, the guitarist said to me, "We go around singing for pennies. It's the only way we can scratch out a living these days." He completed the group by being a blonde. He was tall and thin, and his narrow fingers were made for dancing over the neck of a guitar.

"Oh," I replied shyly. "You're very good."

"Well, we used to be better," said the accordionist. "We used to have a banjo player, a darn good one too, but he hopped the line last week. Now we're a trio instead of a quartet."

"Oh, I see."

"He'll probably be back, though, one of these days. He thought he'd find greener grass on the other side of the fence, but he'll find out soon enough the grass ain't growing anywhere."

The guitarist, waving one long arm toward Papa, said, "We've heard you whistling enough to know you enjoy music. Why don't you sit yourself down awhile and join us in a chorus or two?"

Papa smiled and glanced again at his watch. "Wish I could, friends," he said amiably, "but I'm afraid I can't spare the time right now. Duty calls down at the office."

"Sorry 'bout that, Doc," the guitarist quipped, tossing a glance at the other musicians. "We forgot what it's like to be a regular working man."

"Well, you'll remember soon enough, I hope. In the meantime, let me know if you need anything."

"I reckon I could use a million bucks." That was from the harmonica player.

Papa chuckled. "I'm afraid I can't help you there, friend."

The three musicians laughed and picked up the song where they had left off.

> *Once I built a railroad,*
> *made it run,*
> *made it race against time.*
> *Once I built a railroad,*
> *now it's done.*
> *Brother, can you spare a dime?*

The tune and the words, so appropriately haunting in such a place as this, followed us as Papa and I strode out of the camp and climbed back into the sweltering car. I was quiet nearly all the way home, subdued this time not so much by the heat as by what I had seen. Not only had that afternoon been my introduction to human suffering, as Papa predicted, but also to the strength of the human spirit.

As we approached our house, that sprawling old Victorian, that place where I had lived my whole life, it appeared to me as oddly unfamiliar. It was as though I stood in a new location in order to view the house from a different angle, the way an art connoisseur steps methodically around a statue to study it from various viewpoints. I saw the house now from the vantage point of Soo City, and from this new angle, I saw how much my family had. Not just the house, but so many other things as well. Everything we really needed, and a few luxuries besides. And for the first time in my life, instead of simply accepting that this was the way things were, I felt a pang of guilt that I should be living a life of comfort — even if I did have to sleep in a crowded bed — while other people lived crammed together in a neighborhood of shacks that weren't even as nice as my old playhouse.

"Papa," I said quietly as my father nosed our Buick up the alley toward the garage, "we live in a very big house, don't we?"

Papa chuckled briefly and said, "It's gotten considerably smaller, I'd say, since the in-laws joined us." That was the closest he ever came to complaining about the Dubbins moving in with us.

"Mama said she was going to make chicken and dumplings for dinner tonight."

"I'd say I'm ready for it. My stomach's been growling for hours."

"And this morning I helped her and Aunt Sally make a couple of rhubarb pies for dessert."

"Sounds dandy," Papa said. "Maybe I'll start my meal with dessert."

"But, Papa," I wailed, "we have so much while those people down in Soo City don't have anything. It makes me feel guilty. Maybe we ought to be like them, Papa. Maybe it would be better if we were like them. If we had nothing. Then everything would be more fair."

Papa pulled into the garage — to save time coming and going, he always left the garage door open — and parked the car. Then he looked at me and said, "Well now, Ginny, I can appreciate your feelings. Most people might just be glad it was the other fellow hit by hard times, but a sensitive person like you probably can't look on the suffering of another without feeling guilty that you aren't suffering in the same way. But you have to look at it this way. If you and I had nothing, we'd have nothing to give. And if we had nothing to give, our friends down in Soo City might be just a little bit worse off."

I considered for a moment my father's words and found they made sense. "You're right, Papa," I replied. "I never would have thought of it that way myself."

"Eventually you would have," Papa responded as he opened the door of the car to get out. "We live and learn. For the living you've done, I think you've learned a lot, but you have to consider that you really haven't lived very long."

I thought I had lived a very long time. Thirteen years, after all, was nothing to sneeze at. But I had to consider that for Papa, who was approaching the midcentury mark, perhaps thirteen years didn't look like very much.

As we walked through the alley and across the yard, each of us toting a medical bag, I slipped my free hand into Papa's, something I hadn't done since I'd declared myself Virginia instead of Ginny. But I suddenly felt like holding Papa's hand again.

"Our teacher told us last year that President Hoover said no one would go cold or hungry," I said. "But I think those people in Soo City are hungry, Papa."

"I'm afraid so, Ginny." We stopped by the garden where Papa pretended to check on the progress of the tomatoes, though I knew he was actually stalling to give us a little more time together. "I'm afraid Mr. Hoover's been a bit too idealistic about the situation in our country. He's reluctant to admit to how bad things really are."

"Is he a selfish old man, Papa?"

"No, Ginny. I think he genuinely cares about people. But he lifted himself up out of poverty as a young man, and he thinks other people ought to be able to do the same. What he's not figuring into the equation is that these men aren't facing their own little financial crises but rather one huge economic disaster. They just can't pull themselves out of poverty the way Mr. Hoover did."

"Will Soo City still be there when winter comes?"

"No doubt." Papa nodded. "I can't imagine things will be much better by winter. No, those people are likely to be in that camp for some time."

"But, Papa, what will they *do* when winter comes?"

Papa stuck out his lower lip and thought a moment. Then he said, "They'll be plenty cold, I guess."

The thought of it made me at once both angry and sad. "So they'll not only be hungry, but they'll be cold, too, in spite of what the president says," I remarked dolefully.

Papa didn't say anything, but his concern for his newfound friends was evident on his face. The two of us walked hand in hand to the house. Before we reached the door, I resolved that, like Papa, I was going to give something to the folks in Soo City, and before we stepped inside, I knew what that something was going to be.

Chapter Twelve

Thinking ahead to the winter months, I decided to collect blankets for the residents of Soo City. The very next day I put a box in Papa's waiting room where people could leave donations. The sign I tacked up over the box got right to the point: "Don't let your homeless neighbors freeze to death this winter. Please give blankets!" Men and women were in and out of that office all day, dozens of people every week, at least a hundred every month. I figured some of them would be willing to return with blankets they no longer needed for themselves.

I also decided I would have to take direct action — a fact learned from the host of traveling salesmen who were constantly ringing our doorbell. We wouldn't have had nearly so many brushes and gadgets in our house if those relentless vendors didn't come around peddling them. Like those salesmen, I, too, would have to go door to door to try to drum up blankets for the people in the camp.

I had easily gotten Papa's permission to put the box in his waiting room, but now I'd have to get Mother's permission before I could make the rounds through the neighborhood. First, I spent several days telling her about all the people I'd met in the camp — Mrs. Everhart and baby Caroline, Mr. Lucky and his dog T-Bone, Sherman Browne and the three musicians — and I told her how polite and kind and gracious they'd all been to Papa and me. I assured her they were regular people, just like us, and that I hadn't met anyone there that we had to be afraid of. (I didn't mention Mr. Jones the Red but felt I was still being honest because I hadn't actually *met* him.) I described their homes, the sparseness of those little shanties, the lack of furniture and food and running water and bathtubs. But those shanties were neat and orderly, I emphasized, and I saw a woman working awfully hard doing her laundry in an old tin tub. Those people weren't lazy — no sirree. They were cleaning and cooking and washing and fixing things just like we did. And one of them, Mrs. Everhart, tried to give Papa a beautiful silver brooch with an opal in the middle. "She said it was for you, Mama, but Papa wouldn't take it because he said one day she or little Caroline was going to have a brand-new dress and would need a piece of jewelry to go along with it." As an afterthought I added, "I don't know where she got that pin, but I bet it might have been a family heirloom, handed down from

Mother to daughter for generations. I bet it was the one treasure Mrs. Everhart took with her when she had to leave her home, and just think, Mama, she wanted to give it to *you!*"

Mother didn't appear quite as impressed as I had hoped. She listened mostly without comment while my prattling accompanied our cooking and canning and washing of the dishes. When I finally ran out of things to tell her, I decided it was time to get to the point.

"Mama," I ventured timidly, "a couple of people have left blankets in the box already, but I was thinking — I bet I could get a whole lot more blankets if I went around door to door and asked for them. You know, the way those traveling salesmen do."

"Door to door?" Mother asked incredulously, her large hands pausing in the midst of scrubbing a pot.

"Sure. I mean" — my voice faltered but I forged ahead — "from what I saw, not a single person is set for winter. And there's a whole lot of people down there, you know. The more blankets I collect, the more people will have one. I just keep thinking what it's going to be like for them when winter comes, and it's a terrible thing, Mama. You know how it is to be so cold your bones ache and you can hardly bend your fingers because it hurts so much. But you and me, we can always come inside here and get warm, but those people, when they go inside they might just as well still be outside. So I was thinking, we must have plenty of neighbors who might not chance to get sick this summer and see the box in Papa's waiting room, but who'd be willing to give a blanket if I asked them for it direct."

Mother sighed as she handed me the pot to dry. I took it from her and rubbed furiously while waiting for her response. She grabbed another pot off the stove and dropped it into the soapy water in the sink.

"You're just like your father, Virginia," she remarked. "Always trying to do the impossible. You can't keep all those people warm this winter."

It wasn't the response I had hoped for, but I wasn't ready to give up. "I know that, Mama," I said agreeably. "But maybe I can make some difference, even just a little bit."

Mother scrubbed away at the pot, splashing water up to her elbows and across the bib of her apron. I chewed my lower lip as I put the dry pot away in a cupboard beside the stove.

"I don't even like the thought of you going down to that place," she said.

"Yes, ma'am."

"I'm only going along with your father's wishes."

"Yes, ma'am."

"If I had my way, you'd both steer clear of that camp."

"But they're not bad people, Mama. Really they're not."

Mother paused again in her work and stared out the window above the sink. Her expression made me wonder if she saw something frightening out there, but when I looked to where she was gazing, I didn't see anything other than Aunt Sally puttering in the garden.

Quietly, Mother said, "I just have a bad feeling. . . ."

I waited for her to continue, but she didn't. Instead, she handed me the last pot to dry while she started wiping down the counters. She was no doubt picturing me going around like a little beggar girl, pleading for help from the neighbors — a thought so mortifying as to send her to an early grave.

As a last resort, I decided to grab my mother by her Achilles' heel. In spite of her sometimes crusty exterior, Mother's heart had a big soft spot for children, and my last bid would have to shoot like an arrow right into that particular target.

"Mama," I said, "there are children down there, you know. Little boys and girls

— even a baby. Their clothes have been worn so long and washed so many times there's practically nothing left of them. There's no way those clothes are going to keep the children warm this winter. But maybe my going out and getting an extra blanket or two will make the difference between them staying warm or freezing to death. What if it was Simon or Claudia or Molly? What if one of them was down there in the wintertime with nothing to keep them warm? Wouldn't you want someone to come along and give them a blanket?"

This time Mother sighed so heavily I thought she'd deflate like an old balloon. She wiped the table clean, then rinsed the dishcloth and hung it on a clothespin on the back of the pantry door. She took the dishtowel from me, snapped it open a couple of times, and pinched it into a clothespin below the dishcloth. Then she slipped off her wet apron, and it too was relegated to its hook on the door. When I finally gave up hope of her ever answering me, she said, "All right, Virginia, you can collect the blankets."

I tried not to let her see me smile. I knew my sense of satisfaction would only annoy her.

But I must have really planted a colorful image in her mind of Simon, Claudia, and

Molly freezing to death in the camp, because that same afternoon Mother rummaged through the linen closet and presented me with a wool blanket she had purchased only the year before, saying, "Here's the first one for your collection."

In all my life up to that point, I don't think I was ever so happy as when Mother handed me that blanket. Her coveted permission was granted, her own donation given, and I was in business.

I dug out my old red wagon from the garage, washed it, oiled its squeaking wheels, and generally readied it to make the rounds. I wanted Charlotte to go door to door with me, but she was still sick in bed. (Mrs. Besac had come around to the office looking for a cure, and Dr. Hal had sent her to the drugstore to get some expectorant and Vicks vapor rub.) But then I realized that Claudia and Molly would actually be better for tugging at the heartstrings of our neighbors. Those two little girls dressed up in lace and ribbons were irresistible. They happily agreed to go with me — to them it seemed a great adventure — and even Mother said it might be a good experience for them. "At least," Mother added, "it'll get them out of the house for a while, give them something to do." We all three put on our best Sunday dresses, buckled on our black patent leather shoes over white ankle socks, and tied ribbons in our hair. When Simon said we looked like a bunch of sissies, I knew the adults would love us.

Papa certainly did. We called to him for his approval just as we were ready to leave, the three of us lined up on the front porch with our wagon. Mother's blanket was in the wagon to act as a sort of incentive to our prospective contributors: "If someone else can give, then so can I." Papa said we made him proud, then gave us each a kiss and sent us on our way.

Our first visit was to our long-time next-door neighbors, Ed and Clara Mobley. They were an elderly couple but still spry. Every evening we saw them out for what they called their "daily constitutional" — a walk that took them past our house in one direction at seven o'clock and past our house in the other direction at seven-thirty. They spent a good portion of every day working in their garden — Clara Mobley's homemade pickles had taken first place at the county fair three years in a row — and they volunteered a great deal of their time to church functions and numerous civic activities. I had them figured as exactly the type of people who would want to donate a blanket to the poor.

Molly and Claudia stood on either side of me while I rang the doorbell. The wagon was left in full view at the foot of the porch steps. Because their front door was open to catch the breeze, we could see Mrs. Mobley coming down the front hall from the back of the house.

"Land's sake!" she cried. "If it's not the little Eide girls!"

"Good afternoon, Mrs. Mobley," I said politely as she opened the screen door.

"My, but don't you look fine, all dressed up in those pretty dresses. Come in, come in! What's the occasion, girls? Today's not some sort of holiday, is it?"

Before I could say anything, a voice reached us from somewhere inside. "Who is it, Clara?"

"It's the little Eide girls, Ed," Mrs. Mobley called over her shoulder. "All dressed up and looking pretty as a picture."

Mr. Mobley appeared in the kitchen doorway. "Come on in, girls," he invited cheerfully. "We've just squeezed some fresh lemonade. Come on in and join us."

Claudia and Molly eagerly accepted the invitation. I was eager only to get down to business. But I, too, sat down to a glass of lemonade and a plate of oatmeal cookies, afraid to offend our neighbors by declining.

When we were all seated around their large kitchen table, Mr. Mobley asked,

"Now, to what do we owe the honor of your company?"

"Well, Mr. Mobley," I explained, "my sisters and I are on a mission."

"A mission, is it?" The corners of the man's mouth turned back in one of those grown-up "I'll-play-along-with-it" smiles. "And what kind of mission might that be?"

"We're collecting blankets for the poor," I said with great seriousness. I even thrust my chin out a little as though daring him to smile again.

"Blankets!" Mrs. Mobley dabbed at her moist upper lip with a linen napkin. "My goodness, child. How can you possibly think of blankets when the mercury's just about to burst right out the end of the thermometer?"

I cleared my throat. "It's always prudent to plan ahead, Mrs. Mobley," I said, parroting Mother. "It may be hot now, but winter's going to come before we know it. And there are people out there who are going to be plenty cold unless someone's willing to give them a blanket."

Both sets of Mobley eyebrows went up at the same time. I had their attention. While my sisters gobbled down cookies and guzzled lemonade, I tried to appear sophisticated as I told our neighbors about the residents of Soo City. Mr. Mobley nodded while I spoke as though he already knew all about it, but Mrs. Mobley punctuated my speech by occasionally crying out, "Oh my!" and "Oh, dear me!"

When I finished, Mrs. Mobley rose from the table and said, "I'll check the linen closet right now. I'm sure we must have something. . . ." Her voice trailed off as she disappeared down the hall. Mr. Mobley poured Claudia and Molly more lemonade while we waited. He said we were doing a fine thing and promised to make an announcement about it at the Odd Fellows meeting that evening. I told him there was a box in Papa's waiting room where anyone who wanted could drop off donations.

In a moment Mrs. Mobley returned with not one but two blankets. "I'm afraid they're a bit moth-eaten," she apologized, "but they're still warm."

I thanked the Mobleys for the blankets and for the lemonade and cookies and told Mrs. Mobley I was looking forward to seeing her pickles win another blue ribbon at the county fair in the fall.

Our experience was just about the same at every house we visited that afternoon — which wasn't very many because everywhere we went we were invited in for something to eat. At the Hansens' it was butterscotch cookies. At the Watsons', pistachio cake. At the home of Widow Wilma we were actually served little finger sandwiches and chocolate truffles. And at almost every house, there was lemonade. Tall glasses of pulpy lemonade with plenty of sugar and ice. As with the Mobleys, I didn't want to refuse for fear of offending, but our neighbors' hospitality, however well intended, did take up a great deal of time.

Our only bad experience was when we rang the doorbell at the Oberlyns' house. I didn't know Mr. Oberlyn other than by sight, but he had a reputation for being a grouch. It was kind of an initiation into manhood for the neighborhood boys to break his living room window by throwing a baseball through it and running away before getting caught. They chose Mr. Oberlyn's house because he was the one sure to yell the loudest and swear the bluest streak. His wife, though, was known for being a sweet-tempered soul, so when my sisters and I stopped there on our rounds, I was hoping it would be Mrs. Oberlyn who answered the door.

Unfortunately, she must not have been home that afternoon. We were met at the door by the grouch himself, a slovenly bear of a man who hadn't bothered to put on a shirt but wore only a T-shirt over his hairy chest and large protruding belly. The T-shirt wasn't even tucked into his pants but hung out over the belt like the drooping lower lip of an old hound dog. He looked like we had just awakened him from a nap, but the newspaper he carried in one hand suggested he might have been reading. A day's growth of whiskers darkened his face, and a toothpick poked out from one corner of his down-turned mouth. All in all, not exactly the portrait of friendliness.

We weren't invited in for lemonade and cookies. I had to talk through the screen door to explain why we were there. All the while I was speaking, Mr. Oberlyn gnawed on the toothpick, his thick lips and flabby jowls working lazily to torture that little stick of wood. When I finished my speech, he hitched up his pants, rolled the toothpick with his tongue to the other side of his mouth, and slowly announced, "Little lady, the only blanket I'd give those lazy good-for-nothings would be a Hoover blanket." With that, he opened the screen door and tossed out the folded newspaper. It landed with a slap on the porch not far from Molly's feet. When the door slammed shut again, he said, "If you want it, you're welcome to it."

Molly's lower lip began to quiver, but I checked the tears by making a funny face as we walked away from the house — minus the newspaper. Claudia and Molly both laughed at my contortions, and the man's rudeness was quickly forgotten. At least by them. I didn't let on how much it bothered me to hear someone call the Soo City residents a bunch of lazy good-for-nothings now that I was acquainted with some of them.

But we kept going and, as I said, everyone else was gracious and neighborly and willing to help if they could. Not every household had a blanket to spare, but by the end of the afternoon we headed home pulling a wagon with eight blankets in it, and we were rather proud of our accomplishment.

Our satisfaction, though, was somewhat deflated by the effects of too much lemonade. Molly, who was too shy to ask for a bathroom, had an accident on the way home that left her socks wet and her shoes making squishing sounds as she walked. Mother was none too happy about that, but she was further annoyed by the fact that neither my sisters nor I could eat our supper. We were too full and too nauseous. Papa gave us bicarbonate of soda to help settle our stomachs, but we still felt a little green around the gills when we slipped into bed that night. I told myself I was suffering for a good cause, but as I lay there listening to the occasional moan that escaped one or the other of us, I vowed never to drink another glass of lemonade for as long as I lived.

Chapter Thirteen

We wouldn't have thought it possible, but the summer only grew increasingly hotter, and sweat-soaked clothes and handheld fans simply became a way of life. People were often dropping off into a dead faint from heat exhaustion. It happened everywhere — in the breadlines, on the street corners where people waited for trolleys, during services in stifling church sanctuaries. In our own church, more than one red-robed choir member tumbled over in the middle of an anthem and had to be revived with water from the baptismal fount.

At home our best defense was simply to open the windows against the heat and draw the shades against the sun so that the hotter it grew outside, the more our living was done within the shadows of indoors. We had numerous small oscillating fans around the house — one in the kitchen, another in the parlor, and one in each bedroom — though any relief they gave us was more illusion than fact. Sometimes when Mother got desperate, she bought a block of ice from the iceman when he made his rounds in the neighborhood. We weren't one of his regular customers because we had bought a refrigerator (which we continued to refer to as an icebox) right before the stock market crashed. But when the iceman came down our street, Mother had Simon or me run out and hail him down to see if he could spare a block. Usually he could. He'd haul the block into the house on his back, gripped in a huge pair of tongs slung over his shoulder, and at Mother's instruction drop it into a metal tub in front of the fan in the kitchen. The air blowing over the ice did help keep the temperature down in that busiest and hottest of rooms. Uncle Jim chipped little chunks of ice off the block so we could have slivers to suck on.

When there was enough wind to make the effort worthwhile, Mother hung up damp sheets in the front and back doorways to create a crosscurrent of cool air through the house. It was a popular idea in our neighborhood, and sometimes on windy days you could walk down our street and see white sheets flapping in every open doorway like so many flags of surrender. Another trick of Mother's was to put our pillowcases in the icebox in the morning and leave them there all day to chill. Resting our cheeks against the cool linen at night made it easier to fall asleep. We only hoped we would successfully reach our dreams before all the coolness wore off.

Mother frequently asked me to watch Claudia and Molly for a half hour or so while they played in a tub of cool water. I didn't mind. I'd sit beside that huge bear-claw basin and dip my wrists in the water and lift the refreshing coolness to my face and neck. The girls and I sang and played games, and sometimes when they got carried away with the splashing, I'd come away soaked through to the skin. But the damp material felt so refreshing I wouldn't bother to change into a dry dress.

Rufus, Luke, and Simon often sneaked down to the river without permission to spend a few hours cooling off, but I never went with them. Only after they all began to suffer from ear infections brought on by the river water did they turn instead to the streets downtown where some of the older kids had learned how to open the fire hydrants with a pilfered wrench.

A few times Uncle Jim drove us kids out to a lake about five miles north of the city. When Charlotte finally got over being sick, I was able to invite her along. (She claimed to have had a combination of pneumonia, bronchitis, rheumatic fever, and maybe even a touch of the gout all in one, but Papa himself had gone to see her and said it was nothing more than a bad case of the common cold.) The grown-ups would have come along to the lake if we'd had another car. Papa's Buick was a spacious vehicle but not nearly large enough for everyone. With my cousins, my siblings, Charlotte and me, and of course Uncle Jim, the car was already crowded enough. Simon and Luke begged Uncle Jim to let them make the journey standing on the running boards, but Uncle Jim said that if they fell off and broke their necks he'd have to answer to Papa, Mother, Aunt Sally, and Dr. Hal, and that was far too many people to reckon with. The two boys grumbled but finally sat inside the car with the rest of us. We all just about died of heat stroke on the way to the lake, but the cool water revived us when we got there. Sadly, though, we got so hot and sweaty again on the long drive home that we were really no better off for having made the trip.

Papa ordered us every day to drink, drink, drink. I quickly got back my taste for lemonade, and I must have consumed it by the gallon. All day long, everyone in the house sipped at glasses of water, lemonade, iced tea, soda pop, or milk, sometimes until our stomachs were bloated and we were arguing over the use of the facilities. Papa also instructed us to eat salty foods. As I recall, every dish Mother and Aunt Sally prepared that summer was on the salty side, which made us all the more thirsty.

In spite of our best efforts to stay cool, the heat made us all sluggish and irritable. Mother snapped at us more often, Molly's lower lip quivered more frequently, and Uncle Jim — when he wasn't at one of his union meetings — walked about the house stripped to the waist and cursing the weather. More than once Uncle Jim entered the kitchen and compared the room to Hades — though his language was a bit more colorful — and he claimed we all were suffering the torments of perdition well before our time. Mother took offense at his theology, declaring, "I for one have no intention of spending any time at all in that big inferno underground." Aunt Sally simply ordered Uncle Jim to get out of the kitchen and "for heaven's sake, put some clothes on!"

All of us, from Papa on down, were enervated daily by the heat, and by the time evening rolled around, we could do little more than gather around the radio in the parlor, sip our iced drinks, and pray for rain. We barely had the energy left to wave our cardboard fans, the ones that advertised Morton's Funeral Home where Grandfather Eide's service had been held some years before. Most people in our neighborhood cooled themselves with fans advertising one funeral parlor or another, and in a macabre sort of way, those funeral parlor fans seemed rather appropriate. More than one person died that summer of heat-related causes, and the rest of us were more or less convinced we'd be the next to go.

The heat of those middle months of 1932 was so memorable that to this day I cannot separate the name of Franklin Roosevelt from those steamy nights around the radio when I first became aware of the man. As governor of New York, he had accepted the Democratic nomination for president on the second of July, and all that summer we listened to his campaign speeches over the radio and wondered whether he would beat Hoover in the November elections. All the grown-ups in our household decided that Roosevelt had their vote. They only hoped he could do what Hoover had not yet done — pull the country up out of the depths of the Depression. We listened to his campaign promises in silence, the only noise in the parlor other than the radio being that of Aunt Sally's chair squeaking as she rocked and the clinking of ice cubes against glass as we sipped at our drinks.

The heat did have one advantage, though: People were no doubt more willing to part with their heavy bed covers in the midst of a sweltering summer than they might otherwise have been in midwinter. Blankets were left regularly in the box in the waiting room, and soon the box overflowed.

At the end of the first week, I had twenty-two blankets to take to Soo City. True to his word, Mr. Mobley had made an announcement at the Odd Fellows' meeting, and that resulted in the donation of six or seven of the blankets. The rest were from regular patients of Papa and Dr. Hal. Miss Cole, when I told her what I was doing, returned with a hand-stitched quilt the day after my piano lesson (taken, she hinted, directly from her own hope chest), and old Mrs. Greenaway brought a couple of woolen coverings simply in celebration of the fact that she was still alive. I didn't do any more door-to-door solicitation — Molly had been somewhat traumatized by the loss of her lemonade on a public sidewalk, and I wasn't exactly eager to run the risk of another stomachache myself.

All twenty-two blankets, plus the little red wagon, went with Papa and me the next time we returned together to Soo City. The backseat of the Buick was crammed so full Papa couldn't even see out the rear window. Since it was impossible to drag all the blankets around at once, my plan was to take about a half dozen in the wagon at a time, hand those out, and go back to the car for more.

On the way there Papa said, "You've done a fine thing, Ginny. Some of the people in Soo City are going to appreciate your efforts — even more so later, when winter comes. I say some, because not all will appreciate what you're trying to do for them. I want you to understand that these people are in need, but there's not one among them who cares to admit it, obvious as it is. It's a hard thing for a man to be wanting. It makes him feel like he's failed, like he's not a man at all. And it's very hard for some people to accept what they think of as charity. The funny thing is, if the tables were turned and we were the ones in need, there's no doubt these very same people would do everything they could to help us. They wouldn't think for a minute to just stand by and do nothing while we went without. It's only natural for people to want to help other people, but at the same time it's not equally a part of our human nature to be glad to *get* help. You know how our Lord said it's more blessed to give than to receive — well, when it comes right down to it, it's a whole lot easier on a man's pride to give than to receive, and that's just a fact."

Fearing that all my efforts had been in vain, I asked, "Do you think they won't want the blankets, Papa?"

274

"No, they'll want the blankets. Of course they'll want them. What I'm saying is that they don't want to want them. Do you know what I mean, Ginny?"

"I think so, Papa."

"We have to be able to give to people without at the same time taking away their dignity."

"But how do we do that?"

"It isn't easy. Of course, a lot depends on the receiver. Some people are able to receive graciously, while the pride of others — and that's different from dignity, pride is — won't let them accept anything at all. But I guess the thing is, Ginny, we have to somehow let people know we don't think we're any better than they are, and we have to do it without actually saying so. We're not reaching down to them, just reaching out to them from a place that runs parallel to their own. Can you follow what I'm saying, Ginny?"

"I think so, Papa." I remembered that when Papa gave away the Mason jars of food, he had talked as though the people were doing us a favor by taking them off our hands. But I couldn't say I just happened to have twenty-two extra blankets lying around, and would anyone be so kind as to relieve me of the burden? I frowned and asked, "What do you think I should say?"

"My advice would be to give people an option. Don't tell them you have a blanket for them. Ask them whether they'd like to have one. That way they can decline easily if they can't find it in themselves to accept one."

I thought Papa the wisest man in the world, and I took his advice to heart. We parked again under the shade of the maples at the edge of Soo City. We had been driving as usual with the windows down, and after being briefly battered by the in-rush of wind, we stepped out into air that was heavy with humidity and as still as death. At once my skin prickled under the heat. The taste of dust settled against my tongue, and my throat felt parched by the hot air that I reluctantly drew into my lungs. The weather being what it was, it seemed strange to pile the wagon high with blankets. For the first time I wondered whether the people of Soo City might laugh at me as I pulled my little red wagon through their streets. Maybe I should have waited until the cooler days of autumn to pass the blankets around. But I was here now, and there was no turning back. If people wanted to laugh, they would just have to laugh. I pulled the first wagonload of blankets toward Hoover Avenue while Papa held one hand on top of the pile to keep it from tumbling over.

I asked Papa if we could go to the Everharts' first. Someone had left a baby quilt in the waiting room box, and I wanted to give it to Caroline. As we made our way down the dirt avenue — the baked earth cracked from lack of rain — I felt the eyes of curious onlookers upon me. The men who had the previous week sat smoking in the doorways of their shacks were there again, as if in the intervening days they hadn't eaten or slept or so much as moved. They pulled lackadaisically on their cigarettes, blowing out the wispy white smoke to mingle with the stifling air. Some called out a greeting to Papa; others simply stared indifferently. One hollered, "Whatcha got there, Doc?"

"We've got some blankets for those who want them," Papa explained.

"Little hot for that, ain't it, Doc?"

"Won't be in another few months, Elvin."

"Haven't much thought ahead to winter. Can't hardly think past next week."

"Well, like I said, those who want one can have one, and we'll be collecting more. You gentlemen think about it and my daughter and I will be back around later. We're heading to Mrs. Everhart's now to see the baby."

Another man volunteered, "I can tell you she's still alive and kicking. She gave the camp a display of her lung power last night around midnight. Lungs are healthy, Doc, I can tell you that."

"Thanks for the medical opinion, Charlie," Papa quipped. "A few more months and she should be sleeping through the night."

"That's all right, Doc," Charlie said. "We don't mind the noise. Kind of gives a man hope, in a strange kind of way."

When we reached the Everharts' dwelling, once again Mrs. Everhart's timid face brightened into a sort of relieved joy when she discovered it was Papa and me knocking on her door. As before, she graciously invited us into her home. "The baby's asleep," she said quietly as she opened the door wide enough for us to enter.

"We won't disturb her, then," Papa said, also quietly. I followed his lead and stayed outside the shack. He looked at me and said, "Would you like to explain to Mrs. Everhart what you're doing today?"

I swallowed and, remembering what Papa told me in the car, began. "I've been collecting some blankets, since I was thinking ahead to winter. My mother always tells me to plan ahead." Mrs. Everhart smiled and nodded appreciatively at Mother's wisdom. Lifting the quilt from the top of the pile, I continued. "Well, somebody happened to give me this pretty little baby's quilt, and since we don't have any babies in our house anymore, I was wondering whether Caroline might like to have it."

Rather awkwardly I lifted the quilt up for Mrs. Everhart to inspect — and to take, if she wanted. But instead of reaching out for the gift, she laid her narrow hand across her heart. "Why, if it's not the most beautiful little quilt I've ever seen . . ." Without finishing her thought, she tentatively moved her hand to touch the quilt, running her palm along the squares of material stitched together by an anonymous mother or grandmother.

"I hope Caroline will want it," I said. "Otherwise, I don't know what to do with it."

"Oh, of course she'll want it," Mrs. Everhart replied.

I gave the quilt a slight nudge so that it pressed more firmly against the woman's palm, and finally, smiling, she took it from me.

"Thank you, Virginia," she said. "Really, though, you all have done so much already, I —"

Papa cut her off by asking, "How's the baby been? Is her appetite good?"

"She's been just fine, Dr. Eide," Mrs. Everhart replied proudly. "And my, yes, what an appetite. I believe she's put on a pound or two just in the last couple of days."

"Good, good," Papa said. "And the rest of the family?"

"Everyone's as good as can be expected. Tom's in town again looking for work, but the boys are here." She looked over her shoulder into the dark shack. "Boys? Come on and say hello to Dr. Eide and his daughter."

Two young boys, about eight and six, dutifully came to the door and offered their indifferent greetings.

"And how are you boys doing?" Papa asked.

"All right," responded the older of the two, though in a voice so low I could hardly hear him.

"What do you think of that brewer's yeast I left with your mother?"

The older boy wrinkled his nose, and the younger clamped his shut with his forefinger and thumb. Both shook their heads.

"Doesn't taste so good, huh?"

"They don't like it," their mother said, "but they're drinking it."

Papa studied the two cherubic but dirt-smudged faces. He asked the boys to hold out their hands, which they obediently did. Papa inspected the back of each hand, turned them over gently and inspected the palms, then looked up and down each bare arm. I didn't know what he was looking for at the time, and I can only speculate now that he was checking for the red splotches that came with pellagra. He asked Mrs. Everhart some questions about the family's diet, questions she answered almost apologetically. Papa reminded her that one of the missions downtown handed out milk for children, and Mrs. Everhart remarked that Tom had taken the boys there on occasion, but even so, their thirst for milk was never satisfied.

"If they can get even one glass a day, that would help," Papa instructed.

"We'll do our best, Doctor. It's a long hot walk into town. Tom's the only one who has the strength to do it every day."

Papa gave the woman a few more words of medical advice and another bottle of brewer's yeast, then turned to go. I hadn't been able to take my eyes off the pale round faces of the little boys. They weren't much younger than my own brother, Simon, but they seemed so much smaller and rather helpless and pitiful.

Impulsively, I asked, "Would you like a blanket?"

They stared at me with blank faces, then looked up at their mother for an explanation of what had just been said.

"For the winter," I added. "I have some

blankets here. You can have one if you'd like."

The older of the two took a tentative step forward while gazing almost suspiciously at the contents of the wagon. Then he lifted his eyes to me without lifting his head. "Okay," he said, holding out his hands. I placed a blanket in his arms.

Mrs. Everhart laid a hand on the boy's towhead. "What do you say, Tommy?"

"Thank you," the boy responded mechanically.

I smiled awkwardly. Never had I seen a child so lifeless, as though a plug had been pulled and all the humanness had been drained out of his little body. He must have sensed my curiosity and pity because he and his brother hastily disappeared again inside. Mrs. Everhart offered a few more words of thanks, then shut the door.

Papa and I spent about three hours at the camp that afternoon. At least that's what I figured because three trains went by. I discovered early on that most of the people in Soo City, lacking pocket watches, kept track of the hours of the day by the passing of the trains. It must have wreaked havoc on their schedules when the trains were running late; but then again, I don't suppose the people who lived in the camp had to worry much about the time.

Among those whom we saw and spoke

with were a number I hadn't met on my previous visit. One was a young man called Longjohn, so named because he wore all of his clothes all year round, including his long johns, for fear that someone would steal them. He didn't actually have many items of clothing — a pair of pants, a couple of shirts, three pairs of socks, a light jacket, a cap, and of course the long underwear — but how he could wear it all with the heat the way it was, no one could figure out. It made me feel faint just to look at him. When Papa couldn't convince him to remove at least the extra undergarment, he suggested plenty of water to prevent dehydration. Mr. Longjohn said he preferred bootleg if he could get it. Papa told him he couldn't help him there.

When Mr. Longjohn learned that I was handing out blankets, he said he'd like to have one, but could I put it aside and bring it around to him at first frost? Otherwise he'd have to wear the thing draped over his shoulders like a cloak, and he figured even *he* wouldn't survive that kind of bodily suffocation. I assured him I'd put a blanket aside for him and bring it around when he needed it.

Shoes was a large middle-aged man who managed to earn pocket change by shining shoes, just as his nickname implied. He set himself up on the same street corner every morning and waited for business. There wasn't much, but he did have a few regular customers. Also, his corner being adjacent to one of the busier hotels, he got the business of the out-of-town salesmen who needed to look good to impress their customers. All in all, he got by fairly well and was known to bring back food and cigarettes from time to time for his buddies in the camp. Shoes took a blanket, one that Mrs. Mobley gave me that was thin and rather worn. In fact, when Shoes unfolded it, we discovered moths had chewed a couple of rather large holes right in the center. I tried to talk him into accepting a better blanket, but he insisted this was the best of the lot. I later learned that he had ripped the thing to shreds to use as rags for shining shoes — his plan from the beginning. The immediate need to keep his business going outweighed his future need for warmth in the winter. I thought him prudent and simply put aside another blanket, along with Longjohn's, to give to Shoes when winter came. I never did learn Shoes' real name, nor Longjohn's, either, for that matter.

Another man put his blanket to immediate use by hanging it up in the entrance to his shack as a door. "At least until I can find a nice piece of wood to put up in its stead," said Ross Knutsen, otherwise known as Ross the Hoss for his muscular build and boundless energy. He'd spent most of his adult life working in logging camps in the Pacific Northwest but had ended up in Soo City some months back when he'd headed east in one freight train after another. He said he might be hopping the Soo Line again before winter, not because he held out much hope for finding a job, but just because he felt better when he was on the move.

Quite a number of the men, like Ross the Hoss, predicted their own departures from Soo City in the not-too-distant future. "There ain't no work out there to be had," more than one said. "But a man's got to snoop around anyway, just in case the unexpected turns up." Most of those who had set their departure dates for sometime before winter said they had no use for blankets. "But thank you kindly, anyway."

On the other hand, the women of the camp gladly emptied my wagon of its cargo. They all had children, and it was the children they were thinking of as they contemplated the coming snows. I figured as much, because the one characteristic common to nearly all the women was a look of unrelieved hunger on their faces. It was easy to imagine them giving most of whatever food they had to their children, while eating only enough themselves to stay alive.

Alice Hunt was the woman I'd seen the previous week washing her family's clothes. She had four children. Two were in their teens, she said, and two under ten. Only the youngsters were with her that afternoon. The two older ones were in town with Mr. Hunt, looking for odd jobs to work in exchange for food. "Time was, when Stan and I had our farm," she told Papa, "I'd give a plate of food to every hungry man came round to our door looking for a handout. And now my own husband's one of those men going into town looking for work and asking for food. I never thought I'd see the day. But life's funny that way, ain't it, Doc? Something you don't expect happens and changes everything."

"Life's always changing," Papa agreed, "sometimes for the better. Things won't always be the way they are now, Mrs. Hunt."

The woman shook her head sadly. "I hope you're right, Doc," she said. "For my children's sake, I hope you're right."

I happened to have Miss Cole's quilt with me at the time, so I gave it to Mrs. Hunt, figuring a woman would appreciate it more than a man. "My piano teacher sewed it herself," I explained.

Mrs. Hunt examined several of the patches one by one, running her thick forefinger over the dainty stitches. "Now, why on earth would she want to give it away, I wonder? Maybe she'll regret it. Maybe she'll want it back —"

I shook my head. "She said it was just sitting in a cedar chest picking up the smell and probably wouldn't ever be used for what it was made for. She wanted someone else to enjoy it."

Mrs. Hunt lifted the quilt to her round face and sniffed. "It does smell of cedar," she said, smiling. "I used to have a cedar chest myself, filled with all sorts of quilts and blankets. . . ." Her voice trailed off and her eyes took on the distant look of remembering.

"I hope you'll enjoy sleeping under it, then," I remarked.

"Oh, we will, no doubt," she replied. "Tell your piano teacher I appreciate her gift, will you?"

I tried to give Mrs. Hunt two more blankets for her large family, but she would accept only one, saying she wouldn't feel right taking more than her share.

One man whom neither Papa nor I had met before was Steel O'Neil. When we came across him, he was sitting on an upturned cinder block staring at a photograph. We paused beside him, and without a word of introduction, he looked up and offered us the photo. "My wife and daughter," he explained, a mixture of pride and longing in his voice.

Papa accepted the photo and studied it with an air of genuine interest. "Nice-looking family you've got," he replied. He handed me the photo and held out a hand to the man on the block. "I'm William Eide, and this is my daughter, Ginny."

The man shook Papa's hand and said, "Proud to know you. Name's Pete O'Neil, but around here they call me Steel. Steel O'Neil. Got quite a ring to it, don't it?"

"You've been in the steel mills, then?" Papa asked.

The man nodded. "Twenty years in the mills back in Pittsburgh. That's my home. Left school and started working when I was sixteen and never missed a day till I got laid off."

After some quick calculation, I realized that this man was some ten years younger than Papa, though he looked ten years older. His hair was almost completely gray, and the deeply tanned skin of his face was leathery and wrinkled. His only young feature was his startling blue eyes, with which he stared up at us beseechingly, as if he was afraid we would walk away without giving him a moment of companionship.

He continued hurriedly. "Got laid off

about six months ago and started riding the rails. The Soo line brought me here a couple days ago. Word had it this shack was empty" — he nodded toward the shanty behind him — "so I thought I'd move in for a time. The man who had it before me hopped the line going south. I wish him luck."

The man's story made me think of a hermit crab finding an empty shell and moving in.

"Is your family still in Pittsburgh, Mr. O'Neil?" Papa asked.

"Call me Pete," the man offered. "It's just easier."

"All right, Pete."

The man took the picture from me, stared at it another moment, and nodded. "Yeah, had to leave them behind in Pittsburgh. I'm hoping to find work somewhere and send home most of the money."

It was a tune Papa and I had heard before. It was the theme song of the Depression.

"Your daughter's very pretty, Mr. O'Neil," I volunteered, hoping to say something to cheer him up.

The man nodded appreciatively again, then smiled. "Looks a little bit like you, I think."

Though she looked nothing like me at all — she had long dark hair, fine features, and an enviable smile — the comment endeared me to Steel O'Neil for life. It was a rare day that a stranger implied that I was pretty.

"You must miss your family very much, Pete," Papa said.

The man sighed heavily. "Never spent so much as a night away from them till now. I'd jump on a train this minute if I heard even a rumor there was work back in Pittsburgh."

"You traveling alone, Pete?"

"More or less. You meet people, you know, people that are going your way, and you travel with them maybe a day or two, maybe more. But everybody's going in a hundred different directions, looking for the one road that'll lead to a little bit of pocket change and a hot meal."

"Do you expect to be around here long?"

"Can't say." He looked up at Papa and squinted against the sun. "You don't know of any place in town that's hiring, do you?"

"No," Papa said. "Wish I could say otherwise, but I don't know of a single place that's hiring."

"I thought not," the man said without rancor. "But I think I'll make the rounds of the town and see for myself. It can't hurt."

"No," Papa agreed, "it can't hurt."

"Say," the man peered at us through

narrowed eyes as though we had just come into focus. "You're not from around here, are you?" He waved a hand to indicate that he was talking about the shantytown.

"We live about two miles from here. I'm a doctor —" Papa lifted the medical bag slightly to offer proof of his profession. Apparently the man hadn't noticed the bag before. "I like to stop by a couple times a week to see if anyone needs anything."

"Well, now, that's good of you, Doc. It's not everyone who'd volunteer to set foot in this camp. Can't blame them, though. No one'd be here if they didn't have to be."

Since Papa had led the way for my speech, I said, "I've got some blankets I'm trying to get rid of, Mr. O'Neil. It's going to be pretty cold around here when winter comes. Would you like to have one?"

The man smiled at me, and his blue eyes sparkled. "That's right kind of you, but I'm not needing a blanket. This shanty came with one. Man before me must have left it behind." I was disappointed that I couldn't give a blanket to Steel O'Neil in exchange for his compliment, but when the man spoke again, I was mollified by his request for something else. "I'm not ashamed to say it can get plenty lonely at times, being away from the family and all. I'd be proud if you two came around again, just to pass the time of day."

"We'd be pleased to do that, Pete," Papa said, while I nodded in agreement. "And if you ever need anything, you let me know."

The man held out his hand. "I'll do that, Doc. Thanks for stopping by. And thanks for the offer of the blanket — sorry, I'm afraid I've forgot your name already."

"Virginia," I replied.

"Pretty name," said Steel, thereby gaining another point in my book. "My daughter's name is Elizabeth Lee."

"That's pretty, too," I said.

Steel O'Neil shook my hand and said, "Be seeing you, Virginia."

Papa and I said good-bye, but before we could get very far, Steel O'Neil called to Papa, "Say, Doc?"

"Yes, Pete?"

The man hesitated, pursing his lips thoughtfully. Then sheepishly he asked, "If I wrote a letter to my wife and daughter, you reckon it'd be too much to ask you to mail it? I don't have the money for so much as a stamp."

"You write all the letters you want, Pete, and I'll see they're posted."

The man swallowed, nodded, and raised a hand but didn't say another word. Papa and I moved on, with Papa's whistling and the squeaking of the wagon wheels accompanying our stride. People could hear us coming, and some showed up in their doorways to talk with Papa. I was curious to get a glimpse of John Jones the Communist, but we didn't meet anyone by that name. I figured he must have been away at one of his Party gatherings. We didn't run into Dick Mason, either, so Papa couldn't ask him about the Unemployed Council. The three musicians were nowhere to be seen, as well, and when I asked Papa about it, someone who overheard my question called out, "They've gone to Hollywood to be in pictures and get rich." But the comment was followed by snickers and laughter, and I knew it wasn't true.

We made a stop at Mr. Lucky's house, where Papa changed the bandages on the old man's hands, commenting that the burns were healing nicely. "Another week or so and the bandages can come off for good," Papa announced. Mr. Lucky received the blanket I offered him with his usual drawn-out laugh, an expression of unbridled glee if I ever heard one. He said he'd let T-Bone use it as a bed until the cold set in. "Might just rest my head on a corner of it, too," Mr. Lucky said, "if T-Bone don't decide to hog it all for himself."

"Tell him he has to share," I told Mr. Lucky, a comment that elicited another piercing shriek from the man.

"Didn't share his soup bone with me,"

Mr. Lucky sputtered through his laughter. "Don't know why he'd up and decide to share his blanket with me now."

At the mention of a soup bone, T-Bone's ears perked up, but Papa apologized to the canine, saying the butcher's daughter's ringworm had cleared up, and the remainder of his payment had already been made in cash.

After several return trips to the car, all twenty-two blankets were given new homes. Surprisingly, two or three men approached me for one after I'd run out. I assured them I'd be collecting more and would bring them around soon.

That night we tried to escape the heat by sleeping outside on sheets in the backyard. The heat was less intense outdoors, the breezes easier to catch, and we might have spent more nights outside on the ground that summer if it hadn't been for the parties of mosquitoes that delighted in buzzing about our heads while growing drunk on our blood.

Although Mother refused to sleep outdoors herself ("What would the neighbors think if they saw me sprawled out all over the grass in my nightgown?"), she laid out sheets for the rest of us and, as usual, cooled our pillowcases in the icebox. Normally I didn't go to bed as early as my sisters, but since they wouldn't sleep outside without me, I gave in to their pleas and joined them. The three of us lay down on the cushion of soft grass, one of them on either side of me, and before I could finish telling them the story of Rumpelstiltskin, they were both settled deep into sleep. I lay awake a long while looking up at the stars. I realized that I had never before simply lain on the ground and stared up at the night sky, and I marveled that something as awful as the heat had initiated my first prolonged look at something so beautiful. I was certain I knew now why newlyweds sat on hotel balconies gazing up at the moon and stars. Surely nothing could be more romantic than the heavens stretched out endlessly overhead. Did the people in Soo City, I wondered, ever leave their shanties at night to look up at the sky? But perhaps the view wasn't so grand from there, especially when they had no clean linens between themselves and the ground and no cooled pillowcases on which to rest their heads.

I turned on my side toward my little sister Molly. She lay peacefully, her doll clutched in her arms, her sweet child's breath escaping lazily from her open mouth. She looked as though she hadn't a care in the world, and indeed, I don't believe she had. I wanted it always to be that way for her and for Claudia. I planted a kiss on the warm cheek of first one and then the other before closing my own eyes to sleep. I had begun to drift off when Simon came out to join us. Then Rufus and Luke, Aunt Sally and Uncle Jim, and even Dr. Hal. Papa stayed inside with Mother.

The nine of us lay side by side beneath the stars, surrounded by the chirping host of cicadas and katydids. The last thing I heard before the night songs finally lulled me to sleep was Aunt Sally's voice, speaking to no one in particular, or perhaps simply to the sliver of moon overhead. "I wonder where Jimmy Jr. is tonight."

Chapter Fourteen

On Monday, the first of August, at eleven-thirty in the morning, the workers of the Thiel Grain Mill walked off the job and formally declared themselves on strike. Even though Uncle Jim was no longer employed there, he was with the men when the picket line started to march at noon.

I had been so caught up in what was happening in Soo City that I hadn't given much thought to the grain mill. But now I couldn't help thinking about it. Rex Atwater had come around late the previous evening to let the grown-ups know that the negotiations had broken down and the only alternative left was to strike. Mother told me the news first thing in the morning, and the weariness on her face let me know that she'd hardly slept a wink all night. I'm not sure any of the grown-ups did because they all looked pretty tired and solemn. Uncle Jim left the house early without stopping for so much as a cup of coffee. Mother and Aunt Sally made pancakes and bacon for breakfast, and by the time Papa and Uncle Hal joined us, the tension in the house was heavy as a thundercloud. We ate mostly in silence — Dr. Hal didn't even bother to read to us from Walter Lippmann — and when we finished, Papa went off to the office without whistling, a sure sign that he was worried and distracted.

My brother, sisters, and cousins sat down to breakfast after the rest of us, which was the usual routine. We couldn't fit all eleven in our household around the kitchen table at once, so we fell into the habit of eating in shifts. Aunt Sally laid a platter of pancakes on the table and announced evenly, as though she were speaking of an upcoming church picnic, "Rufus, Luke, the strike will be starting today. We must all remember to pray for your father's safety and for the safety of everyone involved. Let's hope the strike is settled quickly."

"Is Pa going to fight the mill owners, Mama?" Luke cried.

"Only in a matter of speaking, Luke," Aunt Sally said calmly. It wasn't going to take much for her cool exterior to crumble, though, and if anyone was capable of causing the first crack it was Luke.

"Will there be guns and shooting and stuff?" Luke pressed.

"Certainly not!" Aunt Sally snapped. Her face blanched as white as the milk she was pouring into Luke's glass.

"Quiet, Luke," Rufus muttered as he

dribbled molasses over his pancakes. "Don't talk about stuff like that in front of Ma."

Aunt Sally, flustered, set the pitcher of milk down on the counter, removed her apron, and told Mother she might as well start in on the laundry. Mother said she'd be down to join her in a minute, but her words were lost to Aunt Sally's pounding footfalls on the basement stairs as she hurried away. I paused in my dishwashing at the kitchen sink long enough to cast Luke an unmistakable glare of contempt. Luke responded by rolling out the whole of his tongue at me, upon which sat the half-chewed remains of his latest bite of pancake. Mother turned from the pantry just in time to catch him and warned that if he didn't straighten up, she'd see to it that he wouldn't be able to sit down for a week.

After that our morning fell into its usual routine, though our movements were hampered by the lingering cloud of tension. I was pinning shirts and dresses and sheets to the clothesline and wishing my Charlies would come to our rescue when the men of the grain mill walked out shortly before noon.

Uncle Jim stayed at the strike headquarters until late into the night, but that evening everyone else in the house, including Papa, gathered around the radio — cold drinks in one hand and funeral parlor fans in the other — to listen to the news reports of the strike. The event had begun smoothly enough with words the only weapons used on either side. Rex Atwater was quoted as saying he hoped employers and employees could come to a peaceful resolution of their differences. Rufus and Luke hoped their father would be quoted over the radio, too, but he wasn't.

We listened to the rest of the national news — none of which was very hopeful as far as the economy was concerned — and when "Happy Days Are Here Again" started to play, Aunt Sally rose and turned off the radio. She straightened her back and took a deep breath before she spoke. "Beginning tomorrow," she said, "I'll be gone most every morning. I promised Jim I'd help out down at the commissary, serving breakfast and lunch to the strikers." She went on to tell us that the strike machine was up and fully functioning — with the union assured of receiving all the supplies and voluntary support they might need — and the grain mill workers were settled in for the long haul. No one, Aunt Sally explained, could anticipate how long the strike might last, maybe only days, maybe weeks. "While I'm gone, Rufus and Luke," she continued, turning to her sons, "I want you both to make yourself useful around here and do whatever Aunt Lillian might ask of you." She looked at her sister, and the two women nodded to each other.

"Yes, Ma," Rufus and Luke grudgingly consented in unison.

"Harold, when will you be putting in your time at the strike hospital?" Papa asked.

Dr. Hal shrugged. "Whenever they need me, I guess. I'm hoping, of course, there won't be much need for a doctor."

It looked as if Dr. Hal was going to get his wish, because the second day of the strike was quiet, and so was the third. About two hundred men at a time marched on the picket line for two-hour intervals, then returned to the strike head-quarters for a meal or a cup of coffee. When one group of picketers went off duty, another took its place. They were under constant police surveillance, with the uniformed men walking their new beat in stiff and measured steps not far from the strikers. Uncle Jim said it was like waiting for fireworks to go off. But during that first week everything was quiet. Emerson Thiel and his two sons, Albert and Arthur, the owners of the mill, didn't even try to keep the mill open by bringing in strikebreakers. It was as though the owners and the strikers were just kind of sniffing each other out, trying each to see what they could expect from the other side.

We saw almost nothing at all of Uncle Jim once the strike started, and Aunt Sally generally didn't arrive home from the commissary until early afternoon. Dr. Hal was on alert for his call, but during that first week no call came, and he went about his usual business of tending to the daily fare of illnesses and ailments that trotted through the office.

On Wednesday afternoon, the third day of the strike, Papa called me into his office and asked if I'd like to make a run out to Soo City with him.

"But it's only Wednesday, Papa," I responded in surprise.

"Well?" he asked.

"We always go to Soo City together on Friday."

Papa laughed. "It hasn't been made into law, has it, that we go there only on Fridays? I had to pull a youngster's tooth a couple days ago, and I want to check on him and make sure there's no infection. Are you too busy to come?"

I pursed my lips, wondering what Mother would think. "Well, I finished practicing the piano, and I've done the lunch dishes."

"Then let's go," Papa said.

Reluctantly, I asked, "Do you think Mama will mind?"

"Don't see why she should," came the reply, "as long as your chores are done. Besides, the folks down at Soo City are beginning to mind when you *don't* come with me. Whenever I show up alone, there's not a soul who doesn't ask me where you are."

"Really, Papa?"

"Just the other day Longjohn said that when I make my rounds by myself it's like seeing Laurel without Hardy or Burns without Allen. 'It just don't seem right,' he said."

"You mean they like me to come with you?"

Papa laughed again and patted my arm. "Now, what do you think?" he asked.

I was enormously pleased to think I had won the affections of the people of Soo City. I rushed from Papa's inner office out to the waiting room to check the contents of the blanket box.

"Never mind about that now," Papa said. He followed me into the empty waiting room with his medical bag in hand. "We'll take the blankets in on Friday as usual."

The boy who'd had his tooth pulled was the younger son of Alice Hunt. As we approached their shanty, we spotted Mrs. Hunt and one of her daughters sitting directly on the ground just outside the door.

I hadn't seen Mrs. Hunt's eldest daughter before. The two of them sat cross-legged in the dirt with white enamel bowls cradled in their laps, the hems of their dresses tucked down around their knees. Mrs. Hunt was wearing the same gray cotton dress she had on the first time I saw her, and the scuffed tips of a pair of leather shoes stuck out from beneath either side of her wide lap. Her daughter, a thin girl with limp blond hair, wore a sleeveless pale blue dress. She was barefoot and it was the tips of her toes that poked out from beneath her slender thighs. A third and larger bowl sat on the ground between them into which they repeatedly dipped a hand and pulled something out. When we got closer I could see they were shelling peas. I could also better view the daughter's face. Her skin was mottled, perhaps by the heat, and her face was almost too thin, but she was pretty in a raw sort of way. Could she have gone to Charlotte's house and taken advantage of the boxes of cosmetics and jewelry, she would no doubt have been quite pretty. A little mascara to perk up the doleful eyes, a little rouge to highlight the cheekbones, a swish of lipstick to color the lips, a few rag curlers to add some waves to the hair. She certainly had potential. But here in Soo City she was colorless and forlorn, like the camp itself, and a person had to be content to imagine her beauty.

"Good afternoon, Mrs. Hunt, Lela," Papa said as we reached them.

"Well, howdy, Doc Eide," Mrs. Hunt replied.

The girl glanced up and offered Papa a brief smile. Then, the smile gone, her eyes came to rest on me while her mother continued.

"You caught us fixing supper. Got a treat for tonight. Stan came home last night with a couple pounds of fresh peas he picked up for running some errands for the grocer down at the IGA. He's there now, hoping to exchange a few hours' work for some meat or maybe a few eggs. That grocer — he's a good man. Some of us around here would be a lot more hungry if it weren't for that man's generosity."

Papa nodded. "Sam Gallagher's a fine fellow. My wife's been a customer of his for years, and he's always treated us fair."

"More than fair, I'd say, when it comes to his dealings with Stan and some of the other men out of work. Stan says he's seen Mr. Gallagher put aside vegetables and bread and all sorts of food soon as it comes into the store, and then when the unemployed come around hoping for scraps, Mr. Gallagher gives them this nice fresh food saying it's leftovers and too old to sell. Stan asked him why he did it, and Mr.

305

Gallagher said he'd spent too many days watching men digging through his trash bins out behind the store, and it near killed him. He said, 'Here I am surrounded by food while my fellowman starves, and it just ain't right.' He probably don't need Stan running errands for him, probably would give him food just for the asking, but I reckon he wants to help a man hold on to his pride if there's any hope at all of holding on to it."

"That's important in times like these, Mrs. Hunt. Though I'm sure your husband is giving an honest day's work for an honest day's pay."

"All I know is whenever Mr. Gallagher finds something for Stan to do down at the store, Stan comes home looking like he used to look when we had a bumper crop. That makes us all feel a little bit better, that's sure. He ain't so easy to live with otherwise. Anyway, I suppose you're wanting to see Ben?"

"I just thought I'd take a peek in his mouth to make sure there's no infection," Papa said.

"He seems fine," Mrs. Hunt offered. "He's not complaining, anyway."

"Is he here? It'll just take a moment."

Mrs. Hunt moved her round head from side to side. "He went down to the river to play with his brother and some of the other

306

youngsters, but I'll have Sissy run and fetch him. Sissy!" The woman called the name over her shoulder, flinging it like a scolding toward the door of the shack.

In a moment the door opened and a small girl appeared. She was a younger version of the daughter who sat shelling peas, except that her hair was clipped to just below her ears and her face was still ripe with baby fat. Otherwise, she had the same pale coloring, the same wistful blue eyes, the same long limbs and narrow naked feet.

"Yes, Mama?" she asked, her hand resting on the door as though she wanted to be able to shut it quickly and retreat inside again.

"Run down to the river and fetch Ben, will you? The doctor's here to see him."

"All right." The child cast timid eyes up at Papa and moved reluctantly out of the shelter of the dim shack.

Before she could slip away to the river, Papa suggested, "Tell you what, Sissy, why don't I come along with you? That way Ben doesn't have to be called away from his friends, and I can see a number of the children at once."

The child lifted her bony shoulders in a shrug, then turned and led the way, her small bare feet kicking up dust as she walked. I took a step to follow, but Mrs.

Hunt said, "Why don't you sit with us awhile, Virginia? We don't get many visitors around here."

I looked to Papa for guidance, unsure of what he would want me to do. "Go ahead, Ginny," he instructed. "I won't be long."

I was reluctant to sit directly on the ground, but then again I could hardly stand about hovering over these two people, giving the impression I was too good to join them. The image of Mother's Monday afternoon hands — raw and chapped and wrinkled after scrubbing a household of laundry — pricked my conscience as I settled clumsily into the dirt, but I tried to hide my discomfort with an awkward smile. I had come to the camp with the anticipation of seeing friends — after all, people had been asking for me, wanted me to come — but suddenly I felt myself among strangers, and I was shy and ill at ease. Knowing I ought to be friendly and say something, I was appalled to find myself unable to roll so much as a single word off my tongue. I looked to Mrs. Hunt to say something, but she simply sat serenely shelling the peas. Apparently she had exhausted her arsenal of words while Papa was there.

The awkward moment of silence was broken when the girl said, "I seen you around here before with your pa."

Her words sounded almost like an accusation, as if I'd trespassed on private property. I wasn't quite sure how to respond.

"Uh-huh." It was all I could manage.

"You're the one brought around the quilt and the blanket."

"Yeah."

"The quilt smells good. Like cedar."

"I'm glad you like it."

"Your name Ginny?"

"Well, Virginia, really."

"Mine's Lela. My ma says I'm named after some stage actress, but she doesn't remember who it was. She saw her once on vaudeville and remembered the name Lela, so that's what she named me. I'd like to be an actress on the stage or maybe in the pictures, wouldn't you?"

I'd never seriously considered this a possibility for myself. If my dramatic talents were as questionable as my musical talents, I didn't stand a chance.

Without waiting for my answer, Lela went on. "Just imagine being up there on the stage, all dressed up in beautiful clothes with jewelry and lipstick and maybe even a little beauty mark right here on your face" — with her index finger she touched a spot just to the right of her lower lip — "and everyone watching and thinking how pretty and talented you are. . . ." Her voice trailed off and she got that distant look in her eyes that comes from seeing something that isn't there. But then, so abruptly that it startled me, she turned to me and asked, "So who're you named after?"

"Well, um, nobody. At least nobody I know of."

"Oh." She stared at me a moment before going back to shelling peas. "How old are you, Virginia?"

"Thirteen."

"I'm fifteen." The brief smile of satisfaction that curved the end of her lips seemed to say she'd somehow outdone me by being born earlier. "I don't suppose you have a boyfriend, do you?"

"No," I confessed. I shifted my position in the dirt. The hard earth pressing against my ankles had left my feet tingling.

"I had a boyfriend once, but not anymore."

"Thank the Lord for small favors," her mother interjected without looking up from the bowl of peas in her lap.

"Mama!" the girl protested. "There was nothing wrong with Walter."

"There wasn't much right about him, either," Mrs. Hunt countered.

While they argued about Walter for a moment, I wondered whether I ought to offer to help them with the peas, but I was too timid to speak up and too shy to stick my hand into the bowl and just start shelling without permission. I looked beyond the women to the river to see if I could catch a glimpse of Papa. I hoped he'd hurry back.

My attention was pulled back to the girl when she said, "I suppose you live in the city?"

I nodded. "Not too far from here."

"You have a garden?" The girl's lower lip curled downward in a small pout, as if she expected to be disappointed by my answer.

"Oh yes," I assured her. "Tomatoes, carrots, cucumbers —"

"We had a whole farm once, didn't we, Ma?"

Mrs. Hunt nodded.

Lela, apparently unaware that she had interrupted me, continued. "We grew corn mostly. But Ma had a great big vegetable garden practically right outside our back door. We grew everything you could think of. Best tomatoes you ever ate. And squash and green peppers and rhubarb and peas. Better peas than these." The girl shoved her open palm toward me so I could inspect the little green orbs nestled in the creases of her hand. They didn't look like bad peas to me. When she figured I'd gotten enough of a look, she tossed the peas into the bowl on her lap and sighed. "I sure wish we could go back home again.

I miss that garden."

"Ha!" Mrs. Hunt cried, looking up from her work for the first time. "It was like pulling teeth to get you to go out and water and weed. You hated that garden and you know it."

"I did not, Mama!"

"Then how come you said you did every time I sent you out to work in it?"

The girl stuck out her lower lip again. A strand of her dusty blond hair fell forward over her face as she worked, and she tucked it back behind her right ear with a quick movement of her slender hand. "I did so love that garden, Mama," she finally said defensively. "I just didn't know it till we didn't have it anymore."

"You always said you hated living on a farm, hated being a farmer's daughter. All you ever talked about was living in the city. Well, here we are, living in a city right on the shirttail of the city, and you're still not satisfied."

"Well, Soo City isn't exactly what I *meant*, Mama."

"At least you're finally off the farm."

"I just said — oh, never mind." Her cheeks grew all the more mottled as she swallowed her annoyance. Finally she pushed her mother's comments aside and changed the subject. "You wanna get married when you grow up?" When she looked at me, her eyes sparkled for the first time.

"Well, yeah, sure," I muttered. Of course I did. Didn't everyone?

The girl lifted her slender face toward the sky as though her dream castle was floating somewhere just overhead. "I wanna get married and have a big house in the city. I wanna have pretty china and silk sheets to sleep on and a maid and a cook and lots of children and —"

"I thought you said you missed the farm."

"Oh, *Ma*ma."

"The problem with you, child, is you don't know what you want."

"Yes, I do!" Lela retorted. "I know what I want. I want to be happy. Nothing wrong with that, is there?"

She directed this last question toward me in such a way as to make me feel that somehow I ought to rise to her defense. I opened my mouth to speak — though had I actually had the chance I don't know what I would have said.

Before I could say anything, Lela herself interrupted me by adding, "I got dreams that are going to come true, Mama, whether you like it or not."

"We all got dreams, Lela," the woman replied wearily, not lifting her eyes from her hands still shelling the peas. "But that don't make much difference in this world."

Just then I saw Papa approaching the shack from the direction of the river, and I scrambled up quickly from the ground. "Well, here's my pa," I said, slapping furiously at the dusty seat of my dress. "I guess I better go."

"Been nice visiting with you, Virginia," Mrs. Hunt said, looking up at me and squinting against the sun. Her hands, poised to pinch open a pea pod at either end, paused while she said good-bye. "Stop by again sometime real soon, will you?"

"Sure," I promised reluctantly. I didn't like it when grown-ups started talking about dreams not coming true. Mothers, I thought, were notorious for doing that. My mother, Charlotte's mother, Mrs. Hunt. They'd been around longer than I had, long enough to know more than I did, but I told myself that if their dreams hadn't come true it was their own fault. They just hadn't tried hard enough. That being so, what right did they have to scare me into thinking the future might be nothing but one big disappointment?

"Ben looks just fine," Papa called loudly as he approached us. In another moment he had reached the Hunts' shanty, smiling. He always enjoyed being the bearer of good news. "No sign of infection."

"Thanks for checking, Doc."

"I hate to tear Virginia away from you,

314

but I need my assistant —"

"Not to worry, Doc," Mrs. Hunt said. "We've been having a nice visit, but I know you have other people to see."

"I'll be back around in a few days."

"We'll still be here, I'm sure. Well, good-bye now, Virginia."

"Good-bye, Mrs. Hunt. Good-bye, Lela."

The girl cupped her brow with one hand against the sun and looked up at me. She appeared about to say something of importance but only said, "See ya, Virginia," and went back to the peas.

I walked away gratefully, trailing after Papa. Lela Hunt and her mother and their lost farm and their thwarted dreams had left me feeling sad. Fortunately, I didn't have too much time to dwell on it. In another moment a young man came running up Hoover Avenue yelling, "Doc, there's a man cut his hand real bad on a rusty tin can trying to get 'er open. Can you come —"

"Lead the way," Papa said. The man turned on his heels and started in the opposite direction, with Papa and me hurrying after. On one of the smaller roads off Hoover Avenue, up toward the tracks, we came upon the wounded fellow sitting next to a small sputtering campfire, his right hand cradled in his left. The handkerchief he had wrapped around his palm was soaked with blood. The assailing can of beans lay on its side near the fire, half its contents spilled out over the ground. "Lucky you were here today, Doc," the young man said as we reached him. "Otherwise I just mighta bled to death. Just about cut my hand clean in two. Might need a couple of stitches."

"Well, let's just take a look." Papa rolled up his sleeves and cupped his hands in front of me. I knew what to do. Since the beginning it had been my job to pour alcohol over Papa's hands between patients. After he patted his palms dry with the towel, he knelt down on the ground beside the young man while I stood by with the medical bag. I watched my father carefully unwrap the bloody handkerchief and make a cursory inspection of the wound. "Virginia," he said, "hand me some cotton and the bottle of rubbing alcohol, will you? And the bottle of antiseptic." I felt like a bona fide nurse as I opened the black bag and picked out what Papa had asked for. When the hand was cleaned and the bleeding partially stanched with a wad of gauze, Papa inspected it again. A thin red line ran the length of the man's calloused palm. "Don't think you'll need those stitches after all," Papa decided. "The wound's not deep — just long. All the blood made it look worse than it is. But I'll wrap it up good and tight to make sure it doesn't get infected. By the way, I don't think I've seen you around here before. I'm Dr. Eide. And you're — ?"

"Name's Judson Breemer," came the reply. "I only been here a couple of days. Been fortunate enough to take up with Scott here." He looked up at the man who'd rushed down Hoover Avenue to get us.

Papa nodded. I figured he and Scott were already acquainted.

"I've been riding the rails the past couple of months. . . ."

While the three men talked and Papa worked, I inspected the contents of the medical bag, fingering the stethoscope, the bottles of Mercurochrome and aspirin and rubbing alcohol, the lint and cotton and gauze, the applicators and tongue depressors, the syringes with anti-tetanus shots, one of which was used on our current patient. I couldn't help feeling a certain awe at these tools of Papa's trade. The contents of this little bag could help people get better, could maybe even save their lives. That seemed a wonderful thing, and I ran my hand over the worn leather bag proudly.

"Thanks, Doc," the wounded man said as my father stood and stretched his legs and rolled down his sleeves.

"It'll ache for a while," Papa warned, "but I'll leave some aspirin with you. And I'll come around again in a few days to see how it's healing."

That afternoon, Papa made a point of hunting down Dick Mason. We found him in the common pose of the men of Soo City, sitting in the doorway of his shack smoking a cigarette. He had forgone the razor for a couple of days, and the gray of his whiskers made him look surprisingly older. Every time we saw him, I thought he appeared a little bit less like a gentleman and a little more like the regular hobos that had long inhabited the jungle.

Papa settled himself on what passed for lawn furniture around there, an upturned cinder block. I leaned up against the shack, the medical bag resting against my knees. Papa took off his glasses in his customary way and with his handkerchief wiped the sweat off his face before cleaning the lenses.

After a few moments of small talk, Papa asked Mr. Mason, "The men have heard about the strike that started at the grain mill, haven't they?"

Mr. Mason nodded and blew smoke out the side of his mouth. "Oh, sure," he said. "Word gets around pretty fast."

"Have you heard any talk about strike-breaking?"

"Around here?" Mr. Mason shook his head emphatically. He threw the butt of his cigarette on the ground and crushed it beneath the heel of his worn shoe. "We may be down on our luck, Dr. Eide, but I don't think there's a man among us who wouldn't rather starve than be a scab. No, there's been no talk of breaking the picket line, I can assure you of that."

Papa put his glasses back on and thought a moment. "Must be tempting, though. Especially for those who have families to feed."

"Maybe," Dick Mason agreed. "But we know what those strikers are trying to do, and we're on their side. I for one couldn't live with myself if I knew I had a part in undermining their efforts."

"I'm glad that's how you men feel, Dick," Papa said. "I've got a brother-in-law on that picket line, and I have to say my sentiments are on the side of the workers, too."

"Can't say I blame you, Doc."

"I'd be on the side of the workers even if my brother-in-law weren't on the line, though, and that's a fact."

Dick Mason acknowledged Papa's words with a nod.

Papa continued. "I suspect the mill owners will try to bring in scabs at some point, but I'd hate it if any of them were men from this camp."

"Like I say, you don't need to worry there, Doc."

"What's the word on Mr. Jones?" Papa asked.

"He keeps himself busy trying to hold meetings with the men and handing out the *Daily Worker* and pamphlets and other Red propaganda."

"Do the men accept the literature?"

"Yeah, but only to use as fuel for their fires when it comes time to warm up a can of beans."

"So he's not having much luck?"

"A few men meet with him regularly. But if you mean, has he succeeded in forming that Unemployed Council yet, then no. Not that I'm aware of, anyway. He's determined, though. All those Commies are. They all work harder than Billy Sunday spreading their Red gospel. They'd put a lot of church workers to shame."

Dick Mason lighted another cigarette, and Papa talked for a while about the general conditions of Soo City until Mr. Mason interrupted him and pointed briefly with the hand that held the cigarette. "That's him now. Talking with Hoss Knutsen."

All three of us looked down the avenue to where two men stood talking in the middle of the dirt road. I recognized Ross the Hoss, so I deduced that the other man was John Jones. My initial reaction was one of disappointment. I don't know what I expected, but it must have been something other than an ordinary-looking man. Surely, I thought, the Communists must look like Communists, but since I didn't know what Communists looked like, I could only conclude from seeing Mr. Jones that they looked like everybody else. He was a thin man of average height and, from what I could tell, average appearance. Nothing at all about him set him apart from the other men of Soo City. I'd have to tap all the resources of my imagination to make him sound exciting when I described him to Charlotte.

"So that's our Mr. Jones, is it?" Papa asked.

"That's him," Dick Mason said simply.

Papa stood. "Well, guess I'll move on." He extended a hand to Mr. Mason, who shook it.

As Mr. Mason withdrew his hand, his face lighted up with sudden remembrance. "Say, Doc," he said, "I nearly forgot — don't know where my mind's at to forget something like this. A couple days ago the Soo line brought in someone from my own hometown — all the way from upstate New York."

"Is that right?" Papa asked.

"Here I was walking down Hoover Avenue when I saw a man I've known all my life coming toward me. It gave me quite a jolt, I can tell you that. You just don't expect to see someone you know. But anyway, there he was, and I said, 'Alan Getts, what in the world are you doing here?' And he said — easy as you please, just like he'd been expecting to see me — 'Same as you, Dick. I'm looking for work.' Well, we had ourselves a nice little reunion. Stayed up all that night talking about old times."

"Did he have word of your family?" Papa asked.

"Yes, and that's what I'm wanting to tell you, Doc. My wife and kids are fine — or as fine as you would expect, considering the times. But my sister, Marion, took Eugene's death pretty hard."

Eugene, Papa later told me, was Dick Mason's brother-in-law, the man who was killed trying to jump the train.

"See, after Eugene died, I sent word home about it. I was able to get some writing paper and a stamp down at the Lower Street Mission. I didn't give all the details, just that he was hurt while trying to jump the line and died shortly after. But I told them all about you, Doc, about how you came out and offered your services for

322

free. Marion told Alan before he left that if he ever ran into me, he was to tell me to tell you that she was grateful for what you did for Gene."

I thought that Papa would be pleased, but the eyes he cast toward the ground were glazed with a certain sorrow.

"Well now," he said, "I just wish I could have done something for Eugene. The truth is, I didn't do a thing other than call the coroner."

"You came when we needed you, Doc," Mr. Mason said. "That's something."

Papa shook his head. I knew how he hated to lose a patient, even if the patient was already lost before he arrived. He said, "Whenever you have the chance to send word back to your family again, tell your sister she has my prayers, will you, Dick?"

"I'll do that for sure," Mr. Mason promised. "Thanks a lot."

"Is your friend Mr. Getts still in the camp?"

"So far, though I suspect in a few days he'll move on farther west. He says his final destination is California. Not that things are any better there, but he thinks it's his best chance."

"Well, in the meantime if he needs anything, you tell him to let me know."

"I sure will, Doc."

Papa said that as long as we were there

he might as well try to seek out any new-comers to the camp, but before we could get very far, we were waylaid by the three musicians who had once again assembled to keep their vocals geared up. They called and waved us over, and for the first time I learned their names. The harmonica player was Joe O'Hanlon, the guitarist was Oscar Salinsky, and the man who pumped the accordion — affectionately known as Bellowing Bob — was Bob Sbarbaro. All three of them were seated on Soo City lawn chairs, and I soon discovered that Bellowing Bob — an enthusiastic player and foot stomper — had a habit of toppling over and ending up in the dirt, his accordion sprawled across his chest as the last notes wheezed out of it.

"Hey, Doc, how about that song?" Joe O'Hanlon asked. "We're still waiting on you to join us."

"Well now, boys, don't mind if I do," Papa replied heartily.

"Pull yourself up a chair," Oscar Salinsky invited, nodding toward an empty cinder block. Papa complied and seated himself among the men. "How about you, little lady?" Oscar asked, turning to me. "Want to join your soprano to the rest of our voices?"

I flushed at the thought of singing with these men. Bellowing Bob must have noticed my apprehension because before I could say anything, he piped up, "Maybe she'd just prefer to listen and enjoy the music."

I nodded gratefully, and swinging Papa's medical bag slightly against my one leg, I kicked timidly at the dust with the toe of my shoe.

Turning back to Papa, Oscar asked, "What's your fancy, Doc?"

"Let's see," Papa muttered as he rubbed his chin thoughtfully. Then he brightened. "Do you know 'Amazing Grace'?"

"Know it?" Bellowing Bob bellowed. "We practically wrote the song!"

"Tell that to John Newton!" Oscar cried, laughing.

Papa slapped his hands together. "All right, friends, let's give it our best."

Joe O'Hanlon gave a toot on the harmonica to set the pitch, and in a moment Oscar was strumming and Bellowing Bob was pumping and Joe was tooting heartily, his cupped fingers flapping over the instrument. The voices of Oscar and Bellowing Bob met in harmony but were bumped around a bit by Papa's off-key crooning. Eventually they found themselves back on track again and weathered Papa's assault with as much grace as possible. Being Mother's daughter I was somewhat embarrassed. Mother would have argued that singing with a bunch of smelly hobos wasn't dignified, especially for a man of Papa's profession. Yet at the same time I marveled at the complete lack of arrogance that allowed my father to mingle with anyone who might care to call him friend. That was the greatest difference between my parents. Mother, as I've said, lived by her own strict standards of propriety, while Papa probably never once stopped to wonder whether he appeared dignified or not. The rule my father lived by was "Just be kind to people in every situation, and you'll always do right by them."

The age-old song, I had to admit, sounded poignant and sweet as it floated through the dusty streets and the stark shanties of the camp. Here and there men and women paused to listen, and a few even gathered nearby so they could hear better. I pushed my initial embarrassment aside and began to hum along quietly as the men made their way through the song not once but twice. In Sunday school we had memorized a verse from Proverbs that came back to me as I listened to the men sing. "The rich and poor meet together: the Lord is the maker of them all." Papa wasn't rich, but to the men of Soo City he must have appeared to be living in the lap of luxury. So in a sense, here they were — rich and poor, the haves and the have-nots

— meeting together and singing about amazing grace. And though happy days weren't here again, a certain joy was, along with a certain hope. Money or no, house or tin hut, everyone had a reason to be glad.

My father and I came away from the camp smiling broadly that day, and Papa whistled all the way home. The sun beat down on the metal roof of the car, and the all-too-familiar dust blew in the open windows until it nearly choked us, but we were happy and neither heat nor dust could diminish our sense of joy.

But what nature couldn't do, Mother accomplished the moment we arrived home. She met us at the back door and, without so much as offering us a greeting, asked anxiously, "William, have you seen any diphtheria down in the camp?"

Papa cast Mother a puzzled look and said, "No, there's no diphtheria there."

"What about scarlet fever?"

Papa and I stepped into the kitchen, and Papa set his medical bag on the table. "No, Lillian, no scarlet fever either."

"Polio, then?"

Mother was close to tears, and Papa placed both hands on her shoulders to comfort her. "No, Lillian, nothing like that. Now, calm down and tell me what this is all about."

Instead of calming down, Mother raised her voice another notch as she replied, "Well, you must have brought something back from that dreadful place. Both the girls are burning up with fever, and I don't know what it is!"

Chapter Fifteen

Papa rushed off to see the girls, sending instructions over his shoulder that Mother and I were to stay put. Mother stood unmoving as she watched him go, her sensible shoes planted on the linoleum floor, her right hand raised to one flushed cheek. Fear, I discovered in that moment, is as contagious as disease — maybe even more so because it takes only a moment, a few words, or a look for it to leap from one person to the next. All the joy I'd felt coming home from Soo City vanished completely as Mother's fear invaded my own blood. I wanted to assure her that everything would be all right, that the girls had come down with some minor ailment, but I knew that no words could lessen the anxiety of her maternal heart. Besides, what good was consolation from the one at fault? I was the one who had gone to the camp against Mother's wishes, after all, and I was guilty of carrying the illness piggyback into our home and cutting short the lives of my little sisters.

I became light-headed at the thought of what I'd done, and I put my arms around Mother's waist in hopes of receiving a hint of her forgiveness. She received me in her arms and held me to her. I was grateful and felt a sob grab at my chest.

"Mama," I questioned softly, "why didn't you have Dr. Hal look at them?"

"He was called out early in the afternoon and hasn't yet come back," she explained. Her voice was strained, and I knew she was trying to keep a bundle of emotions in check.

"Is Simon all right?" I whispered.

"Yes, all the boys are fine."

"Claudia and Molly seemed fine this morning, too. Maybe a little tired, but —"

"They started complaining only a couple of hours ago. That's when I discovered they had fever. I kept thinking your father would be home any minute."

And I knew what else she was thinking: Papa *would* have been home if we hadn't gone running off to Soo City. I could only wonder how she'd feel if she knew he'd spent the last half hour not doctoring but singing. Singing with a group of hobos while his own two babies lay on their deathbed.

Mother took a deep breath, then turned from me and went to work attacking the dirty dishes in the sink. I barely had time to grab the dishtowel to help when we heard Papa on the stairs, merrily whistling "When We All Get to Heaven." Mother and I gaped at each other in disbelief. How dare Papa whistle such a tune when Death was lurking nearby, threatening to snatch away our little girls!

He further mortified us by entering the kitchen and laughing outright in the face of all our concerns. He threw his big arms around Mother and squeezed her in an uncharacteristic display of affection. "Lillian!" he chided. "You scared us all out of ten years of life for nothing. What's the matter with you? Don't you recognize the chicken pox by now? The girls have got the telltale rash all over them." He laughed again and pinched Mother's cheek. She responded by narrowing her eyes in a frown.

"What do you mean, chicken pox?" she asked, flustered.

"You know." Papa tapped at one of his outstretched arms with the tips of his fingers. "Scabs, itching — surely you haven't forgotten that most enjoyable of childhood diseases. Seems like only yesterday Ginny and Simon were scratching away with it."

Chicken pox! Then I wasn't a murderer! The thought of it was enough to make me want to do cartwheels the length of the kitchen floor — and I might have, if Mother hadn't been there.

Mother pushed a strand of hair off her forehead with the back of one soapy hand. The fear reflected in her eyes refused to be assuaged so easily. "Are you sure, Wil-

331

liam?" she asked. "Are you absolutely certain it's only the chicken pox?"

Papa answered with a question of his own. "Didn't the girls attend a birthday party a couple weeks ago?"

"Yes, at the Ryans', but —"

"That's what I thought. Cindy Ryan came down with the pox only a couple days later. It seems the hostess gave a little gift to her guests, or at least to a lucky few. I've diagnosed chicken pox in a couple other kids, but I'd completely forgotten Claudia and Molly were at the party."

Mother turned away from Papa and rested the palms of her hands on the edge of the sink. She sighed deeply.

The jovial look slid off Papa's face and was replaced by one of puzzlement. "What is it, Lil?" he asked, subdued by Mother's reaction. "I should think you'd be relieved."

Without turning Mother said, "I am relieved. It's just that I worry all the time now —"

"You worry far too much," Papa said, laying a consoling hand on her shoulder.

Mother dropped her eyes and shook her head slowly. The wisp of hair fell across her forehead again and swung like a pendulum marking off time. "I feel as though I'm waiting for something dreadful to happen, William. Every morning I wake up thinking 'Maybe today. Maybe today that terrible thing is going to come.' "

Her words sent shivers down my spine. Mother wasn't one to put much stock in feelings or presentiments. She was far too practical for that. But suddenly, in recent weeks, she'd begun forecasting doom, and her predictions put me on edge.

"Come now, Lillian," Papa said soothingly. "There's no use entertaining those kinds of thoughts. We're all a little tense because of the strike and the heat and, heaven knows, just the way things are in general, but we can't allow ourselves to get overwhelmed. Come on, it's best for you to do something constructive. Why don't you go upstairs and give the girls a nice cool bath with baking soda? It might help both you and them to feel a little better."

Mother shut her eyes as though trying to hold back tears, but then she turned and smiled bravely at Papa. "All right, William," she agreed. "A cool bath does sound like a good idea for the girls."

"I'll finish the dishes for you, Mama," I quickly volunteered, wanting to do something to help Mother feel better.

"Thank you, Ginny," she replied quietly. "When I come back down, we'll put a cold dinner on the table. I imagine everyone's getting hungry."

That night I started sleeping on the

couch in Papa's study. I was immune to the chicken pox myself, having already had them, but I thought the girls would be more comfortable if they had more room in the bed. The couch in the study was old and lumpy, but I marveled that I hadn't thought to spend my nights on it earlier. It was cooler in that room simply because it was downstairs and also because there weren't two little girls curled up beside me generating heat. I was able to sleep much better there. More than that, all night I felt surrounded by the presence of Papa, and sometimes in the early morning, an hour or so before sunrise, I'd awaken to see my father at his desk with his back to me, the small desk lamp shining dimly on his open Bible as he engaged in "the first order of the day." I'd watch him for a few bleary-eyed moments, comforted by his discipline and enjoying his company even though no words passed between us. Then I'd succumb to sleep again with a warmth that kindled in my mind sweet and lingering dreams.

Shortly after Papa diagnosed the girls with chicken pox, their skin began to blister. The first blisters turned into scabs while a second set of blisters broke out. Within a few days both girls itched all over, a misery exacerbated by the heat and their own perspiration. Mother gave them cool baking soda baths twice daily and fed them aspirin ground up in applesauce to try to relieve the itching. She also cut their fingernails way back so they wouldn't scratch off the scabs and cause infection or scarring. I spent part of every afternoon diverting their attention from their physical misery by entertaining them with songs and stories. Though relieved that they weren't suffering from anything more serious than the pox, I remembered my own discomfort from the disease some years before, and I felt terribly sorry for Claudia and Molly and helpless to do them any real good.

At the same time, there was constant speculation among the grown-ups as to when Emerson Thiel might start bringing in scabs to break the strike at the grain mill. Whenever anyone mentioned scabs, all I could imagine was the picket line being crossed by gigantic sores resembling the ones that dotted the skin of my little sisters. The girls scratched their scabs and cried, and on the tenth day of the strike, the tenth of August, the picketers were finally faced with scabs and fought. No one was sure which side started it on that sultry afternoon when the first riot broke out. The picketers said the police swung their billy clubs without provocation, but the police said one of their own was attacked by a picketer. Either way, it was a bloody ordeal.

We were alerted to the rioting by Aunt Sally's cry of "They've come! The scabs have come and the men are fighting!" She had just returned from serving lunch at the commissary. The riot presumably started while she rode home, unaware, on the trolley. As had lately become her habit, she turned on the radio as soon as she stepped into the house in case a news bulletin about the strike should interrupt the usual afternoon serials — which, to her dismay, was exactly what happened. "Lillian, Rufus, Luke — come listen! There's rioting down on the picket line!"

In a moment we all came running from every corner of the house to gather in the parlor. Mother and I, having just finished cleaning the kitchen, rushed down the wide hall toward the radio, wiping our hands on our aprons as we flew. The boys nearly knocked us over as they ran into the parlor from the front porch where they'd been playing marbles. We arrived just in time to hear the newscaster announce excitedly, ". . . and now the police are in front of the Thiel Mill attempting to subdue rioting strikers with tear gas bombs and threats of arrest. Fighting broke out less than an hour ago when police attempted to escort a caravan of pickup trucks, carrying replacement workers, through the picket line. . . ." Mother and I resigned ourselves to the couch, knowing that the fighting could go on for a while and not wanting to miss the news. Rufus, Luke, and Simon sat cross-legged on the floor in front of the radio, looking up at the dial with great anticipation on their faces, as if they were listening to "The Lone Ranger."

"Get 'em, Pa!" Luke cried, slamming a clenched fist into an open palm.

"Hush, Luke!" Aunt Sally scolded. "This isn't a game. Your father could get hurt —" She stopped abruptly, picked up a fan from the coffee table, and nervously fanned herself.

Confirming my aunt's words, the newscaster announced, "There are reports of casualties on both sides, and the city's ambulances have been deployed to transport the wounded to an unconfirmed hospital."

Aunt Sally gasped, and her skin took on the color of bleached linen. She leaned forward in the rocking chair and was listening so intently to the radio that she jumped visibly when the telephone rang.

"I'll get it!" Simon yelled, leaping up from the floor and running to the phone in the hall. We heard him pick up the receiver but didn't hear him speak. After a moment he ran back to the doorway between the hall and the parlor and announced, "They've called Doc Bellamy down to the strike hospital. Doc Wilson's there but there's too many men for him to handle. Some's bleeding real bad! Doc Bellamy said he's on his way."

Dr. Hal must have picked up the extension in the office while Simon got on the line just in time to hear the conversation.

Aunt Sally rose from the rocker and put one small hand over her heart. "Dear God," she whispered.

Mother rose to meet her. "Now, Sally, don't start thinking the worst. We don't know whether Jim's been hurt —"

She stopped when she heard the door to the waiting room open across the hall. We heard Papa say, "Take the car, Harold. Here are the keys," and Dr. Hal replying, "Thanks, Will. I'll be back soon as I can."

Aunt Sally stepped out to the hall to meet him, and for a moment their eyes locked. "Harold —" my aunt whispered.

Dr. Hal was carrying his own new medical bag of shiny black leather. In spite of his pained expression, he looked very handsome at the moment, like a hero in a war movie. Calmly he said, "Try not to worry, Sally. Everything's going to be fine. I'll bring Jim home with me when I come." And then he quickly strode the length of the hall and disappeared into the kitchen. When we heard the screen door slam shut, Mother went to Aunt Sally and put an arm around her shoulder.

"Come on, then, there's nothing we can do right now," she said gently. "Maybe it'd be best to turn off the radio and stay busy."

"No, please, Lil," Aunt Sally fairly pleaded, "I've got to know what's going on."

Mother consented and we all resumed our places in the parlor and waited for further news bulletins. Aunt Sally let off anxious steam by alternately rocking furiously and fanning herself vigorously. Sometimes she tried doing both at once, but she'd end up getting confused and all the more flustered and frustrated, like a person trying to pat her head and rub her stomach at the same time. The boys fidgeted on the floor, trying to be patient between bulletins. Papa stopped by between patients to get updates, standing in the doorway with his hands in the pockets of his starched white jacket and rocking on his heels as he listened to whoever happened to speak up. Mother excused herself now and again to check on the girls or to finish some forgotten chore. I had removed my apron but kept it in my lap. It became wrinkled over the next couple of hours as I rolled it between my sweaty palms. I kept thinking of Uncle Jim standing in the doorway that first night Rex Atwater visited our home, looking out into the falling dusk as though the darkness were an omen of things to come. And I thought too of Mother's unusual presentiments, her feeling that something bad was going to happen. The clock on the piano ticked away the long drawn-out moments of that afternoon.

Just before three o'clock the music of the regular programming was interrupted once again by another announcement. "We have an unconfirmed report that one of the wounded picketers has succumbed to his injuries and died before he could be reached by ambulance. . . ." Aunt Sally stopped fanning and gave out a cry, her trembling fingers resting lightly against her pale lips. At the news, the backs of all three boys went straight as ramrods, and my own stomach fluttered as though invaded by a flock of birds. Mother was with the girls when the bulletin came on, but Rufus, wide-eyed with fear himself, tried to step in as comforter. "It's not Pa," he assured his mother. "I know it's not Pa. He'd never go down so easy."

Aunt Sally nodded but continued to stare at the dial of the radio, mesmerized. The lower rims of her eyes sparkled with unshed tears.

"Don't cry, Ma," Rufus said quietly. I had rarely seen my cousin try to be consoling, and the gentleness of his words soothed my own fears somewhat, if not those of my aunt. "Pa's going to be fine. You'll see. I've just got a gut feeling about it."

The music resumed. Aunt Sally, her lips kneading themselves into a taut line, went back to fanning herself. Mother returned, and when she sat down next to me, I whispered that one man was reported dead.

She shut her eyes a moment, then asked me quietly, "Did they give a name?" I shook my head. Mother looked at Aunt Sally, but my aunt seemed hardly aware of what was going on around her.

At 3:30 another bulletin informed us that the rioting had subsided and the picketers had retreated to the refuge of the strike headquarters. Their plan, we later learned, was to resume picketing the next morning. Meanwhile, in the midst of all the mayhem, a number of the scabs had made it into the mill. Temporary housing had already been set up inside so they could stay in safety beyond the gates and would not have to brave the picket line every day.

Even after the news that the rioting had stopped, Aunt Sally refused to leave the radio. "If only I knew *something*," she said, wringing her hands and pacing the floor in front of the Philco. When Mother suggested she put her mind on other things — like fixing supper — Aunt Sally retorted that she couldn't chance missing any further reports.

"Can you call strike headquarters and ask somebody there about Jim?" Mother asked.

My aunt shook her head. "There aren't any telephone lines running into the warehouse. They have to make their calls from a pay phone at a drugstore several blocks away. Maybe I should catch a trolley and go there myself —"

"You'll do no such thing," Mother interrupted. "You'll only be in the way. Harold said he'd bring Jim home tonight."

And he did, though the clock had continued its agonizing journey and dusk had already begun to spread lengthy shadows across the ground before Luke, waiting and watching at the back door, cried out that the Buick had just pulled into the garage. I stepped to the kitchen window to look on while Luke and Rufus ran out to the yard to greet their father. Uncle Jim flicked the butt of a still burning cigarette into the garden. Then yelling a greeting, he draped an arm around the neck of each boy and together the three of them strode the remaining length of the yard to the house. Aunt Sally stood in the open doorway and finally allowed her tears to flow freely. I don't know whether the tears were triggered by relief at the sight of Uncle Jim or by fright at the bandage that circled his head. Perhaps it was both.

"Jim!" Aunt Sally cried, throwing her arms around him. She let out a wrenching sob and clung to Uncle Jim there in the doorway, the two of them blocking the boys and Dr. Hal from stepping inside.

Uncle Jim shushed his wife and patted her back, saying kindly, "I'm all right, Sally. I'm all right. Don't fret yourself so." Aunt Sally sniffed and stepped back, dabbing at her moist blotchy cheeks with a hankie and forcing her pale lips into a brave but fleeting smile. She took one deep breath to reinforce herself, then grasped Uncle Jim's hand and led him to a chair at the kitchen table. Uncle Jim sat down with Aunt Sally on one side of him, Luke on the other. Rufus sat across the table from his father. The rest of us stood. When the chairs stopped scraping across the kitchen floor and everyone was settled, Aunt Sally tentatively lifted her fingers to the bandage across Uncle Jim's brow. "How did it happen?" she asked.

Dr. Hal answered. "He took a clip from a billy club. Bad enough to need stitches but not so bad that he won't be good as new inside a week."

"Now, don't fuss," Uncle Jim said, taking Aunt Sally's trembling hand in his own. "Harold sewed me up just fine.

343

There's other men hurt worse."

Dr. Hal nodded in agreement. "A few bad bumps and broken bones. Thank God we weren't trying to deal with bullet wounds. Shots were fired, but evidently the police were using blanks. Just trying to scare the strikers, that's all. Still, it was a lopsided affair — the police with their billy clubs and tear gas against a group of men whose only weapons were their fists."

Uncle Jim chuckled. "Some of the strikers were swinging their signs, though. The two-by-fours those signs were nailed to turned out to be pretty good weapons."

Aunt Sally remarked breathlessly, "They said on the radio one man had been killed. I thought —"

"I'm sorry for what you've been through this afternoon, Sally," Uncle Jim interrupted. "I should have thought to try to reach you, but the strike hospital was in such a commotion I just couldn't get away to the phone. After Harold fixed me up, I tried to help out with the other men the best I could. I just wasn't thinking about what you might be hearing on the radio. I'm really sorry."

"Who was it — the one killed?"

"A man named Jeremiah Carlson. One of the finest grain mixers at the mill. Never missed a day of work in more than twenty years — not that I remember, anyway."

"Did he have a family?"

Uncle Jim nodded. "A wife and five children."

"Five children! Oh, that poor woman."

Mother, who had been standing by silently with her hands clasped in front of her, asked, "How could this have happened, Jim? How could it have gotten so out of hand that a man would be killed?"

"A couple of the sheriff's deputies got carried away with their duties," Uncle Jim explained, his shoulders sagging wearily as he spoke. "They just started beating the man and didn't know when to quit. Jeremiah was a big man, but I never so much as saw him swat a fly. I don't know what he did to provoke the deputies, but I reckon it wasn't anything other than the fact that he was there."

Mother turned pale and laid a hand across her chest. Aunt Sally wiped away a couple more tears that had silently slipped down her cheeks.

Rufus, clenching and unclenching his fists on the tabletop, said, "They ought to go to jail, Pa — those deputies that killed that man. They ought to rot in jail."

Uncle Jim cast a sorrowful look across the table at his son. "And just who's going to arrest the sheriff's deputies?" he asked. "Even if they were arrested, there's not a jury in the land that'd convict them of murder."

"But it *was* murder, Pa."

"I know it was, Rufus, but the law don't see it that way."

A hush fell over the kitchen, the quiet that accompanies disbelief. We were all stunned, not quite able to comprehend that something so awful had interrupted the peaceful unfolding of our lives.

The silence was broken after a moment when Luke asked loudly, "Does your head hurt, Pa?"

Uncle Jim, obviously amused by the question, started to chuckle, but his laughter was cut short by one of his usual fits of coughing. When his chest stopped heaving long enough for him to speak, he said, "Sure, it stings a little." Then he added with a sheepish grin, "Especially when I cough."

"I'll get you something for the pain," Dr. Hal said. He turned to the rest of us. "Jim wouldn't take anything down at the strike hospital, though I warned him the pain would only get worse before it got better."

Before Dr. Hal left, Mother asked, "How many men were hurt, Harold?"

Dr. Hal chewed his lip and thought a moment. "Out of two hundred on the picket line, I'd say maybe fifty or so had injuries that needed medical attention. You can imagine that Dr. Wilson and the nurses and I were kept pretty busy. I have to say that Rex Atwater and his men set up a fine little hospital down there in the warehouse. Can't match Mercy, of course, but it's not bad for a makeshift facility."

"How many arrested? Do you know?"

"I can't answer that for sure. I suspect the numbers will be in tomorrow's newspapers, though. Mr. Thiel will want his victory announced, of course, and I'm sure the editors of the morning edition will be all too happy to oblige. Well, if you'll excuse me, I think I'll go rummage through the medicine cabinet — see what I can find."

Dr. Hal headed for the office, and before his footsteps had ceased to echo in the hallway, Luke tugged on his father's sleeve and asked eagerly for more details of the riot.

"Not now, Luke," Aunt Sally replied firmly. "Your father needs to rest. Soon as you take something for the pain, Jim, I want you to go on upstairs and lie down."

"Can't argue with you there, I guess." Uncle Jim lifted a hand to his forehead and winced.

"And I don't want you going back to the line tomorrow —"

"Now, Sally, you know I've got to go back —"

"Please, Jim, not after —"

"My place is with the men —"

347

Papa rushed into the kitchen then, interrupting the debate before it turned into an argument. "Harold says you've been hurt, Jim."

"Just a crack on the head, Will. Nothing serious. You know my old skull's too thick for them to cause much damage," he remarked lightly. "Harold got me fixed up all right."

"I'm sure he did a fine job," Papa said as he carefully lifted the gauze to inspect the stitches. The wound looked like a small length of railroad track cutting across the creases of Uncle Jim's forehead. "Well, good chance you'll be left with a little souvenir of the strike," Papa predicted. "Otherwise, it should heal nicely. You'll have a pretty bad headache, if you don't already." Uncle Jim nodded, and Papa continued. "Harold's bringing you something for the pain, then I suggest you get some rest."

"I was just sending him up to bed," Aunt Sally said. "Come on, we can intercept Harold on the way, and you can take your medicine upstairs."

She helped her husband up, though he accepted her help reluctantly. "I'm fine, Sally. No need to fuss," he repeated. They had reached the kitchen doorway when Uncle Jim remembered his sons. They were both staring after him expectantly.

"Well, come on, then," he said. "Let me get myself stretched out on the bed, then I'll tell you some of what happened."

The boys jumped up as if a spring had ejected them from the chairs and followed after their parents. Simon quietly but just as quickly tagged along. Ever the doctor's son, he was undoubtedly less interested in the riot itself than in the wounded men left in its wake.

Papa, Mother, and I were left alone. We looked briefly at one another, then turned our eyes away, reluctant to speak. Mother untied her apron and hung it on the hook on the inside of the pantry door. She smoothed the wrinkles out of her dress, sighed, and asked rhetorically of Papa, "Where's it going to end, William?" Her expression said that the doom she had predicted would surely come.

The one small fan in the corner turned its head from side to side, giving off mechanical sighs of contentment as it blew warm air across the room. In the glass-covered cabinets along the walls, the plates and cups nestled placidly together like sleeping children. The refrigerator hummed complacently, as though sated by the food in its belly. The whole room was quiet and at peace. And for an odd moment, I envied those objects their untroubled existence and wished that I, too,

could be a piece of wood or a stone or a
bit of metal that could simply be, without
at the same time having to feel anxious or
afraid — even if it meant feeling nothing at
all.

Chapter Sixteen

Sometimes that summer it seemed as though the whole world was reeling from one big terrible hangover after the party of the Roaring Twenties. We had danced in a frenzy through the long night of prosperity, but when morning came in the form of the stock market crash, our muddled roaring was silenced. We found ourselves sick, angry, frustrated, and maybe a little bit sorry for our overindulgence, and we were now staggering about somewhat recklessly, trying to restore order to the ruined party room.

In early August, the farmers in Iowa — having banded themselves together in a group known as the Farmers' Holiday Association — went on strike in an effort to force up farm prices. At that time, hogs were going for three cents a pound; milk, two cents a quart. By August 14, some fifteen hundred farmers, joined by the Milk Producers' Association, were guarding all the roads into Sioux City, virtually halting all milk and livestock deliveries to the market there. The picketers blockaded the roads with spiked telegraph poles and logs and turned back hundreds of trucks. Gallons of milk were poured into roadway ditches, though thankfully some milk was confiscated and distributed free on the streets of Sioux City.

From there the strike spread to Omaha, Council Bluffs, and Des Moines, where strikers used the same tactic of blockading the streets. The governor of Iowa ordered the roads cleared, and a number of deputies were sworn in to reinforce the sheriffs' troops. A few trucks, escorted by armed deputies, were able to make it in to market.

In all areas of the strike, the guns of the lawmen were pointed at the picketing farmers, but no shots were fired. Plenty of men were arrested, though, and hauled off to jail.

From Iowa the strike eventually fanned out across America's farm belt. Farmers in Minnesota, Missouri, Illinois, Montana, Wisconsin, Oklahoma, and Nebraska all organized to strike for cost of production, and all — to some extent or another — withheld their goods from market. Everywhere guns were raised. Everywhere men were arrested. That particular upheaval stretched all the way into autumn before it was eventually settled.

Meanwhile, the rumor mill was busy spitting out endless speculation that the picketers were not actually themselves farmers but were most likely groups of unemployed men led by Communist agitators. Many people genuinely believed that the strikes and riots plaguing our country were about to usher in a Communist revolution. Others played on these fears, using the Communist threat as a convenient excuse to dismiss even the most reasonable demands of the American worker. I've no doubt that the nation's mass hysteria added to the problems that our own local strikers faced down at the grain mill.

As the strike at the grain mill wore on, reports, editorials, cartoons — even advertisements — in the local papers warned of the attempt of a Red takeover there in our own city. One editorial writer called the strike a Communist plot to assume control of the Thiel Mill and called on all men of patriotic persuasion to come forward and be deputized, to join the heroic throng fighting to preserve democracy, freedom, and the American way. Uncle Jim's doleful response to the editorial: "You'd never know that all we're asking for is better working conditions and ten cents more an hour."

Rex Atwater, as he himself predicted, was accused of being a ruthless perpetrator of Communist doctrine, and writers of letters to the editor called on him to go home to Moscow where he belonged. Half- and full-page ads painted a picture of national rebellion and encouraged people not to be hoodwinked by the wily Communists into making contributions to the strike machine. One cartoon, run on the front page of the morning edition, showed a flag with hammer and sickle flying atop the grain mill, with the caption "Thiel Mill, 1933."

Emerson Thiel, knowing a strategic advantage when he saw one, jumped on the anti-Communist bandwagon whole hog. "The strikers," he was quoted as saying, "are trying to make it appear that their central concern is the wage issue. But our workers have always been paid fair wages, comparable to or better than the wages of grain mill workers all over the Midwest. They have no grounds for complaint. No, the real issue here is Communism. The organizers of this strike are Communists, and they've got our workers in their dangerous clutches. They've brainwashed our men into believing that Communism is a better way than democracy. They are hoping that this strike is the beginning of a revolution that will overthrow all existing government!"

Uncle Jim's response to the ranting of his ex-employer: "That yellow-bellied snake knows full well it's not the Reds behind the strike. He's just using that as an excuse not to recognize the union and to turn everybody else in this city against us."

Thiel might not have convinced everyone that our city was in danger of a Communist revolution, but one person he did persuade was the mayor. Mayor Dowling, a weak-chinned, spineless little fellow (it was later uncovered that he gained his office through bribery), sided with the employers announcing, "We won't have our city be known as the birthplace of the American Soviet Republic." Whether he really believed the strike was a Communist-led plot was anybody's guess, but wanting to remain in favor with a wealthy and influential man like Emerson Thiel, he called on the governor to implement martial law.

Fortunately, Governor Borgmann, who had been voted into office on the Farmer-Labor ticket (amazingly, a radical party with identifiable ties to socialism), was reluctant to step in on the side of the employers. Recognizing that the mill workers had some legitimate grievances, he hesitated to implement martial law, asking instead for the mayor to set up a board of mediation. And wanting to remain on good terms with the governor, the mayor set up the board. It was comprised of three supposedly disinterested citizens who would act as a go-between for the employers and employees as they worked out their differences.

The board of mediation seemed a good idea at first, but no matter what compromises the board came up with, they were rejected out of hand by both sides.

And so the workers went on picketing while scabs — many of whom were recruited from out of state, some scarcely old enough to have graduated from high school — continued to be escorted though the picket line. Because of the ensuing riots, only a small percentage of the scabs actually got beyond the front gate. But about three weeks into the strike, the newspapers reported that the mill was running at nearly half capacity.

"How many scabs you think they've got in there?" Dr. Hal asked Uncle Jim one morning at breakfast.

Uncle Jim shrugged as he replied, "Can't be more than a hundred, maybe less. They only try bringing them across the line a couple times a week. So say they've crossed a half-dozen times, and each time a dozen scabs got in — that'd be what, about sixty, seventy men?"

Dr. Hal tapped a cold piece of toast against his plate while he thought. "How could the mill be running at half capacity with fewer than a hundred men?" he asked. "Is Thiel bringing men in at night?"

Uncle Jim shook his head. "Nights are quiet," he said. "We've got men outside the gate around the clock just to make sure the scabs aren't brought in under cover of dark. So far, nothing at all has happened at night."

"Then either Thiel's got more men in there than we think or the mill's not running at half capacity."

"It might be he wants us to think he's doing better than he is. Thiel's got the newspaper on his side. They'll print whatever he asks them to."

"Maybe. But my guess is he's bringing in men we don't know about."

Uncle Jim shrugged again and finished his coffee. "Don't know how he could," he replied as he settled the cup in the saucer. "No, Thiel's just trying to pull one over on us. He may be able to throw a lot of power around, but I'm still of the opinion we've got the upper hand. That man can't turn his grain into money without us, and right now he hasn't got us. He'll be willing to see reason sooner or later."

Down on the picket line, men continued to fight and to be wounded, but after they were pieced back together, they returned to the line. More men were arrested, but when the union's lawyer got them out on bail, they went back to the line. Reinforcements were added to both sides. Businessmen, lawyers, store owners, clerks — all felt the patriotism surging through their blood and stepped forward to allow Sheriff Dysinger to deputize them into the fight against the Commies. While the ranks of the deputies grew, those of the picketers were increased somewhat by a handful of unemployed volunteers — some from Soo City — who joined the picket line. They joined not only because they had nothing else to do, but because they believed in what the mill workers were fighting for. Longjohn was one who joined the line, skivvies and all. Ross the Hoss was another. Judson Breemer, whose hand Papa had tended to, and his friend Scott Larson also marched. Sherman Browne, I heard, took up a sign once or twice. Some of the other men from the camp whom I didn't know also put in hours on the picket line. Though they were in the midst of a battle that probably would have no payoff for them personally, I think marching on the line gave them a sense of purpose.

Uncle Jim returned to the picket line in spite of his injury and in spite of the danger. The attitude of Thiel and his men only fueled Uncle Jim's anger and made him all the more determined to see the union recognized by the mill. Aunt Sally continued going down to the commissary to serve breakfast and lunch, and every afternoon she came home and turned on the radio and took up her vigil in the rocking chair to listen for news bulletins. And the bulletins invariably came, interrupting the music shows and the daytime serials, commanding more attention in our house than the Olympic Games in Los Angeles, a man called Hitler in Germany, and Hoover's inevitable admission that Prohibition wasn't working.

Every morning I wondered whether Uncle Jim would come home again, and every night Aunt Sally cried with relief when he did. We'd all go to bed thankful that he'd made it through another day. And then the whole anxious and agonizing cycle began over again the next morning when my aunt and uncle left the house together to catch the early trolley down to strike headquarters.

Chapter Seventeen

When Charlotte called one afternoon and asked me to come over right away, I couldn't get out of the house fast enough. She said she had something important to discuss with me, and even if that something was how to win over the affections of my cousin Rufus, it had to be better than sitting by the radio waiting for news about the strike. August was winding down to the homestretch, and the whole of it — the last month of my summer vacation — had been mired in the anxiety of what was happening at the grain mill. Because it was a citywide issue, I couldn't get away from it anywhere. At church, talk of the strike replaced the usual pleasantries that floated about the fellowship hall during coffee hour, and Rev. Winchell preached on the blessedness of peacemakers and the evils of greed for three weeks running. At the market, women huddled amid the rutabagas and brussels sprouts to rue the day their husbands had voted to walk out of the mill, and Mr. Thiel himself was properly censured for having created the conditions that started the strike in the first place. At the butcher shop that Mother frequented, Mr. Ramsey was quick to swing his cleaver viciously into the cutting board at the mention of Mr. Thiel's name. Our butcher was sympathetic to the mill workers and made generous donations of meat to the strike commissary. At the bakery, Mr. Bixby, who donated day-old bread to the commissary every morning, repeatedly cursed Mr. Thiel, saying, "If anyone's a Red devil around here, it's Thiel himself! He's the one who wants to keep all the mill workers in chains." Even at the movie theater waiting for the show to start, kids were placing bogus bets on whether or not the governor would call in the National Guard. It was a far cry from the usual talk of who was sweet on whom and how many frogs and snakes had been caught down by the river the previous afternoon.

Our Philco radio ran nonstop from the moment Aunt Sally got home in the mid-afternoon until Uncle Jim returned late at night. There was a time I would have loved nothing better than to lounge around the parlor floor listening to that marvel of modern communication, but during the summer of 1932 I learned to detest the click of the dial that brought that monster to life, the buzzing static that bristled the hair on my neck as the beast warmed up, the tinny music that always seemed so at odds with what we were waiting to hear, and most of all, the deep and disturbing voice of the newscaster who brought the events of the strike all the way across town and into our otherwise quiet home. Whenever a fight broke out on the line, he couldn't simply lay out the facts in a voice of monotonous serenity. He had to embellish his announcements with numerous inflections and exclamation points, as though his dramatic flair were necessary to drive home to our hearts the horror of the situation: "At two-twenty-five on this hot afternoon, tempers flared and fists flew as yet *another* bloody conflict broke out on the picket line outside the Thiel Grain Mill! The clash between police and strikers ignited as lawmen attempted to escort truckloads of workers across the picket line. The ensuing battle led to *countless* injuries and one unconfirmed death. We'll have those exact numbers for you as soon as they're available. In the meantime, *don't touch that dial.* . . ."

The only good news I heard out of that torturous machine all month was that on the sixteenth a second son was born to Charles and Anne Lindbergh. It didn't make up for the kidnapping and murder of the first one, but I was grateful to think that the new baby must surely be a source of joy in the lately troubled home of my hero.

On the afternoon that Charlotte called

sounding more animated than usual, I had just finished practicing my piano lesson when Aunt Sally returned from the commissary and turned on the radio. I thought I might volunteer to pull weeds in the garden just to get away from it for a time, but mercifully the phone rang before I could mention my plan to Mother. Also mercifully, Mother said I could run on over to Charlotte's until suppertime. The strike had upset even the regimented routine of our household as Mother tried to deal with the increase in the size of our family, the strain on our finances, and the frayed nerves of her sister. Though my absence meant a couple of regular chores would go undone, I think Mother was just glad to have one less person underfoot for a few hours.

Charlotte met me at the front door of her house, waving the latest issue of *Life* magazine and chanting, "We're gonna be rich, we're gonna be rich!"

I thought she had lost her marbles for good and said so.

Undaunted, she pointed to the open page and demanded that I read it. The figure $25,000 in type nearly an inch high caught my eye, and I grabbed the magazine from her and read the following headline:

$25,000 in Prizes!

May the best "Blurbs" win.

464 cash prizes each month.

Two first prizes of $500 each . . . Just write a "blurb."

Beneath the headline was a series of pictures of two men in undershirts, one with shaving cream lathered over his face. The soap-free man held a tube of Palmolive shave cream, the lathered man held a tube of Colgate. Their conversation went something like this:

Palmolive man: "Pardon me for bragging, Bill, but Palmolive's the finest shaving cream a man ever used."

Colgate man: "You're wrong again, Walt. Colgate's for me first, last, and always. You can have all the rest."

Palmolive man: "I tell you I've tried them all, and for quick, lasting lather in any kind of water — hot or cold, hard or soft — nothing, absolutely nothing, compares with Palmolive."

Colgate man: "Don't be so cocksure! My beard's as tough as yours, and I never knew what a close shave was till I used Colgate's."

Palmolive man: "Yeah? Well, you'll never know what a *real* shave is till you use an olive oil shaving cream."

Colgate man: "What do you mean,

real shave? I claim it takes a real shaving cream to get these bristles of mine off close to the skin. I'll stick to my Colgate's."

The ad copy then invited shavers to get in on the argument. "Get into this shaving cream blurb contest, men. Who are *you* for — Walt or Bill? Palmolive or Colgate's?" Contest rules and the address of where to send the blurb were printed on the opposite page.

"All we have to do is write a *blurb*," Charlotte cried, "and we're five hundred dollars richer!"

"But, Charlotte, this contest is for men," I pointed out.

"So we send in our blurb under my father's name. So *what?* The judges will never know."

"But, Charlotte," I continued, "we have no idea what it's like to shave." We had in fact tried to shave our legs once, an incident that ended with both of us sporting several bandage strips across our shins.

"Well, *silly*," Charlotte countered, "all we have to do is do it!"

"Shave, you mean?"

"Of *course*, shave!"

Before I could protest further, my eager friend grabbed my hand and pulled me upstairs to the bathroom. She flung open the mirrored medicine cabinet and proudly produced the lather brush and soap dish that her father used while at home. In the dish was a round, nondescript cake of soap, dry and cracked from days of neglect since her father was, at the moment, on the road.

"Which kind is that?" I asked, wrinkling my nose at the thing. "Palmolive or Colgate's?"

My friend looked at the forlorn disk of soap and shrugged. "I don't know," she admitted. But she hastened to assure me that it didn't matter. "Shaving cream is shaving cream. It doesn't matter what we use."

"But I don't think that's shaving cream," I argued. "It's not in a tube like in the ad. This stuff's just plain soap."

Charlotte sighed heavily and glared at me in disgust. "Look, Virginia, do you want the money or not?"

I had to admit that I did. Only a few days earlier Mother had told me that rather than getting my usual new pair of shoes for school, I had to make do with the pair from last year. I never knew exactly how we stood financially — that was something Mother and Papa didn't discuss with us children — but I did know that things weren't quite what they used to be if we couldn't afford my annual pair of school shoes. I suspected it was because our budget had had to stretch to include the Dubbins, and when I thought about going back to school and facing Danny Dysinger with the same old footwear he'd seen all the previous year, I was almost tempted to feel angry with Uncle Jim all over again. But suddenly, here was a solution to my problem.

I looked at the ad again. There were to be six contests in all, this being the first. Six sets of prizes, each set totaling $4,200, would be awarded. The winners of this first contest would be announced the following month. Two first prizes of $500. Why couldn't Charlotte and I be the recipients of one of those prizes? If we split the money, I'd still have the remarkable sum of $250. I could give $225 to Mother and have enough money left over for myself to buy several pairs of shoes — or anything else I wanted!

The second prize was $125; the third, $50; and two hundred runners-up would win the paltry sum of five dollars. I ignored those lesser numbers altogether and set my sights on the top prize. Surely if Charlotte and I put our heads together, we could come up with a blurb that would outdo even that of the most experienced male shavers.

I set the magazine down on the top of

the commode and said, "Let's lather up."

"*Now* you're talking!" Charlotte giggled.

She ran the hot-water faucet until the water was steamy, then moistened the brush and ran it in circles over the soap as she no doubt had seen her father do. While she did that, I removed the razor blade from the safety razor that Charlotte had pointed to in the medicine cabinet, saying, "That's Pop's extra razor. He has a better one he takes on trips, for when he has to look really good."

Once she decided the soap was ready, Charlotte turned her face sideways to the mirror like a man inspecting his whiskers, drew her mouth to one side to pull one cheek taut, and painted her skin with the lather. With one cheek frothy white, she sucked her lips in over her teeth and lathered her chin and upper lip. Then she worked her way over to the other cheek.

"How's it feel?" I asked.

"Good," she replied noncommittally. She lifted her chin and lathered her long white neck. When she finished, she gazed at herself in the mirror and smiled. She looked like an adolescent boy with a cotton beard pressed to his face and playing Santa Claus in a Christmas pageant. "Now you go," she instructed.

I ran the brush in circles over the soap as Charlotte had. Then I used the same circular motion on my right cheek. "Feels nice and soft," I said.

"Yeah," Charlotte agreed. "Kind of like a massage on your face."

"I wonder why men complain about shaving."

"I don't know. Maybe they get tired of it."

"I kind of like it so far."

"Me too."

"Do you have any ideas yet?"

"No."

"Me neither."

Charlotte picked up the empty razor from the rim of the sink. "Maybe if I go through the motions of shaving, it'll help me think."

"Okay. Just do one cheek, then let me try."

Charlotte pulled the safety razor down her cheek and along the line of her jaw, then rinsed off the soap under the running water. She handed me the razor and I did the same.

"Anything yet?" she asked.

"Feels kind of tingly and wet. What do you think?"

"*Soothing* might be a good word. Yeah, we could work that in somehow. Let me do my chin."

I passed the razor back to Charlotte. She held it level to the bottom of her lower lip, then drew it down her chin.

"Think it feels any different when there's a blade in there?" I asked.

"I don't know, but I don't think I want to find out."

"Me neither. But maybe it hurts when men nick themselves. Maybe that's why they don't like shaving so much."

"I always know when my pop nicks himself because he cusses up a blue streak. Mama claims he sets the neighbor's dog to howling, but I don't think that's true, seeing as how none of our neighbors have a dog."

I tried to picture Papa cussing up a blue streak like Mr. Besac. I generally wasn't awake yet when Papa shaved, but I couldn't imagine that his nicking himself resulted in anything worse than a momentary pause in his morning whistle. There was, though, plenty of evidence that he rarely got through a shave without drawing blood. "Sometimes," I volunteered, "my Pa comes to breakfast with little bits of toilet paper stuck to his face — you know, with one red dot in the middle. Mama has to remind him to take them off before he starts seeing patients."

Charlotte had just handed the razor back to me when Mrs. Besac appeared in the bathroom doorway. She looked frumpish, with bags under her eyes and her hair all flattened against one side of her head, as though she had just awakened from a nap. I hadn't even thought of her until the moment she appeared. A cigarette was pressed between her lips, and she lit the end of it with a slender silver lighter. She snapped shut the lighter, inhaled deeply, blew the smoke out one side of her mouth, and picked a tobacco seed from the tip of her tongue, all without taking her eyes off of us. Charlotte and I stood motionless as she stared, each concocting in our own minds an explanation for what we were doing.

Fortunately, we were spared an explanation. The world-weary Mrs. Besac, patron of speakeasies and acquainted with all manner of oddities, simply shook her head and said, "I'm not even going to ask."

We heard her footsteps echo along the hardwood floor of the hall, then descend the stairs. When we decided she was out of earshot, we looked at each other and burst out laughing. Charlotte laughed so hard she had to sit on the edge of the bear-claw tub until she got her breath back. I shut the bathroom door and leaned up against it, trembling with mirth. When we both calmed down, we had only to glance at the other's half-lathered face to break out again into howls of amusement. This went on for several minutes until Charlotte, slapping her thigh, said even as she wailed, "We've got to *stop!* This is im*por*tant! This is *se*rious! We've got to come up with a blurb!"

We allowed ourselves another full minute of laughter, then returned, red-faced and panting, to the task at hand.

We finished shaving, then lathered up and shaved again. We lathered up so many times over the next couple of hours that Mr. Besac's cake of soap was reduced to half its original size. "Doesn't matter," Charlotte said when I pointed out how much the soap had shrunk. "We'll win enough money to buy Pop ten *boxes* of shaving cream."

After three or four mock shaves, I asked, "Which brand of shaving cream are we trying to write a blurb for?"

"Doesn't matter," Charlotte said. "Either one."

"Have you got any ideas yet?"

Charlotte thought a moment. "How about this? 'If it's good enough for Bugs Moran, it's good enough for every man. Use Colgate's shaving cream.' "

I frowned. "How do you know Bugs Moran uses Colgate's?"

"I don't."

"Then you can't say he does."

"Yes, I can. This is advertising. It doesn't matter what you say."

"Even so, I'm not sure most men want

to be like Bugs Moran."

"Rich and powerful? Of course they do."

"But he's a gangster, Charlotte."

"So?"

"I don't think that makes for good advertising. Besides, I thought you decided athletes were more exciting than gangsters."

"Oh yeah." After a moment, she added, "Okay, how about, 'If it's good enough for Eddie Tolan,' " — she was referring to the runner who had just taken the gold in both the 100-meter and the 200-meter dash during the Olympic games in Los Angeles — " 'If it's good enough for Eddie Tolan, it's good enough for —' "

"Think of something else," I suggested. "That's not going to work."

"Well, you come up with one, then," Charlotte demanded huffily. I think she was stung by my offhand rejection of her blurb, but there was a lot of money at stake, and I had to be honest.

"All right," I said. "How about something simple but catchy like 'Use Colgate, it's doubly bubbly.' "

Charlotte repeated the phrase, then turned up her nose and shook her head. Even if she liked it, of course she wasn't going to admit it. She was going to make me work for her approval.

I shrugged my shoulders and tentatively offered another: " 'For skin smooth as an olive, try Palmolive'?"

"Hmm, we'll keep that one in mind. But maybe we should try to come up with something a little more romantic."

"Like what?" I couldn't imagine anything romantic about a shaving cream ad.

Charlotte thought a moment as she absently lathered her right cheek again. Suddenly she exclaimed, "I've got it. 'For an irresistible kisser, get rid of every whisker with Colgate'!"

I scratched my soapy chin with the tips of my fingers. "Not bad," I said. "I like it but the judges might think it's too racy. Besides, men don't like romantic stuff; only we women do. Better think of something else." Remembering what Charlotte said about her father swearing when he cut his face, I suggested, " 'Instead of a scream, let shaving be a dream. Try Palmolive.' "

Charlotte suggested that we think again.

We thought and we lathered and we shaved and we volleyed our ideas back and forth across the bathroom sink, and finally by some act of divine inspiration (or so we thought), Charlotte began, "Pamper the skin —" and I added, "On your cheeks and your chin," and Charlotte concluded, "Use Palmolive." We looked at each other with raised brows, our faces still streaked with drying soap, then said again slowly, this time in unison, "To pamper the skin on your cheeks and your chin, use Palmolive."

"Hey!" Charlotte shouted.

"That's it!" I cried.

We repeated the words again and again, picking up speed each time and snapping along, then tapping along, until finally we moved out of the bathroom and down the hall, chanting our slogan with wild enthusiasm while dancing a kind of improvised rumba. Hands in the air, fingers snapping, hips swaying as we moved up and down the hardwood floor. Whenever we came to "Pal-mo-" we stood in place and gyrated our hips, and then on the final "-live!" we thrust out our backsides in the questionable manner of salon dancers. This went on for several minutes until we noticed Mrs. Besac at the head of the stairs, once again staring at us as she slowly moved her head from side to side. Her footsteps had been drowned out by our own voices, and we hadn't heard her come up the stairs. Suddenly she was just there, holding a half-empty glass of iced tea. Charlotte and I came to an immediate standstill and, at a loss as to what else to do, returned her stare. Bad enough that she had already caught us shaving — but now to find us dancing like a couple of bootleggers' wives? As the color crept into my soap-streaked face, I could only imagine what my own mother would say if she came upon such despicable behavior. After receiving a thorough dressing down, I'd be reciting Thomas Campion poems for the rest of my life. But Mrs. Besac, so unlike my own mother, simply gazed at us with the eyes of a hound dog, looking as if she had just seen the saddest thing in the world. Then quietly, almost under her breath, she violated the third commandment, shook her head once again, and said, "I'll be glad when school starts up again. You kids are going crazy with boredom." She turned and disappeared down the stairs, returning to the comfort of her iced tea and cigarettes on the front porch swing.

Charlotte and I ran into her bedroom and flung ourselves across the four-poster bed, once again exploding into laughter. We buried our faces in the pillows and laughed until we were exhausted. (Charlotte later told me that all that night she kept catching whiffs of her father's shaving cream, and she dreamed that she really did have a beard that she was trying frantically to shave off.) Finally, when we were able to look at each other without breaking up, she said, "Come on. Let's get our blurb ready to mail."

Using her father's ancient Remington, Charlotte typed up the blurb on a plain piece of paper and signed her father's name to it. Then she typed the Chicago address of the contest on an envelope, and we each put up a penny toward the postage. I crossed my fingers while Charlotte kissed the envelope and said, "Make us *rich!*"

When I walked home that afternoon, the skin on my face felt tight from the soap and irritated from the repeated scraping with the razor, but I ignored my discomfort and thought only of the look on Mother's face when I handed her my winnings and the look on Danny Dysinger's face as I pranced about school in my shiny new black patent leather shoes.

Chapter Eighteen

Just after lunch the next day, Simon and I sat side by side on the piano bench practicing a duet. Miss Cole, during a momentary lapse of judgment the previous week, had given us this rather awkward assignment. My brother and I had never before attempted to play together, and Simon's superior skills became even more evident as I fumbled about trying to keep up with him. Time and again we had to stop and start over, and he grew increasingly frustrated until he actually resorted to kicking my shin beneath the piano bench.

"Hey, what's the idea!" I yelled, shoving him hard with both hands.

He managed to catch himself before falling off the bench and took a swing at me with his right fist, hitting me squarely on the upper arm. "A monkey could play better than you!" he cried.

"Could not!" I screamed, though I knew it was true. In retaliation for the swat, I grabbed a fistful of his curly hair and pulled, refusing to let go. He yanked at my bobbed hair, and we sat there locked in a clash of wills, each with a hand to the opposite head, our faces reddening as our anger grew hotter.

"Could so!" he countered. "A *deaf* monkey who was *blind*folded could play better than you!"

"And just who do you think you are?" I screamed. "Ludwig van Beethoven himself?"

"Compared to you I am!"

From the corner of my eye I saw someone step into the parlor, and for a second I thought it must be Mother coming to referee. I immediately dropped my grip on Simon's hair, only to discover that it wasn't Mother but Rufus, wandering in nonchalantly with his hands in the pockets of his overalls. As usual, because of the heat, he wore no shirt beneath the bib. He sauntered over to the piano, pulled a frayed toothpick out of his mouth and pointed it at us. "Hey, Luke and I are going out. You two monkeys wanna come?"

In my sudden excitement, I let the monkey comment slide. This was the first time Rufus invited me to do anything with him since he had moved into our house. Simon had developed a camaraderie with our cousins, but I, who was only a girl, had been largely ignored by the boys.

"Where ya going?" I asked, jumping up from the piano bench.

Rufus leaned toward us and whispered

conspiratorially, "Down to the picket line. We want to see for ourselves what's going on down there."

For a moment I was stunned. My eyes widened in fear and wonder. I thought he might suggest swimming in the river or going downtown to see whether a fire hydrant had been opened. But the picket line? "Rufus, you know we're not allowed —"

"Who's to know?" my cousin interrupted, straightening up and chomping on the toothpick again. "We can say we're going to the drugstore for a soda."

"But —"

"If you don't wanna come —"

"I'm coming!" cried Simon.

Not wanting to let the opportunity get away from me, I echoed timidly, "I'm coming, too."

"Good," Rufus said. "Ginny, you tell Aunt Lil we'll be back in a while. Luke and Simon and me'll be waiting for you out on the porch." Aunt Sally hadn't yet returned from her duties at the commissary, though we expected her home at any time, and my cousins were most likely anxious to leave before she arrived.

I found Mother upstairs putting fresh sheets on the girls' bed. Crossing my fingers behind my back, I told her the boys and I wanted to go out for a soda. Fortunately, Simon and I had been at the piano for nearly half an hour, so Mother was satisfied and gave us permission to go.

Feeling giddy, I ran out to catch up with the boys, who had already started down the sidewalk.

"What'd she say?" Rufus asked when I reached them.

"She said all right."

"Good."

The four of us walked along in silence for a moment, spurred on by a certain unspoken determination to reach the picket line as quickly as possible. But the day was another scorcher and the glare of the sun stung our eyes. It wasn't long before we all began to drag.

"Gonna be a long hot walk," Luke said, shuffling along the sidewalk. Like Rufus, he wore denim overalls without a shirt. I thought the overalls must be hot and wondered why my cousins didn't wear cotton shorts like Simon did. It never occurred to me that they might not have any.

Rufus tossed the toothpick onto somebody's front yard. "Yeah, and we're gonna feel a lot hotter before we get there — unless anyone's got money for the trolley."

I reached into the pocket of my dress and felt my weekly allowance resting there against the seam. Just that morning Mother had given me my usual quarter. I was saving it for Saturday when Charlotte and I planned to see Douglas Fairbanks Jr. in *Love Is a Racket*. But I didn't think twice about pulling it out and impressing my cousin Rufus. If I *had* thought twice, I might have realized why he had invited me along. After all, he knew I had the quarter because he'd seen Mother give it to me.

But I held up the gleaming coin and, feeling like a heroine, cried, "I've got money!"

There was just enough for the four of us to catch the trolley to the warehouse district, a block away from the grain mill, with a nickel left over. Where I was going to come up with enough money to go to the matinee with Charlotte, I didn't know. But I decided not to fret about it just then. An outing with my cousin Rufus — and an illicit one at that — was too exciting to pass up.

We caught the trolley on the next block and found seats at the back. Simon and I sat together in one, Luke and Rufus in another behind us. None of us said a word as we passed through the city streets. We sat as though mesmerized by the soothing air blowing in through the open windows. Whenever the trolley stopped, the heat stung our skin as sure as the biting winds of winter, but we were only uncomfortable until the car jerked into motion again and the wind of locomotion whistled across our faces.

When we reached our stop, Rufus tapped Simon and me on the shoulder, and we followed him out of the trolley.

"Where's the picket line?" Luke asked.

"Follow me," Rufus replied, motioning us on with a sweep of his arm.

We hurriedly trod the sidewalk in single file like a string of sleuths hunting down clues. Rufus was point man, while I brought up the rear. In another moment, we heard the picket line before we saw it. What came to us through the streets of the warehouse district wasn't shouts or grumbling or yelling, but singing — the hum of two hundred male voices hewing out a rough tune. We rounded a corner and there they were, a swarming assemblage of dark-clad men, spilling out over the sidewalk and onto the street, most holding signs, a few wearing sandwich boards, almost all sporting caps in spite of the heat. Their whiskered faces spoke of fatigue and discouragement, and yet they sang, and the shock of coming upon this vast bedraggled choir in the street brought us to a standstill, able only to gape and to listen. I can hear it yet, the sound of their unskilled voices rising together to the tune of "Battle Hymn of the Republic."

When the Union's inspiration through
the workers' blood shall run,
There can be no power greater anywhere
beneath the sun,
Yet what force on earth is weaker than
the feeble strength of one,
But the Union makes us strong.
Solidarity Forever!
Solidarity Forever!
Solidarity Forever!
For the Union makes us strong.

"Wow!" cried Simon quietly, almost reverently.

"You see Pa?" Luke asked.

"Not yet," answered Rufus. "But don't let *him* see *us*. Come on, over here."

Rufus led us to a narrow alley between two buildings across the street from the mill entrance, a position from which we could watch the picket line without being noticed. We crouched against the brick walls of either building, Simon and I on one side, our cousins a few feet away on the other. Though the alley was shaded by the buildings that formed it, the air in there was heavy with heat and difficult to breathe, and the bricks, yielding a pungent odor of cement and dirt, burned hot against our bare arms and legs. It was something like being inside a brick oven, but our discomfort was overridden by our curiosity.

The chorus of picketers sang and marched in measured steps while their reluctant audience, the police and the sheriff's deputies, milled about looking natty and domineering in their starched uniforms and their sidearms of batons and guns and rifles. The lawmen exhibited little expression, but every one of them made me think of a night watchman whistling in the dark, uneasy at the thought of what he may come upon around the next corner. Occasional furtive and menacing glances passed between the strikers and the lawmen. Both sides seemed posed to jump at the slightest provocation.

Adding to the tension were the newspaper photographers and reporters who had come to capture the story, identifiable by their white shirts and loosened ties and the fedoras that sat far forward over their brows to shade their eyes from the glare of the sun. The reporters had small notebooks cupped in their hands on which they scribbled with pencil stubs. The photographers fiddled with their cameras and walked to and fro, seeking out vantage points for their picture taking. Even a newsreel truck was there to record the strike in moving pictures. The cameraman had climbed to the roof of the truck to set up his tripod. He too was getting ready, and the preparation of the journalists defined the climate of the scene: Anticipation. Something was about to happen. Something was about to happen as though it had all been staged and the players in the wings were nervously awaiting the rise of the curtain, the start of the show. A line of patrol wagons sat parked down the street, hinting at the outcome of the final act.

"Is there going to be a fight?" Luke whispered loudly to Rufus.

"I don't know," Rufus said, shaking his head. "Will be, I think, if they try to bring in scabs."

"They gonna try to bring in scabs?"

"How should I know? Just shut up and watch."

"Look, there's Pa!"

Luke stretched out one sun-darkened arm and pointed toward the center of the crowd near the mill gate. There indeed was Uncle Jim, carrying a sign that read "Give us a voice! Recognize the Union!" He was speaking to the striker next to him and nodding his head.

"Don't let him see you!" warned Rufus.

"He's too busy to notice us over here," Luke argued.

"Yeah, well, just keep your head down. That goes for you, too, Ginny and Simon."

My knees ached from crouching in the alley, and I shifted my weight from one foot to the other. The nervousness of the men was infectious, and I pressed my fingernails into my palms as my eyes followed the movements of the picket line. My heart pounded with an overabundance of adrenaline, and I suddenly felt so thirsty my throat ached. I swallowed hard and pursed my lips and tried to keep my mounting fear bridled within my chest.

The song tapered off as a low rumble of mumbling replaced the singing. Hundreds of pairs of feet slapping against the pavement slowed to a shuffle. The picketers looked uneasily over their shoulders. There was a tensing of bodies, a shifting of eyes. The lawmen touched palms to batons and guns and stamped nervously at the gravel and pavement like frightened horses. Whatever they were waiting for wasn't there yet, but it was coming, and they all knew it.

"What's going on?" Simon asked.

None of us answered. None of us knew.

A distant roar of engines blew over the picket line like an icy wind and sent a shiver through the crowd. "They're coming!" one of the picketers cried, and finally all movement ceased as hundreds of eyes, both anxious and angry, gazed down the street in the direction of the rumbling. Police and deputies fell into line about the picketers, weapons poised. The first of the camera bulbs flashed. The film on top of the newsreel truck started to roll. The fedoras swam through the sea of caps as the journalists moved toward the center of the impending action.

But the mill workers stood placidly, like surrendered prisoners of war, watching as a line of vehicles drew near to the mill. The first was a Ford convertible driven by the chief of police, Morton McCormick, and in the passenger seat was Sheriff Clem Dysinger. They were followed by two squad cars, then three pickup trucks loaded down with men waiting to be taken into the mill. Beyond the trucks was a large contingent of policemen and private-citizens-turned-deputies following on foot.

The serpent of vehicles slithered along the street, coming to rest at the edge of the picket line. Chief McCormick left the Ford's motor idling while Sheriff Dysinger stood up in the front of the car, supporting himself against the windshield while holding a megaphone up to his lips. A hush fell over the crowd as the mill workers glared up at the sheriff and waited for him to have his say.

"You men are going to have to clear on out of here!" Sheriff Dysinger began bluntly, spitting his words out through the megaphone and over the heads of the picketers. With his left hand he pulled a folded sheet of paper out of the breast pocket of his uniform and waved it at the crowd.

"What I've got here is a court-ordered injunction, issued on behalf of the Thiel Grain Mill, that prohibits you from picketing —"

An angry roar went up from the throng, interrupting the sheriff's words. Men shouted and hissed, and above the clamor I heard a familiar voice cry, "What good's a strike if we can't picket?" It was Uncle Jim. Other men picked up on his argument, saying they had a right to picket, and no court could deny them that right.

Sheriff Dysinger waved his arms to silence the men. Even from where I crouched in the alley, I could see the two full and dripping moons of sweat in the armpits of his uniform. His thick arms stopped waving when the noise had settled enough that he could be heard above it. "I've got an injunction," the sheriff continued, "and it's legal, and any one of you who disobeys this injunction is facing a jail sentence."

Again the crowd roared, but Sheriff Dysinger went on yelling through his megaphone, and eventually the strikers quieted down enough to listen. "You men might as well recognize the fact that you're beat. Injunction or no, your striking is getting you nowhere. You might as well put down your signs and go on home peacefully or join the men inside and get your old jobs back. Now, Mr. Thiel has generously promised to take back any and all willing to come back, no questions asked." A murmur of dissent rippled through the crowd, but the sheriff ignored it. "I say we've had enough fighting and enough bloodshed. It's time to get this thing settled peaceful-like. You can choose to go on home, or you can come with us right now and return to work. We've got a few men in these trucks willing to work, and Chief McCormick here and I are gonna escort them inside. In the meantime, you men decide what it is you want to do."

Like a politician on the campaign trail, he held up his hands to the crowd, gave one cursory wave, and settled back down in the seat. The police chief began inching the car forward toward the crowd, hoping for it to part like the Red Sea and let them through. The trucks holding the scabs revved their engines.

The picketers suddenly fell eerily silent as they stood their ground in front of the mill gates. Not one striker moved. They glared en masse at the occupants of the Ford, daring the lawmen to mow them down.

For several seconds the two sides stood pitted against each other like a couple of bulldogs separated by a fence, but the stagnant standoff was interrupted and the

fence pulled down when one of the picketers yelled to his fellow strikers, "We
gonna let 'em crush us like bugs?"

"No!" cried the men with one voice, and
like a single creature the men rose up and
lunged forward. In the next moment the
street became a battleground. Police whis-
tles pierced the air as angry hands reached
out and dragged McCormick and Dysinger
from the still idling car. A dozen police of-
ficers leapt to the defense of the two
lawmen. The scabs likewise were pulled
from the pickup trucks and swallowed up
by the crowd. From within the tumult of
billy clubs, baseball bats, knives, and rocks
— for the picketers had finally armed
themselves with weapons — came the
shouts and screams of the fighting and the
wounded. I lifted my hands to my ears in
horror against the shouting, the stomping,
the cries, but I could not turn my eyes
away from the battle out in the street. Just
in front of us, not thirty feet away, an of-
ficer swung his billy club at the head of a
striker. The striker's cap flew off and the
man — one hand instinctively rising to the
wound — staggered forward before col-
lapsing against the asphalt. After a moment
he struggled to push himself up with the
palms of his hands, but the policeman hit
him again, swinging the club against the
man's shoulder blades with both hands,

like a baseball player determined for a home run. With all the breath knocked out of him, the striker reeled and slumped forward, his right cheek landing and coming to rest against the hot pavement.

I cried out against the beating of the defenseless man. Rufus crawled across the alley and put his hand over my mouth — for what reason, I don't know. My cries could never have been heard above the tumult in the street. I pulled his hand away frantically and yelled, "He's dead! He's dead!"

"Maybe he isn't," Simon countered. He looked at me with eyes wide with compassion. He was trying desperately to console me and keep me calm. "Maybe he's still breathing."

The man lay alone and ignored in the street, his attacker having gone off to batter someone else.

"Come on, Simon," Rufus said, "let's get him out of the street."

I grabbed my brother's shirt. "Don't go out there, Simon."

But he pulled away and ran with Rufus to the wounded man. Luke came and crouched beside me, watching the riot intently and saying nothing. I wanted to scream again, but I was paralyzed by the gruesomeness of the event playing itself out in front of me. Adding to my confusion was the flashing of cameras here and there like so many lightning bugs on a summer night. *Why are you taking pictures!* I wanted to scream. Cameras were meant to capture smiling faces, family portraits, sunsets, flowers — not blood, not anger, not the evil of man against man. Why would anyone want to record this? Why would anyone want to remember this?

Trembling, I pressed my cheek against a sun-baked brick to steady myself. I closed my eyes to shut out the scene and pressed my palms over my ears to dull the noise, but it was no use. On the dark screen of my own eyelids I saw the panorama of that harsh summer played out — the doleful line of hungry men outside the soup kitchen, the homeless and penniless in the shanties of Soo City, and now the fierce bloodshed outside the mill gate. Everything I knew about life was suddenly turned upside down. It was as though an error had been made in the cutting room, and an awful and terrifying movie had been spliced onto the happy, romantic film advertised on the theater's marque. I'd bought a ticket for the romance, and here it was interrupted right in the middle by some tragic picture I never would have chosen to see. All I wanted was to get back to the original film, to be again the girl who gazed at sunbeams in search of angels, and who spun a globe to find out where she was going on her honeymoon.

By the time I dared open my eyes, Rufus and Simon had dragged the wounded man onto the sidewalk only a few feet away from the alley. Simon had a hand on the man's neck trying to find a pulse. Luke and I, still on our hands and knees, crawled over to peer at the victim sprawled out on the pavement.

I cast a fearful glance at Simon. "Is he dead?" I asked.

Simon shook his head. "He's still breathing and I feel a pulse. Good thing that last one was across his back and not his head. He's bleeding pretty bad, though, from that first wallop."

Rufus, who'd been supporting the man's head and shoulders as the boys carried him off the street, uncurled his fingers to reveal two red and sticky palms. I heard him curse under his breath as he wiped his hands on the sidewalk, painting two red patches there with the blood of this wounded stranger.

"What should we do, Simon?" I asked breathlessly.

My brother didn't answer, but in a moment he had removed his shirt and was wrapping it around the man's head. "This might stop the bleeding a little," he said. As I watched Simon at work, a sense of pride pierced my terror, and I smiled in spite of myself. My brother, only nine years old, seemed already to be fulfilling his destiny, and I knew this moment foreshadowed what he was to become. He was so very much like Papa, and I thought, *They are good people, always trying to fix the bad that others have done.*

Simon was gently tying the shirt's short sleeves together to form a kind of tourniquet when Luke, pointing out toward the crowd, cried, "Fire!"

The four of us turned to where Luke was pointing. In the midst of the struggling crowd there wafted a thick haze of smoke, rising as placidly above the tumult as Wordsworth's lonely cloud.

"It's not fire," Rufus, narrow-eyed, hissed angrily. "They've thrown tear gas. They're trying to blind the mill workers. Another unfair advantage."

We watched as the assaulted men screamed and staggered, their hands lifted to their smarting eyes. Some rubbed their eyelids frantically, trying to wipe away the searing gas, but in vain. A group of police wearing gas masks appeared as from out of nowhere and surged into the crowd, grabbing at the blinded men and subduing them with repeated blows of their billy clubs. When the beaten workers had fallen to their knees or collapsed completely on the street, they were handcuffed and carried off to the patrol wagons.

I turned to look at my cousin Rufus, who was clenching and unclenching his bloody fists. He was muttering under his breath, and it sounded something like "Gotta help Pa. Gotta help Pa."

In the next moment, Luke yelled, "There's Pa! There he is. He's taking on two of them at once!"

Uncle Jim alternately swung his fists at his assailants and lifted his arms to ward off the blows of their clubs. "It's not fair, two against one!" Luke cried, and Rufus must have thought so too because before any of us could protest, he had sprinted up from the sidewalk like a track runner and darted into the midst of the fray. The three of us watched him wide-eyed and openmouthed. I realized only slowly that I held my arm straight out in front of me, instinctively reaching for my cousin, trying to pull him back from the battle. Resignedly, I let my hand fall to my side.

"Kill 'em, Rufus," Luke muttered.

"He's gonna get killed himself," Simon replied soberly.

I could only whisper a prayer wrenched from the very center of my heart. "Oh, God. Oh, God." And that was all. I was scarcely aware of the tears streaming down my face as helplessly I looked on. The same instinct that had sent Rufus into the battle was inside me: Someone I loved was being attacked, and I wanted to rip apart his attackers limb by limb. It wasn't right. It wasn't fair. Didn't those policemen know what they were doing? This wasn't just another picketer. This wasn't just any ordinary man. This was my Uncle Jim. My fun-loving, caring, hardworking, Mouth-Happy, beloved Uncle Jim.

"They got Pa handcuffed," Luke replied solemnly.

Out on the battlefield Uncle Jim struggled against the restraint. Rufus swung at one of his father's captors, but in a moment the swarming crowd swallowed them up, and they were hidden from our view.

"I gotta help, too!" Luke cried, standing up.

I knew how he felt, for I, too, wanted to rush out there and swing my fists blindly until all my rage was spent, but I grabbed one of Luke's legs, Simon the other. "You stay right here!" I ordered. "We never should have come. We never should have —"

My words were cut off by a shot ringing out through the crowd. Luke stopped struggling and stiffened, almost as if struck himself by an unseen bullet. We heard another shot and then another. "They're shooting," Luke said quietly, announcing the obvious. I felt the muscles in his leg tremble.

Simon squinted behind his glasses and looked out over the crowd. "Just blanks," he said. "Uncle Jim said they just ignore the guns anymore. They all know the police are only trying to scare them."

Just in case, we took cover again in the alley and listened for more gunfire. In spite of the tear gas, the fighting continued as fiercely as ever. The crowd actually grew as reinforcements were added to both sides, lawmen surging in from one side, strikers from the other. Word of the riot must have gotten back to strike headquarters because dozens of men wielding baseball bats, clubs, and knives joined the throng from the direction of the warehouse district. By now, a host of wounded men lay moaning or unconscious in the streets. The police went about collecting them as quickly as they could and hauled them away like so much deadwood. Other bleeding strikers were carried to vehicles that had arrived, tires screeching, from the warehouse district. I figured they were being taken to the strike hospital. Man after man fell and was carried in one direction or the other toward the union's rented warehouse or toward the long line of patrol wagons. I had a good idea which direction Uncle Jim was going.

For several minutes no more shots were fired, but then another shot rang out, and a great roar of anger went up from the crowd. One of the strikers on the edge of the crowd facing us suddenly threw up his hands and thrust out his chest as a look of surprise crossed his face. The man staggered and tried to stand but sank to his knees instead. He lifted his right hand to his chest where a red spot appeared on his shirt like a bud, then spread like the opening of a rose. With his quizzical eyes still open, the man fell face forward onto the street, shivered a moment, and then lay still.

"They killed him," Luke said flatly. "That was no blank. That was a real bullet."

"Yeah, that was real," Simon confirmed with a nod. "Looks like he was shot in the back and the bullet went clean through."

Staring immobile at the freshly fallen corpse, I suddenly felt detached from the scene around me. Surely this was all pretend, a carefully arranged scene. Surely the man running the camera on top of the truck would cry "Cut!" and the action would stop. Surely the man facedown in the street would push himself up again, wipe the dust from his pants, and go off whistling.

"He can't be dead," I said, shaking my

head. Still unable to take my eyes from the corpse, I grabbed Simon's hand. "He's not dead, is he, Simon?"

Before Simon could answer, two men, obviously mill workers, rushed up to their wounded companion on the sidewalk, the man Rufus and my brother had dragged off the street. One bent over him and, as Simon had done earlier, felt his neck for a pulse. The other gently touched the wounded man's head and said, "Lookit here, someone tied a shirt —" He interrupted himself when he spotted us crouched between the buildings. "Hey," he yelled, "what are you kids doing there? Are you crazy? You go on home! Go on, git! You wanna get yourselves killed or something?"

The other man, more concerned about his downed companion, said, "Come on, Joe, let's get him to the car." He lifted the man's legs around the knees while Joe slid his arms under the man's shoulders. Without waiting to see whether we left, they hurried their wounded toward the car and the strike hospital.

Simon squeezed my hand. "Come on, Ginny," he said. "I think we'd better get out of here like the man said."

Numb and senseless as a sleepwalker, I let Simon pull me up and drag me out of the alley. Just beyond our hiding place the sidewalk glistened with the blood of the wounded man who had just been hauled away. I walked up against the front of the building to avoid the crimson spot.

Simon yelled back over his shoulder, "Come on, Luke. We gotta get out of here."

Luke shook his head and made no move to get up. "I'm staying put."

Simon started to protest, but before I knew what was happening he suddenly cried out and fell to the sidewalk. "Simon!" I cried, dropping to my knees beside him. "Simon!" Fresh tears broke loose from the cistern of horror inside me and mingled with my screams. Though I couldn't see the wound, I was sure my brother had been shot, and that he was dead.

Chapter Nineteen

Like the corpse in the street, Simon lay with his forehead pressed to the hot cement, his shattered glasses straddling a crack in the sidewalk a few feet from his head. I wrung my hands, wondering what to do. Then, to my surprise, Simon moaned. Tentatively, he raised one hand to his head. He was bleeding, I finally realized, from a wound just beside his right brow, and I wondered whether a bullet had sliced his skull and entered his brain. I thought that I might faint, but I forced my trembling hands to turn my brother over on the sidewalk. By now Luke was beside us, holding a rock.

"This is what hit him," my cousin explained. "It landed right at my feet."

I looked at the rock, then at Luke's face. "Are you sure it was a rock that hit him?" I asked. "Not a bullet?"

Luke snorted. "If it'd been a bullet, it would've blown his head clear off. Your head's still there, ain't it, Simon?"

Simon sat up, and when he did, blood dripped from his cut brow and onto his bare chest. "Yeah, it's still here," he moaned. "I know it is, 'cause it's killing me."

I let go a great sigh of relief and would have thrown my arms around my brother if it hadn't been for the blood. Still shaking, I lifted my cotton skirt and ripped a jagged piece of material from the thin attached petticoat. "Here, Simon," I said, pressing the cloth against his forehead, "hold this on the cut."

He obediently pressed the improvised bandage to his head, then asked, "Where's my glasses?"

On hands and knees I retrieved them from the sidewalk and held them out to Simon. Both lenses were shattered and the frames were bent. Simon slowly lifted the tangled object from my palm.

"They broke my glasses," he said mournfully, and he sounded so pitiful I started to cry again. Then he said, "Oh, it's all right, Ginny. Don't start bawling. Let's just get out of here. You coming, Luke?"

"Nope, I'm staying."

"You're crazy."

"I gotta see what happens to Pa and Rufus."

"But Aunt Sally will die if she knows you're here," I protested. Luke shrugged. It would be impossible to persuade him to come home with us. Nodding toward the chaos in the street, I relented, saying, "Look, just don't go out there, all right?

403

Stay put in the alley."

"All right."

"Promise?"

"Yeah, now, go on. You better tell Ma that Pa's been arrested."

"Can you walk?" I asked Simon.

He nodded and stood, pressing the torn cloth to his head with one hand and clutching what was left of his glasses with the other. I put my arm around his bare shoulders, and together we hurried away from the scene of the riot. I felt for the nickel in my skirt pocket.

"Let's try to catch the trolley," I said breathlessly as we made our way toward the warehouse district.

"You got money?"

"Just a nickel."

"Which one of us is going to walk home?"

"Neither. The driver's got to let us both on. You've been hurt."

I felt Simon's shoulders lift as he shrugged. "You can ask him, I guess."

We had to wait only a couple of minutes at the stop before the trolley arrived. I pushed Simon ahead of me up the steps to the driver, where I held out the nickel in the palm of my hand. I felt like Oliver Twist as I pleaded, "Please, sir, I only have a nickel, but my brother's been hurt and I want to get him home. My father is Dr.

William Eide, and he's good for the other nickel."

The motorman was a huge fellow with a full-moon face and a thick neck that bulged out over the back of his sweat-soaked collar. He gazed at the pitiful picture Simon and I made and said kindly, "Keep your nickel, little lady, and you and your brother have a seat. I'll take you where you need to go."

I was tempted to throw my arms around his thick neck, so sorely did I need that bit of human kindness at that moment. His words caused a fresh batch of tears to well up in my eyes, and I could scarcely catch my breath to thank the man. He nodded toward the seats and said, "Go on, now. I've a schedule to keep, and the sooner we get the lad home the better."

Simon and I turned and started down the aisle, realizing for the first time that we were not alone on the trolley and must appear as quite a spectacle to the half-dozen or so passengers who stared at us quizzically. Only one man, absorbed in his newspaper, seemed not to notice the wounded, half-naked boy and the weepy girl who accompanied him. I sniffed loudly and slid into an empty seat. Simon sat down beside me. The curious eyes pressed heavily on my back, and my face burned in anger and humiliation. Yes, I was crying, and yes, I had begged the driver for a ride, but didn't these people know what was happening only blocks away? How dare they complacently go about their business while men were being beaten and killed in the streets. What right had they to stare at *me* as though I were the strange one!

Simon seemed not to care about our fellow passengers. He sat indifferently nursing his wound, but I cried quietly all the way home, wiping my eyes and nose with the back of one hand.

Just before our stop, Simon mumbled, "We're going to catch trouble from Mama, Ginny."

I sniffed and replied vaguely, "I don't care." Suddenly Mother's wrath appeared amazingly mild compared with the violence I'd just seen.

"We shouldn't have gone," he continued, shaking his head slowly. "We shouldn't have done it."

Maybe not, but we *had* gone, and there was no covering up that fact now.

"I wish they hadn't busted my glasses," Simon continued. "Everything's blurry without them."

"Papa'll get you a new pair." I sniffed loudly, then asked, "How's your head feel?"

"Hurts some. But I think the bleeding's stopped."

"Maybe you'll have a scar like Uncle Jim."

"Maybe. If I'm lucky."

When we reached our stop a couple blocks from home, we again thanked the driver. He said, "Have your father clean that wound with a little peroxide. That oughta take care of it." A paternal smile lighting his round face, he patted Simon's shoulder with his doughy hand before we exited the trolley.

Simon and I approached the house with a sense of foreboding, not for ourselves, but for Aunt Sally — because of what we had to tell her. We found her and Mother, as we expected, seated in front of the radio, listening for bulletins about the riot. When we arrived, a daytime drama was playing and the radio's volume was turned down low. Aunt Sally was sitting in the rocking chair with a linen handkerchief pressed to her forehead. When she saw us, she gasped and her face blanched even paler than it already was.

Mother jumped up from the couch, crying, "Simon! What happened to you?" She rushed to Simon, and lifting his chin with one hand, she removed the strip of my petticoat from his forehead. Gazing at the wound, she asked, "How did this happen? And where on earth is your shirt?"

"I was hit with a rock, Mama," Simon

explained. "It smashed my glasses to bits." He held up the shattered spectacles for Mother to see.

"A rock? On your way to the drugstore?"

"No, ma'am."

Aunt Sally interrupted, "Where are Rufus and Luke? Lillian said you four went out together."

"They didn't come back with us, Aunt Sally," I confessed reluctantly.

"Then where are they?"

I looked hesitantly from my aunt to my mother. I didn't want to admit where we had been — where my cousins *were* — but as I had already realized on the trolley, it couldn't be avoided.

Mother, impatient with my hesitation, insisted, "Speak up, Virginia. Tell us what's happened. Then I want to get Simon cleaned up. Of course, your father isn't here to tend to this cut. He always seems to be absent at the worst possible moments."

"Where is Papa, Mama?" I asked.

"Harold got called down to the strike hospital about an hour ago, and your father decided to go with him. The reports have been that there's a bad riot going on down at the grain mill, the worst yet."

Simon nodded his head and replied sheepishly, "We were there. We saw it."

Aunt Sally gave a brief anguished cry

and held her handkerchief up to her open mouth. Mother's face grew stormy with anger and concern. "What do you mean, you were there? Didn't you tell me you were going to the drugstore for a soda?"

My heart beat rapidly and my palms grew sweaty. "Rufus and Luke wanted to go to the grain mill," I explained, trying at least to pass some of the blame along to my cousins, where I thought it properly belonged. "They wanted to see the picket line."

"Dear God in heaven!" Mother cried. "Have you completely lost your senses? There've been reports of gunfire. Don't you know you could have been killed!"

Aunt Sally leaned forward in the rocking chair and asked anxiously, "Is that where the boys are now?"

"Yes, Aunt Sally."

Before I could add more, Simon volunteered the dreaded information. "We saw Uncle Jim handcuffed. Two policemen were beating him and they handcuffed him. Rufus went out to try and help him."

"Rufus —" Aunt Sally started. She stopped and looked up at Mother in disbelief, then patted her upper lip with the cloth she clutched in her hand. "Rufus went out into the fighting?" she asked hesitantly, as though afraid of the answer.

Simon and I nodded in unison. "We

couldn't stop him," I explained.

"And Luke?"

"He stayed in the alley — we were watching the riot from an alley across the way," said Simon. "We tried to get him to come home with us, but he wouldn't come."

"I made him promise to stay put, though, and not go out into the street," I said, hoping to bring some comfort to my aunt. I don't think I was successful.

Aunt Sally's lips moved but no words came out. She slumped back in the chair, shut her eyes, and held her hands over her heart. In a moment, two tears slid out from beneath the closed lids and slithered down her face. "Oh, Lillian!" she moaned.

Mother left Simon to take her sister's limp hand. "It'll be all right, Sally," Mother said. "It sounds like Jim's been arrested. That means he's out of the fight. I guess he'll be taken to jail, but at least he'll be safer there than on the picket line."

"Yes, I suppose you're right," Aunt Sally agreed. "But, Rufus —" A sob clutched her chest. Her shoulders heaved forward as she gave in to it. "They said on the radio three men are dead already —"

I saw in my mind the man who was surprised by the bullet, how he looked as though he'd only received a bit of news he couldn't quite believe, and how he dropped to his knees and spent the last moments of his life trying to make sense of the blood oozing from the wound in his chest.

Mother patted her sister's hand and sighed. "We can pray, Sally. Rufus was foolish to do what he did, but we can pray for his safety."

Aunt Sally took a deep breath and held it as if she were trying to breathe in courage from the air around her. She let it out slowly, then whispered, "All right, Lillian. All right. I'll try to pray."

After a quiet moment, Mother said, "Virginia, you stay here with Aunt Sally while I take care of Simon."

She crossed the room to Simon, and I sat down obediently on the end of the couch near Aunt Sally's rocking chair. Just before Mother and Simon stepped out into the hall, Aunt Sally, trying bravely to smile, asked, "What *did* happen to your shirt, Simon?"

But before my brother could explain, I spoke up in his defense. "There was a man lying hurt in the street not far from us. Rufus and Simon pulled him up to the sidewalk. A policeman had hit him in the head and he was bleeding, so Simon took off his shirt and wrapped it around the man's head like a bandage."

Aunt Sally nodded in satisfaction. "Well, you're your father's son, aren't you, Simon?"

Simon beamed and smiled broadly. Mother, her arm around Simon's shoulder, seemed less impressed. Her only response was to say, "I hate to think of what you children saw down there."

She disappeared with Simon into Papa's office. Aunt Sally and I sat in silence, waiting for news. My aunt stared tensely at the radio while I peered at her from the corner of my eye. Her face remained ashen and even her lips were white, and I could see the pulse thumping in the hollow of her slender neck. The clock on top of the piano continued to tick away the minutes above the sheet music that Simon and I had tried to play together only a few hours before, when we were young.

With the waves of reinforcements that came in on both sides, the riot lasted more than four hours and was finally quelled only when the governor called in the National Guard. It had been a slaughter in the streets. The last numbers we heard that night were eight dead and more than five hundred wounded. Among the fatalities were five mill workers, two policemen, and one deputy sheriff. The latter was a man who had been deputized only the day before. His actual vocation was that of selling life insurance. A young man, he left behind a wife and two small children.

It was well after midnight when Papa and Dr. Hal returned from the strike hospital, bringing Luke with them. Luke had made his way to strike headquarters by following the cars that were hauling away the wounded picketers. He knew Dr. Hal would be there and could eventually give him a lift home.

Mother, Aunt Sally, Simon, and I were still in the parlor, our tense vigil having been interrupted only long enough to eat a bite of dinner and put Claudia and Molly to bed. Simon, who hadn't wanted to go to his own room, was asleep on the couch with his bandaged head resting on Mother's lap. Aunt Sally sat in the rocking chair, fanning herself with one of the funeral parlor fans while staring intently at an invisible spot on the wall. I was curled up in one of the wing chairs, drowsy but avoiding sleep, fearing the dreams that might come when I shut my eyes.

Neither my mother nor my aunt had asked me to go into detail of what I'd seen at the grain mill, and I didn't want to tell them. If I had had to put it into words, if I had had to say, "I saw a man die," then I could no longer deny the reality of it. The death would become fact, and I couldn't pretend that it wasn't so. And it was just too awful to believe.

Mother allowed me to stay up with her

and Aunt Sally, knowing instinctively that I needed to be near them. We had turned off the radio a couple of hours earlier. Mother was reading aloud from the Psalms while Aunt Sally and I listened. At least I tried to listen, but I found it difficult to concentrate on the words. The scenes from that afternoon kept wanting to replay themselves in my mind, and I had to consciously push them away.

Only when we heard the faint crunching of the Buick's tires over the gravel in the alley did Mother abruptly stop reading and Aunt Sally turn her eyes from the spot on the wall.

"They're home," Mother announced mildly, as though they were returning from an ordinary house call. She closed the Bible and put it aside, then lifted Simon's head gently from her lap and slipped out from beneath his sleeping form.

Aunt Sally jumped up from the chair and left it momentarily rocking without her. Still clutching her tear-moistened handkerchief to her heart, she rushed across the parlor toward the kitchen, with Mother and me following.

"Oh, Luke! Thank God!" I heard Aunt Sally exclaim in the next moment, and when I got to the kitchen, she was down on her knees with her arms about her youngest child. She was crying again, and her shoulders shivered as she sobbed.

"Aw, I'm all right, Ma," Luke assured her. "You don't have to cry." His hair stuck up in all directions, and his eyes had the glassy look of interrupted sleep. One side of his overalls was undone, and the bib hung lopsided in front while the strap trailed him like a tail.

Aunt Sally continued to cling to Luke as she looked up at Papa and Dr. Hal. Both men appeared heavy with fatigue. Their faces sagged under the weight of overwork. I'd never seen Dr. Hal look so middle-aged, nor Papa so old. Funny, you could leave the house one age and only a short time later come back another.

"Where's Rufus?" Aunt Sally asked anxiously.

"He's all right, Sally," Papa said softly.

"But where —"

"He was asleep on one of the cots at the strike hospital by the time we left, so we decided to just let him be. Harold will go down in the morning and bring him home."

"But is he hurt?"

Dr. Hal shook his head. "Nothing serious. Just some cuts and bruises. Worst thing is a bump on the back of his head. Must have been a billy club that knocked him out, but there was so much going on at once that he's not sure exactly what hit him. By the time he was brought to us at the strike hospital, though, he was talking and coherent and aching to go back out into the fight." Dr. Hal let go a little sniff of a chuckle. "Of course we didn't let him go, and finally he gave up and fell asleep. He was one of the lucky ones — lucky he wasn't hurt bad and lucky he didn't get arrested."

"But what could he have been thinking to go out there in the middle of a riot . . . ?" Her voice trailed off. Still on her knees, she looked at Luke.

"They were beating up on Pa," Luke explained. "You couldn't expect Rufus to just stand by and watch, could ya?"

Aunt Sally dropped her head. "Oh, Rufus," she whispered.

Mother, ever practical, stood at the pantry door tying on her apron. "You men must be starving," she said. "Sit down and let me fix you something to eat."

"I'm starving too, Aunt Lillian!" Luke cried, pulling away from his mother's grasp.

"I figured as much. Go on and have a seat. It won't be a moment." While Mother pulled three plates out of the cupboard, Papa and Dr. Hal seated themselves wearily at the table, dropping their medical bags on the floor beside them. Papa briefly rubbed his forehead with both hands, then acknowledging my presence for the first time, he smiled up at me. I stood shyly against one wall, not quite sure I belonged in this group but wanting to. Wanting, most of all, simply to be in the same room as Papa.

Luke scrambled into a chair, and Aunt Sally sat down at the table beside him. Tentatively, her words almost a whisper, she asked the question that was on all of our minds but we dreaded to ask. "Any word about Jim?"

Dr. Hal sighed. "He wasn't at the strike hospital. Word has it he was taken to jail."

"A lot of men were arrested today," Papa added. "Those jail cells are going to be plenty crowded tonight. They'll probably be taking the overflow to the next town, maybe even to the town after that."

Mother set heaping plates of cold chicken, potato salad, and homemade bread on the table, following those with three large glasses of lemonade. Luke and Dr. Hal ate hungrily. Papa picked at the food and chewed thoughtfully.

"I'm surprised you didn't have to stay down there all night," Mother stated.

"Well, Dr. Wilson and all four nurses are still there. And of course the worst cases were farmed out to the hospitals — every hospital in the city is packed to the gills about now," Papa explained. "The strike hospital isn't set up to do complicated surgery, and a good number of men needed bullets removed."

"Will did take out one bullet," Dr. Hal interjected. "Rex Atwater caught one in the shoulder. He refused to leave headquarters, though. He knew he'd be arrested if he did."

"How is he?" Mother asked.

"As well as can be expected, I think," replied Papa. "He's as stubborn as a mule, that one. He wouldn't even accept chloroform. Said he needed to stay alert, so I had to operate without —" He looked up at me again and interrupted himself. He didn't like to go into too many details about his work when his children were around. "Well," he continued, stabbing his fork into a piece of potato, "there's always the risk of infection, but my instinct tells me he'll pull through without complications."

Aunt Sally's voice held a hint of anger when she commented, "I hope that Rex Atwater isn't married. That's all I have to say about him. And if he is, God help his wife."

Dr. Hal chewed and spoke at the same time, one cheek bulging with food. "We were plenty busy, though, I'll say that — even with the number that were sent to hospitals. We left dozens of men sleeping on the floor of the warehouse because there weren't enough cots to go around.

"There's been an injunction issued against picketing, you probably heard," he continued, glancing up at Mother and Aunt Sally. "So it looks like there won't be a picket line tomorrow. But even if there weren't an injunction, I don't think there's enough men able to stand upright to keep the strike going."

"Nevertheless, Rex is determined to keep it going," Papa countered. "Though in my estimation, the mill workers are beat."

"I hope it's over," Aunt Sally said quietly. "Even if the workers lost, I just hope they decide to call off the strike."

Silence settled over the kitchen, broken several minutes later when Simon staggered drowsily into the room, rubbing his eyes and yawning. "Hi, Papa!" he said when he saw our father sitting at the table.

Papa held out a hand and beckoned him over. "Come here and let me see that cut."

"Did Luke tell you —"

"He said you had a little mishap with a rock."

"My glasses got broken, Pa."

Papa lifted the bandage on Simon's forehead and inspected the wound beneath. "Well, it's not deep," he determined. "It looks like your mother cleaned it well. As for the glasses, we'll get you down to the optician tomorrow and have another pair made." Papa patted Simon on the shoulder. But then he looked at my brother sternly, or as sternly as Papa could, and said, "You were wrong to be down there, Simon. You know that, don't you?"

Simon nodded dolefully. "Yes, Papa."

My father looked up at me to include me in his reprimand. "You too, Ginny."

"Yes, Papa," I said. The scene before me started to swim as my eyes glazed over with tears. I thought I had used them all up, but I was wrong.

"You too, Luke," Aunt Sally added. "You know the grain mill was off limits to you and Rufus."

Luke, his mouth full of chicken, mumbled, "Yes, Ma."

"It was very wrong to tell your mother you were going one place," Papa scolded, "then go to another place where you had no right to be."

Luke must have told him about our scheme, perhaps trying to place most of the blame on me as I had done to him and Rufus.

Papa continued. "I'm very disappointed in both of you that you'd conspire to lie and disobey us."

Nothing cut me to the quick more keenly than to disappoint Papa. I promised myself in that moment that I would try never to do anything wrong again.

"I have a feeling that just as virtue is its own reward, this evil has been its own punishment. You're no doubt sorry you went down to the grain mill today, after all that's happened."

The tears coursed freely down my cheeks. "Yes, Papa," I said, with Simon echoing my words.

"And I can trust you not to do any such thing again." It wasn't a question; it was a statement.

"Oh yes, Papa," we agreed.

Our father nodded, satisfied, though I had an idea Mother was mulling over the possibility of some additional punishment. I would accept gladly whatever punishment she doled out, hoping it would help to wipe out the memory of what I'd seen.

"Why don't you children go on to bed now," Papa ordered quietly. "It's been a difficult day for all of us, and we need our rest. Time to dry those tears now, Ginny. A person can't sleep and cry at the same time."

I was a little embarrassed to be crying in front of everyone. I sniffed loudly and wiped the tears off my cheeks with both hands.

Luke didn't help me feel any better when he said, "Aw, you know how girls are. She's been bawling all day."

"That's enough, Luke," Aunt Sally intervened. "Time for you to get into bed, too."

My cousin rose from the table, carrying a chicken leg away with him. He and Simon and I said good-night and gave kisses all around, even to Dr. Hal, as that night it seemed somehow appropriate. As we turned to go, Simon suddenly said, "Oh! There was a man with a shirt around his head —"

Dr. Hal chuckled and wiped his mouth with a napkin. "Was that your shirt, Simon?" My brother nodded. "We wondered how a boy's shirt got around that man's head, didn't we, Will?"

"Did you see him, then?" Simon asked anxiously.

"Yup. He's asleep down at the strike hospital right now," Dr. Hal said.

"I wanted to help him. . . ."

Papa smiled. "You no doubt helped to stop the bleeding. That was an important first step in saving his life."

Dr. Hal winked at Simon from across the table. "Good job, Dr. Simon," he said.

Simon, smiling broadly, stood basking in the glow of the older men's praise until Mother brought him back to earth by saying, "That still doesn't make it right, though — your being where you didn't belong. Off to bed now, all of you."

As we left the kitchen, I heard Aunt

Sally ask, "What do you think will become of Jim?"

But I didn't hear the answer, if anybody had one to give.

I was exhausted in body and soul but was still awake a few hours later when Papa came into the study for "the first order of the day."

I think I startled him when I said, "Papa?"

He turned from his desk to peer at me though the dimness of the room. "You awake, Ginny?"

"Yes."

"Can't sleep?"

"No."

"Still thinking about things?"

"I guess so."

"Would you like me to fix you some warm milk?"

The thought made my stomach turn. "No thanks, Papa."

"Well, try to get a little sleep."

Papa turned back to his Bible and I lay quietly a moment, unwilling to close my eyes. I had been thinking about the man who was shot, and that Simon might have been hit by a bullet instead of a rock, and that I myself might have been downed by stray gunfire. It was the first time in my short life that I actually realized my own

423

mortality — and the mortality of those I loved.

"Papa," I asked, "does it hurt to die?"

My father turned back around to look at me, chuckling and frowning at the same time as though not quite sure how to react to such a question. He laced his fingers together and rested his hands over the back of the chair. "Well, that depends," he said. "Sometimes death is painful, but other times — most often, I think — people just kind of drift away peacefully."

I remembered that Grandfather Eide had simply fallen asleep one night and never awakened. How different a death from the man I'd seen gunned down in the street. Still, either way, it was a frightening prospect. "Are you afraid to die, Papa?" I asked.

Papa took a deep breath and let the air out slowly. "I'm in no hurry to leave you and your mother and all the people I love — but, no, I wouldn't say I'm afraid, exactly. I know where I'm going."

"You'll climb the sunbeam up to heaven?"

"Well —" Papa paused to smile. "I don't know for certain how I'll get there. I only know that's where I'll end up."

I pursed my lips and thought a moment. My eyes wandered to the window. The last darkness of the night was fading as morning began to rise. "Sometimes," I said, "it's hard to believe there's really such a place, and that we'll ever be there."

"As strange as earth might seem to someone not yet born," replied Papa. "But when we wake up in heaven, it will seem just as natural and familiar as waking up right here at home. Maybe more so, since that's where we really belong."

"Do you think so, Papa? Do you think it will all be familiar when we get there?"

"Yes, I think so."

"But still, I'm glad to be here with you and Mama and Simon and Claudia and Molly."

"I am, too."

"And I hope everything gets back to the way it was . . . before the strike and everything."

"Things will be better soon."

"And I hope Mama's bad feeling about Soo City goes away."

"Well, maybe if we could convince your mother to come to Soo City with us sometime, she'd see there's nothing to be afraid of."

"She'd never come."

"Maybe not. Still, none of us needs to spend time fretting over things that haven't even happened. And now, young lady, you need to shut your eyes and try to get some sleep."

"All right, Papa. I'll try."

"Sleep well, then, Ginny."

He turned toward the desk, adjusted the small lamp, and leaned over the open pages of the book. I gazed at his beloved figure across the room, wishing there was no other place than here, and no time other than this very moment.

Chapter Twenty

Aunt Sally always said things happen in threes. If she broke one drinking glass, she was bound to break two more. If she pricked herself on her sewing needle while darning a sock, she was destined to suffer two additional wounds before the stitching was done. If she was gripped by a sneeze that left her ears ringing, two more explosive sneezes were sure to follow.

While it was a rule that even Aunt Sally admitted had its occasional exceptions, it did seem to apply when it came to the men in our family getting whacked on the head. First Uncle Jim had that patch of railroad track laid across his brow when his head collided with a billy club and Dr. Hal had to stitch up the wound. Then my brother Simon stepped into the path of a flying rock that left him with a pretty cut on the side of his forehead. Finally, cousin Rufus, in the midst of the riot, took a thump from an unseen assailant that raised a plum-sized knot on the back of his scalp. That thump also left him unconscious, and like Dr. Hal said, it was lucky he was rescued by the mill workers and carried off to the strike hospital rather than handcuffed by the police and hauled off to jail.

So that was three, and according to Aunt Sally's reasoning, I figured we were done with the whole mess and life would return to normal. It certainly seemed so, anyway. The only person unable to accept the fact that the mill workers were beat and the strike a lost cause was Rex Atwater. As stubborn as the proverbial mule, he refused to surrender even after the governor instituted martial law and continued to oversee the strike machine from his bed in the warehouse hospital. There were a number of mill workers who remained loyal to him. While Mr. Atwater and the union lawyer tried to get the injunction against picketing repealed, some of the men got around it by invoking their constitutional right to peaceable assembly. They showed up in front of the mill gates without signs and simply stood there, sometimes singing, sometimes talking quietly among themselves, deftly ignoring the National Guardsmen who patrolled our city streets with rifles and machine guns. In this way, the strike limped on for another week, but it was only a token demonstration. Thiel had no reason to pay attention to the men who continued to demand a union. His mill was running just fine without the men and without the union.

The mill was operating normally with a

force made up partly of scabs and partly of former workers who had given up and returned to their jobs beyond the gates. Thiel, true to his word for once, accepted back all who wanted to return — at the same hours and wages as before the strike. When the former workers went in, word got out that Thiel had built up his work force during the strike by smuggling men in on the same trains that hauled in the grain.

"It was really so simple," Dr. Hal said when he learned of Thiel's scheme. "I can't believe I didn't think of that." Dr. Hal was still putting in time at the strike hospital, following up on the men as they recuperated after the final riot. It was there he learned about what was happening behind the scenes while the strikers were marching in front of the gates. "The scabs," he explained to us later, "that Thiel recruited to cross the picket line were only a front. It didn't really matter whether they got through the line or not, since Thiel was bringing the real workers in on the trains. Those scabs were brought around to the picket line just to get the strikers rioting. That was their whole job, and they were paid pretty well to do it."

"But those men, those scabs, didn't they know they might get hurt? Killed, even?" I asked, appalled. After all, I had seen firsthand what happened when they tried to cross the line.

"Sure they did," Dr. Hal replied. "But they figured a little money in their pockets was worth a beating."

"But why, Dr. Hal?" I asked. "Why did Mr. Thiel want to start those riots?"

"Because, Ginny, rioting means men will be wounded and men will be arrested, and the more men out of the way, the less men on the picket line. That way, Thiel figured, he could undermine the strike. And he figured right."

On the evening of Friday, September 9, the strike finally ended with one last gasp and a long drawn-out sigh when several hundred National Guardsmen, a battery of light artillery, and a detachment of machine gunners surrounded the warehouse that served as strike headquarters. The military stayed outside while their colonel went in to meet with Rex Atwater and the other union organizers. The colonel asked that the warehouse be evacuated without resistance. Finally admitting defeat, the strike leaders — including Rex Atwater — allowed themselves to be taken into custody while the remaining mill workers, members of the women's auxiliary, and other strike sympathizers who happened to be there at the time broke rank and drifted off in various directions. After that, the city settled back into normalcy, and martial law was repealed.

Some of the mill workers who stuck with Rex Atwater till the very end simply returned to their old jobs after his arrest. Others left the city in search of better opportunities elsewhere, though their prospects were questionable. Rumor had it that a few, disillusioned with capitalism after Thiel's victory, pledged allegiance to the Communist Party and devoted the rest of their lives to the revolution that never came.

Uncle Jim and the others who had been arrested languished in jail because there was no money left in the strike coffers to bail them out. Again the rumor mill, working overtime, had it that the men would be slapped with long prison sentences. But we read in the newspapers that a trio of lawyers from the Grain Millers Union was pleading with the governor for leniency. Chances were good that our farmer-labor governor, thinking ahead to the next election, would comply. It was men like those awaiting trial who would be voting him back into office.

While waiting for the trial date to be set, Aunt Sally insisted I move back into my own bedroom.

"Nonsense," Mother said. The three of us were in the kitchen canning tomatoes when my aunt offered me my room. "Where else will you sleep, Sally?"

"I'll sleep on the couch in Will's study, where Ginny's sleeping now," Aunt Sally replied firmly.

"You won't be comfortable there," Mother argued.

"I can't sleep in that bed without Jim. Really, I prefer the couch."

My heart gave a little leap for joy. I'd have my room back, my own place. I could sleep in my own bed and move my two Charlies back to the dresser mirror and again see the morning sun coming in through the windows.

"Well, if that's really what you want," Mother conceded, "then all right. But you'll move back into Ginny's room when Jim comes home."

Aunt Sally sighed as she wearily peeled tomatoes. "Who knows when that will be," she said quietly. And she was right. None of us knew.

School started the following week, and while Charlotte and I walked to the school yard that first morning — I in my old shoes but wearing a new dress of my own making — I realized as I began my eighth year of education that I wasn't dreading the start of classes as I once had. Always before, even with the regimented schedule Mother imposed upon her children, summers had been a magical time and I hated to see them end. It was with great reluctance that I would bid farewell to the warm sunny days, to the exhilarating sense of freedom that came when I awoke and knew the whole day would be spent right there at home, away from school and lectures and tests and all the annoying social intricacies of cliques and, even at our young age, the wearisome rap-tap-tapping of the pecking order. At school, a person was always having to prove herself: her intelligence, her athletic ability, her social graces. But at home a person could just relax and be herself because there was nothing to prove. She was accepted just because she had been born and she was family.

But this summer everything had been different. Not the family, really, but things in the wider circle of life. Just as the sun, once a warm friend, had nearly crushed us with the full strength of its heat, the economy, once a prosperous ally, had trapped the country in its still crumbling structure and nearly left us all flattened in the dirt. I had seen those most affected by the times — the hungry down-and-outers in the soup line; the men and the families in Soo City; the mill workers rioting outside the gates in a bid for higher wages and shorter working hours. I had seen a man die, shot in the back by one whose job in former days had been to protect him.

No, it had been no ordinary summer, and though I knew I would continue to visit Soo City at times with Papa, I was content to put the summer behind me and move forward. I could not pretend that none of it had happened. It had happened, all right, and the country and our city and my family — and I — would never quite be the same. We had all of us felt the heel of the Depression's boot pressing down on us. But I for one was ready to piece together the thread of my life that had been snipped in two by the summer, ready to go back to the place I had been before the summer began. I thought that in school, in the midst of the books, the chalk dust, the wooden desks with the names carved into the tops, I could regain a sense of order and well-being. Unlike other years, I was surprisingly ready to turn my attention to my studies, to my school friends, and of course — for hope springs eternal in the human heart — to the pursuit of romance in whatever adolescent forms it might appear.

I could not, however, continue to allow myself to be sweet on Danny Dysinger. His father was my uncle's enemy, and I had no business hoping for any sort of alliance, however innocent, with such a one as he. Already I had replaced him as prospect number three when Charlotte and I spun the globe. Should I pull number three from the jewelry box, I'd be honeymooning instead with Buster Keaton, at least until I could set my sights on some other boy at school. And if Danny tried to flirt with me between classes — and I was smugly certain that he would now that my hair was bobbed — I would simply have to stick up my nose and walk away.

As it turned out, I needn't have come up with any such resolve. On the first day of school (and for many days afterward) Danny Dysinger paid no attention to me at all. He seemed to have forgotten we had shared a box lunch during the fund-raiser for the Lower Street Mission. I was secretly hurt that he would forget so easily and angry that I didn't have the opportunity to rebuff his advances. He left me with no means of dignity at all. I could only stare at him from across the room, feeling on the one hand as traitorous as Juliet in love with a member of the opposing tribe, and on the other hand as undesirable as Leah, whose husband, Jacob, threw fits of disgust when he discovered he'd been tricked into marrying her.

After school that first day, I went home with Charlotte to do the globe and talk about the boys in our class. She had gained no more encouragement from Mitchell

Quakenbush than I had from Danny Dysinger.

"Like Mama says," Charlotte explained in a huff, "men are fickle. One day they tell you they love you, and the next they can't even remember your name."

Not that Mitchell Quakenbush had ever told Charlotte he loved her. As far as I knew, he had never paid Charlotte any attention at all — hadn't even shared her box lunch at the fund-raiser. But our imaginations were fertile in those days, and sometimes we confused our dreams with reality.

"Well, let's spin the globe," Charlotte suggested.

We spun and found ourselves transported to the far corners of the earth with men who could do nothing less than pledge eternal devotion. My finger landed on Tahiti (or close enough) and from the jewelry box I pulled number three. For the first time I found myself honeymooning with my substitute for Danny — Buster Keaton. Charlotte sailed off to the Mediterranean with Eddie Tolan, the Olympic runner to whom she'd lately taken a fancy.

We sighed contentedly and began to rummage through the shoe box of cosmetics. We powdered our faces and darkened our eyelashes and rubbed lipstick over our lips, and suddenly, right in the middle of everything, I was struck by the overwhelming sense of the unreality of this game of make-believe in which I found myself a willing participant. I was playing the game because I had my whole future ahead of me, and I had the youth and the adolescent mind-set to believe that my life should unfold just as I desired. But I had spent a whole summer pining over Danny Dysinger only to have it come to nothing. And now I suddenly could see that dreams are dreams and life is life, and that only too often the two bear little resemblance.

The hand that held the tube of color to my lips paused in midair. "Charlotte," I said quietly, "do you think it'll ever really happen?"

My friend must have been preoccupied with thoughts of sailing the Mediterranean, for it took her a moment to respond. "What?" she finally asked, reluctant to be pulled away from her visions. "Do I think *what* will ever happen?"

"You know, the traveling, the excitement, the romance. Do you think it'll ever really happen?"

"It better happen," Charlotte stated firmly, "or I'm going to kill myself."

But I think that was the moment my one foot, still caught in childhood, made a definitive move over the line toward adulthood, because it was then I began to realize that life might very well turn out to be quite different from our dreams, and that happiness, too, might be something completely other than what we had always imagined it to be.

Chapter Twenty-One

"Papa?"

"Hmm? Yes, Ginny?"

"What *is* going to happen to Uncle Jim and Mr. Atwater and all those other men in jail?"

Papa drove with his left elbow out the window. He glanced into the rearview mirror, then stretched his left arm straight out to let the driver behind us know we were turning. After a summer of such signaling, Papa's left arm was considerably darker than his right.

When we'd made the turn, Papa said, "I can't say for sure, of course, but chances are some of them will serve prison sentences."

"But why, Papa?"

"Because rioting is a criminal offence. It's against the law. What makes it worse is that a couple of police and a deputy sheriff were killed."

"But so were five mill workers — no, six! One was killed in the first riot, remember?" Papa nodded. I continued. "Will the police who killed them go to prison, too?"

"No, they won't go to prison. That's not considered murder, Ginny. The lawmen were only doing their job."

"But that's not fair, Papa."

"Well, it certainly doesn't seem fair, does it?"

We were quiet for a moment. Then I asked, "Do you think Uncle Jim is one who'll serve a prison sentence?"

"I can't say for sure," Papa repeated. "The union lawyers are working pretty hard on behalf of all the men in jail. It may be that they'll persuade Governor Borgmann to be lenient. We can hope so, anyway."

Uncle Jim had been locked up for three weeks now, and it seemed strange to have a relative behind bars. Jail was for criminals, and Jim Dubbin wasn't a criminal — no matter what the law said about rioting. Rioting hadn't been his intention. He had wanted only to make a better life for himself and for other working men. But somehow the plan had taken a turn for the worse, and Uncle Jim ended up where he didn't belong.

We all missed him, but we didn't talk about him much. It was too painful. It was almost as if by not talking about him, we could pretend he wasn't in jail, that he'd be coming home anytime now, that he'd walk through the front door with those great strides of his just as he used to.

The grown-ups visited him in jail, but

Uncle Jim didn't want us children to see him there. Trying to remain optimistic, he said he'd see us when he got home. Aunt Sally always returned from these visits looking sad and wistful, but instead of talking about her husband, she'd say something like, "I wish Jimmy Jr. were here. Do you suppose he knows how much we miss him?"

It was a Saturday afternoon near the end of September, and Papa and I were on our way to Soo City. Mother still didn't approve of our visiting the shantytown but relented without too much fuss whenever Papa said I was going with him. I think she still had her bad feeling, but I didn't hear her say as much. Before I could leave the house, though, I had to have my homework done, my piano practicing finished, and my chores completed. I had had a busy morning, but I didn't mind. I read my English lesson and figured my math problems at my own desk in my own room, where — curtains drawn back and windows thrown open wide — I paused occasionally to look for angels on the sunbeams slanting in. I'd seen none, and yet I wasn't disappointed. They must be here, I thought, because life was peaceful again. The strike was over. Uncle Jim was in jail, but I tried to look at the bright side even of that. It was better than being dead. Aunt Sally, though still concerned about Uncle Jim's future, had stopped crying. The radio no longer played endlessly while we gathered anxiously about it, fanning ourselves with funeral parlor fans. Life had regained its composure, had evened out to a more easily navigable flow.

Though I still saw the dying man in my dreams, I had gotten over some of the horror by recounting the event in detail to Charlotte. She was the only one, besides Simon and my cousins, who knew that I'd seen a man shot to death. Mother, Papa, and Aunt Sally had never asked about the riot — maybe they'd been afraid to ask. If the boys ever spoke of it to them, I wasn't a part of the conversation. And yet I needed to tell someone about the shooting, so I poured the scene into the listening ear of my friend. She was sympathetic and, needless to say, more than a little envious.

"Wow, Virginia," she had said admiringly, "you've — well, you've *lived!*"

As we made our way to the shantytown, Papa whistled against the wind, cooler now that summer had passed. As usual, he whistled Christmas tunes, and even though we were no longer at the height of the summer heat, the notes of "The First Noel" still seemed out of place against the early autumn landscape. The trees were just beginning to succumb to fall colors —

here, a hint of red, there, of yellow — and the first few leaves had begun spiraling to the ground. Each evening when dusk settled in we relished the refreshing night breezes, the forerunner of a colder season. It wasn't here yet, but the world hinted at its coming.

In the backseat of the car lay six wool blankets, neatly folded. It wouldn't be long now before the folks in Soo City would need to wrap themselves up against the frigid weather. Whenever I went to the camp, I handed out as many coverings as I could. Still, as men and even entire families came and went, there always seemed to be someone else who needed a blanket before winter.

Listening to Papa whistle, I let my mind wander and found it going around in circles from the riot, to school, to Danny Dysinger, to Charlotte, and back to the riot again. I wondered what Uncle Jim was doing to pass the time behind bars, and I wondered whether Mr. Atwater was sorry he hadn't become a shoe salesman or a railroad conductor or something equally as routine and safe.

"Papa?"

The whistling stopped. "Yes, Ginny?"

"Why does Mr. Atwater keep trying to organize unions when he just gets beat up and shot and arrested?"

A little smile of amusement formed on Papa's lips. "Well, because he's doing something he believes in. I'm sure he finds a certain satisfaction in it."

"But he could get killed one of these days if he keeps getting shot at."

"There's always that possibility, I suppose."

Papa parked the car in our usual spot on the outskirts of Soo City. Before we got out, I remarked, "I don't think unions are worth getting killed over."

"It's all in how you see it, Ginny. To Mr. Atwater, it would probably be worth it. You see, it's not the unions that are so important to him, but the men who make up the unions. Mr. Atwater is making sacrifices for the people he cares about."

I considered this a moment, then replied, "Still, if you ask me, I wouldn't die on purpose for anything."

"It isn't easy, but many people do. Maybe not completely on purpose, but they take the risk. Soldiers die for their country. Martyrs die for their beliefs. Union organizers die for social justice. They allow their lives to be sacrificed for what they think is a greater cause."

We got out of the car and opened the back doors on either side. I took three of the blankets in my arms — we hadn't brought the wagon this time — while Papa grabbed the other three along with his medical bag. We walked past the "Welcome to Soo City" sign. I still hadn't decided whether that sign was blasphemous or not, but over the months as I saw people come and go, I had come to appreciate their illegal dependence upon the Soo line. If they didn't hop the trains, how would they get from here to there in search of opportunity? The soles of their shoes were too thin to carry them to all the places where those great train wheels were rolling every day.

As we sauntered through the orderly squalor of the shantytown, I thought about Papa's words. "The mill workers who died in the riot — in a way they were martyrs, weren't they?"

Papa, shifting his medical bag from one hand to the other beneath the bulky blankets, said, "Not everyone would think so, but yes, they certainly died for what they believed in."

"Then maybe that's better than dying in a plain old accident or just of old age."

"The poets might hail it as more noble, I guess. Afternoon, Mrs. Hunt, Mrs. Conley," Papa said, greeting the two women who were washing dishes together outside Mrs. Hunt's shanty. Ever since Roy Conley had settled his family into the camp a short time before, Mrs. Conley and

Mrs. Hunt had become inseparable. I thought it particularly nice that Mrs. Hunt had found a friend. Now she had someone to visit with all the time.

The women greeted us, saying they were happy to see that the blanket brigade had returned. Papa asked them how their children were, and they assured him all were fine. I didn't see Lela around anywhere and was thankful for it. She and her questions had a way of making me nervous.

Papa and I walked on. "Even if it's a more noble way to die," I said, picking up the thread of our conversation, "I hope I don't ever have to be a martyr."

Papa let go a swift chuckle. "I wouldn't put that on the top of your list of worries right now," he remarked.

There were a couple of new men in the camp that Papa wanted to visit first — he'd met them earlier in the week, and one of them was suffering attacks of asthma — but before we could hunt them down, we came across Dick Mason sitting alone on a Soo City lawn chair in front of his shanty. He was reading a day-old newspaper while an unlit cigarette butt dangled listlessly from his lower lip. When he saw Papa, he folded the newspaper and waved us over. "Pull up a brick," he invited. "I've got to talk with you, Doc."

Papa put the blankets and his bag just

inside the door of Mr. Mason's shanty, then upended a couple of cinder blocks for the two of us to sit on.

Dick Mason shook Papa's hand and tipped his weathered fedora at me. "Got news for you, Doc," he began. "It may mean something, or it may mean nothing at all. I don't know. But Mr. Jones has got himself a sidekick, a fellow by the name of Ernie Armstrong. The two of them have been working overtime trying to get the men to stage a hunger strike down in front of City Hall."

Papa's eyes narrowed behind his glasses. "A hunger strike?"

"One of the missions downtown has run out of money and is no longer giving out food. That was one of the places the men were dependent on for a square meal, and last week it had to shut its doors," explained Mr. Mason. He hadn't removed the cigarette butt, and it flapped between his lips as he spoke. "Of course, there's a couple of other breadlines still moving, but the men are afraid the same thing will happen there. We all know those breadlines are depending on charity, and when all you've got between you and starvation is another man's generosity, you know you're skating on thin ice. Now Jones and Armstrong are squawking about how it's the federal government's job to take care of us, and the government's not lifting a ringed pinky on our behalf. They say Hoover would just as soon let us starve as use federal funds to feed us. Which I suppose is true — I've never been a Hoover man myself, and you can be sure I'll be backing Roosevelt in the next election. Anyway, Doc, the men are hungry. And to tell you the truth, they're more scared than ever. They're scared for themselves, and they're scared for their families."

Papa sat forward with his arms on his thighs, his fingers laced between his knees. "I don't suppose the strike down at the mill did much for their morale either."

Dick Mason shook his head and spat the butt out onto the ground. I imagined it was something he'd never done at home in front of his wife before the Depression turned him into a temporary drifter. "The men are —" He started to use an expletive, but remembering my presence, he cleared his throat and started again. "The men are plenty angry about it. Some of them were on the picket line, you know." Papa nodded. "Every man in Soo City was on the side of the strikers, and they took the loss personally. Longjohn came back from that last riot, but Ross Knutsen and George Samuelson are both behind bars. Yeah, the men are pretty sore about it all.

And for Jones and Armstrong, it's just given them more fuel for the fire. 'See how the government treats its workers,' they say. 'See where capitalism has gotten you.' "

Mr. Mason paused to fumble around in his shirt pocket for another cigarette. He didn't have a pack of them; rather, he drew out three that had already been smoked to some extent and picked out the longest one. I decided he must have picked them up off the street in town. I shivered as he lighted the tobacco with the last match in a dog-eared matchbook, imagining the dirt the man had just placed between his lips.

He continued. "If you're going to be a Red, now's the time, I guess. If I didn't know better, I'd say the time was ripe for a revolution. I don't really think it'll happen, but those who want to believe in it have got good reason. Things have never been worse for the capitalist."

Papa squeezed his fingers together, then cupped his knees with the palms of his hands. "No use worrying about a Communist takeover because it's not going to happen," he stated flatly. "Anyway, that's the larger picture. What we have to be concerned about is the smaller picture, that is, what's happening right here. What do you think the chances are, Dick, that there will be a hunger strike?"

Dick Mason took the cigarette out of his mouth and scratched his forehead with his thumbnail. "I frankly think chances are good," he confessed, "judging from the atmosphere around here lately."

"Have any definite plans been made for a strike?"

Mr. Mason shrugged his shoulders while taking a long drag of the cigarette. The smoke came out while he spoke. "I'm not sure, but I don't think so. The scary thing is, where once the men weren't willing to give Jones the time of day, now they're starting to listen to him. That's what hunger and anger will do to you. Suddenly a man doesn't have the same convictions he had when he was comfortable, and the Reds know how to take advantage of that."

Mr. Mason smoked quietly while Papa rubbed the back of his neck with a handkerchief. I rocked casually on the cinder block while watching a couple of scrawny chickens strut their way across Hoover Avenue. The lack of meat on their bones was probably what kept the birds alive. They weren't worth the effort to kill, pluck, and cook. All down Hoover Avenue, the usual group of men sat in their doorways smoking. Some, like Dick Mason, read outdated newspapers to stay in touch with a world to which they no longer belonged. Other men squatted around small fires, warming their predictable lunches of canned beans. I heard a baby cry and knew it must be Caroline Everhart. From somewhere across the dusty avenues, the sound of singing reached us. The Soo City trio was at it again. They were still waiting for the Soo line to bring them back their banjo player. So far, he hadn't shown up. In the distance a train whistle blew, and I thought, *Maybe there's the banjo player now.* One never knew.

I heard what Papa and Dick Mason were saying, but somehow it stirred up little concern on my part. Papa said there'd be no Communist takeover, and if Papa said it, then that was that. I was tired of worrying about the Communists — I was tired of worrying, period — and I just wasn't going to do it anymore. The worst was behind us now. Things were still bad in Soo City, but they were better for my family, and that was what mattered to me at this point. We'd done our bit for social injustice. The requisite number of males in my family had taken their lumps on the head, and now it was time for us to get back to enjoying life as much as possible. I admit I felt more than a little selfish, but all the anxious days beside the radio had left me worn out.

Of course, I was sorry the mission had closed and the people of Soo City had one less resource for food. That being the case, I wasn't so sure a hunger strike was a bad thing. Why shouldn't the men make a show on the steps of City Hall to let the government know they were hungry? Nothing was bound to happen otherwise, not if they just sat around here smoking cigarettes and reading yesterday's news. And just because the grain mill strike had failed didn't mean a hunger strike would fail. I wasn't on the side of the Reds, but obviously something needed to be done. If the men of Soo City chose to voice their complaints on the steps of City Hall, I'd hope for the best for them, but I didn't want to get emotionally involved. It had nothing to do with me.

Or so I thought.

Chapter Twenty-Two

For a moment I thought the sun had gone to my head and I was seeing things the way a nomad dying of thirst sees a mirage in the middle of the desert. After all, it was one of those unusually hot days in late September, and our class had already been out in the heat for more than half an hour. In another ten minutes the bell would ring to call us in from recess, but by then — if what I was seeing were in fact a figment of my own making — surely I'd be nearly prostrate with sunstroke.

I rubbed my eyes and looked again, but the vision didn't fade. Danny Dysinger, his hands in his pants pockets, was strolling purposefully across the school grounds, and he was heading in the direction of where I sat with Charlotte and two other girls. Tagging Danny like a shadow was Philip Messner, a scrawny, nasal kid who was forever trying to prove his manhood by following the bigger boys around and thrusting himself into the midst of whatever argument, debate, or fistfight they might happen to get into. Philip had been known to run half the length of the school to jump on top of two boys wrestling in the hall, just to pick up a few bruises he could wear like a medal of valor. He had a way of sniffing out the action, and if he was trailing Danny — if in fact Danny was really there — that meant something was up.

My friends and I sat on a patch of brittle grass discussing the movie *Love Is a Racket*, with Douglas Fairbanks Jr. (Even though I'd spent my allowance on the trolley to get to the grain mill, Papa later slipped me enough under the table so that I could go to the picture with Charlotte as planned.) We were debating about whether love really was a racket when Rosemary patted my knee and said, "Say, Danny Dysinger's headed this way. What do you suppose he wants?"

So it was true. Rosemary had seen it too, and now Charlotte and Jean both shielded their eyes from the sun and stared off in the direction from which came Danny Dysinger and his slightly asthmatic shadow.

Suddenly Charlotte swung around and looked at me with raised eyebrows. "He's actually going to *say* something to you, Virginia!" she whispered. "Maybe he's going to ask you out."

My resolve to no longer be sweet on Danny Dysinger was easier said than done. As he approached us, a sudden fear whirled in my chest, and I thought I might faint. The thought flashed through my mind that I'd never live it down if I fainted right there in front of everybody. I grabbed my skirt with both hands to ground myself in the conscious world and said in response to Charlotte's remark, "Oh, I don't think so. . . ." But before I could say more, Danny was there, kicking at the dry grass with the toe of one leather shoe and smiling down at us with an insincere grin.

"Having a party?" he asked, pushing his hands farther down into his pockets. "I mean, with a capital P, that is."

Philip Messner snickered and snorted, though he probably had no more idea of what Danny was talking about than we did. He aped Danny by thrusting his hands into his pockets and kicking at the ground. A tuft of grass got caught between the sole and the toe of his shoe, but he didn't notice.

I looked up longingly into Danny's face. It was difficult to believe that this good-looking boy had come from the likes of Clem Dysinger. Not a hint of the father marred the son's appearance. Where the sheriff was overweight and doughy, Danny was slender and lithe. While the sheriff's face hung heavy as a hound dog's, Danny's was sleek and narrow like a greyhound's. The sheriff was a colorless fellow, with wishy-washy hair and nondescript eyes, but

Danny's hair and brows and eyes were a deep brown, the color of maple wood that's been smoothed and polished. The features of his face were well-proportioned: wide-set eyes, narrow nose, a pleasant, inviting mouth that revealed perfect teeth when he smiled. I knew the face well; its portrait had hung on the wall of my mind for months. And now here it was in the flesh.

But the taunting look on the face that hovered above me was hardly in keeping with my dreams.

Charlotte narrowed her eyes. "What on earth are you talking about, Danny?" she asked sharply.

"Oh, don't you know?" he replied with mock politeness, the grin on his face melting into an undeniable sneer.

"Know what?" Rosemary put one small fist on her hip as a gesture of defiance.

Danny nodded down at me and stated flatly but accusingly, "Ginny's father is a Communist."

"Yeah, he's a Communist," Philip echoed. He snorted again.

My friends and I squawked in unison, I loudest of all. I jumped to my feet and clenched my hands into fists.

"What do you mean, calling my father a Communist?" I cried.

Charlotte jumped up beside me. "Start

explaining!" she yelled. My best friend's face was nearly as red as my own.

Danny Dysinger was unperturbed. He shrugged nonchalantly. "My pa says yours is a Commie. Says your uncle is, too. And Dr. Bellamy, too. He says the whole lot of you are bloodsucking Reds."

I couldn't believe what I was hearing. And coming from the boy I had spent all summer dreaming about!

"That's a lie!" I was so angry I was trembling.

Charlotte tapped on Danny's chest with two fingers. "You'd better take that back, Danny Dysinger, or you'll be sorry."

Danny laughed outright. "Whatcha gonna do, beat me up? I'm not gonna fight a girl!"

"Fight a girl!" Philip echoed. Spittle flew from his mouth as he laughed.

Rosemary and Jean were both on their feet by now, muttering threats about having older brothers who would gladly do them a favor. Danny Dysinger was only amused. "Whatcha mad at *me* for? I'm only telling it like it is."

"Yeah, he's just telling it like it is," Philip said.

Charlotte turned to the offensive follower. "Oh, you shut up, Philip Messner, you stinky little sewer rat."

"Hey —" Philip cried, but Danny quieted him with a wave of his hand.

"Don't let them bother you, Phil," Danny said. "They just can't face the truth."

"It's not the truth!" I countered. "My father is *not* a Communist!"

"Then why's he spending all his time down at that squatter's camp? He's not getting paid, is he?"

"No, but —"

"Then he's doing it because he's a Red."

"He's not! He's doing it because —" I paused, unable to continue. Why *was* Papa doing what he was doing? Why *did* he go to Soo City?

"Simply because," Papa had told me, *"it makes me happy."* Not for any noble reasons, he had said, but just because it made him happy.

But what would that mean to Danny Dysinger and his sewer rat sidekick? If I told them what Papa had said, the boys would only laugh all the harder. I finished lamely, "Just because my father goes down to the camp — well, it doesn't *mean* anything."

"My pa says it does," Danny continued. "He says those poor people ain't paying him, but maybe Moscow is."

Charlotte shrieked with feigned laughter. "Now, that's so stupid it's downright *funny.*"

458

"Nobody's paying him," I threw in. "He's just doing it."

"Nobody does something for nothing," Danny said.

"Yeah," Philip added. "I bet Moscow's paying him."

"Aw, why don't you just crawl back to where you came from?" Charlotte suggested.

"Hey —"

"It's not just what he's been doing down at the camp," Danny said, ignoring Philip's attempt at self-defense. "My pa says he was down helping out at the strike hospital too. Everyone knows the strike was started by the Reds. It said so right in the newspaper. If your pa was on the side of the strikers, he was on the side of the Reds."

It was getting more and more difficult not to swing my already clenched fist at Danny. His rejection of me was bad enough, but his spreading lies about Papa was too much. It was the worst thing he could possibly do.

I found myself screaming at the top of my lungs. "Your father's a liar!" My outburst turned heads all over the school yard, but I didn't care. Everything within me wanted to defend my father, no matter the cost.

To my continued frustration, Danny remained complacent. "My pa only calls 'em like he sees 'em," he said mildly.

"Yeah?" Charlotte said. "Well, your father's calling this one wrong. Besides, he's a rotten sheriff, and my father said he wouldn't vote for your father next election if the only other person running was Al Capone."

"Hey!" Philip whined. "You gonna let her talk about your pa like that, Danny?"

Danny once again shrugged his shoulders annoyingly. "What do I care what she thinks about my pa?" Then, looking at me, he concluded, "At least my pa's not a Red."

That did it. Though I couldn't see straight for the tears that were blurring my vision, I nevertheless swung my fist in Danny's direction only to end up sweeping the air. Danny must have seen it coming because he stepped back and held up his hands.

"Whoa!" he said. "I didn't come here to start a fight."

"Well, what *did* you come here for?" Charlotte cried. "Why don't you both just go on and leave us alone?"

As Rosemary and Jean joined Charlotte in throwing out words to defend me, I willed the tears in my eyes not to spill over onto my cheeks. But my will wasn't enough to keep the teardrops from slipping out and trickling down the side of my nose. I hastily wiped away the evidence of my humiliation — and my broken heart — and as I did I glanced in Danny's direction to convince myself that he hadn't noticed my tears. To my surprise, the mask of smugness on his face had been replaced by something very similar to concern, and Danny started to say, "Aw, Ginny, I didn't think —"

But Charlotte cut him off with a shove to the chest and the warning, "Just leave her *alone*, you big bully, or I'll make you sorry you were ever born."

Good old Charlotte. I could always count on her to stand up for me, even if it meant threatening a member of the stronger sex. I had no idea how Charlotte would make Danny sorry he'd been born, but no doubt she could pull it off somehow.

Just as my friends and I turned away from the boys, the bell called us all in from recess. Charlotte saddled up beside me and put her arm around my shoulder. "Good thing you already picked someone else for number three," she said. "I wouldn't send my worst enemy on a honeymoon with that creep."

I sighed forlornly. All summer long I had wanted Danny to pay attention to me, to talk with me once school started up, and now when he did, it was only to insult my father. Again I was reminded — in the cruelest of ways, it seemed — how very different real life turns out to be than what we dreamed.

Sniffing loudly and wiping one last tear from my cheek, I asked, "Did your father really say that about Al Capone?"

"Naw," Charlotte said, shaking her head. "But you can be sure he won't vote for Sheriff Dysinger next election — not if I have any say about it."

I wanted to tell Charlotte she was a good friend, the best of friends, but I knew she'd only be embarrassed and shrug it off. Instead, I swung my arm up over her shoulder, and entwined like two vines of the ivy that climbed up the school's brick facade, we walked on to class.

But disappointment hadn't finished with us yet. After school I walked home with Charlotte where we found the latest issue of *Life* magazine on a table with the other mail in the hallway. Charlotte dropped her school books on the table, scooped up the magazine, and said, "The contest results should be in this issue. Come on!"

I followed her up the stairs, our shoes tapping out a hurried rhythm on the steps. From the kitchen Mrs. Besac wailed, "Try to be a little less noisy, will you? I've got a pounding headache." But, completely unsympathetic toward her ailment, we ignored her. All we could think about was the vast amount of money soon to cross our palms.

We threw ourselves onto Charlotte's bed, and my friend then licked one thumb and hurriedly flipped through the pages of the magazine. "Here it is!" she hollered excitedly. As her eyes moved down the page of contest winners, she muttered her father's name over and over, "Luther Besac, Luther Besac."

"Do you see it?" I asked. I held both hands in the air with fingers crossed.

"Not yet," she said. "Luther Besac, Luther Besac. Come on, you've got to be here somewhere."

She turned the page. Then she slowly lowered the magazine to the bed as her eyes moved up to my face. I gave her a questioning look, unwilling to uncross my fingers and drop my hands.

"Did you see his name?" I asked tentatively.

"It's not here." Charlotte spoke the words breathlessly, as though she couldn't quite believe it.

"You mean, we didn't win anything?"

"Not even five lousy dollars."

I let my hands drop to the bed. For a moment neither of us said anything.

"But it was a good slogan," I groaned. I felt like crying again. There would be no crisp greenbacks for me to present to Mother and no new patent leather shoes for me to show off at school. And I had been so sure. . . .

Charlotte, muttering something about it being a stupid contest anyway, flung the magazine across the room. "Let's do the globe," she suggested, swinging her feet off the bed and grabbing the globe from the vanity table. Then pulling the jewelry box out of the drawer, she brought both it and the magic orb back to the bed.

Charlotte twirled one of her short curls around her index finger. "Go on, you spin first. But I just hope you don't land in the Dead Sea again this time," she said, referring to where I'd landed the day before. "It's really hard to be romantic when you're floating around the Dead Sea."

I spun, but without enthusiasm. I might as well end up in the Dead Sea, the way I felt. If not even Danny Dysinger was a part of my life, then what did Charles Lindbergh, Charlie Chaplin, and Buster Keaton have to do with me? Why should I dream of winging off to some exotic place to honeymoon with them? None of them even knew I was alive.

Suddenly spinning the globe seemed a ridiculous game, a childish game. I laid a hand across my stomach, moaned slightly, and mumbled that I wasn't feeling well.

Charlotte, not wanting me to be sick all over her frilly pink-and-white bedspread, suggested that I go on home.

I did, but instead of entering the front door of our house, I entered the side door that led directly into Papa's waiting room. Fortunately, no one was there, and I sat down in one of the empty chairs. If anyone found me — like Mother — I decided I would say I was checking the blanket box for donations.

Of course, I wasn't really. I just wanted to be near Papa. He was in the inner office — perhaps checking the supplies in the medicine cabinet or reviewing some paper work. I didn't know. But he was there. I could hear him whistling Christmas carols beyond the adjoining door. I sat in the waiting room for about ten minutes, listening. That was all I needed to believe again that life was good and happiness possible.

Chapter Twenty-Three

We didn't know about the hunger march until the morning after it happened. We might have learned about it the previous evening had we bothered to turn on the radio, but we were no longer so keen to listen to that bearer of bad news. Even with the strike over, we were wary of the Philco and kept our distance from it for a while. The march had taken place more than twelve hours earlier, and some of the men from Soo City had already spent their first night in jail before Papa read the news account in the morning paper over breakfast.

Papa and Dr. Hal sat at opposite ends of the kitchen table, each with a section of the newspaper spread open before him. I was the only other one at the table enjoying the pancakes and molasses. Mother and Aunt Sally both puttered about the kitchen, preparing for one of the last canning days of the season. Since it was Saturday, Claudia, Molly, and the boys hadn't bothered to get out of bed yet.

Dr. Hal was biding his time with the sports page until he could get his hands on the section Papa was reading. Before leaving the table, he would have to have his daily dose of Walter Lippmann. As I mentioned, Dr. Hal had a fondness for reading aloud from Lippmann's column, thereby punctuating our morning with news of how much deeper into the Depression our country had sunk. Whenever Dr. Hal blurted out, "Hey, listen to this —" I'd immediately try to set my mind on something else so as not to fall into a depression myself.

But this morning it wasn't Dr. Hal who read to us from the newspaper. It was Papa. He had just raised his coffee cup to his lips when his eyebrows rose above the rims of his glasses, and he said quietly, "So they've done it." He set the coffee cup back in the saucer without drinking.

Dr. Hal looked up from the sports section. "Done what?" he asked.

"Dick Mason said the Communists were trying to organize a hunger march at City Hall, and he was right. They marched yesterday afternoon. I can't believe we didn't get wind of it somehow."

"Should have listened to the news last night," Dr. Hal said. "I would have if I hadn't been called out. You get too busy and you start to lose track of what's going on."

Yes, I thought, *and the same thing happens if you're just too scared to know.*

Mother turned from the sink to cast

Papa a dubious look. "Do you mean to say Communists were able to organize a protest?"

Papa nodded. "There've been a couple of men trying to set up an Unemployed Council for some months now. Looks like they succeeded. According to this article, about three hundred men and women showed up at City Hall saying they were hungry and demanding relief."

"Not all from Soo City, were they?" Dr. Hal asked.

"Couldn't have been," Papa said, sticking out his lower lip. "No doubt some were from the shantytown, but they must have gotten people from all over the city to join them."

"Papa," I piped up, "how come Mr. Mason didn't tell you it was going to happen? You told him to let you know if there was going to be a march."

"He's been gone for the past week, though he's supposed to return today. He found temporary work just over the border in Wisconsin."

"But even if you'd known about the march," Dr. Hal interjected, "what could you have done about it?"

Papa shrugged. "I don't suppose I could have done much of anything. You can't stop three hundred hungry people."

Mother sounded slightly exasperated

when she asked, "So what happened?"

"More violence, I suppose," said Aunt Sally, who had been quiet until now.

Papa nodded again as his eyes scanned the article. "Says here, 'A delegation of unemployed, led by John Jones, alleged head of the Unemployed Council, demanded of City Manager Thomas Simington that the authorities furnish immediate relief for the men and their families. Jones rejected a request by Mr. Simington for the names and addresses of the members of the Unemployed Council. Jones and the delegation returned to the marchers, a group of some three hundred men and women, and excited the crowd with antigovernment rhetoric. From City Hall they led the crowd on a raid of two businesses on nearby Third Avenue — Elkton Grocer's and Owensby Bakery. The owner of the bakery, Owen Owensby, suffered a broken arm when he was attacked as he drew a revolver and attempted to keep out the angry demonstrators. The shelves of the grocery store and the bakery were stripped of their goods, and windows in both establishments were broken. Local police hastily assembled an emergency squad and dispersed the crowd with tear gas. Thirty-seven men who were trapped in the wrecked stores were arrested. Six women were released. Among those arrested were John Jones and Ernie

Armstrong. The police said Armstrong was one of the speakers who harangued the crowd at City Hall before the demonstrators descended on the stores.' " When he finished reading, Papa folded the newspaper and lifted his shoulders in a sigh.

Mother asked wearily of no one in particular, "Will it ever end?"

Papa tossed the paper across the table to Dr. Hal and said, "I guess I'll find out more this afternoon when I make my rounds at Soo City."

I took a sip of milk, then leaned toward my father and asked quietly so that Mother wouldn't hear, "Can I go with you, Papa?"

I should have known it was no use. Mother heard and, answering for Papa, replied firmly in the negative. "No, you may not go, Virginia. Certainly not today, after what's just happened at City Hall."

"But, Mama —"

"I said no, young lady, and that's final."

It was just as well. I was supposed to go to the movies with Charlotte in the afternoon, and she'd be cross with me if I backed out. She'd been waiting all week to see Lowell Sherman in *What Price Hollywood?* Lately Charlotte had been thinking about becoming a movie star, and she thought the show might give her some ideas on how to break into film. As for Soo City, Papa could tell me everything when he got back, if there was anything to tell.

Both Papa and Dr. Hal got up from the table without asking for a second helping of pancakes. Dr. Hal must have lost his appetite for Walter Lippmann, as well, because he left the newspaper on the table where Papa had tossed it.

I spent the morning doing chores, working on my school lessons, and practicing the piano. After lunch, Charlotte came by so we could walk together to the theater. Her father was out of town again, and her mother, though always ready with an opinion about the times, didn't in fact pay much attention to the news, so I knew Charlotte probably hadn't heard about the hunger march.

"You mean a bunch of Reds busted up a couple of stores downtown?" she asked when I told her what Papa had read in the paper that morning.

"Yeah, a grocery store and a bakery."

"On Third Avenue?"

"I think that's right. You know, Elkton Grocer's and Owensby Bakery."

"I've been to both those places a million times!" Charlotte cried. She quickened her pace. "Come on! Let's go see how busted up they are."

Charlotte took off running and I called out, "But what about the movie?"

"We can miss the cartoon and the newsreel. This is important!"

I hurried to catch up with my curiosity-seeking friend. We sprinted toward downtown until we arrived panting at Third Avenue.

A policeman, his hands clasped together behind his back, lingered in front of the grocery store. He paced the sidewalk, stopping momentarily to glance from the wrecked grocery store to the ravaged bakery across the street, then satisfied that both places were free of looters, he continued pacing. Pedestrians walking past the stores, taken aback by the destruction, stopped, shook their heads, talked among themselves, and exchanged comments with the policeman before moving on. Even cars slowed as they passed by in the street, the occupants fairly hanging their heads out the open windows to get a better view. More than once the policeman had to blow his whistle and wave the traffic on to prevent a backup on Third Avenue.

Charlotte and I paused a few yards from the policeman and gaped at the broken windows. Someone had swept up the glass on the sidewalk, but a few small shards remained, glittering in the sun. We timidly approached the grocery store to peer in through what was left of the plate glass window. Peaks of glass pointed upward from the bottom frame of the window and downward from the top, reaching toward each other like the columns of stalactite and stalagmite in an underground cavern. Through the hole we saw the aisles of the store strewn with debris — wilted vegetables heaped upon splattered fruit, canned goods scattered amid broken glass bottles. Two men, appearing to us like shadowy figures from where we stood in the sunlight, moved about inside, cleaning up.

Wide-eyed, Charlotte and I gazed in disbelief at the mess.

So, I marveled, there really *are* Communists in this city. And here is the evidence of their existence.

All the while the strike at the grain mill had been going on, the Communists had been a kind of nebulous group to blame, a smoke screen for the real issues at hand. Surely patriotic, freedom-loving Americans wouldn't pull a stunt like that, it was thought. Oh no, only Communists would call a strike and talk about workers' rights. It was kind of like the kid blaming the mess in his room on goblins or elves — on something that doesn't really exist.

But this, these two wrecked stores, was the work of the Commies. The goblins were real. They hadn't had anything to do with the grain mill strike, but nevertheless, they were real. And they were busy.

The silence into which Charlotte and I

had settled was interrupted by the policeman. "All right, girls," he said, not unkindly, "you've seen all there is to see. Move along now."

Like a couple of dumb sheep, we obeyed, making our way along Third Avenue to the theater a few blocks east. We paid our quarters and sat through the movie, but after viewing the destruction of the hunger march, even Charlotte thought the picture somewhat dull and unreal in comparison.

When Papa got home that evening, I asked him what he'd found out at Soo City. He said that of the three hundred marchers, less than fifty had been from Soo City, and only a half dozen of those arrested were from the shantytown. "No one you know," Papa told me, "though you may have seen some of them once or twice."

I asked him about Steel O'Neil, Shoes, Mr. Lucky, Sherman Browne, Longjohn, the three musicians, everyone I could think of, and he assured me they were all fine. None of them had been involved in the hunger march. Dick Mason had returned from Wisconsin and, after taking inventory, told Papa that the men who'd ended up in jail were rascals anyway, and Soo City was better off without them.

"With Jones and Armstrong out of the

picture," Papa predicted happily, "life should be much quieter for everyone from now on."

My father was a smart man and made us all feel better with his words of assurance. But as it turned out, he was not a very good barometer of things to come.

Chapter Twenty-Four

Charlotte and I usually walked home from school together, but after the last bell on Monday, she headed downtown on an errand for her mother, and I was left to walk home alone. But I didn't mind too much. The autumn leaves were dropping from the trees, and I enjoyed listening to their swishing and crunching as I strolled through the mat of crisp colors on the sidewalk. It was a music I could never quite hear over Charlotte's chatter.

I wasn't walking really, but rather shuffling, barely lifting the soles of my shoes from the sidewalk so as to produce the loudest swish-swish possible from the leaves. The noise was delightful and I almost started to whistle along with it as Papa would have done, except that I was interrupted by someone calling my name.

"Ginny! Hey, Ginny, wait up!"

To my great surprise and even greater horror, I recognized the voice of Danny Dysinger.

Not bothering to turn around, I continued walking and swishing all the louder. Ignoring him gave me a deep sense of satisfaction, but the feeling was short-lived.

Danny Dysinger was not one to be easily put off. He came panting up behind me and tugged at the shoulder of my dress, saying, "Ginny, are you deaf or something? I said wait up."

I pulled my shoulder away briskly, as if I'd been shocked by static electricity. "My name's Virginia," I stated firmly, "and what do you want?" My mouth had suddenly gone dry and the last word rolled clumsily off my tongue.

"Listen," he said, "I didn't mean to make you sore the other day. I wish you wouldn't hold it against me."

Giving him my wildest stare of disbelief, I responded, "You call my father a Communist and expect me not to get mad?"

Danny belched out something between a laugh and a guffaw. "Aw, Ginny," he explained, "it was just a joke."

My eyebrows jumped up toward my hairline. "Some joke!" I cried.

"Aw, I didn't mean nothing by it."

I shook my head and walked on. I was still sweet on Danny and there was no denying it, but I couldn't bring myself to accept his fumbling apology.

Still not ready to give up, though, he tugged again at my shoulder. "Aw, Ginny —"

"Virginia!" I hissed.

"All right, all right. Virginia, then.

Listen, I'm trying to tell you I didn't mean nothing by it."

Lifting my chin half an inch higher, I argued, "It's your father's fault my uncle's in jail. My uncle Jim's a good man, and your pa put him where he doesn't belong."

"My pa was only doing his job," Danny countered. "Any sheriff would've had to go out there and arrest the strikers."

"Maybe so," I said, "but just because your father's the sheriff doesn't mean he can go around calling people names. Your father said my father and my uncle and Dr. Hal were all Reds, didn't he? He said those awful things and it's not true."

"Yeah," Danny admitted, sounding sheepish. "He said it, but I know it ain't true. I know your pa's not a Red. And not your uncle or Doc Bellamy neither."

"Then why did you say it?"

"I don't know, Gin— I mean, Virginia. You can be sore if you want, but listen, I got to tell you something. Something important."

He paused. I waited for him to go on, but he didn't.

"So what is it?" I asked stonily, adding a heavy sigh to accentuate my contempt.

Danny took a deep breath, and I noticed his chest quivered nervously. His lips puckered a moment as though he were trying hard to spit the words out. Finally, he said,

"I heard my pa talking with some men yesterday. They didn't know I was outside the door, but I was and I heard everything."

I let the feigned contempt drop from my voice. Danny had captured my curiosity. "Yeah?" I asked. "So what did they say?"

"They said the hunger riot was on account of the people down at the shantytown. They said those tramps were responsible for busting up the grocery store and that bakery."

"That's not true!" I cried. "Most of those people that rioted weren't *from* the shantytown!"

"I'm just telling you what I heard," Danny said defensively. "My pa said those tramps are vermin that need to be got rid of for the good of the city. He said the shantytown is really a Red village, a miniature Moscow sitting right there on the banks of the river. So my pa and his men — they're going to run them out, Ginny. They're going to run them out and burn the camp down. They're going to do it tonight after dark."

Stopping abruptly, I stared at Danny in horror. My heart pumped wildly and my limbs became so weak I thought I might drop the books clutched in my arms if my knees didn't buckle beneath me first and leave me in a heap on the sidewalk. "Danny Dysinger," I asked quietly, "are

479

you telling me the truth?"

"I swear, Ginny," he said solemnly. His walnut-colored eyes were wide and fearful, almost pleading. "That's what I heard them say." Hurriedly, he added, "Listen, I know what you're thinking. You're thinking you got to warn them. But it's too late. Pa's already got some of his men posted down there at the camp disguised as tramps. Three deputies wandered into the camp this morning looking like all the other bums down there. They're all riled up and just aching for action, Ginny, and I'm telling you they won't act kindly toward anyone who tries to interfere." Danny paused and looked at me long and hard for a moment. "I know your pa goes down to the camp a lot to help out, but I'm giving you fair warning: don't let him go down there tonight. Make sure he stays home. What's gonna happen down there ain't gonna be a pretty sight."

I was momentarily stunned into silence, but finally I managed to mumble, "You can't let your pa do this, Danny. He's got it all wrong. The people in the camp — they're good people. You have to stop him, Danny."

Danny shook his head slowly, almost sadly. "I can't stop him, Ginny. He and his men — they've made up their minds. You got to understand. . . ."

His words trailed off and a look of helplessness crossed his face. Suddenly I did understand. Danny was afraid of his father. He knew his father was doing something wrong, but Danny felt incapable of confronting him. And so he was trying to have some influence over the situation in the only way he knew how — by telling me.

And now that the burden had been passed to me, I was equally staggered by its weight. Without another word to Danny, I turned and ran, half stumbling, my legs limp with fear. Behind me I heard Danny call out my name, "Ginny! Ginny!" but I didn't stop and I didn't even turn my head to look. Breathless, gasping for air, my books heavy and awkward against my chest, I ran, feet pounding recklessly on the sidewalk. Tears stung my eyes until I was half blind, and I moved through the dizzy streets by instinct, like a homing pigeon. When I reached our house at last, I flew through the front door, pulled myself up the stairs with the help of the banister and flung myself across my bed. My school books went soaring through the air and landed on the floor with a thump that alerted Mother. In the next moment she came to my room and settled her ample body on my bed where I lay weeping. Though I didn't lift my face from my arms, I felt the bed sag to one side with her weight, and just the sense of her presence was comforting.

"Why, Virginia," she said, sounding almost startled. But her voice was laced with a soft note of compassion. "What on earth are you crying about?" She reached out one hand and patted my tangled hair. I longed to lie there beneath her soothing touch and tell her everything, shifting the weight of Danny's warning over onto her strong shoulders.

But I couldn't tell her, of course. There was no question about that.

Neither could I simply say it was nothing. One didn't throw herself across the bed weeping for no reason. I hated to do it, but I would have to lie.

Lifting my tear-streaked face from my arms, I said, "I didn't do well on my lessons today, Mama."

Mother almost laughed, but it came out more like a chuckle. "Well, for heaven's sakes, Virginia," she replied, the note of compassion becoming a flat chord of amusement. "You don't have to get so upset over something like that. It's not the end of the world. We all have a bad day now and again."

I tried to nod bravely. "I know. It's just that I want to do well."

"Of course you do," Mother agreed. "But crying isn't going to get you any-

where. Come on, now, dry your tears."
She rose from the bed — that side of the
mattress sprang up again — and gathered
up my books from the floor. "Here you go.
Why don't you spend the next hour
studying before you come down to help
with dinner?"

I sat up and wiped at my cheeks with the
back of one hand. "What about the
piano?" I asked.

"You can let that go for today," Mother
replied. "It sounds as though you need
some extra time with your books, and
that's more important." Had the circumstances been different, I would have been
jubilant to be excused from practicing the
piano, but that afternoon I felt no joy at
all. As it was, I would have gladly practiced
an extra half hour if only the day had suddenly become like every other.

Mother placed the books on my desk
and gave them a swift pat. "Come on. The
only way to do your lessons well is to
buckle down and get to it."

I dragged myself from the bed and wearily crossed the room to the desk. "All
right, Mama," I said. I sat down and
opened a book, not even noticing which
one it was. "Call me when you want me to
set the table."

I followed Mother with my eyes as she
left the room, longing to call her back,

longing to ask her what I should do but knowing that if I told her of what was about to happen in Soo City, she'd tell Papa, and Papa would undoubtedly go down there to the camp, and then . . .

For the next hour I sat unmoving, staring out the window, so lost in thought I didn't even see what was beyond the glass. I was facing the worst dilemma of my life: Should I tell Papa what I knew, or should I remain quiet?

There would be consequences either way.

If I didn't tell Papa about the upcoming raid, our friends in Soo City might end up hurt — or worse. At the very least, they would all lose their homes. Most people might not see it as a great loss, the destruction of those makeshift shanties furnished with the scantiest of goods. Nevertheless, it was all those people had. The burning of the camp would leave them with nothing.

On the other hand, if I did tell Papa, *he* might end up hurt — or worse. The thought of anything happening to him was one I couldn't bear.

My mind vacillated like a metronome beating time on top of a piano: back and forth, back and forth, Papa and Soo City, Papa and Soo City.

Papa, I told myself, was valuable, was indispensable. His patients needed him, his family needed him, *I* needed him. I had an obligation to protect him.

And yet the people down at Soo City were no less valuable. Maybe they were poor, maybe they were jobless, but still they were *people*. I thought about Mrs. Everhart and baby Caroline. I thought about Mr. Lucky and Sherman Browne. I thought about Dick Mason and Alice Hunt and Steel O'Neil and Longjohn and Shoes. I thought about the three musicians and how grand they had sounded when Papa sang "Amazing Grace" with them.

They were all there at the camp, going about their lives — cooking, washing, singing, reading the newspaper — preparing for the evening and the night, completely unaware that this night was not to be like every other. They didn't know. But I knew.

I knew there were three men among them at this very hour, disguised as transients, who thought them less than human, who considered them vermin. I knew that darkness would bring more men, armed men, angry and unreasonable men, men who had hate in their blood. They would come seeking revenge for the destruction on Third Avenue, and it was the innocent residents of Soo City who would pay. These residents — my friends — were helpless, and there was no one to help them. No one, except, perhaps, me.

I wanted to save them. I wanted to run to the camp and warn them, to cry out like a modern-day Paul Revere, "The sheriff is coming with his men! Get out! Get out while you can!"

But the truth was, I was afraid. I was afraid not only for Papa but for my own self. I had seen the deputies at work. I had seen men beaten and battered and even shot. I had seen blood on the streets and on the sidewalk, and I believed the sheriff and his men to be so ruthless as to swing their batons or point their pistols at even a young girl if she stood in the way of what they wanted to do.

I dismissed all thoughts of going to Soo City myself. I hadn't the courage.

Oh, if only Dick Mason had never come to our door looking for help! If only Papa had never gone to Soo City that first time! Mother had been right in her presentiments of doom. Something bad was going to happen. It was happening now.

My head felt as though it were spinning, spinning like the leaves that spiraled downward from the trees in front of the window. There was Papa, and there were the people of Soo City. I could protect one, or I could give warning to the other. But I couldn't do both.

From far away I heard Mother call me down to chores, but for a moment I could only watch, transfixed, as the occasional leaf broke free from a branch and gave itself over to the wind. For the tree, one small loss, and then another and another, as it slowly succumbed to winter's long sleep.

Papa joined us for dinner, something he was rarely able to do. The whole of our immediate family sat around the table that night, my parents, my brother, my two sisters. Aunt Sally and her boys would eat when we had finished and made room for them at the table. Dr. Hal, out making a house call, would join them if he got back in time. But for now, it was the six of us. Gathered around the dinner table the way most families gathered to eat in those days. A regular Norman Rockwell picture. Molly, between bites of food, sang "Twinkle, Twinkle, Little Star" in her childish, high-pitched voice. Mother reminded Molly repeatedly that we don't sing while we're eating, and the rest of us were warned to keep our elbows off the table. Simon, energized by Papa's presence, rambled on about what he'd learned in science class that day, and Papa, listening intently, swatted absently at a fly that buzzed about the kitchen.

Each bite of food I swallowed landed like

a rock in the pit of my stomach. I finally gave up and resorted to pushing a pea around my plate with the prongs of my fork. *It's just like every other night,* I chanted to myself in a desperate bid at make-believe. *Just like every other night, just like every other night. . . .*

Papa noticed my mood and the fact that the food on my plate was going everywhere but in my mouth. "What's the trouble, Ginny?" he asked.

As was Mother's habit, she answered for me. "She said she didn't do well on her school lessons today."

Papa smiled kindly as he sliced away at the pieces of fried Spam on his plate. "Don't let it bother you," he said. "We all have a bad day once in a while."

"That's exactly what I told her," Mother replied with a satisfied nod.

Oh, if it were only so simple as all that! I looked up at Papa with pleading eyes, wishing I could throw myself across his lap and tell him everything I knew. More than that, what I really wished — what I wished desperately — was that I knew nothing at all about the raid. I wished that I, too, could go about the evening in blissful ignorance, not knowing what lay ahead.

But there was no cure for knowing. I knew, and that was that.

"Don't let him go down there tonight,"

Danny had warned.

No, I couldn't. I couldn't let my papa put himself in danger by going to Soo City.

They'll be all right, I told myself in one last vain attempt to rationalize what I was doing. The Everharts, the Hunts, the Conleys, all of them — they'll have to move on, but thousands of homeless are wandering around the country all the time. Danny said Sheriff Dysinger and the deputies were going to run them out, but that doesn't mean they'll hurt them. No, they'll just scare them off. Then everyone will just move on and find someplace else to live. Maybe they'll even find work if they're forced to go somewhere else. . . .

Later that night when I kissed Papa before going to bed, he gave me a long hug and said, "Good night, Ginny."

I couldn't bring myself to wish him a good-night in return. In spite of my frail endeavors to minimize and even to dismiss the threat to Soo City, I knew it would not be a good night. It would not be a good night at all.

Chapter Twenty-Five

I couldn't sleep. I tried to pray, but I couldn't do that either. I just kept thinking, *Dear God, dear God,* and nothing would come after that.

My mind kept drifting down to Soo City, wandering from shanty to shanty, seeing everyone I had come to know over the summer. I wondered who might be sleeping peacefully, curled up beneath the blankets I had given them; who might be reading or working by lantern or candlelight; who might be sitting on a doorstep or an upturned cinder block, just looking up at the stars and smoking a cigarette. Was little Caroline asleep in her crate or just now being sung to sleep in her mother's arms? Was Mr. Lucky stretched out on the dirt floor of his slightly charred shack, his head resting on T-Bone's furry rib cage as on a pillow? Were Joe and Oscar and Bob sitting beside a late-night campfire, swapping stories about the past, dreaming aloud about the future? Was Lela lying awake among the tangled limbs of her three younger siblings, wondering when her interrupted life would begin again?

They were all there in the little ramshackle city by the river with only their usual fears to haunt them in the dark: Where will my food come from tomorrow? Will I find work? Will I ever see my family again? These fears had become familiar, acceptable, like an arthritic knee one has learned to live with. They lay there in their safe assumption: "It's just like every other night. Tonight is just like every other night."

And for all they knew, it was. But I knew otherwise.

I wondered when their night would be broken in two, shattered by the sheriff and his men. Was it now? Was this the hour the lawmen were descending upon the camp and forcing out the residents like cattle from a pen?

Mother came upstairs to bed at ten-thirty. Papa followed at eleven o'clock. The house was dark and quiet except for the usual night sounds outside — the katydids, the occasional passing car. I listened to myself breathe. I felt my heart beating in my chest. I didn't know what a man felt like as he waited for his executioners to come, but I thought it must be something like this.

Dear God, please, God . . .

Fear hovered over me thick as fog, weighing down on me until I felt myself choking. Still, the minutes dragged on.

Papa slept. Mother slept. Everyone slept. I sat up in bed trying to catch my breath, then pushed back the covers and crawled out. The room was chilly, filled with the brisk air of an October night, and I instinctively reached for the robe that lay across the foot of my bed to throw it on over my cotton gown. But I stopped myself and left the robe where it lay. Stepping to the window, I pressed my forehead against the cold glass. I stood there unmoving, the soles of my bare feet planted on the raw boards of the hardwood floor. The wind seeped in through the cracks of the window frame and made me shiver, but I didn't wrap my arms about myself for warmth. I wanted to be cold, to suffer, if even only just a little bit, to pay penance for what I had done by not doing anything.

Outside, the night shadows played upon the grass. The moon was just a fragment of a shining planet in the sky. I looked up at the stars sprinkled like glitter across black paper and heard Molly's tiny, sweet voice:

> *Twinkle, twinkle, little star,*
> *How I wonder what you are. . . .*

The universe was so vast, so expansive, and the world, and Soo City, and I — so small. *Oh, God, dear God. . . .*

For a long while I watched and waited. I

strained to hear any unusual sounds, any cry in the dark, any indication that what had been forewarned had come to pass. And then, finally, there it was: the sound of rushing footfalls on the sidewalk, one pair of feet pounding the pavement in front of our house. The footsteps gave way to a panicked rapping on the front door and an unfamiliar voice calling out, "Doc Eide, Doc Eide!"

The light went on in my parents' room, casting a subdued glow into the hall. In the next moment, Papa, his clothes already thrown on over his pajamas, rushed past the open door of my room. The knocking went on and on. I almost thought I could feel the house trembling under the attack. "Coming!" Papa called as he hurried down the stairs. I followed, my bare feet slapping against the floor, but paused at the top of the staircase.

Mother, in her robe and slippers, shuffled up behind me and, stifling a yawn, said, "Go back to bed, Virginia. It's nothing you need to concern yourself with."

She thought it was just another call for the doctor, an anxious father-to-be or the son of a man taken sick. She thought it was just someone come to ask the doctor to rush to another bedside, but she was wrong.

Papa opened the door and an ill-clad youth came tumbling in, clutching his cap. I didn't recognize him, but I knew he had to be from the camp. Of course he would be the one elected to come. He was young and long-legged and able to run quickly. He stood there in the hallway panting and gasping for breath.

"Andy!" Papa said in surprise.

"The camp's burning!" the young man cried. "Some people's been hurt. You gotta come!"

The commotion had awakened both Aunt Sally, who was sleeping in Papa's study, and Dr. Hal, who slept on a rollaway in the back room of the office. They entered the hall from either side, like two actors making an entrance from opposite wings. Dr. Hal, like Papa, was already dressed.

"What's going on, Will?" Dr. Hal asked.

"I'm not sure." To Andy, Papa said, "Now, calm down and catch your breath. What's this all about?"

The young man's shoulders still heaved. He squeezed his cap more tightly in his hands, making of it one narrow bit of cloth. "Some men came. They started driving everyone out and set fire to the camp."

"Harold, get my bag, quickly," Papa instructed.

"I'll go with you, Will."

"No, better if you —"

"I can help, Will."

The two doctors looked at each other for one brief moment. "All right, then," Papa conceded. "Get both our bags. Let's go. Andy, we'll take the car."

Danny's words came to me then, screaming in their intensity: *Don't let your pa go down there tonight!* I flew down the stairs, stumbling and clutching at the banister, crying out, "No, Papa, no! You can't go! You can't!" Mother behind me called out my name, but I kept on without turning around.

My father looked at me, puzzled. I rushed to him and threw my arms around his waist, as if to physically restrain him. "No, Papa! You can't go down there!"

"Ginny," Papa said quietly, shaking his head, "what's come over you?"

"It's Sheriff Dysinger, Papa. It's the sheriff and his men. You can't go down there! They'll kill you if you do!"

Papa unlocked my arms from around his middle and, holding me by the wrists, took one step backward. "What do you know about this, Ginny?"

Tears burned my eyes and coursed down my cheeks, and Papa's face became a blur. "Danny told me. Sheriff Dysinger's son. He said there wasn't any way to stop —"

Papa shook me, one brief shake of anger. "When did you learn about this?"

"This afternoon — he told me — on the way home from school —"

"Why didn't you tell me, Ginny?" Papa's cheeks flared red. I had never seen him so angry, had rarely ever seen him angry at all, and it frightened me into silence. When I didn't answer, he repeated sternly, "Ginny, why didn't you tell me?"

Papa and Dr. Hal and Mother and Aunt Sally and the boy from the camp all stood there waiting for my reply, but I couldn't speak. I heard the words in my mind but couldn't bring them to my tongue. *I wanted to protect you, Papa! I stayed quiet for your sake!* I stood mute as a statue, my mouth open dumbly, staring up at my father.

He let go of my wrists, almost thrust me aside, and took his medical bag from Dr. Hal. Without another word, the three men moved quickly through the hall toward the back door. Mother, Aunt Sally, and I stood immobile on the cold hardwood floor and watched them go. We heard the slamming of the door, followed a minute later by the starting of the car engine, and finally the crunching of tires over gravel in the alley. Then everything became so quiet I could hear the faint ticking of the clock on the piano, the clock that measured off all the desperate hours of our lives.

I lifted my eyes slowly to Mother's, afraid of what she might say. But instead of reprimanding me, she held out her arms and invited me in. "Why, you're cold as ice, Virginia," she whispered. With the belt of her quilted robe, she wiped away the tears on my cheeks.

It was past midnight, but Mother decided she and I ought to get dressed, just in case. She insisted I put on a wool dress and sweater, thick socks and shoes, and though I balked, I did it.

Mother and Aunt Sally, who stayed in her gown and robe, sat at the kitchen table drinking coffee and talking in low tones. The boys had woken up briefly but were sent back to bed after receiving an evasive explanation as to what the commotion was all about. I paced the front hall, periodically checked the clock on the piano, went to the back door to watch for car headlights in the alley, then went back to the front hall.

"Quit pacing," Aunt Sally pleaded during one of my trips through the kitchen. "You're making me all the more nervous."

I retreated to the front door and looked out at the street. I stood unmoving for several minutes in the hopes of appeasing Aunt Sally. Then I continued pacing, my footsteps echoing loudly through the otherwise quiet house. At two o'clock I paused in the kitchen doorway and asked, "Should I have told him, Mama?"

Mother only sighed, looked at me sadly, then got up to pour herself and Aunt Sally more coffee. I went back to the clock on the piano. Two minutes after two.

"He'll be all right," Mother assured me on my next trip to the back door.

"Do you really think so, Mama?" I asked, my forehead pressed up against the glass in the door.

"Yes," she said. But from the sound of her voice and the fact that she wanted us dressed "just in case," I knew she didn't think so at all.

I walked the length of the hall again and looked out the front door. Then I went into the parlor to look at the clock. I thought about wandering into Papa's study, but I wasn't sure I could bring myself to do it. While I stood by the piano debating, the voices of the women in the kitchen drifted to me, and I caught snatches of their conversation.

"I had a feeling all along," Mother was saying, "that no good would come of this. I tried to tell him. . . ."

". . . nothing you could say or do to persuade him," Aunt Sally responded. "Once Will makes up his mind, that's it."

". . . see that his responsibility was here, with his family and his practice. . . ."

". . . know him well enough to know he had his reasons. He thought it was important, thought he could help."

I sauntered back to the kitchen and settled myself in a chair at the table. Both my mother and aunt looked across at me in silence, unwilling to continue the conversation I had interrupted. I wanted to tell them what Papa had told me about why he spent time at Soo City, but before I could say anything Aunt Sally spoke again.

"Every time I think it's all over," she muttered, "something else happens."

For a moment the three of us were quiet. I listened to the clinking of the spoon against the porcelain cup as my aunt stirred sugar into her coffee.

Then she continued. "It kind of makes you wonder where God is in all of this, doesn't it?"

I wanted to believe He was there with us, and also at the camp with Papa, and everywhere anyone needed Him that night, but all I could picture was a distant throne somewhere beyond the stars.

Dear God, I thought. *Please, God, look down from heaven. . . .*

A sudden furious rapping at the front door interrupted my prayer. Mother stood and rushed down the hall, with Aunt Sally and me right behind her. She opened the door to find the same young man who had stood there two hours earlier. His face was streaked black with soot, and this time I smelled the smoke on his clothes. His hands, now empty of the cap, flailed wildly. "Mrs. Eide, the doc's been hurt bad. The other doctor, the young guy, took him to the hospital in Doc Eide's car. He told me to ask you if you can get to the hospital right away."

Without a word to the winded messenger, Mother turned to me. "Run next door and ask Mr. Mobley to drive us," she said evenly, as though she'd been expecting the news all along.

Mechanically, I did as I was told. I was so overwhelmed by feelings that I couldn't feel anything anymore.

Chapter Twenty-Six

Dr. Hal was waiting for us just beyond the double glass doors of the hospital lobby. With numerous expressions of thanks for giving us a ride at such an hour of the night, we sent Mr. Mobley back home to bed. He offered to stay with us in spite of his sleepwear — when he'd learned that Papa was hurt, he'd grabbed his car keys and flew from the house in his robe and slippers — but Mother assured him we'd be fine. Before he left, he lightly touched the top of my head with his big paw of a hand and said he'd not be sleeping but praying. Mother thanked him again, and I hoped that our neighbor would be better at persuading God down from his throne than I had been.

Dr. Hal led us to an empty waiting room, where, with an abrupt flash of his palm, he indicated that Mother and I should sit. We lowered ourselves onto a couch. Both of us balanced on the edge as we leaned toward Dr. Hal, who settled himself in a chair across from us. It was only then that I noticed one sleeve of Dr. Hal's shirt was missing, torn from the shoulder. His clothes were filthy, smudged with dirt and ash, and like the messenger, he smelled of smoke. His face, too, was dark with soot, and on either side — from temple to jawline — a streak of sweat sliced through the black like a river. What was most unnerving, though, were the splotches of blood that dotted his clothes as if someone had flicked a huge paintbrush at him. Brownish dots, like rust, lay splattered on the white of his shirt, on the tan of his pants. On his right thigh were four long stripes where he had obviously wiped his fingers. He was a macabre portrait of modern art, the creation of a fatalistic artist whose desire was to capture death on canvas.

"How is he, Harold?" Mother asked, her voice trembling with the anxiety she was no longer able to hide.

Dr. Hal pressed his hands together between his knees. "It's impossible to say at this point," he began, sounding less like a relative than a doctor. "He's in surgery right now to remove a bullet from his leg. It shattered his femur — that is, his thighbone."

A shattered thighbone. That didn't sound so bad to me. Lots of people had been shot in the leg or the arm or even the shoulder and had recovered just fine. Now, a chest wound — that was a different story altogether. If a person was shot in the chest, everyone had a right to start worrying. But a leg — pshaw, that would heal easily enough! Papa might be left with a limp, but all the cowboys and the gangsters in the movies that were shot in the leg —

Mother interrupted my mental stream of solace by asking Dr. Hal, "Did he lose a lot of blood?" Her eyes traveled over Dr. Hal's clothes as she asked the question.

"Yes," Dr. Hal replied. "Evidently the femoral artery or the vein, or perhaps both, were involved. But even that isn't our greatest concern at the moment." He paused and took a deep breath. He wasn't quite able to keep eye contact with Mother. "He sustained a head injury, the full extent of which can't be determined right away —"

"A head injury?" Mother echoed, sounding incredulous, not quite believing Papa had suffered such a wound. "Did he strike his head when he fell after he was shot?"

Dr. Hal shook his head. "No, Lillian. I wasn't with him when he was hurt, so I didn't see what happened. Will and I had gone off in different directions once we reached the camp to try to help whomever we could. By the time we got there, more than half the camp was burning. It was absolute chaos — people running, screaming —"

"But what of William?" she interrupted.

"What exactly happened to him?" Mother shut her eyes momentarily, as though to keep her patience from escaping.

Dr. Hal sighed. He rubbed his thighs with his open hands, like a public speaker with sweaty palms. "There are indications Will was beaten with a blunt object — a stick of wood, maybe. Or a billy club. Or it could have been the butt of a gun. It's hard to say for sure. But apparently he was beaten after he was already down."

Mother gasped and lifted one trembling hand to her lips. "Who would have — who *could* have done such a thing?" she asked, her voice barely a whisper.

"I don't know," Dr. Hal responded morosely. For a moment, he seemed like a relative again rather than a doctor. He looked at me as he confirmed my words to Papa some hours earlier. "We do know it was the sheriff and his deputies who pulled off the raid, just like Ginny said. But as to who actually did this to Will — I simply don't know."

"Just how bad is he, Harold?"

"Again, I can only confess that I don't know. When I reached him, he was still conscious but just barely. Fortunately, in the midst of all that chaos, I was able to hear the cries of the man who came across Will just as his assailant ran off. The man just kept screaming for help, saying Doc

504

Eide was down." Dr. Hal paused and shook his head. He took a deep breath before continuing. "So the good thing is that I got to Will right away. I tied a tourniquet around his thigh with my shirt sleeve to staunch the bleeding, but it was obvious that wasn't the only thing I was dealing with. Will had been beaten pretty badly — he's bruised all over, and there's a possibility that his right arm is broken. X-rays will clarify that. Anyway, the man who alerted me to Will was somehow able to hunt down a blanket" — at the mention of the blanket, he glanced at me to acknowledge my unwitting contribution to Papa's rescue — "in one of the shanties that was still standing, and we used that as a kind of hammock to carry Will to the car. I hated to move him like that, considering the condition he was in. No telling the damage —" He stopped abruptly and stared at his hands. Suddenly he looked very young, almost like a child who'd been caught disobeying and was bracing to accept his punishment.

When he didn't continue, Mother assured him, "You did the right thing, Harold. There wasn't anything else you could do."

Dr. Hal nodded and exhaled so heavily I thought every last bit of oxygen must have been drained from his body. "As I say, our greatest concern is the head wound. There appears to have been just one blow to the head, but it was a hard one. Right about here, running along the right side of his scalp." Dr. Hal ran his fingertips through his disheveled hair to indicate the spot. "Will hasn't been through the X-ray department yet. They wanted to get him into surgery for the bullet wound as quickly as possible. But they did take a few pictures with a portable machine, the quality of which isn't as good as what you can get with the real thing, but good enough to reveal that there is a fracture of the skull. It appears at this point not to be depressed — that is, bone didn't collapse into the brain, which of course is a good thing. What happens to the skull itself doesn't matter very much. Like any other bone the skull can be expected to heal pretty easily, barring infection. What matters is the damage to the brain, and that's what's in question at this point."

Mother and I were silent for a moment, unable to take in what Dr. Hal was trying to tell us.

Finally, tentatively, Mother asked, "Well, when will we know something, Harold?"

"With an injury like this," Dr. Hal explained, "it's impossible to know anything right away. Diagnosing head trauma is always a matter of observation, a matter of time."

Mother moistened her lips with her tongue. She was breathing faster than I thought she should. "You say he's in surgery now."

"Yes."

"What about the anesthesia? What will that do —"

"They'll use a local. It won't have any affect on his brain."

"Oh yes. Yes, of course. I should have realized." Mother squeezed her hands together and pursed her lips. "The man who alerted you to Will — did he see who did this?"

Dr. Hal's eyes hung heavy with regret. "I'm afraid not, Lillian. It was dark. The man — the assailant — was running away. I don't even know the name of the man who called me over to Will. I wish I'd asked for it now, but there was so much confusion, I couldn't think. Anyway, I asked him if he saw who did this, if he had any idea at all, and he said he didn't."

The thought of Papa lying helpless while one of Sheriff Dysinger's deputies, or maybe the sheriff himself, beat him until he was bruised and broken — the image was more than I could bear. From the moment the young messenger came to our door until now, I had moved in a daze, but talk of Papa being battered by that faceless assailant re-ignited my emotions. They sizzled to life like a flame crawling along a fuse, then exploded into rage. I buried my face in my hands and wept, falling forward into my own lap.

Mother's arm curled around my back as she drew me to her. I leaned my head against her chest, my anger and grief spilling out and leaving moist, salty spots on Mother's plain cotton blouse. How long she allowed me to cry, I can't say. I lost all track of time.

"There, Ginny, hush now," she said repeatedly, stroking my hair. "It'll be all right."

To Dr. Hal, she remarked, "I shouldn't have brought her with me. It's too much. She's too young —"

"Why don't I drive her home —"

"I'm not too young!" I objected, pulling away from Mother and sitting bolt upright. Wiping my wet cheeks with my palms and sniffing loudly, I said, "I want to stay here where Papa is. Please, Mama, please let me stay."

Mother's mouth was a thin line. Her shoulders sagged. "It's against my better judgment, but all right, you can stay. Go find a rest room and wash your face while I call Sally and let her know what's going on."

I did as I was told, then returned to the waiting room. The thought occurred to me that we'd spent much of the past several months just waiting for one thing or another. Waiting around the radio. Waiting for news of the strike. Waiting for word about Uncle Jim. And now, waiting to see what would happen to Papa. We were living out our days in one huge waiting room.

"Did you call Aunt Sally, Mama?" I asked.

"Yes."

"Was she awake?"

"Of course. She was sitting right there by the phone."

"What did she say?"

"That she'd be praying."

"What's she going to tell Simon and Claudia and Molly when they wake up?"

"She'll tell them that your father is going to be in the hospital for a little while but that they mustn't worry."

"I hope Molly doesn't cry."

"Aunt Sally will know what to do if she does."

"Mama?"

"Yes, Virginia?"

"I can't help but to be worried, even if it's a sin and I'm not trusting God."

Mother was quiet for a moment. Then she said, "It's not a sin to be worried, Virginia. We can't help worrying sometimes. But in spite of what we feel, we can still trust God to do what's right."

After that, we didn't talk much. Dr. Hal got himself a cup of coffee — Mother declined his offer, saying she couldn't possibly drink any more coffee that night — and paced the room as he drank. Sometimes he stopped at the window and stared out at the night sky, just as I had done earlier in my room at home.

Twinkle, twinkle, little star,
How I wonder what you are. . . .

Oh, God, dear God, up above the world so high, please look down and see us. . . .
Mother pulled a small Bible from her purse and read to herself. The trembling fingers with which she turned the pages were the only evidence of the turmoil in her heart. I lay on the couch, my head on her lap, and drifted in and out of sleep. When I slept, I had wild, disjointed dreams in which I was clubbing a defenseless Sheriff Dysinger with a baseball bat. And when I awoke, I was sorry that my hands were empty and that the sheriff was no doubt by now sleeping soundly in his own warm bed at home.

Papa was on the operating table until almost dawn. With the first dim lightening of the sky, the first faint stirrings of birdsong, a nurse came by the waiting room to tell us

510

Papa was being settled into a special care ward, and that the doctor would be along soon to speak with us. I could read nothing at all in her face, though I tried desperately to discern some sign of hope. Mother tried to ask her how Papa was, but the nurse would only say that the surgeon would answer all our questions very shortly.

We heard his footsteps in the corridor before we saw him. When he appeared in the doorway, a wave of nausea rippled through my stomach. Here he was, the man who had come to tell us about Papa, the messenger of Papa's fate. While we waited at least we had a cushion of time in which we could dream and pray and hope for the best, but now that time was up, and there could be no more hopeful conjecture. The doctor was here, and like it or not, we had no choice but to listen to what he had to say, to hear the truth about Papa's condition. I thought fleetingly of the messengers in ancient Greece who were executed for bringing bad news. Though I had always considered it unfair that they should die for simply doing their job, I suddenly understood the desire to have the bearer of bad tidings snuffed out so he couldn't come around again.

Dr. Hal walked across the waiting room with his right hand extended to greet the surgeon. He introduced Mother and me.

The surgeon shook Mother's hand and offered a polite but formal greeting. He was a man by the name of Dr. Rawls, whom neither Mother nor I had ever met before, though we were acquainted with many doctors through Papa's practice. A heavyset, middle-aged, weary-looking man, he was still dressed up in his surgical garb, his mask still tied about his thick neck and dangling beneath his chin like a discarded feed bag. His hair was hidden completely by his white cap, the rim of which was darkened with sweat. His ample gown had a bib of sweat across the front and, worse, splatters of blood. Papa's blood. First there was a little bit of Papa on Dr. Hal, I thought, and now there's a little bit of Papa on this doctor, too. It was strange and disconcerting to see my father's lifeblood where it didn't belong. It had flowed through Papa's veins, and it ought still to be traveling that old familiar route, not adorning the clothing of these two men.

Mother and I had stood to greet the doctor, but he invited us to sit again. When the four of us were seated, Dr. Rawls began speaking in low tones. He assured us that the surgery on Papa's leg had gone reasonably well, but, as Dr. Hal had already pointed out, the head injury was an even greater cause for concern.

"The first twenty-four hours will be critical," Dr. Rawls explained. "Of those patients who die of brain injury, more than half die within the first twenty-four hours. We've already called for a neurologist to conduct a full examination tomorrow — er, later this morning. The results of his exam will give us a better idea as to what we're dealing with here. Of course, it's after twenty-four to thirty-six hours that we may begin to see symptoms of delayed or secondary increased intracranial pressure."

As he talked, I noticed Mother's jaw working, as though she were trying to chew on the doctor's words to make them easier to swallow.

"If there is swelling, it could be the result of hemorrhage or edema, or perhaps both. No doubt the neurologist will want to perform a lumbar puncture as soon as Dr. Eide has stabilized to determine whether there is blood in his cerebrospinal fluid. . . ."

I didn't know what the doctor was talking about, and furthermore, for reasons I couldn't quite pinpoint right at the moment, I didn't like him very much. I only wanted to get away from him and his statistics and his medical mumbo jumbo as quickly as possible. Mother must have felt the same way, because she interrupted the man by asking, "May I see my husband now, Dr. Rawls?"

The doctor denied Mother's request with a shake of his head. "Better if you didn't," he replied stiffly. "Not while he remains in the post-op ward. Go home and rest first, and when you return, you can see him. In the meantime, we'll call you if there is any significant change in his condition."

Mother, stunned by the doctor's refusal, started to protest, but Dr. Hal stopped her by patting her shoulder. "Dr. Rawls is right, Lillian," he said. "Come on, I'll take you home. After Will's had a chance to recover a bit from the surgery, we'll come back and see him."

Mother's mouth closed up like a nutcracker's jaw snapping on a hinge. She stared at Dr. Rawls with steely eyes, a gaze I had learned to fear early in life. But, to my surprise, she didn't argue. Without saying anything at all — without even the pretense of propriety or a single word of farewell — she turned to go.

But Dr. Rawls stopped her with one more statistic. "Do keep in mind, Mrs. Eide," he said, "that seventy percent of head injury cases are treated successfully, and a full recovery is made."

He smiled wanly, offering us one small hint of his humanity. But neither Mother nor I received affably his attempt at encouragement. In spite of the fact that the doctor's statistics were in our favor, all I could think about was the thirty percent who weren't so lucky.

As we walked out of the waiting room and down the long white corridor of the hospital, I held on to Mother's hand and felt — in spite of my earlier protests — like a child again, in fact, wished indeed that I were, holding her hand as we walked to the park or to church or to the store as once we had done.

We arrived home a weary lot that morning. Dr. Hal, in spite of his lack of sleep, opened the office and saw patients. Mother let me stay home from school to rest. She put on her apron to prepare breakfast, but Aunt Sally shooed her off to bed, saying she could take care of everything until Mother awakened.

When I crawled into bed, the morning sun was just beginning to peek in through the east window of my room like a candle tentatively taking the flame. I lay awake and watched, knowing I wouldn't see the angels if they came, but hoping they were climbing down the sun's ladder, anyway, to come and help us.

Chapter Twenty-Seven

It was dark when Mother slipped into my room and seated herself on the edge of the bed. I was only vaguely aware of her presence at first, frowning, I think, as I felt the bed shift to one side under her weight, unhappy at the intrusion into my sleep. The higher toward wakefulness I climbed, the more confused I became. What was happening? Why was Mother slipping into my room like this in the middle of the night? I felt her hand on my arm.

"Ginny, time to wake up now."

Time to wake up for what? For school? I had always awakened on my own. I didn't need Mother to wake me. Had I been sick? What day was this? What was going on?

And then I remembered.

"Mama!" I cried, fully awake. "What time is it?"

"About eight o'clock."

"Eight o'clock at night?"

"That's right."

"Have I slept all day? More than twelve hours?"

"Yes, and no wonder —"

I threw back the covers. "I have to get up and see Papa!" How, I wondered, could

I have slept so deeply and for so long while Papa lay suspended somewhere between life and death in the hospital?

Mother tightened her grasp on my arm. "I was just at the hospital," she said.

"What?" I couldn't believe she would go without me. "Why didn't you come get me? Why didn't you let me go with you?"

Her face was little more than a shadow in the dark room, and I couldn't see her expression. I reached over and turned on the lamp beside the bed. Mother's face appeared strained and wan, but otherwise she was calm. "Your father's still in the special care ward," she said quietly, "and you wouldn't have been allowed in with me."

"You saw Papa?" I asked. Mother nodded. "How was he, Mama? How did he look?"

"Well, not quite like himself." Mother tried to smile, but her effort didn't amount to much.

"Did you talk with the doctor?" I was anxious to know everything, though Mother seemed reluctant to tell. "Did you talk with that neurologist they were going to call in?"

"Yes, I saw him. His name is Dr. Murphy. He seems like a nice sort of fellow. More personable than Dr. Rawls, anyway."

"But what did he say?"

Mother lifted her shoulders and let them fall again. "That we can't know anything for certain yet."

"But Dr. Rawls told us *that* much!" I sputtered. "I thought a specialist was supposed to know more than a regular doctor. What was the use of calling him in if he can't tell us more than that?" I was beginning to feel irritated by the entire medical profession.

"Like Harold said, it takes time to assess the damage of head trauma."

"Couldn't Dr. Murphy tell you *anything?*"

"He said that your father has some reflex movement and that his pupils respond to light. Those are good things, he said."

I was almost afraid to ask, but I forced myself to form the words. "What are the bad things, then?"

Mother thought a moment, her mouth turned downward in a visible frown as if she were mentally sifting through the vast clutter of information the neurologist had dumped at her feet. "Your father's age, for one thing."

"Papa's not old!" I cried.

"Of course not. But I guess most people over forty-five don't recover as well from head injuries."

More statistics. I clenched my teeth. "He doesn't know Papa," I said. "He doesn't know that Papa's different. . . ."

I let my words trail off as Mother patted my hand. All she said was, "Well," and I knew what she meant. I lowered my eyes to the quilt that covered my bed and tried to anchor myself by following the pattern in the stitches that connected the squares. After a moment, I asked, "What else did the doctor say?"

"He said a lot of things, Virginia, most of which neither you nor I can fully understand. I'm finally learning that for a doctor's wife I'm woefully ignorant when it comes to medicine and the human body." She attempted to smile again. "I know about childhood diseases, but that's about it. Though that's debatable, too, since I didn't recognize chicken pox in the girls when all the symptoms were laid out right under my nose."

Mother spoke wistfully. Personally, I didn't blame her for not knowing what she had never learned, but she seemed keenly disappointed in herself. Nevertheless, it wasn't Mother I was concerned about at the moment.

"Mama," I ventured timidly, "did the doctor tell you whether or not Papa would be all right?"

"No, Virginia," Mother replied quietly, "he didn't tell me that. He can't answer that question, I'm afraid."

"No," I said, "I didn't think he could."

Suddenly Mother stood. "Time for you to eat something," she said. "Everyone else has had supper already."

"But when can I see Papa?"

"Possibly tomorrow. I don't know for sure."

"You won't go back to the hospital without me, will you?"

"I don't like the thought of keeping you from school, but no, I won't go to the hospital without you. Your father needs you more than you need to be in school. We'll arrange for your lessons to be dropped off at the hospital for a couple of days. Come on, now, let's get you fed."

I got up then and, sitting alone in my bathrobe and slippers at the kitchen table, tried to eat the scrambled eggs and toast Mother made for me before she disappeared to put the girls to bed. Though I hadn't eaten all day, I wasn't particularly hungry. I chewed slowly, thinking about what a strange place the kitchen was when there was nobody in it. Kind of like a church sanctuary without a congregation. The room was meant to be occupied, was built for bustle and activity, was where life was supposed to be going on. But now it was quiet and empty. Even the electric fan was still, turned off and unplugged after having worked so hard for so many months. The dishes had been washed and put into place behind the glass-door cabinets, the plates and bowls in stacks, the teacups dangling from little hooks, appearing unused. Even the refrigerator, tired of humming, was silent. Quiet as a tomb, I thought. The whole room was so quiet that even the scraping of my fork against the plate and the crunching of toast between my jaws was an annoying and grating noise. I couldn't remember the last time I'd eaten in the kitchen alone. I couldn't remember *ever* eating in the kitchen alone. And the fact that I was there by myself, eating scrambled eggs in my pajamas at eight-thirty at night, meant that everything in my life had changed. I looked about the room nervously, fearing that at any moment the door to the pantry, or the door to the basement, or the door to the backyard would fly open and something evil would pounce in upon me.

But what came into the kitchen a moment later was my brother, Simon, and when I saw him I sighed openly with relief. Simon was here, and a little bit of life was just the same as it had always been. Maybe he'd sit down and we could talk awhile, give each other a boost of encouragement. We'd experienced the riot together and had come away closer to each other for it. Now we could face together what had happened to Papa. Even though he was just a little boy, he had a certain strength about him, and heaven knew I needed that strength now.

But my hopes quickly toppled into little crumbs of dread when Simon acknowledged me with one long stare of contempt and said nothing. I knew what he was thinking. Papa had gone to the camp and had the life nearly beaten out of him, and Simon blamed me. I watched him reach for a glass from the cupboard and fill it with milk from the bottle in the refrigerator. A pain hung in my chest as heavy as lead and pulled my shoulders down.

"I didn't want Papa to go down there, Simon," I defended myself quietly.

"You knew about the raid," he accused, turning from the refrigerator so quickly that some of the milk in his glass splashed out onto his hand. "You should have stopped him."

"I wanted to stop him, but I couldn't. You don't understand —"

"If Pa dies, it'll be your fault."

His words hit me like a club across my sagging shoulders and knocked the breath out of me. *He's not going to die!* I wanted to yell, but the words caught in my throat. Simon's angry face became a blur as my eyes clouded with tears.

I ran up to my room and cried myself to

sleep, but even then I slept only fitfully between each fresh onslaught of tears.

The next morning I awoke abruptly at dawn and realized that at just about that same time the day before, Dr. Rawls had come to meet us in the waiting room at the hospital. *The first twenty-four hours will be critical,* he had said, and this was it, the zero hour. The first twenty-four had passed and as far as I knew, Papa was still alive.

Throwing back the covers, I climbed out of bed and bundled up in my bathrobe and slippers against the morning chill. I might have enjoyed the cool weather after the unbearable heat of summer, but at the moment I gave it little more than a passing thought. I had to find out about Papa.

As though in answer to my unspoken question, the telephone rang just as I entered the upstairs hall. I rushed down the stairs, hanging precariously on to the banister, while Mother, already up and dressed, moved quickly from the kitchen to pick up the extension on the table near the front door. I arrived breathless and anxious at her elbow. She only glanced at me, then turned away so I wouldn't distract her.

"I see," she said. "All right. . . . Yes, I see. Yes . . ."

Light-headed with fear, I wanted to beat on Mother's broad back to get her attention, to get her to turn toward me so I could read her face. What was the person saying? Was Papa all right? Had he taken a turn for the worse? Mother's voice, calm and even, gave not a clue.

"Yes, we'll be there as soon as we can," she concluded. "Thank you."

She slowly returned the receiver to the cradle, seeming to barely possess the strength to carry out the task. She finally turned her eyes to me. I met her gaze.

She didn't smile. "Eat some breakfast and dress quickly, Virginia," she instructed. "Your father's out of the special care ward and the doctor says we can see him."

"Is he awake?"

"No, not yet."

"But is he better?"

"Enough to be moved from special care."

"When will he wake up?"

"Don't ask me questions I can't answer, Virginia. Run upstairs and get yourself ready to go."

A half hour later, while Mother put on her hat and Dr. Hal warmed up the car to drop us off at the hospital, I ran into Simon in the hall. He was just coming down to breakfast — Aunt Sally was frying eggs in the kitchen — and he was carrying a pile of school books under his arm. He walked by me without saying a word, as if I wasn't there. His accusations of the previous night came thumping down on me again, and I bit my lower lip to keep from crying. But to my surprise, Simon stopped short of the kitchen doorway and turned to look at me.

"Ma tells me you're going to the hospital to see Pa," he said.

"Yes, he's out of that special ward. The hospital called."

He was trying to look angry but without much success. Simon was never able to be anything other than genuine. I knew from the look on his face he was sorry for what he'd said, though he'd never go so far as to admit it. Instead, he requested, "Tell Pa hello for me, will ya?"

"Sure, Simon. I'll tell him."

"Tell him I wish I could come myself."

"All right."

"But I can't, seeing as how the hospital rules says I'm not old enough."

"I'm sure he knows about the rules."

Hoisting the books up higher under his arm, he turned toward the kitchen again. But he paused and said over his shoulder, "Tell him I'm expecting him home by my birthday. That gives him a whole two weeks and three days to get better. I think that's enough time."

I couldn't respond in words, my throat

was so choked up. But I nodded and gave my brother a half smile, and he went off to get a plate of Aunt Sally's eggs.

Papa had been moved into a private room on the wing of the hospital that was named after my grandfather. It was a first-floor room, overlooking the hospital grounds, where patients' families strolled to calm their nerves and patients themselves were wheeled to sit in the sun on warm days or in the shade of one of the maple trees.

As we walked from the lobby to Papa's room, I noticed that Mother and I were the only civilians on the floor, that is, the only ones not dressed in the white uniform of the army of healers. We were the oddities because it was still only midmorning, and visiting hours — noon to two o'clock and six o'clock to eight o'clock — hadn't begun. The rules were being bent for us not only because we were the family of Dr. Eide, but because Mother was the daughter of Theodore Foster. Our double-edged status of privilege allowed us free access to Papa now that he was out of special care.

Mother lectured me through the length of the corridor on how I ought to behave. "You must be brave, Virginia. There's to be no crying while we're with your father. I don't want to upset him."

Because Papa hadn't yet awakened, I didn't think he'd know whether I cried or not. But Mother seemed convinced otherwise, and for that reason — just in case she was right — I promised myself I wouldn't cry.

We finally reached the door of Papa's room, and while I paused on the threshold to gather my courage, Mother marched right in, leaned over the figure of Papa on the bed, and kissed the corner of his mouth. She didn't have to bend over very far because the head of the bed was elevated to a nearly forty-five-degree angle. A small ice pack crowned the top of Papa's head, and I thought he could have looked rather comic — like one of the Laurel and Hardy duo complaining of flu — if the situation hadn't been so grave.

Mother pressed her fingers lightly to one of his cheeks and said, "We're here, William. Virginia and I have come to be with you." She went on talking to him softly while I made my way to the bed, the tapping of the heels of my shoes against the bare floor an annoying din in the quiet building. When I reached the bed, I followed Mother's lead and kissed Papa's cheek. The bristle of his whiskers against my lips startled me. I had never known Papa's face to be anything other than smooth and fragrant with aftershave. I drew back suddenly, thinking, *This isn't Papa.*

And, indeed, the man in the bed bore little resemblance to the father I knew. Beneath the sandy whiskers, his usually ruddy cheeks were a pasty gray. His face looked small, his closed eyes naked and impish without his glasses. Both eyes were cradled by black-and-blue crescents, like two soft-boiled eggs served in eggcups. His nostrils and the inside of his ears were painted red with iodine. I didn't know why then, but I would shortly learn that meningitis poses a serious danger to head injury cases, and that this particular precaution was taken so that the germ-carrying microbes wouldn't enter Papa's head via these passages. A large bandage circled his head so that between the bandage and the ice pack only a tuft or two of hair stuck out on top of his scalp, like grass springing up between the cracks of a sidewalk. Even his ample body appeared smaller somehow, lying there beneath the crisp hospital linens. Since the sheet was pulled all the way up to his chin, his broken arm and shattered leg were tucked away, and I guess in a way I was rather glad that I couldn't see the whole mess at once.

Aunt Sally had always said that things happened in threes, but this time she was wrong. Papa was the fourth in our family to receive a head wound in this war called the Depression, and his injury was the most serious of all.

"Don't just stand there gaping, Virginia," Mother chided. "Say hello to your father."

When I cast a dubious glance at Mother, she drew me aside. In a whisper she said, "We don't know how much he can hear, but maybe if we talk to him as though everything were normal, it'll help to bring him around."

Everything was not normal — everything was very far from normal. I had promised not to cry, and that was hard enough, but to talk as though nothing were wrong — that was a whole different story. It seemed too much for Mother to ask of me, but wanting not to disappoint her, I said, "I'll try, Mama."

When we returned to Papa's side, though, and I opened my mouth to speak, nothing came out. I was paralyzed by the strangeness of talking to a sleeping figure. It seemed like talking to a photograph or to the tombstone of someone who obviously wasn't around to listen anymore. I glanced up again at Mother. She nodded at me to go on, like a mother bird nudging the baby out of the nest with her beak. Drawing in a deep breath, I told myself I couldn't exhale without including words with the air. I gathered together a few words in my chest, pushed them up to my tongue, and said, "Hello, Papa. It's me. It's —" I almost said Virginia. But somehow using my full given name didn't seem right. To Papa, I was Ginny. I had tried so hard to get him to call me Virginia, yet now I wondered why. What I wouldn't have given at that moment to hear him call me Ginny again. "Papa, it's Ginny," I said finally. "Mama and I are here. We're fine. Everyone's fine. Simon says hello. He and Claudia and Molly miss you. They wanted to come, but you know they're not old enough. I'm glad I could come, Papa. The hospital is breaking the rules for us, you know, because you're special. Mama and I can come whenever we want and stay as long as we want, so we'll try to be here as much as we can, if Mama doesn't make me go back to school too soon. . . ."

The longer I spoke the more easily the words came, but just as I began to feel comfortable talking with someone who couldn't hear, Dr. Rawls arrived and interrupted us, lumbering into the room like a polar bear up on his hind legs. He tossed a greeting to Mother but seemed not to notice me. After studying Papa's chart and hanging it back up on the foot of the bed, he said, "Well, we performed the first lumbar puncture early this morning and discovered very little blood in the spinal fluid, which is a good sign. Of course, we'd like the fluid to be clear, but there wasn't enough blood to cause undue concern at this point. According to the manometer reading, there's a moderate increase in intracranial pressure, but again, there's no real cause for alarm as yet. We'll keep an eye out for increased pressure, of course, as there's a good chance of edema setting in, maybe even hemorrhage. In the event of either or both of these, we can begin a regiment of regular lumbar drainage and hypertonic solutions. . . ."

I stood there openmouthed, listening to this robotic recitation and understanding not a word of it. My eyes turned to Papa lying nearby on the elevated bed with iodine in his nose and an ice cap on his head, and I felt increasingly annoyed at Dr. Rawls and the highfalutin medical terms that dripped from his tongue like so much late-afternoon-staff-meeting dialogue. I didn't want to hear about lumbar punctures and spinal mercury manometers. I didn't want to hear about cranial trauma and meningitis and subdural hematomas, about concussion and contusion and compression, and about all the other disasters that Dr. Rawls was babbling on about. I didn't want to hear a series of meaningless statistics and speculations. What I wanted was to push aside this onslaught of medical rambling, to sweep it away like so much unnecessary clutter, and to get right down to the important question: Was my father going to be all right?

But the fact was — and I knew it even then — in spite of the man's impressive knowledge, the best that Dr. Rawls could offer us when faced with such a question was, "I don't know."

Mother must have been just as disgusted with the doctor as I was because when he left, she said, "Well, we'll have to have Harold interpret all that mumbo jumbo when we see him."

At regular intervals throughout the day, we were interrupted by the sudden appearance of doctors, interns, nurses, technicians, orderlies. Papa's temperature was taken, his pulse checked, his respirations counted, his blood pressure measured, and the results dutifully recorded in the chart at the foot of his bed. His eyelids were lifted and his eyeballs assaulted with lights. His one good leg and his one good arm were repeatedly thumped, his reflexes measured. His heart and lungs were listened to, his chest tapped. The bandages around his thigh were cut away, the wound checked, fresh bandages applied. The same was done to his head. His nostrils and ears received fresh coats of iodine. His ice cap was carted away and brought back bulging with fresh ice. Once or twice he was given an injection of this or that. There seemed an endless parade of white-clad people coming in and out of the room, working over Papa the way all the king's horses and all the king's men tried to put Humpty together again.

I prayed these people would be more successful with Papa than all the king's men were with Humpty-Dumpty.

During those moments when Mother and I were left alone with Papa, we talked almost constantly, sometimes to each other, but mostly to Papa. And all the while we talked, we watched for any small movement — a pressing of the hand, a fluttering of the eyes, a twitching of the lips — anything to tell us that Papa was there, and that he was trying to make his way back to us.

Chapter Twenty-Eight

Mother allowed me to miss one more day of school so I could stay with her at the hospital. We arranged for Charlotte to drop off my lessons at the nurses' station in the afternoon, which would enable me to remain caught up with my homework.

That second day was even longer and more tedious than the first. Mother and I went on talking with Papa about everything we could possibly think of: family news, updates on his patients from Dr. Hal, tidbits of interest from the newspaper, what I was studying in school. I even recited for him some of the Thomas Campion poems I'd memorized that summer as punishment for cutting my hair. Never in my life had I prattled on so much, and the fact that I was speaking to someone who wasn't even conscious made it all the more tiring. About every hour or so we interrupted these strained ramblings to read long passages to Papa from his Bible. While this saved me from having to think of anything original to say, it was almost even more emotionally taxing than the forced monologues. Papa's Bible was crowded with notes he'd written in the margins in his cramped but tidy script. Dr. Hal often kidded him about his handwriting, saying he ought to work on making it more illegible if he wanted to be respected as a doctor. I used to laugh at that joke, but now it fell flat as I gazed at Papa's Bible notes and wondered whether he had written the last of them.

Throughout that long day the doctors and nurses came and went, the former looking stern and professional, the latter casting us sympathetic smiles. Still, no one could tell us anything definite about Papa's prognosis, and I sensed an aura of apology hanging about these professionals, a silent and embarrassed apology to Mother and me for their inability to predict the future.

There was no change in Papa's condition. He went on sleeping and gave us no indication at all that he could hear us, or that he knew we were there.

Dr. Hal came around in the late afternoon shortly after Charlotte dropped off my homework. I was sitting on the floor with an open book in my lap, almost relieved to have this connection to the normal world, my former life, when Dr. Hal entered the room. With some reluctance, I shut the book while Dr. Hal took Papa's pulse, listened to his heart, shined a light in his eyes, and did a few other of those medical things. It was time to return to Papa, to listen to what Dr. Hal had to say. When he finished his cursory examination, Mother motioned him out into the hall. I followed.

"I've gotten the opinions of Dr. Rawls and Dr. Murphy — more or less," Mother said evenly, "but I want to know what you think, Harold."

Dr. Hal shuffled uneasily. "Well, Lillian, I have to agree with what those two have already told you. We can't make any predictions at this point. We just have to wait and see. I know that's frustrating — believe me, I know. Waiting is the hardest thing to do. But right now, thankfully, things don't look too bad."

"Then why isn't he waking up? I can't believe it's a good sign when a man's been unconscious for two days."

"Actually, Lil, with a head injury like Will's, several days of unconsciousness can pretty much be expected. A coma is a body's way of healing itself. It's not necessarily a bad thing."

Mother's shoulders lifted and settled again. "If you say so, Harold. But I can't stop thinking of all those terrible things Dr. Rawls said might still happen — edema and blood clots and brain hemorrhages and meningitis. And, Harold, what about permanent brain damage? Dr. Rawls said nearly half the people who survive this kind of injury end up damaged for life, while ten percent are totally incapacitated. Totally incapacitated, Harold! Just what is William going to wake up to be? What —"

"Lillian, listen to me. For your own sake, don't pay too much attention to Dr. Rawls' statistics. His numbers just don't mean that much — not when it comes down to the bottom line, anyway. And, you see, the bottom line is this: Every head injury case is unique, or, as one of my medical professors used to say, 'a law unto itself.' There isn't one case that's exactly like another, which makes it almost impossible to predict what's going to happen. Just because some people are left with permanent damage doesn't mean that Will is going to end up one of them. It's possible, yes, but let's not assume anything until we have more to go on."

Mother's forehead wrinkled, and she lifted sad eyes to Dr. Hal. "But it's also possible, isn't it, that he won't wake up at all? He won't die and he won't get better — he'll just go on sleeping."

Reluctantly, Dr. Hal agreed. "Yes, it's possible. But right now, in William's case, it doesn't appear probable. Chances are good he'll start to come out of the coma in another day or so."

"And the longer he sleeps?"

Dr. Hal sighed, as though he'd just been

checkmated. "The longer he sleeps, the less likely it is he'll wake up. But listen, Lillian, at this point we might as well keep expecting the best. For William's sake, keep your hope up."

Mother gave a brief and tentative smile but then asked timidly, almost like a child, "But, Harold, can't you just tell me —"

"Doctors aren't God, Lillian," Dr. Hal interrupted, anticipating Mother's question. "You, of all people, know that."

Mother gazed at Dr. Hal in silence, probably wishing as I was that she could pull a definite forecast out of him. Wishing that he would say, "Just a day or two more of sleep and he'll be fine. All the tests indicate there won't be any permanent damage." Even if he couldn't say that, even if he had to say instead, "He won't be waking up again," it would be better than the not knowing. If we *knew* he was going to remain comatose, or even to die, then we could begin to adjust to our loss. But this not knowing, this dangling in suspense between hope and despair, was almost unbearable.

But as Dr. Hal said, he wasn't God. And there wasn't a doctor in the world who was. Only God was God. And only God could decide what would happen to Papa.

Dr. Hal laid a hand on Mother's upper arm. "Why don't you and Ginny come home with me now? It's been a long day for both of you."

Mother looked at me for my opinion. "Let's stay awhile longer, Mama," I said. It was hard to be there, but it was harder to think about leaving.

Mother nodded. "Would you mind coming back later this evening, Harold? I know I'm completely neglecting everything at home, but I'd rather stay here with William just now."

"Of course," Dr. Hal said.

"The children — are they all right?"

"Everyone's fine. Well, a little sad and a little confused. Molly keeps asking where you and Will are. It's tough explaining it all to a three-year-old without telling her too much. Claudia seems more accepting of the situation than Molly. In fact, she tells Molly not to worry because you'll be home soon and maybe you'll bring them some candy if they're good." Dr. Hal smiled wistfully at the thought.

"And how do you think Simon's holding up?" Mother asked.

"Harder to tell with him. He doesn't say much, but I think he's scared. You kind of have to expect him to be."

"I know they need me at home, but —"

"Will needs you here, Lillian. Don't berate yourself for wanting to be with your husband."

"Yes, well, maybe I can spend a little extra time with the children tonight, or tomorrow morning. Just to reassure them."

"All right," Dr. Hal said, shrugging, "but you've got Sally and me to help take care of them, too."

"Yes, I know, and I thank you, Harold. It just seems everyone is overburdened right now. You, trying to hold down the practice by yourself —"

"Don't worry about that, Lil —"

"— and Sally taking care of the children and the house. How's she doing, do you think? Is she managing all right on her own?"

"Of course, but then again —" Dr. Hal paused to smile — "she's not really on her own. I mean, the neighbor ladies are starting to bring food around and offering to help with chores, and the menfolk are stopping by to see if there's anything that needs fixing. I think Sally's going to have all the help she needs for a while."

"Oh!" Mother said. "How kind of everyone to help out. I must make a point of thanking them when all this is over." She paused a moment, then added, "Is Sally finding the time to visit Jim?"

"She spent an hour with him just this afternoon. The Mobleys volunteered to watch the girls while she was gone."

Mother nodded, satisfied. "They've always been good to us, the Mobleys. Is there any news about Jim?"

I felt a momentary twinge of guilt whenever anyone mentioned Uncle Jim. From the moment Papa was hurt, very few of my waking thoughts were centered around my uncle. He was still in jail, his future still uncertain, but at least he wasn't hurt, and he wasn't in danger of dying. I couldn't afford to expend any of my energy worrying about someone whose situation seemed relatively safe. All my worrying was done for Papa.

Dr. Hal shook his head. "Nothing yet. The lawyers are still working on it."

"Poor Sally. I hope we know something soon."

"She told Jim all about Will, of course." Mother nodded. Dr. Hal went on. "Jim's taken it hard. Broke down and cried right there in the jail cell in front of a dozen other men. He said being behind bars had been almost bearable until it was those same bars keeping him from Will's bedside. He said he'd sure like to be here, but since he can't, he sends his love."

Mother smiled weakly. "And we send ours to him."

Once we had all been together in one big house that seemed small and crowded at the time. Now all I wanted was for us to be there again, crowded or no, instead of having to send messages of love to places like the city jail and Mercy Hospital.

"Well, Harold." Mother sighed. "Why don't you pick us up around eight o'clock or so tonight?"

"I'll be here," Dr. Hal assured her. "And don't worry. Try not to worry about anything."

We were all talked out, I guess, by the time the first shadows of dusk fell. I was on the floor again, cross-legged, my geography textbook cradled in my lap, my other books scattered on the floor around me. Mother sat in the chair beside Papa's bed and said nothing. She simply sat, holding his hand. Every so often I looked up from my book to take in the scene across the room — my father lying silently on the bed, my mother sitting silently beside him.

Mother's face was a mask, offering no clue as to the thoughts running through her mind. I tried to imagine her feelings by picturing myself sitting beside the bed of a wounded Charlie Chaplin or Charles Lindbergh. It was as close as I could come to knowing what it would be like to be in danger of losing the one you loved. And though I knew it wasn't really the same at all, because they were only a dream to me, while Papa was very real to Mother, it gave me some idea as to the depth of Mother's personal tragedy. "Will and Lil," she had written all over her school books. "Will and Lil." And there had never been anyone else for either of them. Should Papa die, the largest chunk of Mother's life would fall away, and she'd never get it back. It made me dizzy to imagine the wide open space that would enter Mother's life with Papa's absence. A space so large you could get lost in it and never find your way home again.

Out in the hallway beyond the open door of Papa's room, the members of the hospital staff passed by in blurs of white. Medicine carts that needed oiling squeaked by, wheelchairs rolled past, stretchers rumbled along. All the hurried movements beyond the door presented a stark contrast to the dimly lighted hush of Papa's room. We were the theater patrons, Mother and I, watching life playing itself out upon the stage, wishing that we, too, could be a part of it. But we were consigned to this place of watching — and waiting.

The thin blanket spread out across Papa's chest lifted and fell with his every breath. "We have to watch for changes in respiration," one of the nurses had explained to us earlier. "It could be cause for concern if it speeds up or slows down, or especially if it becomes stertorous." When I looked at her blankly, she smiled and said, "That is, it becomes loud or labored, kind of like snoring. That's a bad sign." Since her warning, I'd been intermittently watching Papa breathe. It made me feel that I was doing *something* to help take care of him.

Mother's eyes moved from Papa's face to the slightly opened window and back again.

I stared down at the book in my lap, but I didn't read. My mind drifted elsewhere, out of the hospital room and through the city streets toward home. Home where Simon and Claudia and Molly, Aunt Sally and my cousins, and Dr. Hal were. Life was going on there, too. Real life, like the happenings out in the hall. Every day Aunt Sally cooked and cleaned, the older children went to school, the younger children played. Dr. Hal saw patients. The same as always. I missed home. I missed the routines of our lives, all the otherwise unnoticed customs — meals together around the kitchen table, and evenings together on the porch or around the radio, all the untroubled hours of work and play and rest. How sweet all those simple things seemed now. How much I longed for that completely unromantic but loveliest of lives.

And how central Papa was to all of it. Papa sitting at his desk in the morning taking care of the first order of the day. Papa whistling as he shaved, as he worked, as he waited for his warm milk at night. Papa sitting beside me on the porch swing, listening patiently to all the small details of my life, as though I was the most important person in the world. It was Papa's love and his joy and his presence that colored all my days and made them beautiful.

If it were all to end now, I thought, it would be a bitter ending. If Papa never awoke, if he were to die tonight, or tomorrow, or the day after that, his last conscious feelings for me would be of anger and disappointment. After all the years of resting secure in his love, I couldn't bear the thought that our relationship would end at such a point. I saw him as he was the night of the raid, peering down at me through narrowed eyes, his face crimson with anger. *"Why didn't you tell me?"* he had demanded as he shook me. *"Why didn't you tell me?"* I wanted to defend myself now, to point to his wounds and say, *Because I love you, Papa! Because I love you and I didn't want* this *to happen. I was trying to protect you.* I wanted to hear him say it was all right, that he loved me too, that he understood why I didn't tell him about the raid on Soo City. . . .

In spite of my determination not to cry, I felt the tears pressing against my eyes. I kept my head bent over my geography book so Mother wouldn't see. I peered hard at the open pages, but they suddenly appeared as disjointed as a kaleidoscope in motion. Then two tears slithered down my cheeks and landed with a splash on the map of the United States in my lap. I thought that in another moment I would have to give up and simply give in to the grief, but before I could break down completely into uncontrollable sobs, my sorrow was interrupted by an unexpected commotion. The sound came through the partly opened window, from out on the hospital grounds. All at once there was a blur of voices, people talking in low tones, a ripple of laughter, then the blaring of instruments and a chorus of off-key voices. Mother straightened up as though someone had called her name, and she looked over at me. We frowned at each other across the room.

"Now, what on earth —" Mother began, but before saying more, she settled Papa's hand gently on the bed and rose from the chair. I brushed away the tears on my cheeks, pushed my geography book aside, and scrambled up from the floor to join her at the window.

We stood there motionless, not quite believing what we saw. Out in the pale evening light, gathered on the leaf-strewn grounds, was a picket line. A whole string of people milled about, carrying signs and singing, but it wasn't a picket line like the one that had marched and sung about solidarity in front of the grain mill. It wasn't a picket line like the ones that gathered in cities across the country to demonstrate against hunger and unemployment and low wages and unfair working hours. No, this was something altogether different from the uprisings that had plagued our nation for months.

"It's some of the people from Soo City, Mama," I whispered. "That's Joe blowing on the harmonica and Oscar playing the guitar. And the man playing the accordion — they call him Bellowing Bob. Down at the camp they sit on cinder blocks while they play, and sometimes Bob gets to pumping so hard he falls right off the block. Oh, and the woman there holding the baby — that's Mrs. Everhart, and the little baby is Caroline. You remember, she's the one Papa delivered not too long ago. And that's Mrs. Everhart's two boys and her husband, too. Standing right behind them is Sherman Browne — he's the one who pulled stork duty when Caroline was born because Mr. Everhart was too nervous to come himself. And there's Dick Mason — he came to the house when his brother-in-law was run over by the train. Remember, Mama? He was the first one ever to come to our house from Soo City.

And look, there's Shoes and Longjohn and Mr. Lucky, and that's Mr. Lucky's dog, T-Bone." The very people who, by staying quiet, I hadn't stepped forward to help.

Where they had come from and how they had found their way to Papa at the hospital, I had no idea. To my shame, I realized that they had been brushed aside right along with my worries about Uncle Jim. I hadn't even wondered what had become of them, so caught up was I in my own father's welfare. After the raid, they had simply disappeared from my mind as quickly as they had disappeared from the riverbank — without one thought or prayer from me. But now, suddenly, here they were, singing "Amazing Grace" and holding makeshift signs of cardboard with charcoal lettering. GET WELL SOON, DOC EIDE and WE'RE PULLING FOR YOU and GOD BLESS YOU, DOC. Even T-Bone wore a sandwich board, one side of which said DOC EIDE: FRIEND TO MAN AND BEAST and the other: T-BONE LOVES SAWBONES.

They were a motley crew, dirtier and more disheveled than ever. Their clothing was torn, their hair matted and flying in all directions, and all ten of Longjohn's toes stuck out of the ends of his tattered shoes. They also carried the wounds they had suffered in the raid: an arm in a sling here, a black eye there, a hand or a foot or a knee wrapped in crude bandages. Even their voices were harsh and raspy, still bearing the effect from the smoke of the fire. They were the sorriest group of musicians I had ever seen, and yet they made the sweetest music I'd ever heard.

Mother, who hadn't spoken up till now, remarked quietly, "Oh, Virginia, aren't they dreadful?"

But she said it with a kind of awe. Her chin quivered and her eyes glazed over with the first tears I'd seen since our ordeal began, and in those few moments Mother must have understood what Papa saw in these people Jesus called "the least of the brethren." She must have seen what it was that took Papa back again and again to their camp to be among them.

And I did, too. When I looked at them as they stood there in their peculiar picket line, I saw the long-handled spoons that Papa had told me about. The instruments and the voices and the improvised signs and the tears on people's faces — these all were long-handled spoons, held up now to Papa's lips with the life-giving stew that Papa couldn't reach for himself. Unlike me, these people understood the riddle of those strange utensils, had probably understood it long ago, and had somehow — in their own way — been feeding Papa across the table all along.

Suddenly, Mr. Donner, the hospital administrator, appeared on the grounds, taking long strides toward the group while waving his arms dramatically. "This is a hospital!" he cried in an angry stage whisper. "We must have quiet here! Either you leave at once or I'll call the sheriff."

At that, Mother flung open the window as wide as it would go and shouted through the screen, "*Mis*-ter Donner! You will do no such thing! I think the sheriff's done quite enough, thank you. These people have come to sing, and sing they will!"

I couldn't believe it. Here was my very proper mother, standing arms akimbo, yelling at the top of her voice to the hospital administrator.

Mr. Donner, I think, couldn't quite believe it either. He looked around frantically for the source of this unexpected censure until he finally spotted Mother in the window of Papa's room. The Soo City singers had stopped singing, and Mr. Donner's suddenly timid voice came to us from out of the abrupt silence.

"M-Mrs. Eide!" he stuttered apologetically. "I was just trying —"

"You leave those people be," Mother warned. "Let them do what they've come to do."

The man, red-faced, glanced at the dubious singers. He did a double take when Bellowing Bob, the accordionist, bowed and tipped his cap. Mr. Donner responded with a frown. Then moving in his long-legged strides toward the window where we stood, he didn't stop until he practically had his nose pressed up against the screen. "But, Mrs. Eide," he said as he ran his thin fingers through his hair, "I have to think of the other patients. We can't have these — these *people*" — he spat out the last word as though he considered it a misnomer — "disturbing the residents of this hospital."

"Then they will just have to sing more quietly," Mother replied adamantly. She had that look on her face that meant her decision was final.

Mr. Donner took out a handkerchief from his breast pocket, wiped nervously at his brow, and sighed heavily. He looked from Mother to the singers and back to Mother again. "All right," he conceded. "They can sing, but only very quietly and only for a short time." Then gathering up the pieces of his shattered authority, he added sternly, "And no instruments!"

As the administrator stalked off, Mother slipped me a placid smile. "I knew I'd be glad one day that Father funded this wing," she said. Actually, she'd been proud all along, but now Grandfather Foster's generosity had proved really useful. I smiled at Mother in return and took her hand.

The Soo City singers moved closer to Papa's window, and Joe O'Hanlon stepped forward, took off his cap and squeezed it, together with his harmonica, in his large hands. He looked at me and nodded a greeting, then said to Mother, "The doctor was always coming around doing for us, ma'am. We wanted to do something for him in return. It ain't much, but we know how he favors music. We thought he might like a song or two."

Mother took a deep breath before speaking, appearing to collect herself. When she spoke, her voice was strong and even. "I thank you good people for your thoughtfulness," she said. "I wonder whether I might ask a favor of you?"

"Of course, Mrs. Eide," Joe agreed eagerly.

"Dr. Eide had —" Mother stopped and corrected herself. "Dr. Eide has a special penchant for Christmas carols. I know it's not yet the season, but I wonder whether you might —" Mother stopped when she saw each face in the crowd brighten into a smile.

"It would be our pleasure, ma'am," Joe replied. He returned his cap to his head and, as self-appointed conductor of the group, instructed, "Let's start with 'O come, O come, Emmanuel.' I heard the doc whistling that one enough to reckon it's one of his favorites. Listen up, now, here's the note."

He tooted on his harmonica — an effort that did little to get the group on key — and in the next moment Papa's room was filled with something resembling the songs of Christmas.

We listened to those *a cappella* whisperings for the next half hour while night settled over the hospital grounds. And as the darkness came on, a certain light slipped in as well — a light that began to dispel the inner blackness of our fears, for the singers brought Christmas to us. It didn't matter that it was October and not December, or that what was tumbling from the sky was autumn leaves and not snow. Christmas had come.

> *"O come, O come, Emmanuel,*
> *And ransom captive Israel,*
> *That mourns in lonely exile here,*
> *Until the Son of God appear. . . ."*

Emmanuel: God with us. Not up in the sky somewhere beyond the twinkling stars. Not so far away that the earth appears a little speck of dirt hung slipshod in the uni-

verse. But here. Right here. In this city . . .
in this place . . . in this room.

> "O come, Thou Dayspring, come and cheer,
> Our spirits by Thine advent here;
> Disperse the gloomy clouds of night,
> And death's dark shadows put
>   to flight. . . ."

I had wanted to shout at Him, to reach
my hand up and rattle heaven, to demand
His attention: *Oh, God, dear God, I'm here!*
But it seemed only futile, and I questioned
His ability to hear me, to see me, to answer me. He who was up above the world
so high, like a diamond in the sky. But
then, suddenly, unexpectedly, the people
from Soo City had slipped onto the hospital grounds, and in spite of the rags they
called clothes, in spite of their poverty, in
spite of the failures that clung to them like
so much lint on an old jacket, they had
brought God with them.

When the notes of the last song subsided, Joe O'Hanlon tucked his harmonica
into his jacket pocket and said, "Well, Mrs.
Eide, I reckon we'd better be moving
along."

Mother took a small step closer to the
window and placed her hand on the
screen. "I wonder, would you —" she
started. She had the same look on her face

as when she sometimes watched Papa go off to Soo City, that look of wanting to call him back but wondering whether she should. "Well," she continued, "would it be an imposition to ask you to come back tomorrow?"

Oscar Salinsky strummed a chord on his guitar. "We'll be here, ma'am," he promised.

Mother thanked them, and good-nights were exchanged all around.

"God bless you, Mrs. Eide."

"See you tomorrow, Virginia."

"Take good care of the doc."

"We'll be praying."

"Sleep well, everyone," Mother called out.

They turned to go, and too late I wondered to ask them where they were going, where they had come from, where they would sleep.

I never did find out.

Chapter Twenty-Nine

Mother sent me back to school starting Friday of that week. Of course I didn't want to go. I wanted to stay with Papa. Mother tried to console me by saying I could come to the hospital straight from school and spend the rest of the afternoon and evening there with her. She instructed me on where and when to catch the trolley and gave me the nickel fare in the morning before I left the house.

That first day back at school, I felt like the bearded lady at the circus, a misfit to be stared and gawked at. Of course my friends Charlotte and Rosemary and Jean welcomed me back into the fold, and my teacher, Miss Howard, pulled me aside and offered words of consolation and encouragement. But most of the kids regarded me from a distance, with furtive stares and barely concealed whispers.

"Her pa got shot."

"His head's all bashed in like an old pumpkin."

But the one that really bothered me was "They say he might die any minute now." The fragmented whispers followed me wherever I went. I clenched my jaw and forced myself not to cry, thinking, *Let them say what they want. What do they know, anyway?*

Danny Dysinger tried repeatedly to catch my eye in class, but I ignored him. He had wanted to help in his own way, I knew, but I couldn't get it out of my mind that it may have been Danny's own father who wielded the blow to Papa's head when he was already down.

Good old Charlotte spent most of the time between classes and at recess with her arm around my shoulder like a mother hen tucking a chick beneath her wing. She didn't offer me any sympathy, for which I was grateful, but repeatedly made statements that began with "When your pa gets better . . ." or "When your pa gets home . . ." She didn't entertain the possibility of any other outcome, and she wouldn't let me either.

Saturday gave me some relief from the curiosity of my classmates, though it was another day spent from morning till night at the hospital. I realized on Saturday that during those hours I was away from Papa, it was easier to hope for his recovery, much easier than when I was with him. Because when I stood beside his bed and looked upon the gaunt and vacant face that didn't resemble my father at all, I'd think, *How can he possibly ever be Papa again?*

Sunday morning Mother insisted that we all go to church, and Rev. Winchell's prayer — "O Lord, comfort the good doctor's wife and children at this, their hour of trial . . ." — and the sympathy of our fellow congregants just about killed us.

"Oh, Lillian, you're holding up so *well*. I remember when my Harry died. . . ."

"God will never give us more than we can bear. . . ."

"There's a purpose in this — someday you'll see. . . ."

". . . and your children so young, but God takes care of His own. You won't be alone, Mrs. Eide. . . ."

Mother and I dragged ourselves to the hospital that afternoon with the condolences of our fellow churchgoers hanging like chains around our necks and threatening to choke us. "They mean well, Virginia," Mother explained. "Try not to let their words bother you."

But bother me they did, and I was in a deep funk until early evening when some unexpected guests showed up. Mother and I had just returned from supper in the hospital cafeteria when Charlotte and Mrs. Besac appeared in the doorway with small cloth bags in their hands like a couple of trick-or-treaters. Only instead of asking for handouts, they were bearing gifts, and instead of being all made up, Mrs. Besac was alarmingly colorless. I think she knew she'd offend Mother if she came around wearing her usual rouge and lipstick. My friend and her mother stood in the doorway awkwardly, not quite sure what to do, until my own mother finally said, "Mrs. Besac, Lottie, how nice of you to come. Please come in."

Mother stood to greet Mrs. Besac, and all the while the latter was apologizing for having shown up unexpectedly. "We called your house," she explained, "and Mrs. Dubbin told us you were still here and to just come on over."

"Of course," Mother responded. "I'm so glad you did."

Her words surprised me because I was well aware of her opinion of Mrs. Besac. And yet I should have known that Mother would hardly turn up her nose and send the woman away. Charlotte and I smiled at each other as our mothers exchanged pleasantries.

"Won't you sit down?" Mother invited, pointing to the one chair beside Papa's bed. "I can get some more chairs —"

"Oh no, really, I can't stay," Mrs. Besac interrupted. "I just wanted to bring Lottie around and give you this." She pulled out of the bag something all wrapped up in wax paper and handed it to Mother. "I made some bread this afternoon. It's banana bread. I don't know whether you like it —"

"Why, yes, of course," Mother said, accepting the loaf. "Banana bread is one of our family favorites. Thank you so much."

"You know I hate to cook, Virginia," Charlotte blurted out, "but I tried to make you some cookies. They're chocolate chip. I don't think they turned out so good, but anyway, here they are."

"I'm sure they're very good!" I said as I took the little bag she handed me, though, in fact, I could imagine she had forgotten some vital ingredient like the sugar. But I didn't care.

Mrs. Besac appeared flustered as she stood near Papa's bed. She kept dropping her eyes, seeming afraid to look at him. "I wanted to tell you, Mrs. Eide," she said, clenching her hands together, "that I really am sorry about what's happened to Dr. Eide. He always treated me good whenever I came to him with a problem, or whenever Lottie's been sick. And, well, I'm not a praying woman, Mrs. Eide, but ever since I heard the doc was hurt, I've been asking God to help him. Lots of good people are praying for him, and well . . ."

Her voice trailed off, as though she'd simply run out of words. Mother smiled at her then, not a false smile prompted by propriety, but a genuine smile.

"Thank you for your prayers, Mrs. Besac," she said gently. "That means so much to me. And it will mean a great deal to Dr. Eide, too, when he wakes up and learns you were praying for him."

Mrs. Besac's face flushed slightly, but she returned Mother's smile. "Well," she said, sounding relieved, "I'll be back when visiting hours are over to pick up Lottie."

"Are you sure you won't stay awhile?" Mother asked.

"Thank you, but I can't. Lottie," she said, turning to Charlotte and me, "you be good and don't bother Mrs. Eide."

"I'll be good, Mama."

"I'll meet you out front at eight."

"All right, Mama. And, Mama?"

"Hmm? Yes, Lottie?"

"It's Charlotte."

Mrs. Besac sighed and exchanged a knowing glance with Mother before walking out of the room. Mother stood there holding the loaf of banana bread in her hand and staring at the doorway through which Mrs. Besac had just passed. There was a gap a mile wide between the two women, but I decided Mrs. Besac had just laid the first brick in the foundation of the bridge that might one day connect them.

Charlotte walked over to Papa's bedside and looked down at him with a sorrowful expression in her eyes. "He doesn't look very much like his old self, does he?" she asked quietly. She didn't wait for an answer before looking up at Mother and saying, "But don't worry, Mrs. Eide, he's going to be all right. I can feel it in my bones."

"Thank you, Charlotte," Mother said. She finally placed the banana bread on the side table and settled herself in the chair beside Papa. I'm not sure she put much trust in Charlotte's bones, but she smiled at my friend as though she were Dr. Rawls himself telling her Papa was bound to wake up any minute now.

"You wanna take a walk, Virginia, just around the halls?" Charlotte asked.

I looked at Mother. "Can we, Mama?"

"All right, but do it quietly. This is a hospital, remember." When my friend and I headed for the door, Mother called, "You'll be back in time for the singers, won't you?"

"Of course," I said. "You want to hear the singers, don't you, Charlotte?"

"The Soo City singers?" Charlotte asked. "Sure I do! We'll be back soon, Mrs. Eide."

Out in the corridor, we threw our arms around each other and started to walk. "Think we'll see anything gory?" Charlotte asked expectantly.

"Naw," I said, shaking my head. "They pretty much keep the gory stuff hidden as much as possible."

"The only time I got to be in a hospital, besides right now, was when my great-aunt Bernice was dying of a gall bladder attack. I only got to see her before she was dead, though, and not after, so it was hardly worth going."

I remembered the dead man I'd seen in the street during the riot in front of the grain mill. "Well, I can tell you, Charlotte, people look a whole lot better alive than dead," I assured her. "But if you're really all that interested in it, maybe you should think about becoming an undertaker."

"Naw," she said, shaking her head. "I'm not going to become anything. I just want to get married. I spun the globe last night even though you weren't there, and you know where it said I'm going on my honeymoon? Saudi *Arabia!* Can you beat that? Maybe I'm going to marry one of those rich sheiks over there — you know, the ones that wear those towels over their heads even though it's hotter than blazes. . . ."

We walked on, talking about our dreams, our hopes for romance, our wish that a handsome new boy would enroll at school and fall madly in love with us. So for a time, with Charlotte at my side, I almost forgot where I was and why I was there. Friends can do that, bring a bit of real comfort in a time of distress like balm on a wound. When I saw the clock above the nurses' desk and realized the Soo City singers would be performing soon, I steered us back to Papa's room.

The group had already arrived by the time we joined Mother at the window. "Do you want to munch on some cookies while we listen?" I asked Charlotte. She said she did, so we each grabbed a couple from the bag. We offered one to Mother but she declined, saying she'd already had a slice of banana bread, and it was delicious.

Charlotte and I both bit into a cookie — they were pretty good, after all — and chewed contentedly while the singers fumbled for their key and started to sing. Our chewing slowed down, then stopped altogether as we listened to the group singing about the little town of Bethlehem. Charlotte moved her head in time to the music and seemed to enjoy the show. After another song or two, she asked, "Do you think they can do 'I Found a Million-Dollar Baby in the Five-and-Ten-Cent Store'?"

"Well," I explained, "mostly they just do hymns and Christmas carols and stuff like that."

Charlotte stared at the group a moment,

then lifted her shoulders in a shrug. "Well," she replied decidedly, "that's all right. I like 'em anyway."

Good old Charlotte.

Chapter Thirty

Every day as soon as the bell rang at the end of the last class, I gathered my books, reluctantly disengaged myself from Charlotte's arm, and ran to catch the trolley to the hospital. It was the time of year when everyone was making little bonfires of the autumn leaves in their yards, and on those afternoons when I stood on the street corner waiting for the trolley, the scent of burning leaves hung heavy in the air. Normally I loved that distinct fragrance of autumn and inhaled it as deeply as I did the aroma of spring flowers. But now the scent of those innocent fires conjured up in my mind images of destruction, of Soo City in blazes, of Papa being beaten against the backdrop of the flaming shanties. Even autumn was a stranger and not the season I had always known.

I was glad when the trolley came and swallowed me up into the scent of my fellow passengers' various perfumes and tobaccos. But my relief at escaping the burning leaves was always short-lived. As soon as the driver shut the doors and the car jerked forward into motion, I remembered where I was going. I wasn't escaping the Soo City fire; I was heading right for it. With the passing of each block, with every turning of the trolley's wheels, my fears grew. *Maybe, by the time I get there, he'll be dead,* I'd think. *Or maybe he's dying now, this very minute, and he'll be gone before I arrive.* By the time I'd reached the hospital, I'd be so wound up I could hardly breathe. I'd hurry through the lobby and past the nurses' station to Papa's room, but before I came to the door, I'd stop and take a deep breath, trying to prepare myself for what I'd see. Every day it was the same. Papa was still lying in the bed, his chest still rising and falling. *Not yet,* I'd think, light-headed with relief. *He's still here. I can still hope.*

And yet as the days passed, the chances of his waking up became slimmer. Edema set in on the sixth day, causing pressure on his brain, which was relieved through regular lumbar drainage. He was also given repeated injections of dextrose, a hypertonic solution used to deplete fluid in the tissues, thereby combating the edema. While Papa's fluid intake was restricted, he was watched for over-dehydration, and the whole routine became a delicate balancing act. And, of course, all the while, we were still on the lookout for blood clots, hemorrhaging, convulsions, meningitis, and so forth, any or all of which could develop at any moment.

Although at first I hadn't wanted to hear all the medical mumbo jumbo Dr. Rawls insisted on throwing at us, I eventually made up my mind to try to understand as much as I could about what was happening to my father. Ignorance may be bliss, but I could no longer pretend that Dr. Rawls' big medical terms had nothing to do with Papa. They had everything to do with Papa. And so I asked Dr. Hal again and again to explain Papa's symptoms and the measures taken to relieve them. And again and again Dr. Hal patiently obliged, always ending his simple lectures with an assurance or two that Papa would come around.

Still the days slipped by, and Papa didn't come around. Though they didn't downgrade his prognosis from guarded, the doctors and nurses began to pass in and out of the room as solemnly as if my father were already laid out in his coffin. After a while I no longer looked to any of them — save Dr. Hal — for reassurance, for they seemed determined not to give it.

During those interminable hours at the hospital, I turned often to Mother for consolation and strength. I knew she was afraid, of course — how could she be otherwise? — but if she gave up hope, then I, too, would give up hope, and even without my saying so, she knew that. At the same time, she needed me to encourage her as well. We were like two playing cards leaning up against each other to form a teepee, one thin paper edge touching the other in so fragile a construction that the slightest movement of air could topple it. And if one of us fell, the other would certainly fall as well. So almost unconsciously, we buoyed each other up with a certain simple liturgy of hope. I'd say — and it'd be a statement, not a question — "It's still possible he'll wake up, isn't it, Mama." And she'd respond quite confidently: "Yes, Virginia. With God, anything is possible." Even as Papa's recovery became more and more improbable, the fact didn't change that with God anything is possible. That was the only hope we had.

While Mother and I held each other up, the two of us were together reinforced by the daily appearance of the Soo City singers. Every evening at six o'clock they gathered outside Papa's window, and every evening the group grew larger as more and more of the scattered residents of the burned-out shantytown learned of my father's plight and came back to offer what help they could. They had somehow scraped up a couple of hymnals so they wouldn't have to improvise so much on the words of the songs. Like clockwork they assembled there — minus the signs, the guitar, and the accordion — and though they appeared weary and hungry and almost without hope for their own lives, for half an hour every evening they put all thought of themselves aside and sang to Papa.

The days were cool and the nights were downright chilly, but not even the cold deterred the singers. They hugged themselves and warmed their fingers under their armpits and stamped their feet between songs, and sometimes their breath wafted like little clouds in the early autumn air, but on they sang. Mother opened Papa's window only a crack when the Soo City singers came around, then she and I put on sweaters and pulled an extra blanket up around Papa's chin to keep him warm. Whenever we did this, I thought of all the blankets I had collected for our friends in the camp, and I was sad to think that, before the cold of winter had even had a chance to set in, all those blankets had become fodder for the sheriff's fire. All except, perhaps, the one that Dr. Hal had used as a hammock to carry Papa to the car after he was wounded.

Mother and I weren't the only ones to gain encouragement from the Soo City singers. Their arrival soon became a ritual that other patients and their families looked forward to as well. Shortly before six, we'd hear people in the halls say, "It's almost time," and wheelchairs were pushed closer to windows, and those people who were ambulatory shuffled in their hospital slippers down to the dayroom to listen. Even some of the nurses and orderlies paused in their work for a few minutes to turn an ear toward the singers on the lawn. On occasion we'd hear someone call out, "Would you mind singing —" and one song or another was requested. The singers would riffle through the hymnbooks till they found the song, then Joe O'Hanlon tooted a note on his harmonica, and the choir quietly serenaded their grateful audience. I think even Mr. Donner, the hospital administrator, came to appreciate the singers. He never said so, but once I saw him at his own window in the opposite hospital wing, his hands behind his back, his head nodding slowly in time with the music.

And every evening after they sang, before they went away to wherever it was they went away to, they stopped to ask about Papa.

"Any change for the better, Mrs. Eide?"

"None yet, but we don't give up hope."

"He's a tough one," someone would offer. "He'll pull through yet."

And someone else would say: "Any man deserves to live, it's Doc Eide."

And still another: "I'd trade places with

him if I could. He means that much to us."

Words of consolation, encouragement, prayers were passed through the crack of the open window, then, "We'll be back tomorrow, same as always. Take good care of the doc."

Papa's Bible, which Mother and I continued to read aloud, reminded me that God was near, not on a distant throne. Not only near but here. Here in the room where Papa lay, where Mother and I spent so many hours waiting and wondering. But while I prayed for Papa, I remembered the Lindbergh baby, and that in spite of the prayers of thousands, he hadn't been returned home safely. He had been found dead and decomposing in a field. And I knew that God wasn't obligated to answer my prayers for Papa in the way I wanted him to, either.

Papa had told me — and I thought often of his words — he wasn't afraid to die, that when he died he knew he'd just be going home. I believed that, too, and yet I wasn't ready to let Papa go. We still needed him here with us — Mother and Simon and the girls and me. And his patients needed him. So many people needed him. How could God take him from us now? But I knew if Papa could speak he'd say, "Now, look, Ginny, God knows what's right. What we can't understand we have to take on faith."

I'd try, if Papa died. I'd try to take it on faith because surely I would never understand.

Time dragged on, and every hour seemed a day, and every day a week. Restless nights were followed by weary days at school, then the trolley ride to the hospital, the afternoons and evenings with Papa, the nightly assembling from out of nowhere of the faithful Soo City singers. Each time I entered Papa's room, I looked for some small change for the better. I watched for any movement he might make, listened for any word he might try to speak — but there were none. Rather, he seemed only to grow thinner, paler, weaker, as though fading away.

The morning of the fourteenth day was gray and overcast, adding dismay to my already struggling spirits. Everything always seems worse when the sky is covered over, the sun hidden.

Just as I reached the bottom of the stairs on my way to breakfast, I overheard Mother and Dr. Hal talking at the kitchen table. I could see them, but they didn't see me. I sat down on the stairs to listen.

"Why isn't he waking up, Harold?" Mother asked.

"I don't know, Lillian," Dr. Hal said, so quietly I almost couldn't hear.

"You expected him to be awake by now, didn't you?"

"I thought he probably would have come out of the coma by now, yes."

"It's not a good sign, is it?"

"It's not necessarily a bad sign, Lil."

"Level with me, Harold."

"I'm telling you what I know."

There was a moment of silence, then mother said, "Dr. Rawls and that other doctor, Dr. Murphy, they must be doing something wrong."

"They're doing everything they can."

"What about surgery, Harold? Some sort of operation?"

"Surgery isn't called for, Lil. There's nothing a surgeon can do. We don't know the exact injuries to the brain, but opening up Will's skull and taking a look inside isn't going to tell us any more than what we already know. As a doctor's wife you must have heard it a million times: Medicine is an art, not an exact science. That's what they were always telling us in medical school, and I've since found it to be true. Healing the human body isn't like fixing a broken car. I wish it were that easy, but it just isn't so. There are too many variables, too many unique complications to each case. But you have to believe that everything that can be done for Will is being done."

There was another quiet moment before Mother said, "It's just hard for me to stand by . . . it seems I ought to be doing more."

"We all feel that way, Lillian. A situation like this leaves everyone feeling helpless."

"I know you told me that even if he opens his eyes, he may still be in a coma, may still be unaware of everything around him. But I really feel strongly, Harold, that if he would just open his eyes, I could get through to him somehow."

"Well, it would be a good step forward if he'd open his eyes. But like I said —"

"I know. We can't know at this point how much permanent damage . . ." Mother's voice trailed off. The legs of her chair scraped across the kitchen floor as she rose to pour herself another cup of coffee. "Fourteen days, Harold. Two whole weeks — and he hasn't even opened his eyes once."

"Well, granted, it's more common for people to open their eyes early on, whether they're out of the coma or not, but it's not unknown for people to go two weeks without opening their eyes. I heard of —"

"Harold," Mother interrupted. She settled her coffee cup loudly on the counter and stood looking out the window above the sink. "We're grasping at straws, aren't we? I mean" — she turned to look at Dr. Hal — "you don't really have much hope left, do you?"

Dr. Hal sat still as stone, like a child playing statue at the sight of a bee. As though, if he were perfectly quiet, he might somehow blend into the scenery, go unnoticed and not get stung. But slowly, very slowly, he lifted his face toward Mother, but what he said I couldn't hear, he spoke so low. Mother's face, though, told me what my ears had failed to pick up. Dr. Hal was loosening his grip on hope.

He pushed back his chair from the table, said a few more words to Mother, then left the kitchen. When he passed me in the hall, I looked up at him from where I sat on the stairs. Our eyes met, but only briefly. He turned abruptly away so that I wouldn't see what was written on those two dark mirrors. But I already knew. Mother had had a premonition. She had stood at the door with her hand upon the screen watching Papa go, fearing there was something there in Soo City that would keep him from ever coming back. And now her fears appeared to be justified.

After that, I dragged my heavy emotions with me all through the day, from the first morning bell to the last afternoon bell when I was finally able to leave school and go to the hospital. The sky had remained overcast all day, and only during that brief ride did the sun momentarily discover a break in the clouds, pushing its golden shimmering rays earthward from heaven. Aunt Sally's ladders. I looked for angels. How I longed to see angels coming to help. But then I remembered — Aunt Sally said those sunbeams were also the ladders that souls climbed up to heaven.

I didn't cry out, and I didn't feel fear. Rather, what filled my heart was the greatest sadness I had ever known. *Oh, Papa,* I thought. *Don't go, Papa, please don't go.*

The clouds shifted, filling in the gap, and the sun withdrew the fingers with which it had touched the earth.

I was sure then that Papa was gone. He had climbed up the ladder of light and the sunbeam had been pulled back up into heaven behind him, the door to heaven shut and padlocked as Papa disappeared inside.

The trolley rumbled on its way. A middle-aged woman with a Pekingese got on and plopped down in the seat beside me, holding the small dog in her lap. I offered her a wan smile, but the woman sniffed and didn't return it. Her haughtiness, which at any other time wouldn't bother me, was almost enough to make me break down and cry. It was a busy hour for the trolley, with people getting on and off at every stop, filling up the seats and even standing in the aisle. Most of them were traveling home from work, from shopping, from appointments. I envied them, going about what I imagined to be the mundane routines of their lives, uninterrupted by something as awful — as final — as death. I felt cut off from them all, isolated by my grief, the only one among them touched by tragedy. If only one of them, I thought, would turn around and see me and know that something was wrong. If only I could say, "My papa's dead," so that they might answer, "You don't know for sure yet. Don't say that until you know for sure." But no one noticed me, and I had to go on looking out the window and waiting for my stop as though nothing in the world were wrong.

When I got off the trolley in front of the hospital, my knees were so weak they threatened to buckle beneath me and leave me in a heap on the sidewalk. But I mustered up whatever strength I could find and managed to drag myself beyond the double glass doors into the lobby. The sterile smell of disinfectant assaulted me and turned my stomach. I scanned the room. The lobby was quiet and orderly. No one rushed about as though someone had just died. The nurse at the front desk smiled in my direction when she noticed me. She wouldn't have done that, I thought, if Papa were gone.

And indeed, in spite of my fears, when I reached his room I found Mother sitting placidly beside the sleeping figure of my father, the same as always. The tableau was the same; it hadn't changed. I had expected a different scene, was so sure that the curtain had opened on a new act. *But you were wrong,* I told myself. *The sunbeam came, but Papa didn't climb up it.*

I gazed upon Papa's sleeping figure with quiet acceptance, thinking of how I had always tried to write the outcome of the story — by spinning the globe, by dreaming and wishing, by fearing and doubting. Always trying to set the story line, always trying to lay out the plot. Yet I could speculate and guess and conjecture all I wanted, but in the end, the fact remained that I wasn't the author of the play. Someone else was, thankfully.

"How is he, Mama?" I asked quietly.

Mother closed the Bible in her lap. "No different," she replied. "I'm glad you're here."

After an hour, a cold, sparse rain began to fall, and I was afraid our friends from Soo City might not come. But they came — improvising, as always. Instead of umbrellas, they held leaves of newspaper over their heads. Only Mrs. Everhart stayed away to keep baby Caroline protected from the damp chill, though Mr. Everhart was there with the two boys.

"You'll catch your death of cold," Mother warned the singers. "Perhaps for tonight you should —"

A barrage of mild protests interrupted her.

"A herd a wild horses wouldn't keep us away, Mrs. Eide."

"Gotta see how the doc's doing."

"It wouldn't feel right, not coming round like always."

"Little bit a rain never hurt no one."

And so, huddled beneath the dripping papers, they sang. Dick Mason and Joe O'Hanlon and Oscar Salinsky and Bellowing Bob Sbarbaro. Alice Hunt and her friend, Mrs. Conley, their husbands and all their children. Steel O'Neil and Shoes and Longjohn and Sherman Browne. Mr. Lucky and T-Bone, who contributed an occasional yelp. And a number of faces that I didn't recognize — whiskered faces, dirt-smudged faces, gaunt faces, weary faces. But, to me, the faces of angels nevertheless. I decided then that these so-called good-for-nothing loafers, these Red vermin, these human parasites and pampered poverty rats — these very ones must have been the angels that climbed down the sunray ladder that afternoon to bring us the hope of heaven.

I still think so, because that evening, sometime during the second stanza of "O Holy Night," Papa opened his eyes.

Epilogue

I have always attributed Papa's recovery to the work of God, of course, but I've never questioned that He chose to send some of His healing grace through that unlikely group of musicians. Papa said he didn't hear the singing until after he woke up, but the funny thing was, as soon as he opened his eyes, he turned his head toward the window where the Soo City singers were gathered. Mother and I knew at once that the opening of his eyes wasn't just a reflex, but that Papa was aware, that he had made a connection with the waking world. And he was back with us.

From the day he opened his eyes, Papa's recovery was steady but slow. All through that long winter and the following spring, he struggled to regain speech, movement, and dexterity. At first he spoke as though his mouth were full of cotton, but that eventually improved. Some words gave him trouble for a long time, but one word he could pronounce without difficulty from the beginning was my name. I just about choked on my joy every time I heard him call me Ginny.

Sometime early on in Papa's convalescence, Mother and I confessed to him how frightened we had been when day after day went by and he didn't wake up. Mother, in an uncharacteristic attempt at humor, chided, "If you were going to wake up anyway, at least you could have done it sooner and saved us all a great deal of worry." To which Papa quipped, "Now, Lillian, you can't blame a doctor for grabbing a little extra sleep when he can. That was the first uninterrupted sleep I've had since I hung out my shingle."

I also confessed to Papa my fear that he would die while still angry with me. Papa thought about that for what seemed a long while. Finally, he took my hand and said, "Ginny, you were becoming a lovely young lady so fast I forgot that in some ways you were still a little girl. You were a little girl faced with a terrible decision the night of the fire, a decision that would have been hard for anyone to make. I know now why you chose not to tell me about the raid. If I'd been in your shoes, I'd have done the same thing for my own father."

"Then you're not angry with me anymore, Papa, about what happened that night?"

"Of course not, Ginny. I stopped being angry the minute I reached Soo City and saw the fire. Then I was angry at the people who pulled the raid, but not at you.

I knew you were just trying to protect me."

"That's right, Papa! That's right! I was just trying to protect you."

"I'm so sorry you had to be afraid I'd die angry with you. But I'm glad I'm here to tell you that you mustn't ever think that way again. I've told you before, and I don't want you to forget, that there's nothing greater than my love for you. You understand that, don't you, Ginny?"

"Oh yes, Papa," I cried, throwing my arms around him, "but I'm awfully glad you're here to tell me again!"

Life began in earnest, then, to settle back into a normal routine. For me, that meant going to school, doing chores, visiting Charlotte, and spinning the globe (even though I no longer took the game seriously). One thing that didn't resume, however, was my laboring over the piano. While I was visiting Papa in the hospital, Mother realized I didn't have time to practice. She called Miss Cole to tell her that my lessons would have to be put on hold indefinitely — though no doubt all three of us knew they'd never start up again. I think I heard the echoes of Miss Cole's sigh of relief from all the way across town. Simon continued taking lessons and went on to become quite skilled, and later even Claudia and Molly showed more talent for the instrument than I ever had. Mother must have been satisfied that three of her four children exhibited talent because she never again suggested that I take music lessons, and I never did.

Papa continued to improve, though he was never able to walk again without leaning heavily on a cane. The bullet that shattered his thighbone left him with a nasty limp. And his hands were never quite as strong as they had once been, but since he wasn't a surgeon, that didn't seem to matter too much when it came to his work. He resumed his medical practice in the summer of 1933, and his first rounds included a trip to Soo City. By that time, the little community down by the river had been reestablished for some months. The charred remains of the burned-out camp had been dragged away, the ashes raked over, and new scraps of tin and wood — whatever one could lay a hand on — had been hauled to the riverside and fashioned into shanties. The town was built up roughly along the same dirt roads, except that the main street was renamed Roosevelt Boulevard — a designation that evoked greater hope than Hoover Avenue ever did. Those who made their homes in the camp were largely those who had been there before. They came back to Soo City simply because they still had nowhere else to go. Also, the Soo line kept bringing new residents while it continued to carry some of the transients away. Some time that spring the railroad brought back the missing banjo player, so the Soo City trio once again became a quartet.

I accompanied Papa the first time he went limping back into the camp. He was no doubt heard before he was seen. He approached Soo City whistling "Joy to the World" — slightly off-key, as usual, but loud and clear. You would have thought he was the King of England the way those people flocked to greet him. We'd no sooner passed the "Welcome to Soo City" sign (the original placard still hung from the same tree) when one person after another started hollering that Doc Eide was back. As word traveled quickly over the "Soo City telegraph," people rushed forward out of their shanties and down Roosevelt Boulevard to meet us. They were all there: the Everharts, the Hunts and the Conleys, Dick Mason and Sherman Browne, Steel O'Neil and Shoes and Longjohn, Joe and Oscar and Bellowing Bob and the recently returned banjo player, and Mr. Lucky and T-Bone. T-Bone barked and wagged his tail so wildly he could hardly keep his hind legs on the ground. And there were many others — some whose names I was never quite sure of, others whose names I've forgotten over the years. Papa hobbled forward, his left hand clutching the cane, his right hand extended, and in the next moment he was swallowed up by the crowd and hidden from my view. I stood there on the outskirts of it all, holding Papa's medical bag and feeling very proud. On that hot and dusty afternoon, I made a promise to myself that one day I would be just like Papa.

During the months Papa was recovering, Dr. Hal was the only wage earner among us. It was quite a responsibility for a man of twenty-seven to be the sole provider for twelve people, but somehow he did it, and we always had everything we needed.

I say twelve because late in that fall of 1932, we got Uncle Jim back as well as Cousin Jimmy. Before the jailed strikers could be brought to trial, the governor pardoned them and sent them home. Governor Borgmann was voted back into office in the next election; Sheriff Dysinger was not. I'm not sure whatever became of Clem Dysinger, because after he lost his place as sheriff, he moved his family away from Minnesota. I was glad to see him go and told Papa I hoped Ex-Sheriff Dysinger never showed his hound-dog face in our town again, even if it meant losing Danny for good. Furthermore, I added, I'd consider it just desserts if he couldn't find a job and ended up in a shantytown himself.

Let him see what it felt like to go hungry and sleep on the ground while everyone with jobs was calling him a pampered poverty rat and a Red vermin.

Thinking Papa would agree with me, I was chagrined when my father frowned and said, "Now, Ginny, two wrongs don't make a right, you know. Sheriff Dysinger shouldn't have raided Soo City the way he did, but we can't allow ourselves to go on feeling ill will toward him."

"But, Papa!" I protested. "He might have been the one to beat you senseless and leave you for dead!"

"Then he's the one we need to forgive, isn't he?" Papa asked quietly.

I narrowed my eyes and huffed a bit. "Have *you* forgiven him, Papa?" I asked.

Papa offered me a sheepish grin. "Well, Ginny, I'm trying. There are those moments when I still want to spit fire at the thought of him, but when they come I just have to forgive Clem all over again. Eventually I'll have the matter settled."

It went against the grain, the thought of forgiving a man who had brought so much harm to my father and my friends. But I'd already promised myself I was going to be like Papa, and this gave me the chance to get started. Papa explained that if we went on hating Clem Dysinger because he hated the people of Soo City, then we were all caught up in a cycle of hate that spun around and around and never accomplished anything. "Only forgiveness can break that cycle of destruction," Papa said. It took me a while of teeth-grinding contemplation and no little bit of brooding, but I finally told Papa that I, too, was willing to forgive Sheriff Dysinger for what he'd done.

So anyway, as I was saying, Uncle Jim came home, and not long afterward Jimmy Jr. found his way back to us on the Soo line. He had gone first to the Dubbins' old house and found it deserted, but he figured right away he would find his family living with us. He showed up on our doorstep half starved and bone thin, but it didn't take long before Mother's and Aunt Sally's cooking filled him out again. We were all so glad to have him back, especially Aunt Sally, that we didn't mind his being one more mouth to feed and one more body needing a place to sleep. He entertained us for months with his stories of riding the rails until Uncle Jim made him stop when Luke started talking about hopping a train and heading west.

Neither Uncle Jim nor Cousin Jimmy could find steady work for quite a while, but we told ourselves it would just be a matter of time before the new president got the clogged wheels of the economy oiled and moving again. Even before he was elected, President Roosevelt was talking about his New Deal, a "three-R" plan that would offer relief, recovery, and reform for the country. All sorts of agencies were formed under the New Deal, two of which helped our family directly. In 1935, my uncle got a job through the Works Progress Administration that earned him sixty-three dollars a month, and the following year Jimmy Jr. went off with the Civilian Conservation Corps and began mailing home fifty dollars a month. With Papa, Dr. Hal, Uncle Jim, and Jimmy Jr. all contributing to the household kitty, we felt downright rich again.

Of course, when Uncle Jim came home from jail, I once more ended up on the couch in Papa's study. I didn't have a room of my own again until 1937, when Uncle Jim could finally afford to move his family to a small house not far from ours. Even then I had my old room back for only my final summer at home before I left for nursing school — at which time Claudia took it over. It didn't matter. If the only thing the Depression took from me was one small room, then I was blessed.

Even though prosperity eventually returned to our country, we never quite made it back to those wild and carefree days of the Twenties. It was as though we had left the innocence of childhood behind and grown up into the responsibilities of adulthood. America became a superpower, a world leader, and discovered that life means facing things like cold wars and hot wars, civil rights battles and women's rights battles, a decline in values and an increase in apathy, and what the writers came to call angst. I grew up, too, and discovered how the overarching troubles of the world affect the individuals who live in it, and that sometimes the dreams of youth are flattened out and reshaped by the larger circumstances of life.

For me there were no European honeymoons, no gondola rides through Venice, no midnight walks beside the River Seine. I never knew what it was to sit on a hotel balcony staring up at a full moon with my newly wedded husband. Charlotte married, of course — three times, in fact — and sent me postcards from each of her African honeymoons. Those postcards were generally slow in reaching me, since they had to make their way into the jungle, up over mountains, or across deserts, depending on where in Central or South America I happened to be working at the time.

When I inevitably neared the half-century mark, I abandoned all hope of marriage and resigned myself to the ranks of Miss Cole and the other spinsters I had so pitied and secretly feared. But it wasn't with grief that I gave up my dream. Rather, I felt only a sense of wonder that the single life could be so fulfilling.

It was, of course, just when I accepted my solitary existence that I finally met my husband, a fellow medical missionary who — whether by sheer coincidence or by some divine whimsy, I've never known — was named Charles Chaplen. Spelled one letter different from the Charlie of the silver screen, but nevertheless pronounced the same. "Dear Charlotte," I wrote, "you'll never believe who I met wandering around the wilds of Guatemala. . . ." She wrote back asking whether his feet stuck out like a ballerina's and if he could walk more than three steps without falling down. She later sent matching canes and bowler hats as a wedding gift when I told her Charlie Chaplen and I were engaged.

Charles proposed to me late one night while we were scrubbing for emergency surgery. When I said yes, we elected not to seal the engagement with a kiss, for fear of spreading germs. The next day he presented me with a silver ring he had bartered for in the marketplace in Guatemala City, using the Spanish he was only just learning (he was a newcomer to the mission field) and finding out later he'd ended up spending more than the original asking price. He slipped it on my finger while we sat in a leaky dugout canoe that threatened to capsize and toss us into the waters of Lake Amatitlán. It had been our intention to watch the sun set over the mountains from this romantic vantage point, but a storm blew in and left us soaked and shivering before we could paddle our rather dubious vessel back to shore. We were married in the chapel on the hospital compound, and contrary to our original plans for a brief escape, we spent our wedding night tending to the victims of a devastating fire in one of the nearby villages. Nevertheless, the sweetest words I ever heard were muttered in the midst of the chaos that night when Charles asked of one of the orderlies, "Manuel, get my wife some water, will you? She looks like she's about to faint." That was the first time Charles called me his wife.

It was not exactly what I had dreamed of as a child while spinning the globe with Charlotte, but I was far happier than I ever could have imagined all those years before. My husband and I, until our recent retirement, spent twenty years together immersed in poverty, hardship, filth, and disease — and, more importantly, in the incomparable joy that arose from the midst of it all each time we discovered we had offered a sliver of desperately needed hope that otherwise might not have been there.

And that is what I tell my grandnephews and grandnieces — all the grandchildren of Simon, Claudia, and Molly — when they ask me why I chose to spend my life as a missionary nurse working among "those uncivilized people in the jungles of Latin America." I remember Papa and give them the truest answer I know to give: "Because it made me happy."

About the Author

Ann Tatlock is a full-time writer who has also worked as an assistant editor for *Decision* magazine. A graduate of Oral Roberts University with an M.A. in Communications from Wheaton College Graduate School, she has published numerous articles in Christian magazines. This is her first novel. She and her husband make their home in Minneapolis in a house overlooking one of the 10,000 lakes in Minnesota.